FLAT

An Edgy Tale of Accidental Discovery

By Neal Rabin

For Timmy & Dave

Published in the United States by
Ponderosa Publishing, LLC
This is a work of fiction. Names, characters, places, and incidents
either are the product of the author's imagination or are used ficti-
tiously. Any resemblance to actual persons living or dead, events, or
locales are entirely coincidental.

"Human beings are works in progress that mistakenly think they're finished."
Daniel Gilbert

Flat Main Characters

Lanning Delaford – *Captain of the L'Aquila, adopted son of Molly Cortez*

Molly Cortez – *Adoptive mother of Lanning Delaford, head baker Algeciras palace*

Felipe Cortez – *Sailing master of the L'Aquila, son of Molly Cortez*

Filippa Beaufort – *Spanish courtesan*

Contigo – *Butcher at Algeciras palace*

Marco Bellini – *Head chef Algeciras palace*

Don Burducci – *Local mafioso*

Shafi – *Berber apothecary*

Destemido – *Pirate captain of the Queen of Sheba*

Lorenzo Espinosa – *Best friend of Lanning Delaford*

Longshort – *Boatswain of the Queen of Sheba*

Nantucket – *Native American passenger on the L'Aquila*

Hector – *Crew member of the L'Aquila*

Roderick Gagnez – *Viceroy of Algeciras*

— Chapter 1 —

NIGHT MOVES

IBERIAN PENINSULA – SEPTEMBER 14, 1519 – SUNDAY

A starless night was faintly lit by a pinprick beam escaping from a fingernail moon. Save for this single gossamer filament, an inky blackness engulfed the far western edge of the Mediterranean Sea. A small, cargo laden, two-masted xebec was slowly making its way from the tip of Northern Africa. It had reached the half-way mark towards its home port of Algeciras at the far end of the Bay of Gibraltar.

A slight favoring breeze from the south kept the seas smooth and the progress slow but steady.

Four of the six-man crew lazed about the deck in various states of approximate sleep. Working hard to remember the Tangier whore he spent one weeks' pay on the previous night, one lovesick sailor wedged himself up against the bow rail. With the sails tied off holding the wind, the drowsy helmsman kept a casual heading for his home port while gnawing on a foul-tasting, weevil pockmarked, sea biscuit.

Three bound stacks of hand-woven Berber robes shared cargo space with fourteen wooden crates evenly split between sugar and dates. Stashed in the far corner of the small hold, next to a pile of rocks used for added ballast, stood three unmarked, wax-sealed oak casks.

They never heard a thing.

Hanging double the sail in the wind, the caravel's captain skillfully maneuvered his boat silently amidships of the lolling xebec. Shifting to a hard left rudder, the boats crossed bows. In a split moment, ten hooded men, faces masked by black scarves, leaped over their own starboard rail, much to the surprise of the recently spent love machine who was knocked cold by a swift sword hilt to the head. The helmsman tabulated his odds, then quickly raised his arms in surrender. The invaders, repeating the Renaissance classic sword hilt to the head, and sedated him along with the rest of the bewildered crew.

Once the boat was secured, the captain made a quick study of the cargo.

"Are you kidding me? DATES...and ROBES? I'm swimming in dates and robes. What the hell am I supposed to do with this shit? Open a day spa?"

One of the crew, holding a lit torch, haltingly approached the captain. He spoke in an unintelligible, muffled tone, "zzz use e of zzz"

"Drop your kerchief moron, I can't understand a word you're saying!"

"Right. Sorry sir. There's hummus. And lots of it. Crew loves hummus sir. I mean it's a few barrels of the stuff, but still, do we keep it?"

The captain rubbed his forehead at the pathetic haul for the effort and potential consequences risked. "Take it all, then cut us loose."

"So, burn the boat sir?"

"Why?" came the captain's curious reply.

"Well, um, it is customary. I mean, I thought we always, did."

The sailor eagerly anticipated the prospect of dropping the first torch and blazing the ship.

"Considering they haven't done anything to us, and we've already screwed up their night, we probably don't need to burn them alive sailor. Let's wrap this up and move along."

"Aye sir."

Clearly disappointed, the sailor slowly moved off to follow the orders.

The captain's irritation with the night's work flared up. He kicked the nearest dog.

"Crewman!"

The man stopped in his tracks. He turned back to face the captain. "First off, do me a favor. Stop calling me '*sir*.' This isn't the Portuguese navy. You're a pirate! For god's sake, try and act like one! Show at least a little disrespect for authority."

"I'm trying sir. That's why I brought this." The seaman waggled his torch at the captain. "I figured, given your reputation, 'the Fearless One', you'd want to make a statement."

It's true the captain had a much-deserved reputation for unprovoked violence, but not tonight. He did however sense that the seaman had mocked his resolve.

"You're new?"

"Yes sir. First trip."

"Navigation?" The captain thought he had seen him manning the wheel at one point during the evening.

"Yes sir, plus carpentry and, uh, also lute."

"Lute?" The response arrived coated in sarcasm which, completely escaped the enthusiastic sailor.

"Been playing since I was a lad."

"Versatile."

With a sigh of relief, the man lowered his guard. "Thank you, sir."

"What genius supposed we needed a musician on board? As if a useless cargo weren't enough, now we need someone to sing a merry tune about it afterwards?"

His mind made up, the captain shrugged his shoulders in resolve. "No matter. Over the rail you go."

"Sorry?" The sailor looked confused. He slowly backed away from the captain and the port side rail.

The captain issued his final ultimatum to the shrinking crewman, "Quick as you please. Over the rail, or I can run you through straight away."

The captain drew his saber from the scabbard at his waist and calmly extended it towards the now petrified seaman.

"Choose."

The man dropped his own sword on the deck and ran to the rail.

"Hand me the torch please. Wouldn't want an accident at this point," said the overly accommodating Skipper.

"Thank you, sir, er...Captain."

Quite content with himself after he heard the splash the captain leaned over the rail, and with a bemused shout, issued his terms.

"Follow us best you can. If you last the hour, you can have your old job back."

Holding the torch, he walked back towards his own ship searching for the Boatswain— his 2nd in command.

"Longshort!" he shouted. "Longshort, where the hell are you?"

The captain's longest, closest friend, guardian, and confidante, Longshort, stood a Portuguese 500 real coin over six feet tall with drooped shoulders, a crooked thrice-broken nose, scraggly D'Artagnan greyed goatee and, mostly gray hair. Longshort had witnessed the sailor drop over the rail then drift back with the current. He made a quick run to the caravel's stern and surreptitiously tossed a line down to the swimmer, motioning him to remain quiet and hold on. Taking stock of the state of things between the two boats, he cut loose a small oar boat the caravel was dragging behind it as well.

"Here Captain. I'm here," he hailed.

Longshort gingerly navigated the gap between the two bound together boats and approached the captain.

"Shall we talk about how hard it's becoming to find good help these days?" Longshort mused.

"He mocked me."

"That can happen."

"According to the book of Longshort, discipline must be maintained," the captain said.

"Noted. Some years ago, I crewed for a..."

Knowing where this tale was headed, Destemido cut Longshort off at the knees.

"We don't have time for one of your instructional tales. Daylight's coming."

"Thank you for giving him the option of a workout versus a funeral at sea. Orders?"

"We're not getting paid enough to put up with this crap. Cut us loose," spat the captain who was tapped out on patience.

Longshort spun around to head back to the caravel. The captain waited a beat, then began a frustrated walk across the deck of the ransacked xebec. Standing on the port rail before leaping the growing gap between the two vessels, he dismissively tossed the still-fluttering torch onto the deck strewn with half-conscious sailors. He hopped over the rail, giving the command to "come about" as he heard the screams and the occasional splash recede in their wake.

"Hummus all around," came the order from the foredeck.

⊷ Chapter 2 ⊶
FIRST SERVE

A *small, spinning leather ball*, stuffed with a combination of imperial poodle hair, domestic piebald sheep clippings, sawdust, plus a royal handful of collected castle lint, flew high into a cloud-dotted, azure sky.

Almost drowned out by the Regal Flute, Lute & String ensemble perched upon a nearby balcony, came an alto shout from ground level.

"TENNIS!"

Lanning Delaford had just launched a whistling, sky-high power lob off Charles number Five's royal tennis court. It being spring in Andalusia, Lanning had instinctively calculated the transient ocean breeze into his shot. He watched as the ball floated weightless at the pinnacle of its flight. It hung there on his side of the net in divine stillness – a frozen moment defying the entire weight of the known world. Then, as planned, the breeze nudged it on the shoulder, directing the balls' downward arc deep onto the opposing side of the net.

"It's completely inconclusive, you know."

Prince Ferdinand, the gawky, handsome-ish in a Hapsburg inbred royal way, sixteen-year-old younger brother of the newly minted Spanish King Charles V stood on his half of the tennis court. He waited with complete disinterest for Lanning's lob to reconnect with gravity and return to earth.

"Move your feet Highness!"

Of course, Lanning knew the prince had little interest in the game at hand, his lessons, or much of anything beyond royal pursuits of leisure.

"It's simply not always the case," said Ferdinand, standing

apathetically stationary on the court.

"I give up. What is?" Lanning replied, already certain he knew the topic in question.

"What goes up does not necessarily guarantee it."

"Yes, it does, Highness. It has come down, just there. See...three, four, five. It has bounced away from you yet again."

The ball rolled off the court, and into the drainage well at the back of the enclosure. It came to rest in a neat, orderly line, along with the ten other testimonials to royal disinterest that had preceded it.

The prince continued his treatise. "Not always, is the point."

"In what case?"

"Why on the other side of course. It is utterly inconclusive at best."

"So you've said. The other side of what, Freddy?"

The prince set his firm jawline, pushed his shoulder length blonde hair back off his forehead, then pointed his racquet straight down. "THIS! Beneath us," he stressed stomping his size ten shoe on the court, "the underside?"

Lanning calmly shook his head. He had wrestled and resolved for himself the very same question since childhood. This had been a recurring debate between student and teacher for some time. "It's not flat, Highness."

"Wiser men believe differently, Lanning. We don't question those things we haven't experienced. I, although royal, and virtually perfect in every way by birthright, am not a man of science."

"Science actually is conflicted on the matter, Highness. I guess you'll have to rely on your own perfection to choose what is correct and what is *mierda del toro*!"

Despite his age and scant portion of athletic talent, the prince possessed a diligently trained intellect. It was by courtesy of private tutors spanning several countries, and professions from wet nurse to court elders to present company. Lanning mostly enjoyed their sparring matches and often engaged the youngster's penchant for competitive argument. Today he had other pressing matters.

The prince parried, "I do not question the existence of the rainbow, yet I know I shall never bathe in either end of its spectrum. I do not question God's power over mortality, yet other than dispatching the random, bellicose Turk or interloping Moorish squatter by my sword, I am powerless to control God's will."

Lanning knew the day's tennis lesson had now been usurped by the prince's urge for verbal fisticuffs. His attention span had shrunk to its bare minimum, forcing him to try and cutoff the discussion with haste and a tactical amount of grace.

"Two caterpillars were clinging to a tree branch," began Lanning.

"Ugh. An allegory?" The prince moaned his disapproval.

Lanning spread his arms in a welcoming gesture. "Since you don't want to play tennis, you leave me no other option." He continued, "Two caterpillars hanging out talking about their day. As they were talking, a butterfly floated by. One caterpillar said to the other, 'You'll never get me up in one of those things!' 'Why not,' asked the other caterpillar. 'I'm terrified of heights, and always will be. I never want to fly. Squirming is my primary choice of transport.' The other one nodded in agreement, 'I hear you brother. I don't want to be a butterfly either. Bein' a worm is totally where it's at!'"

The prince discarded his racquet and sloughed over to a bench on the side of the court. "I am not arguing against curiosity."

"You simply think God expects us to accept all things without question. What happens to imagination?" asked Lanning rhetorically.

As happened frequently, the teenager grew suddenly weary of the engagement.

"I take your point. Brain switching off…now. Let's drink!"

"I just had breakfast! Don't be such a *prince*. Ten minutes more," Lanning urged.

The two men had been on the court for a skoosh under one hour, with infinitesimal progress. Lanning had other places to be, but one does not rush royalty without peril. He might offer a healthy dose of back talk, but the crown owned all the hours of the day if it so chose.

"Lanning, sip with me," whined the prince, regressing further back in childhood.

He motioned the reluctant Lanning to take a seat next to him on the royal bench. A watchful attendant leaped into action from his courtside seat. Grabbing a four-poled canopy, the attendant placed it over the bench. Another servant delivered two glasses of generously poured chardonnay. The artificial shade covered both men.

Lanning pondered the scope of his impending post-tennis responsibilities. Downing wine at nine in the morning would severely hamper the remainder of his day. He reviewed a hit list in his mind while faux-sipping from his goblet. Get home, change clothes, get to the dock, check the cargo from the previous night's shipment, find his crew, load cargo, get new provisions—and, oh yeah, find the money to pay for all of that other stuff.

"Charlatan! You waste the fruit of the vine," jabbed the prince.

"No one can drink this early in the day."

"Hah! Assumption proven wrong." The prince said loudly slurping his wine.

"For that matter, why must we have the lute & flute brigade whittling away during your lessons?"

"I'm a royal," replied Frederick. "Along with merciless, dispassionate behavior, debauchery, and, in my case, disdainful German lessons at noon, merriment is a formal obligation of the job."

"Sorry Freddy, but I've got a full day, and I know you've got your day too," said Lanning.

Fortunately, the prince found Lanning's nickname amusing. Lanning put his wine glass down no longer needing to pretend. The prince snapped it up, emptying it down his throat like a bucket of water tossed on a dry fern.

"You don't appreciate the freedom you have," lamented the prince.

"Same time day after tomorrow?" asked Lanning.

"I detest this game, but it too *is* a royal requirement from brother Carlos, pardon, his royalness, Holy Roman King, Emperor, God, and whatever other titles he's sporting these days. Fine. Yes. We are '*on*.' I know you know we realize we are not a naturally gifted athlete?"

"Your Highness has gifts. We'll keep looking for them, is all."

Lanning chuckled and served a friendly elbow into the prince's rib cage. A sudden shout came from the terrace overlooking the royal court.

"I see you, **Delaford!**"

A squashed, rotund human, with seven surviving strands of strategically placed fish-wire hair flattened against his bald head, bellowed over the balustrade. Roderick Gagnez, Andalusian Viceroy for the Bay of Gibraltar, had a distinctively nasal tone to his voice. It made him sound like he was suffering from a permanent head cold. Since his birthplace and formative years had been spent in Madrid, no one understood his non-sequitur French accent. The French affect generally showed up at random discordant moments inversely related to Gagnez' ongoing battle with self-esteem. It was symptomatic of his position at the ass end of a long line of Imperial Spain sycophants.

"Ewe should not be *ear*. Why are you NOT. IN. TANGIER!"

The prince signaled Lanning with a quick wink. Although only sixteen, his royal bearing of righteous entitlement had already taken firm hold of his demeanor. Ignoring Gagnez, Lanning stretched out on the bench to enjoy the entertainment.

"Be gone, Monsieur Lickspittle! You presume to interrupt our exercise?" said the prince dismissively.

As he spoke, he waved his right arm towards the Viceroy, and offered a conspiratorial smile to Lanning.

Gagnez raged on. "You are SEETTEENG DOWN! Drinking WHINE!!"

"Mongrel! You doubt the word of the heir to the Spanish throne? Be off before we become bored with your very existence."

Refusing to turn around, the prince whispered to Lanning, "Rather enjoyable diversion, yes? Has he gone?"

"Afraid not," answered Lanning. "In truth, it looks as if the man might explode."

"Let that impotent, sycophantic, dim-witted flesh balloon burst. Would be more entertaining than a flute solo. Ha-ha."

While Lanning had surely enjoyed the prince's hijinks, he knew the shield of royalty would not protect him beyond the palace grounds.

"Allow me a moment, Highness?"

The prince nodded, as Lanning stood up and approached the fuming Gagnez.

"Do not think for a minute I don't know you're ducking me Delaford!" said the red-faced official in a more hushed voice minus Gaelic overtones.

Lanning maintained his cool temperament in responding to Gagnez.

"But I have it, Your Goodness. You shall no doubt have it by supper. My other boat will be unloading in the harbor as we speak. Besides, what is the gain in dodging you? As you can see, at the moment I'm engaged with the prince, who would sooner see you detonate than listen to us jousting."

Outgunned by all but the kitchen spit boy, Gagnez' efforts were perpetually sabotaged by his own greed and incompetence. It drove him mad with anxiety, and like his spherical physique, nourished an always expanding inferiority complex.

"Everyone is out to swindle me! You promised the same only yesterday," Gagnez said.

"As I'm sure the Viceroy is well aware, shipping and delivery are a relative science dependent upon conditions of sun, moon, sky, wind, and water. I ask only for patience, my Lord."

Lanning, along with everyone else at court or in service of it, had read the playbook on Roderick Gagnez. Winning being his singular mission in life, "Rod" practiced a zero-sum gain strategy. Life's gifts held no meaning for him unless they came at someone's expense. Tragically, in an age of shifting loyalties, regional power plays, and the rapidly spreading influence of Machiavelli's page-turning *Idiot's Guide to Despotic Power Maintenance*, Gagnez' meager intellect was publicly, nakedly, overmatched.

Gagnez owed his present station in life along with his waning shreds of self-esteem to the sustaining gift of nepotism. His claim to power relied upon the genetic tether to his grandfather, Gregorio Alfonso del Campo Gagnez. Ferdinand and Isabella, the recently large and in-charge royals, had required the services of Grandpa Gagnez's private regional army. In order to keep the Moors from expanding their foothold in Granada during the final act of the fifteenth century, an agreement was forged. It included certain favors along with buckets of royal treasure. The *favors* were granted. They extended up and all the way down to the bottom dweller of the Gagnez family tree. Voila, Monsieur-Señor Viceroy of the backwater region known as Algeciras.

Rod suppressed his feelings of mortification by obsessive serial eating. His latest compulsion was a mixture of mashed chickpeas, ground hulled sesame seeds, olive oil, a squeeze of fresh lemon juice, sea salt and a healthy amount of fragrant garlic. Gagnez adored hummus. The glutinous haze of a private hummus feast quelled his anxiety and allowed his world to make sense for a brief moment. In Rod's mind, the most glorious orgasmic hummus of the 16th century came from the dark land a mere fifty kilometers away from his door. Only one man knew the exact location of the Tangier chef who made vats of the stuff specifically for the Viceroy of Algeciras. That man was wasting time teaching tennis to the obnoxiously entitled, Prince Frederick.

Lanning was well aware he held the trump card in their fragile relationship.

"A pox on you! Twice!" blurted the frustrated Viceroy.

Lanning knew Gagnez was more bluster than action. "And on you sir!" he returned the salvo.

"I caution you against trying my patience, lad." Gagnez huffed away from the terrace and waddled back into the palace.

A tittering laugh caught Lanning's attention. Swiveling away from the departing anger balloon, he caught a glance from a youthful, olive-skinned girl with wavy auburn hair. She stood tall and lean, dressed in a flowing, green gown. From her spot on the balustrade, she had observed the proceedings for her own entertainment. Lanning caught her eye with his raised brow. She nodded, smirked, curtsied, then headed back inside after the Viceroy.

"Who was *that*?" Lanning asked the prince.

The prince let out a cynical grunt. "Ugh, Filippa Beaufort! The only thing to like about her is her scent. She smells like a summer night!"

"Very romantic, Freddy!"

"Trust me, she's a waste of time."

"As in, spoken for? Because she actually looks like a good use of time to me."

"My friend, you truly have no clue as to the true freedom of day, world, and life you enjoy so dismissively! No matter, I do hope someone remunerates you for showing up day after day, week after week for futility in teaching me the tennis," said the prince.

Lanning appreciated the thought. Even though the prince's concern felt more akin to noticing an un-watered shrub than true compassion for his livelihood.

"Do I get paid? Is that what that means?" teased Lanning. "Hell yes, I get paid. Not enough, but your Exchequer Minister, tosses me a sack of coins every week."

"You'd like more?"

Who couldn't use more money, especially when asked so innocently by the Royal? Lanning did not want to take advantage of his relationship with the prince for something as miniscule as tennis lessons. There might come a time when his friendship with Prince Frederick would have greater advantage.

"I'd prefer some fresh-squeezed juice after the lesson!" Lanning joked as he gathered his things, "Would you mind if I pay my mother a quick visit?"

"As you choose, but the flautist has a solo coming up, and there's still half a liter of sauvignon left."

"See you in a couple days, Freddy."

"Cheers!" The prince raised yet another glass of wine in a departure toast.

Lanning left his racquet on the bench, made his way off the court, then down and around the side of the palace. He headed for a set of stairs leading to the bottom floor, where his mother, Victoria "Molly" Cortez, worked as the palace baker.

Pushing open the pitted, six-inch thick wooden door he found his Rubenesque mother seated on a three-legged stool before a large, flat table. Rolled out in front of her lay a giant slab of dough. Flour covered the table, the dough, Molly's apron, and Molly herself. She had heard the footsteps and looked up to meet Lanning's gaze walking in.

"Really? You wore that to see the prince? Does your mother still need to dress you?!"

"Hi Molly." Lanning ignored her critique.

"This is the palace. You need to start dressing for success."

"I'm here to hit balls, not dance at one. It's tennis."

"I can't keep up with your new-fangled ideas. Give me a hand?"

Molly lifted one end of the weighty dough, motioned for Lanning to grab the other end, and do likewise.

"Mom, it's a sport... like baking..." They grunted while flipping over the dough slab. It landed back onto the table with a deep, whapping thud.

"Ha ha!" She wiped her hands on her apron.

"What's this monstrosity of dough about to become?"

"It's my royally delicious *pan rustico*! A palace favorite. Ask me why I'm making it today."

"I'll bite. Why are you making this today?" Lanning boosted himself onto the worktable.

"Che cazzo! Get the hell off of that table, boy!" Marco Bellini, the Italian head chef of the palace, had appeared as if by magic.

Bellini stood halfway between five and six feet tall. Head man for less than a year, he was Molly's only source of discontent. She tolerated his pugnacious contempt for the veteran kitchen staff, ignoring his moodiness and steering clear of his domain in the upper kitchen.

"Sorry Señor Bellini, that is my fault. He was giving me a hand with the rustico."

"Do we need to hire more help for you, or perhaps, you are getting too old for the work?"

"Hey now," Lanning said.

Bellini stroked his chin deciding how best to counter Lanning's provocation.

Molly stepped between the two men. "Señor Bellini, can I help with something upstairs?"

A devious smirk flashed across the man's face.

"Nothing of you is required. I'm off to meet the king's butcher."

Bellini brushed uncomfortably close to Lanning on his way out the door.

"Keep your boy in line!" he said before slamming the door shut.

Lanning scowled, "Bastard. I should kick his ass!"

"And end up in the stocks, or worse. I don't think so, son of mine," said Molly harshly.

"Weird. Did you see he's missing part of his little finger?"

Molly carried on with her work.

"What an asshole. How do you take that abuse?"

"Never mind him," Molly said. "I've got an opportunity for you, but you better go home and change first."

"Change? I'm on my way to the docks. Got to check last night's shipment and make sure it's delivered to the Viceroy. These two boats are wearing me out, not to mention draining my funds. I need to ready the L'Aquila for the trip to Tangier tomorrow, then find the money to pay for all of it."

"Exactly why you're going to put something presentable on. You can't look like a common thief and meet these people. Hightail it back before supper."

Lanning knew that once Molly had her mind set, the discussion was over. Begrudgingly, he gave her a peck on the cheek.

"Love you, Mol!"

"That's MOM to you!"

He flashed her a smile before heading out the door and up the stairway towards the tennis court.

Chapter 3
MARVIN GAYE SAYS...

Walking across the grounds to retrieve his racquet, Lanning heard two raised voices spitting a cascade of curses. Bellini stood inches away from a stocky, balding man waist-wrapped in a blood-soaked apron.

Feet squarely planted, the palace butcher, Contigo Sousa, stood by his single horse-drawn wagon. A steady rivulet of blood seeped off the wagon's underside, a macabre renaissance marker for freshness. Contigo had delivered a cartload of spit-ready carcasses. Sheep, steer, pig, and venison were packed against each other like cordwood. Wedged alongside in all the available cracks lay a healthy variety of fowl ranging from ducks to geese to swans. Tossed over the top of the entire ensemble like some ornamental throw rug lay a single dolphin corpse.

Lanning's olfactory senses assured him the dolphin was well past any reasonable freshness date. Maybe that's what this was about. He covered his nose as Bellini flashed a "get the fuck out of here scowl" his way. Lanning hoped nothing they argued about would blow back on his adoptive mother. Only his concern for Molly had slowed his walk.

Back on the tennis court, Lanning retrieved his racquet along with a leather pouch brimming with coins. "YES," he thought, "Thank you Freddy!" His next obstacle would be finding a fast way down the hill to the Algeciras docks. Once outside the palace grounds, he broke into a jog. After ten minutes, he heard a wagon approaching from behind. Contigo, the butcher, in his now empty, red-stained, wagon was heading his way. Lanning waved his arms. Contigo pulled to a stop.

"Climb in."

Lanning jumped up sitting to the left of Contigo. He couldn't help noticing the sloped shoulders and the acute level of exasperation in Contigo's voice.

"I heard some of that. It didn't sound good," Lanning said.

"Look at this insulting shit." Contigo shoved a purse of coins towards Lanning, who was now sitting beside him on the wagon. The pouch was three times larger than the one bulging in Lanning's pocket.

"That guy's a first-class prick. I gather he shorted you?"

"We have a history. Carving up nature's beasts wasn't my first goddamn career choice you know!"

Contigo whipped the reins against his horses' haunches in frustration. The wagon picked up its pace. The horse glared back at its owner as if to say, 'Yo Blood Merchant, kindly work out your anger issues somewhere other than on my aching, wagon-pulling ass.' Contigo understood the silent message. He expelled a regretful sigh.

"Sorry, Bado."

Lanning didn't know the butcher well, but had seen him around the castle from time to time. He'd never seen him angry.

"Now I've made you uncomfortable," Contigo said.

"No, I'm okay," Lanning lied.

"Yes. I've made you uncomfortable. Darn it. I'm sorry. You don't need to ask about my job, or my family situation, or how that misguided missionary from hell, Torquemada, destroyed all of us. Bless the holy spirit, and the Jesus for picking up the slack with his cross bearing, plus the whole crucifixion deal, which was more about the Romans, definitely not the Jews. Praise God. Sorry."

"Uh... Sure, I think I get that," Lanning stammered.

"You have no damn idea." Contigo looked around and raised his arms. "You think *this* was my first choice? I'm Portuguese. My family is blown all over the map, thanks to that bastardo! Watch your mother's ass. Watch your ass, too. I'm so damn sick of this godforsaken country."

"You don't talk like a butcher. What about my mother?" Lanning asked.

"Forget your mother right now. I mostly meant literally watch your own ass. When they come, grab the reins, and keep us heading straight. Bado will do the rest."

Lanning had been watching his own ass for quite a few years, ever since his father had died. Contigo was weaving an un-trackable collection of non-sequiturs in his direction. He felt confused, but then realized Contigo was motioning behind and off to the right side of the wagon.

Lanning pivoted and saw a dust cloud growing larger by the second. Five horses with riders swinging blades suddenly exploded from the cloud, bearing down on the wagon. Lanning grabbed the hilt of his sword and began swallowing gulps of air, hoping to bank some additional courage prior to certain attack. His father, a soldier, had spent many hours training him in the skill of sword play. Sure, it wasn't his real father, Lanning thought as his mind spun off into paranoia. "Maybe that means he trained me half-hearted? Shit, what if I suck at swordsmanship." Happily, he had never faced a true test of his skills. Two against five did not make for the best odds.

Contigo tracked the unfolding events and calmly handed him the reins.

"Hmmm, I thought there'd be more. Stay straight."

"More?" Lanning said. "Maybe we can reason with them? Probably just want money. Isn't that better than facing death or maiming? We're not heroes."

They could feel the thundering hooves of the approaching band. Kerchiefs covered the men's faces below their eyes. Ignoring Lanning's remarks, Contigo reached behind him into the wagon and pulled out a broadsword –- twice the width of a normal foil –- plus a single shot matchlock pistol. He coolly prepared the gun for firing without paying much attention to the oncoming robbers.

As the riders approached the rear end of the wagon Contigo leaned over to Lanning. "Don't be shy, lad. Give Bado a little shake of the reins."

Lanning exhaled preparing himself for the unexpected. His bladder tightened. Fear clenches body parts. Fear of death has the highest clench factor in the fear catalogue. Time had never been in such viscerally short supply. What if he only had moments to live? Five men coming for more than his money. His breath, his heartbeat, his dreams, his future? Everything he had ever contemplated suddenly burst into his mind. He had plans. He'd had setbacks and delays, but hadn't felt defeated or overwhelmed. Five against two? For the first time he pictured his own death as an imminent reality.

"Stop thinking about bullshit. You are going to survive this," said Contigo.

How did Contigo know the contents of his brain? Lanning realized there was far more to the man than he'd noticed. However, that reflection would need to take a back seat to his self-preservation, which strongly recommended he do whatever he was told.

Whipping the reins as instructed Lanning again craned his neck to the rear of the wagon. The lead rider had dramatically closed the distance, and was relentlessly bearing down on them. Had this been the summer Olympics in another time, the soon-to-be victim might have competed for a gold medal in the high bar. Sadly, in 1519, fate had made other plans. With exquisitely imperfect timing, Lanning watched the lead rider jump from his horse, laying out in a perfect Jager Pike position. His fervent hope: catch the rail at the back of their bloody meat wagon, plant two feet for a perfect ten-point landing, then launch himself at Lanning, and cleanly slice his carotid artery with one swipe of his rapier.

Feeling the whip of the reins, Bado lurched, then exploded with shocking speed, accelerating to triple their previous pace. The frozen expression on the attacker's face foretold the result of his bold move. As his designated landing zone disappeared, the amateur gymnast hit the unforgiving packed dirt and gravel of the road in a full spread-eagle belly-flop. A deadly two step by his own rental horse completed the failed aerial routine. In a swift mortal sequence, his grey mare stomped its front hooves directly onto the man's chest and groin, caving in both with a deadly crunch. One down.

Contigo let out a maniacal belly laugh before turning in a practiced motion to fire the single shot from his matchlock. The streaking lead pellet caught the next rider square in the neck. The bullet ripped cleanly through his windpipe while dodging the cervical spine. Contigo's precise aim left the bullet a nice reservoir of remaining velocity. It took up permanent residence in the groin of the next tailgating rider. Three down.

Lanning's spirits lifted. With newfound optimism, he recalculated the day. For any sane man, watching all this carnage unfold would surely be sobering. He hoped the two remaining riders would recognize that the fickle winds of fortune had surely winked at them. He hoped they would reflect on their poor showing thus far, and decide to save their greed for another day.

"They'll give up," he said.

Contigo shook his head. "Not hardly."

Maybe the final two men had minimal skill sets and simply could not find another decent profession to pursue. Mid-Renaissance job fairs and community college re-training programs being few and far between, their options were severely limited. Maybe they were part of a long family tradition of larceny, violence, and bad parenting. Maybe they were simply morons.

Contigo recognized a different truth: they were paid assassins out for a healthy ambush commission. Whatever their reasons, or lack of, the two surviving raiders maintained their steady approach to the wagon.

"No job is worth this," said one bearded hombre galloping along on an Appaloosa.

"After what they just did to Evan! No fucking way. That guy's gotta pay," answered the larger fellow riding a chestnut mare.

"I don't give a shit about *Evan*. Besides, I've got dinner plans. I say we blow this off."

"Ride," came the terse command.

"Look behind us. Three down! The other guy is only driving. It's the two of us now, and we just met. How do I know you know what you're doing?"

"You're no nun, pal. A job's a job. Take the left side and kill that big fucker. I'll go right and lay out the kid, then come back to help you. If you turn tail, you're as good as dead."

"This is messed up. And NOT worth it," grumbled the man as he whipped the Appaloosa across its haunches and picked up speed.

Lanning watched as the riders split sides. One approached on the left, the other on the right. He pulled his sword, anticipating the battle to come.

"Remember," Contigo repeated his hand motion, drawing an imaginary line directly ahead of them, "STRAIGHT. I'll have this wrapped up in another minute or so."

Contigo hopped into the back of the racing wagon with surprising deftness. He held his balance against the uneven ground passing beneath the wooden wheels. His right hand gripped the broadsword while his left flipped open a small oak box lodged against the buck-board. Rummaging through the box piled high with all manner of disemboweling tools, both sharp and dull, he pulled out a well-worn meat cleaver along with a rusted iron mallet.

"Were you expecting this?" asked Lanning.

"Convenient tools of the trade son." He handed Lanning the mallet. "Might come in handy."

The driving hooves of the horses rapidly closed in on the bounc-ing, rattling wagon. Contigo flipped the cleaver in the air briefly before catching it by the wooden handle. He let it fly end over end. It stuck the right-side rider with a perfect bullseye deep into his chest, explod-ing his heart. The rider had a frozen moment to gaze down and do the math. His realization of waning mortality would be emblazoned in Lanning's memory until his own light faded out. The rider surrendered to his fate, falling from the chestnut mare and hitting the ground, rag-dolling to a lifeless, rolling stop.

"Goddamn! You dirty bastard!" shouted the last rider.

Keeping impeccable balance despite the terrain change, Contigo shifted toward the wagon's left side rail. He raised his double-bladed longsword, expecting to meet the rapier of the last rider. The appaloosa and rider pulled even with the racing wagon. To Contigo's disbelief, the robber pulled out his own matchlock pistol. Staring at a point-blank shot straight to his face, Contigo flashed on his daughter as he braced for certain death.

Unaware of Contigo's impending peril, Lanning focused on his only job. Keeping the wagon straight. He saw that the road ahead veered to the left towards town, creating an unexpected navigational conflict. By the word "straight" did Contigo mean in reference to the general landscape, or to the existing well-worn road? Given that Contigo was engaged in a life-threatening clash, Lanning figured it was up to his discretion. He opted for the literal definition. He let Bado in on his decision by gently pulling on the reins. Disregarding the road, he maintained a straight path through the scrub brush unfolding directly in front of the wagon.

Lanning turned and saw the pistol come out. He laid the reins to Bado. With no time to spare, Lanning aimed the iron mallet. It hurled end over end. He felt good about its trajectory as it traveled through space and time. In the world's most poorly choreographed moment Bado lurched the wagon off road into the scrub brush. The rider watched bemused as the mallet sailed harmlessly by him disappearing in a cloud of dust behind the wagon. By the time he turned back to fire on Contigo, the gap between the wagon and horse had quadrupled. He fired anyway. The bullet grazed Contigo's right shoulder which only pissed him off more.

"I told you to keep the wagon straight!" Contigo shouted.

"I saved you," yelled Lanning.

"I guess," said Contigo glancing at the trickle of blood seeping through his shirt.

The rider adjusted his course back towards the wagon, swinging his rapier. An angry, but delighted to still be alive Contigo, grabbed his basket hilted long sword, eagerly waiting for the rider to approach.

"You're dead, old man," declared the approaching rider.

Contigo lightly nodded and prepared himself.

Their blades clashed over the wagon's rail with a metallic scrape like nails on a chalkboard. Surprising the final attacker, Contigo leaped onto the appaloosa behind the rider. He pulled a short, serrated knife from his belt. Reaching around the shocked man he slit his throat in one clean, deadly motion before shoving him off the horse. Contigo pulled back on the horse's reins, bringing it to a stop. Bado needed no prompting, and brought the wagon to rest alongside his master.

Contigo flipped off the Appaloosa, cut the saddle ropes along the horse's belly, took off the bridle, then slapped it in the hindquarters. The horse galloped off towards its new life of freedom.

"Need a piss? I know I do." Contigo moved beside the wagon to relieve himself.

"You're either the most dangerous butcher in Andalusia, or not really a butcher at all," said Lanning.

"I have experienced treachery before," said Contigo, climbing back into the wagon.

"Treachery? Bellini? Has this got something to do with Molly?"

"Nope. Not talking about that anymore," Contigo said.

He grabbed the reins, letting Bado know it was time to move on.

"You can't drop a bomb like that on me, then clam up!"

"I don't want you to overreact to something I said off the cuff."

Lanning cut him off. "Five guys tried to kill us! Definitely *fairly* unusual for me!"

"It was me they wanted. You were inconvenient. Doesn't change this shit country or my situation at all." answered Contigo.

They rolled along in silence, Contigo brooding and muttering to himself, while Lanning stared vacantly at the passing scenery. They saw two sentries still as sphinxes guarding a pharaoh's pyramid, either that or they were both fast asleep. Their presence signaled the archway announcing the entrance to Algeciras proper. Had he chosen to stay straight Contigo could've easily dropped Lanning off by the harbor. After passing the gates, Contigo yanked on the reins to make a sharp right turn, then pulled to a stop.

Contigo looked Lanning directly in the eye. "Kid, I'd rather die on my feet than live on my knees."

"A colloquial expression?"

"Actually, that's more of an aphorism. My poetic way of express-ing the truth."

"Why not just say what you mean and forget the poetry?"

Contigo cut him off. "Son, the world may be well and truly flat, but what comes around still goes around. Nuf said, right?"

Lanning hopped down off the wagon.

"Can't say I get the metaphor, or even what the hell you're talking about. And now I'm pretty nervous about the entire content of the conversation. I hope things improve. For you anyway."

"Tell Molly I said hello. Praise Jesus." He shook the reins, "Let's go, Bado."

Chapter 4
STROLLING

Despite the inauthentic, animated, outpouring of Jesus love, Lanning figured Contigo for a Marrano, a Jew who'd converted to Christianity to save himself from the hellfires of the Inquisition twenty years earlier. The carnage inflicted on the Jews and their families left open wounds scattered all across Europe from the Atlantic to the Med, reverberating as far north as the Russian border.

Trying to self-soothe himself away from the near-death misadventure, Lanning rubbed his neck. As if getting the kinks out would remove the experience from his permanent memory. He rubbed and walked down the dirt and gravel main street into Algeciras. Avenida Virgen del Carmen ran the length of town, beginning from Lanning's drop-off point, banking slightly rightward, down to the water before finally winding up at the bustling seaside quay. The street ran roughly two muddy spring or dry summer miles. Del Carmen, wide enough for two-way cart traffic, supported a random amalgam of chickens, goats, the occasional wandering cow, and dogs a-plenty. The foot traffic cruising up and down the avenue consisted of merchants laden with goods; delivery men; drunken, horny, or sated sailors coming or going; half-naked children; and the odd mystery traveler. Lanning considered himself in it, but not of it. His private nature and post-skirmish shakes kept him navigating along the edges.

With no modern zoning laws to impede or govern construction, commerce, or anything else, the street was lined with everything from brothels to fruit stands, dry good shops, lean-to homes, and of course, pubs. Lanning spotted his favorite pub from a few blocks away. The Squirrel & Mutton occupied a corner at the intersection of Calle

Mimosa and Avenida del Carmen.

Lanning curled into a nearby alley to relieve himself. As he peeled back his trousers, his ears detected the cold steel slide of a rapier slowly departing its scabbard. Given the neighborhood, Lanning half-expected it. Luckily the skill of the swordsman lacked a bit of style. Lanning sensed he had options.

"Can you give me just one more second?" Lanning requested with his back still turned.

"Uh...sure?" came the hesitant response.

A rather unexpected scraping sound gave Lanning enough time to complete his business and put himself back together before turning around, braced for a fight.

"I'll take that fat purse if you please." An imposing scuff of a man with broad shoulders, a layover belly, spotty red beard covering chipmunk cheeks and a bald head stood blocking the exit. His tone had a touch of frustration tempering the seriousness of the predicament for Lanning. The man continued struggling to pull his rusty sword the rest of the way out of its sheath.

"You've got to oil a rapier, friend. If you don't take care of it properly, it's going to keep rusting." Despite the threat, Lanning maintained his calm.

"Take care, bold midget! It'll still run straight through your innards whenever I get it out." The brigand struggled once more to remove it from the scabbard.

While the man was distracted with his equipment malfunction, Lanning managed to steal a few precious coins out of his sac, slyly dropping them in his left boot. Still the threat was real.

"First of all, this is a man-bag, not a purse. A purse is insulting. Why do you want it? How about I give you a few coins for your trouble, enough to get some oil for that sad scabbard, and we call it a fair and successful robbery?"

The man changed colors to match his beard. Lanning could tell the direction this was headed.

"Purse or life? You choose, little man. It's all the same to me, except for the mess."

Lanning gave it one more shot, "I could pull my own sword, then we'd see what's what, my overheated friend."

"Fine with me," answered the man mightily struggling with his weapon.

"Well shit!" said Lanning. "Do we both think it's worth the cost? How about this. I'll toss it over if you step to the side and let me pass."

"Don't be fooled by my size sprite. I'm quicker than I look."

The red beast jogged over to the side of the alley opposite Lanning's pissing position. "Toss it high and be on your way."

Even though he had managed to safeguard some of his much-needed coins, Lanning hated conceding defeat. He tossed the bag high in the air and scooted past the robber, back onto the main drag. He heard the man calling after him.

"Manage your bladder better next time, Elf! These streets are treacherous for your kind. Hahaha!"

Fifty feet down the block in front of a lean-to reeking from open septic and humming with kids, Lanning stopped to cinch his waist rope and re-secure his sword.

"I'll take whatever coins you've got on you, if you please."

'Impossible!' thought Lanning. 'Same voice, same manners?' In disbelief he looked up to find the very same man he walked away from only moments before.

"Are you touched? You just robbed me not one minute ago!" Lanning said in disbelief.

This time Lanning was prepared to draw his sword and battle

it out, despite the daunting physical odds against him. However, the beast in front of him was suddenly preoccupied. He had turned to look back up the street crowded with people.

"Damn it! Hector!" He screamed at the top of his lungs.

"HECTOR! What the hell?"

Lanning witnessed his mugger tromp down the street toward him once again.

"You guys are fucking brothers?!"

"Twins," answered the man. "And he's poaching my turf."

As he spoke, Hector walked up to the two men. "Don't bother. He doesn't have shit," said the smirking brother.

"AGAIN, Hector?" yelled the twin.

Hector wore the guilty expression of a ten-year-old boy caught with his hand in the cookie jar.

"But Lonzo, I was way over there." Hector pointed up the block.

"No, you weren't," chimed in Lanning. "You were 50 feet up the street!"

"You just lied to my face?" declared Lonzo. "If you're going to lie to me, what do we have? Brothers don't lie to brothers!"

A scrawny, pale skinned girl with tousled red hair stuck her head out the window of the ramshackle house behind the men. "Dad?"

Lanning jumped back a pace. "You live there?" he said pointing at the lean-to.

"Maybe," said Lonzo.

"Hi Uncle Hector," said the girl before launching into a wheezing, hacking cough.

"That's a pretty sick kid," said Lanning.

Lonzo appeared unconcerned. "What makes you say that?"

"Because she looks like shit, and NO ONE anywhere wants the plague again," Lanning shot back.

"I feel great. We're all lean. Dad says we're athletic."

"Get back in the house, Vicki." Lonzo glared at Lanning. "Listen, friend, she certainly does NOT have **the** plague as you call it. It's a common cold, and she's a little hungry. I'm being a good father trying to provide for my kid, uh, kids. And now you, who claim to care so much about the population at large, don't want to donate a little to the cause? What a hypocrite!"

"First of all, this was a mugging, not a fund raiser, and I already gave to your brother's cause. Right, Hector?"

"I don't see any of *his* money, which is another whole thing," said Lonzo.

Hector was trying to keep up with conversation. It all passed him by like a train running through a station without stopping. "I didn't get much from this guy, but…"

Lanning's frustration with the family drama had reached the boiling point. "Fine, take a couple reals. You two can sort it out. I'll be on my way. Buena suerte kid, and for Christ's sake, go see a damn doctor or at least a capable dentist!" He tossed a couple coins to the girl hanging out of the window, finished knotting his belt, and took off down the street.

"Appreciate the kindness! See you again." Lonzo shouted after him.

"Not damn likely!" Lanning fired over his shoulder.

Twenty paces down the street feeling a grumbling in his stomach, Lanning headed towards the Squirrel & Mutton. A tender, slow-roasted leg of mutton sounded like a great idea to him right now, yet somehow, he knew better.

Chapter 5

THREE DRAGONS WALK INTO A BAR...

"Welcome to the Squirrel & Mutton."

The buxom "waitress" at the door, stood five feet one in every direction. She had packed herself into a fashionably belted burlap bag, circa medieval times. Her uniform was tattooed with enough ale and blood stains to look like a sixteenth-century Jackson Pollock.

"You should know right up front: there's no mutton."

"That's not news, Doris. Why don't you forget the mutton and change the name of this place to the "Squirrel & Ale"?

Life in Algeciras was difficult. Simply being alive for consecutive days represented a monumental achievement for the commoner class like Doris. The ability to make a living on top of surviving wars, pestilence, rampant communicable diseases, and royal taxes was a luxury. Humor was in short supply and generally reserved for the well-off, the victors, or the dimwitted. Doris' disposition landed somewhere in the mix.

She answered Lanning with a blank stare, "Table for one?"

The large dark room had no windows and a series of well-worn alderwood tables with benches packed wall to wall. The overwhelming smell fused stale ale, burned animal flesh, and moldy bread into a symphonic mélange of dank nausea. Today's lunch crowd contributed a healthy portion of regional body odor to the mix.

"Down front, okay?" Doris asked while navigating between the tables.

"Not really. No."

Doris completely disregarded Lanning's reply as she bumped her way down front. The Squirrel & Mutton hosted weekly entertainment.

It served as an ideal distraction from customers paying too much attention to the food-proximity items served on the toxic, lead-filled, iron plates in front of them. No real concern to anyone, as cancer had quite a few years head start on healthcare.

"You're in luck today," she said. "Aside from this pathetic first act, Otis the Lute Master is the headliner. He rarely comes on tour. Wait this guy out and you're in for a real treat."

"Lady and gentleman, we are in luck, my best pal Lanning Delaford just sat down. Great timing, buddy."

Twenty-three-year-old Lorenzo Espinosa stood in the center of the feeble candlelit stage. He wore a traditional green, purple, and gold motley hat sporting three folded-over points, topped by a single bell at the end of each point. In his right-hand Lorenzo waggled a marotte, a symbolic ruler's scepter bedecked with a carved boar's head, the symbol of a graduate. Fulfilling a life-long ambition, Lorenzo was in his final semester at the little-known Algeciras Court Jester Academy. Lanning knew of his friends' obsession, but hadn't realized he'd be stumbling into the pre-exam tune-up session for Lorenzo's graduation performance, two weeks hence.

Reluctant, and somewhat embarrassed at having been called out to the room, Lanning sheepishly took his seat.

"You wanna hear the special?" Doris asked.

"Not at all. Mutton and ale combo, please."

"You'll like the squirrel. It's only three days old."

"Squirrels don't have much meat. Sure you have enough?"

"Oh, we always have plenty of squirrel. If you're skittish, we have some tuna lying around, but it's not on the chef's recommended list."

"Tuna sounds better than squirrel."

"We can chisel off a piece for you if you're feeling suicidal."

"Squirrel please."

"I'm gonna bring you a little something new to drink. You'll like it. By the way, I'm off at dusk. You still know there's more to me than burlap."

Recalling a drunken night several years earlier, Lanning let her last comment drop on the floor. Doris walked away with a wink, leaving Lanning at the mercy of his pal's routine. He hoped Lorenzo was smart enough to play the fool, but had his doubts. Lorenzo usually preferred simply being the fool. An incompetent Jester shared the same life expectancy as a mace bearer in an archery battle.

Lorenzo leaned over, and pulled an empty chair up on stage. He took a seat and stared out at the room. The Mutton and Squirrel teemed with noise. Roaring laughter and loud men's voices mixed with clinking metal tins, and hard tack plates, wooden chairs scraped along the floor, and a throng of constant yelling between the front of the house and the kitchen. The only person paying any attention at all to Lorenzo was Lanning. They made eye contact as Lorenzo launched into his well-practiced routine.

"Three dragons walk into a pub,"

He paused, waiting for the room to catch up. He waited a bit longer, then hit the punchline.

"There were no survivors."

There were also no laughs. Silence swept the room. Faces turned toward the lone performer who stared back at the crowd, unflinching.

"No?" Lorenzo said. "Damn! That was my best joke. This could be challenging."

"What do you call a man with no arms and legs carried by a knight?"

Lorenzo allowed for brief pause before letting loose the punchline, "Lance!"

"Ha-ha..." he chuckled. "Still, no? How about this one: A

barbarian, a rogue and a wizard are sitting in a sinking boat. The rogue is hiding and the wizard teleports away, so the barbarian jumps overboard himself."

"You suck!" came a booming voice from the middle of the room.

"Where's Otis?" shouted another.

"What the hell is wrong with you?" groused still another.

Already fairly drained from his near-miss experience, Lanning started to worry that he might need to protect his pal. He lightly gripped the hilt of his sword, just in case. Doris air-dropped his plate of food and waddled off.

Lorenzo had set the bait, waiting for the appropriate moment to style into his real routine. He keyed in on the heckler. "God, I truly hope nothing is wrong with me. I'm really trying to take better care of myself. I am. Lately, I've been worried about growing old during the pre-Renaissance. Aren't you? Think about this. No one, as in NOT ANYONE cares about you! My friend Manfred died from a splinter. A splinter, for God's sake.!"

Lorenzo rolled out three fingers in coordinated sequence, then held them up to underscore his point, "Infection, fever, dead. In THREE days. I know, crazy. Used to take at least two weeks for that shit to kill you."

"I'm terrified of the common cold. Remember the plague? Guess I don't have to tell you guys that sucked. I gotta stay healthy. I recently stopped smoking— I've been smoking since my first job shoveling horse manure in the royal stables. I know, what connections did I have to score such a great job? I was six, so my day rate was pretty low. But I was lucky. Anyway, I remember stealing some tobacco from my twin sister and hiding it under my hay bed in the bag I made from Shawn, my recently dead pet goat. His ball sac."

A few chuckles dotted the crowd.

"No, this is true. The next day, when I came home from the stables, my mom was holding up the pouch. 'I found your treasure, Mister!'" Lorenzo imitated his mother's high-pitched raspy voice.

"I felt like a bad pirate. I mean, a great pirate would have buried his prize on a deserted island in a deep hole, dug by three men, who he then killed, and tossed onto the chest. Then he would've covered the whole gruesome mess with dirt. Like a pro! Stuffing tobacco into a ball sac under some hay, in your parents' house that you share with six other kids, three goats, six chickens, and your dead grandmother—honestly, we thought she was really tired for a couple weeks—is, well, kind of pathetic. Right?"

"The whole aging thing scares me. Not just staying healthy, but the circle of life thing. I'm bound to be a terrible father. My kids should have someone filled with energy, tossing them up on my shoulders and running around the block. Me, I'm dog-tired all the damn time at twenty-three! The world will probably look like absolute horrible shit to them. That's no way to bring them up."

"Kids today have no idea what's coming at them in the future. I didn't take care of myself when I was a kid because I just figured I'd live forever. I was invincible. Me and my pals, we'd do crazy shit. Wanna dive into the castle moat? Sure, that looks fun. What's a moat? I dunno, but I'm hot. Let's dive. Lucky for me, my buddy Manolo went first. Turns out it's actually pretty foul. Maybe you guys know this already but it's a cesspool! Plus, it's only like two-feet deep, so not refreshing at all. Not really worth the effort. Manolo died of an absolutely wicked horrible, massive infection within a week. So, lesson learned, I guess."

The room filled with laughter.

"Kids think, wow, the future...all mysterious. It could be any-thing right? There'll be superfast ships blasting straight to the edge of the world. Then they'll what? I guess they'll flip over? I could be on the

underside of the world…We're gonna be able to walk right off the edge
and stick on the bottom. There's probably all kinds of wild shit on the
other side. Naked women, free food—plenty of actual MUTTON!"
He glared at the back kitchen area, and chuckled.

"They'll be real bathrooms, everything we can imagine. But I'm
not the guy to go searching for that. No chance. You could simply hit
the edge and fall over into some abyss. End of story, or worse, I could
end up like Manolo."

"Yeah, I definitely need to take better care of myself. You don't
die when you're old, you just feel shitty the whole time. This aches,
that hurts, why am I coughing, I can't piss in a straight line anymore,
I don't want sex! Oh my God, is that part of it?"

"So yeah pal, I am trying to take better care of myself. You all
do the same. You've been a fantastic audience. If I made you smile or
contemplate the truth about life—tell a friend. If I didn't, order the
tuna next time. Thank you so much, and enjoy the squirrel!"

The room, including Lanning, burst into a well-deserved round
of applause. The act certainly suffered around the edges, but Lorenzo
had potential. He bounced off the stage, dropped his motley hat on
Lanning's plate, and sat down. Lanning had a fork full of squirrel
ready to go.

"Are you crazy? Don't eat that shit! It's over a week old!"

"All of it? I'm hungry."

"You can eat the plate. It's safer."

Lanning knocked the plate on the table, broke off a piece of it and
tossed it in his mouth.

"Not bad. Some kind of stale bread thing?"

"Non-toxic is all I know. Just take it with you and let's get out
of here."

Lanning dropped his fork as Bernardo the lanky, tattooed, owner and unwilling emcee, hopped onto the stage.

"Bang your cups together as the Squirrel & Mutton welcomes the sonic stylings of Otis and his Lute extraordinaire…"

The boys began making their way out of the dim pub. As Lorenzo pulled the door open into the broad daylight of Avenida Virgen del Carmen, Lanning heard a voice he knew all too well.

"Brother! I've been hunting your ass all over town. You had better get your tail down to the boat right now. You know who has been raging for an hour."

"About what?" asked a perplexed Lanning.

—•— Chapter 6 —•—
HUMMUS

"DELAFORD! You are destroying my dreams! Why do you insist on vomiting upon my generosity, defecating on my kindness? I have aspirations well beyond this shit-hole town I am forced to live in. You are killing my family's future, one deck board at a time."

"Don Espinosa, calm yourself. I have it here in my pocket. Well, most of it anyway," offered Lanning.

Figuring Espinosa was after the boat rental money, Lanning reached inside his pocket and pulled out his sac of remaining coins from the palace. Espinosa waved him off.

"WHERE is my BOAT?" he demanded. "You are missing a BOAT! My BOAT! I see what remains of your pathetic crew, but NOT MY BOAT! Did it fall over the edge? Disappear into the abyss between here,"

Espinosa emphatically pointed down at the dock with two open hands before extending his arms in a plaintive gesture towards the open sea to the south,

"or THERE?"

Lanning turned to his crew which was strung out in a pathetic, beaten wad along the dock. Lorenzo, seeing his enraged, red-faced father, tried to disappear in plain sight. He sheepishly removed his motley hat, scrunching it behind his back while strategically sliding away from the firing line. He found a nesting spot within the slouching clump of Lanning's crew. He watched sympathetically as his father continued to batter Lanning.

"As we can all PLAINLY SEE the BOAT is not tied to this creaking, rotting, piece of shit dock! Please tell me this is simply a parking problem, and I will take your rent money, buy us both beers, and allow you to breathe another day."

Oscar Espinosa, a short tempered, hot-headed, legendarily ruthless businessman, lived his life as a myopic misanthrope. He had a very small circle of trusted family members, did not tread beyond that circle, and did not give a damn about anything or anyone else outside his sphere. He was completely content with that immutable world view. The only person securely resident within the Espinosa circle of life was his wife, Antonietta. Lorenzo's admittance to the tight circle was dependent on his father's level of disappointment with his life choices, as judged on a bi-weekly basis.

Espinosa had fashioned a life of never-ending adversarial conflicts for thirty-two years. From the moment he arrived those many years ago by need over choice, he reviled Algeciras. He longed to return his own Basque roots in Northern Spain. Not once in his fifty-five years had anyone ever confused his behavior with any sentiment approximating kindness. His reputation was solidly anchored by the absence any act related to the genus of generosity. Don Espinosa, the one-eyed, northern Spain transplant, rented out a fleet of 'pre-owned' (like 14th century pre-owned) wooden objects closely resembling boats. His small fleet of trashed xebecs and dilapidated caravels, all long past their prime had produced an abundant cash flow for over twenty years. The cash Espinosa generated from his business was squirreled away in his *castle fund* for an eventual triumphant return to his beloved northern Spain. As the pile of carefully nurtured retirement funds approached completion, representing his overdue exit from the torture of Algeciras, Lanning lost a boat! To Espinosa, Lanning had not simply lost a boat; he had unrepentantly shattered and firebombed his long-cherished, singular dream of happiness. At this late date, whether or not the coast's most disagreeable man could ever actually bump into contentment and recognize it, was a longer-term issue.

The Espinosa rental fleet included both the missing xebec and, like the L'Aquila currently lashed to the dock, a couple of caravels. Both types were small, meagerly outfitted, two or three-masted vessels rigged with lateen sails. Each mast increased in size from the one aft of it. To any sailor unfamiliar with Espinosa's pathetic fleet of rentals and their current state of flotation, these boats were classified as 'caravela latina'. Lanning often referred to Espinosa's boats in public as 'caravelas detestas,' and in private as 'caravelas mierdas.'

Lanning preferred the L'Aquila as his primary cargo ship for the short run between Algeciras and Tangier. It was a more substantial boat than the missing xebec. A caravel could comfortably carry thirty tons of anything that fit in its eighteen-foot-high hold. Not only did it hold far more cargo than the missing vessel, but it possessed a shallower draft, creating an agile nimbleness in the water. Nimble speed was an asset in avoiding the omnipresent threat of pirates that loomed between the two cities.

Fully aware of Espinosa's temperament, Lanning made it a habit never to be delinquent on his rent. For the surprising news of a missing boat, he had no solution to abate Espinosa's fury.

"At last," thought Lanning. "Someone steps up for me!" Rodrigo (Rory) Garza, his head sporting a bump the size of a late summer melon, wobbled over towards Lanning. He rubbed his throbbing head with one hand while pulling his tattered clothing together with the other as he attempted to gather his wits.

"Lucky to be alive. Could-a, probably should-a been burned, drowned, and fish food by now. I tried to tell 'im."

"He's drunk," dismissed Espinosa.

"Always. But he's not crazy. Can I at least hear him out?"

Lanning didn't wait for Espinosa's answer, since he really did not need his permission.

"What happened? Where's the Antonietta?"

The particular M.I.A. boat, namesake of the queen of Espinosa's inner circle, had added a healthy dose of unwanted sea salt to the open wound. Rory spent the next few minutes detailing what he remembered from the previous night's pirate ambush. He ended by pointing to the oar boat tied up and lolling on the swells hitting the end of the dock.

"So, your crew got drunk and burned my boat to ashes," concluded Espinosa, dismissing the harrowing tale in its entirety.

"Not what I said at all," protested Rory.

"Not what he said in any way!" echoed Lanning.

"I expect immediate payment or replacement!"

"Gentlemen, when you plant a tree, every leaf that grows will tell you, what you sow will bear fruit."

Lanning and Espinosa turned towards the gray-haired, olive-skinned man wearing a Moorish cloak. The man approached them with open arms. The oldest friend of Lanning's father Gonzalo, Shafi had been a fixture in Lanning's life from childhood. His was an omni-present voice of reason, calm, and acceptance that Lanning had learned to trust in the absence of his adoptive father.

"Uncle, maybe not the best time?"

"Zip it, Balthazar!" Espinosa angrily turned back to Lanning, "Another drunk? Do you pick your crew by vintage? Here's what's going to happen. You have one day to find my boat, and that's only because my son likes you. I see you cowering back there Lorenzo."

Lorenzo expected his father had seen him, but the fear of his wrath had kept him shrinking in the back. On hearing the word "cow-ering," Rory had nudged Lorenzo to inspire some courage. Lorenzo, embarrassed by his own behavior, slowly stood up and crept forward.

"If you do not find the boat, and I mean the entire boat, you will pay all rent due on both boats, or I will give them to the next person in line. You will repay the loss of the Antonietta by paying me fifty percent of your receipts on shipments, until all reparations are made for the loss of my property. Questions?" Espinosa in no way planned on entertaining any questions.

A shell-shocked Lanning Delaford swallowed hard. Don Espinosa was attempting to impose a draconian agreement on him. His welling anger guided his left palm over the hilt of his sword. One easy lunge, and Espinosa would be gone. Who would blame him? The man was a bully. His crew would grab the corpse, weigh it down with improvised ballast, then gleefully toss the Don off the pier to meet his maker at the bottom of the harbor. He might even get a parade down Avenida Virgen del Carmen. Problem solved in under a minute. Lanning suddenly felt a calloused, warm hand covering his own. He released the grip on his sword as Shafi gently patted him on the back.

"That's not entirely fair, Señor Espinosa, but I believe you already know that. Here is the rent for the L'Aquila, as due. We will talk tomorrow," said Shafi, gently lifting the pouch from Lanning's other hand.

Espinosa scanned the dock witnessing Lanning's crew standing in defiance. Perhaps he realized the numbers were not in his favor, or maybe a glimmer of some ancient, long-dormant kindness bubbled up in his brain. More likely, pre-Darwinian survival adrenaline knocked some sense into him.

"Keep that damn invading Berber away from me."

"He's lived here forty years," Lanning defended.

"But he's not FROM here, is he?"

"Dad, we're not from here either." Knowing his father would only get angrier and more irrational, Lorenzo stepped in to try and settle things for Lanning.

"I don't trust anyone in a damn robe! The only thing worse is a Jew."

Lanning glanced at Lorenzo who rolled his eyes and shook his head. "Please don't," Lorenzo whispered.

Espinosa glared at Lanning waggling his index finger. "As sure I'm standing here, you will pay me my money tomorrow!"

"Father." Lorenzo stepped forward. "We can talk about this tomorrow. Take the money."

Lorenzo opened his father's palm as Shafi dropped all of the recently received advanced earnings into it.

"Tomorrow is coming soon," Espinosa said wagging a finger.

"It'll be here tomorrow," said Lorenzo, still trying to calm down his father.

"Hello down there!"

All eyes turned to see a strikingly handsome, dapper stranger approaching from the quay.

"Is this a good time for a chat?" he inquired with haughty entitlement.

The gentleman continued strolling down the dock towards the assembled grump squad.

"This seems like a friendly gathering of kindred souls. Which one of you is the captain of this mighty vessel?" he inquired.

To Lanning's eye, the gentleman sported the look of a Flemish nobleman, but lacked the distinctive guttural accent. Lanning, and virtually every other longtime resident of Algeciras, held a deep-seated contempt for the interloping Flemish. He and Espinosa were of one shared mind when it came to the new King's voracious foreign handlers.

"Gentlemen, have no apprehension. I am of Basque heritage."

"That's one thing going for you," said Espinosa.

Noting the common background with a quick wink, the man

removed his feathered hat, bowed gracefully, and announced, "Lieutenant Ignatius Loyola at your service."

He paused, allowing time for the implied trumpet fanfare and spread of imported Chinese fireworks to herald his presence.

For Lanning, the vacuous conceit of this stranger provided a much-needed release of tension. He laughed, as did Don Espinosa. To Loyola, whose cup of hubris runneth way over, the mockery proved disappointing, yet not debilitating.

The eventual Saint Ignatius had not yet made his considerable mark on the history of mankind, nor had history yet made its mark on him. His shape shifting moment with destiny would occur in only a few short months. Loyola had spent a host of formidable years partying in Castile at the court of Ferdinand and Isabella before their deaths. There, he developed a refined taste for all things courtly. As a robust, virile, and ravenously horny young man, he rightly construed every action as foreplay. Life existed as foreplay. Debauchery became his daily lifestyle choice. Loyola had his pick from a multitude of regal activities. He enjoyed gambling, dueling, drinking, and all the trappings of chivalry. The young man grew into a true courtesan: self-centered and contentious in equal measure chased with the invincible conceit of youth.

Currently in between deployments fighting for crown and country, Lieutenant Loyola had arrived at the Algeciras dock searching for a quick adventure and resumé builder across the channel in the exotic Kingdom of Morocco. The metro-sexual, thirty-year-old had grown into a full-blooded nobleman and warrior of some repute. Unbeknownst to him, fate and the Iron age were about to meet for drinks over his muscular left leg in three months' time. The blind date occurred during a particularly vicious fight defending the Spanish garrison at Pamplona against French invaders. Ignatius had no one to thank for this apparent misfortune but himself - but that's a tale for another day.

"Lieutenant Ignatius Loyola?" He repeated with a measure of incredulity. "Surely some of you have heard of me. My exploits have achieved some small level of renown in the kingdom, yes?"

"No," deadpanned Lanning. "If you're looking for Madrid it's that way," he said pointing north. "This is Algeciras, where the weak are killed and eaten!"

Lanning's crew filled the air with laughter.

Loyola proved a quick study. He reassessed his surroundings, found the humor, and adjusted.

"Captain, I assume? Apologies. At least I have provided some entertainment for your crew and...your father?" He respectfully bowed to Espinosa.

"Hah!" grumped Espinosa. "You waste our time."

"I will get to my point directly. I seek passage to Tangier, and am willing to pay for the privilege." Loyola pulled out a pouch and jangled it in front of Lanning.

"We carry cargo, not peacocks," dismissed Lanning.

"But," Shafi said usurping Lanning's authority. He stepped forward to smoothly snag the pouch from Loyola's open hand. In the briefest of moments, he determined its value. "We do enjoy the occasional guest as well!"

"Fortuitous timing can never be ignored, right Captain?" said Shafi.

The hint was fumbled, but not lost on Lanning, whose brain had rapidly turned into a three-ring circus juggling cascading events. He quickly did the math. The money he now owed to the detestable Don Espinosa, combined with his commitment to the equally awful

Roderick Gagnez, whose prepaid shipment of hummus was now likely at the bottom of the Gibraltar Strait, totaled Shafi's advice. Lanning knew he'd landed in a mad scramble for all the cash he could rally. For good measure, toss in his impending appointment back at the palace to further complicate a day in breakdown before the sun had hit noon.

"Uh, yes. You are, of course, quite right, Uncle. However, this," His hands drew a rapid series of imaginary circles in the air, encompassing everyone and everything, "will need to take a pause— not a lengthy pause, but a simple time out, while I tend to other pressing matters."

Lanning steadily backed away.

"Uncle make ready to sail," he loosely ordered.

"When?" asked Shafi.

"Splendid." said Loyola.

"You better be back by tomorrow, Delaford!" harangued Espinosa.

"Father! Please..." implored Lorenzo, moving to shepherd his father off the dock.

"Ah, now I see, wrong father," Loyola said realizing his error.

"When," Lanning fumbled. "How about soonish? But not right away, later...after a bit, tomorrow with the tide. I'm sorry I've got to get back to the palace," shouted Lanning, now moving onto the quay.

"I shall accompany you sir." Loyola proclaimed; neither expecting, nor waiting for approval from Lanning.

"Remember, Lanning," Shafi said, "the purpose of life is to be defeated by greater and greater things."

"In that case, Uncle, I'm having a phenomenal day."

"Older man, you have much to offer. I must study you at a deeper level," said Loyola to Shafi.

Chapter 7

THE ART OF TIPPING — PART I

GENOA — 1480ISH

"Grab yourself a candle, boy."

Marco Bellini, an acknowledged, reviled, irredeemable, narcissistic, asshole did not slide out of the chute like that on day one. He had a minute.

"Grab yourself a candle, boy." His dad had said it twice in between the f-bombs he lobbed at the local mod squad invading their one-room home on a Sunday.

You can never know which lessons a kid absorbs at the time they occur. Sometimes there are simply too many lessons happening at once to properly sift the usable from the horrible.

"Can't beat timeless, portable light when you need it," his dad had added on the day they hauled him off to debtors' prison...again.

"I'm going. Get your bastard hands off me! Son," he squeezed in his last words while being heel-dragged out the door, "Always brace for the worst; and don't forget a match!" Not the ideal childhood weekend with Dad.

That was the last time he encountered his father. His mother, claimed by the plague, meant he had been winnowed down to zero parents, Marco got a job at the age of nine.

* * *

Ten years hence, Don Burducci gulped down the remnants of his fourth Peach Lady. The well-crafted cocktail perfectly suited his epicurean food romance. He downed the brandy-soaked peach wedge lining the rim as a final flourish. Sated and entranced, he placed the empty glass down on the convenient end table. His fleeting moment of peace ended abruptly.

"Put down that knife you idiot!"

Exasperated, the Don tossed his extra fluffy, full length, sheep-skin blanket onto the stone floor. Gathering his expansive frame, he rose from his chair in the corner of the villa-sized kitchen and stormed to the granite countertop.

"Stronzo!" He grumbled, grabbing the razor-sharp knife away from the teenage Marco Bellini.

"You are incapable of learning anything. How many times must I show you?"

"I'm trying Don Burducci," whined the intimidated adolescent.

"Patience. Everything takes patience," scolded the impatient Don. "Remember, we serve others best when we serve ourselves first."

About the time Columbus had bamboozled Ferdinand and Isabella into funding his dream exploitation cruise, and many years before securing his position of authority at the palace in Algeciras, Marco Bellini served a dual apprenticeship with the founder of Genoa's most prosperous lamb exporter. Casa di Costelotte, a second-generation family business, was ruled by the iron-fisted, triple X-sized, Burducci. The Don had gleefully observed the zeal of nineteen-year-old Bellini while visiting his slaughterhouse one spring afternoon.

After a few months, the repetitive task of slaughtering lambs on a daily basis took its toll on the typical hourly worker. Not Marco. After six months on the job, he displayed an increase in both output and enthusiasm. His rapacious blade speed indicated a prodigy-level of callousness that signaled a higher calling to the observant Don.

"Kid, you've got gifts. Your talents are surely being wasted here. Let's make that your last lamb. Finish up and come with me."

Bellini turned doe-eyed upon hearing the offer. In his mind, he'd just won the perpetually rigged Italian lottery. At long last, someone of consequence had recognized his skillset. He quickly slit the last lamb's throat, dropped his blade, and turned for approval to the Don.

"Nice," said the Don as he headed for the main office.

As the blood pulsed out of the dying animal's body, Bellini followed the Don. He never looked back.

The conglomerate Casa di Costolette encompassed several businesses. Not content with being a regional lamb purveyor and wool exporter the enterprise stretched to include the more iconoclastic, lucrative, yet dubious enterprises of regional security, and, yep, extortion. The Don knew precisely where his young protégé's skillset would be best applied.

"You're on the path. Pay attention," said the Don.

Over the next four years, the Don schooled Bellini on all manner of Renaissance chicanery. In addition to his studies on extortion techniques, blackmail, and the fine art of the skim, young Marco honed his skills at close combat. He possessed a natural gift for concealment. He employed the assassin's best friend—a stiletto blade. Bellini wielded the needle-sharp point sitting atop a whisper-thin blade, unfettered by any ethical compass. This ruthless reptilian behavior could not be taught, but as the Don already knew, it could be nurtured. Nature enhanced by nurture fused at the pointy end of Bellini's blade.

Part of the young man's training was plenty of kitchen time. Don Burducci was a passionate chef. One could put knife skills to good use in the kitchen, and reap the benefits over a sumptuous meal. He instructed his student on the Genovese culinary arts precisely as they had been taught to him.

Rarely were kind words exchanged between the two. Don Burducci viewed Bellini as a piece of raw, un-sculpted marble. Somewhere inside, after removal of any extraneous pieces, lay his Platonic ideal of toxic purity. Or not. An errant chisel, or an unseen fissure buried beneath the outer layer could collapse any imagined potential for perfection. Training was a calculated crapshoot. You win some; you lose some. Best to fail as fast as possible and avoid disappointment. Fortunately for Bellini, he had performed well over the four years Burducci invested in him.

On this particular evening, the Don was observing his pupil prepare a regional classic dish - La Genovese. To make it properly required a deft knife hand matched with the aforementioned quality of patience. Two lessons in one for Bellini. A simple dish of onions, a bit of pancetta, an inexpensive cut of braising beef, some herbs, and a dry white wine. The process, which takes hours, yields an elegantly lush, creamy sauce, tasting of caramelized onions and pot roast, mostly savory, but combined with subtle traces of sweetness.

"The onions must be sliced translucently thin," counseled the Don.

Marco allowed his perpetual anxiety to slacken for a minute while watching the Don cut perfect slice after perfect slice of cippolini onion. Forgetting his place, he dropped his guard and tried to make conversation with the man who had taken such a keen interest in his future.

"Don Burducci, why do they call you 'Peaches?'"

Seemingly ignoring the question, the Don continued slicing, then glanced over at the teenager. "Put your hand over here on the cutting board. I want to show you the proper method."

Bellini came close to the Don and lay his right hand down on the board.

"No, no," said the Don, "you are right-handed, correct?"
Bellini nodded.

"For proper technique anchor your left hand on the table, fingers spread for support, like so."

The Don gently demonstrated by fanning the fingers of his hand along the cutting board. Bellini abided the instruction, spreading out his fingers. In a single flawless motion, the Don brought the chef's knife down upon the carving board, severing the top joint of Bellini's little finger in a split second.

"You forget your place, boy!"

The Don nonchalantly swept the fingertip off the cutting board into the trash along with the remaining pieces of uncut onion. Bellini remained expressionless, in shock over the unforeseen penance. The Don tossed a towel to the boy, motioning him to wrap up his bleeding finger.

"It's always easier when they don't expect it. Now clean yourself up and finish the sauce."

Tuition for Don Burducci's institution of higher learning was fully paid through personal sacrifice, the tip of one finger being the least of the price Bellini paid. Except for that one time, no one ever referred to Don Burducci as 'Peaches' to his face again. Bellini spent many hours in the kitchen learning how to cook, but more importantly, how to create a bountiful life on the stiletto sharp edge between shrewd cunning and dumbass avarice. Patience and ambition often contend for mind share in students of any profession. Marco proved no exception.

One day Marco would return the lesson and the blood-soaked cloth to his mentor.

Chapter 8
RENAISSANCE BASE JUMPING

Lanning, accompanied by his shadow, Ignatius Loyola, made his way up the quay along Avenida Virgen del Carmen towards the palace. Hoping to ditch his tag-along Lanning set a no-nonsense pace one notch below speed-walk.

"Captain, are we to walk or run? You seem conflicted," asked Loyola.

"It's less than five kilometers. If you need a rest, feel free to pull over."

Sensing weakness, Lanning accelerated.

They both heard a small commotion erupting from the nearby Plaza de Paloma, Ignatius veered over to investigate. Lanning ignored it.

"Be forewarned, Peacock. Crazy begins there," counseled Lanning.

"All men shall have their day! The Inquisitor is long dead," proclaimed Loyola, heading towards a small gathering of Algeciras locals.

"Only ONE despicable is burning in hell. It doesn't mean there won't be another to take his place standing in the wings," Lanning piped into the breeze.

"So...you're a tankard half empty kind of guy," replied Loyola.

Loyola continued veering over to investigate the crowd. Realizing he couldn't exactly abandon his only paying passenger, Lanning slowed his pace. He lagged several steps behind Loyola, fighting a memory-induced rising bile in his throat.

He walked by a dwarf asleep on the grass. The man had a rope fastened to one wrist. The other end held a beige bichon frise — a typical Andalusian dog. "Ugh," Lanning thought. What a total embarrassment as a species, let alone a regional representative. Couldn't Andalusians have selected a better breed of dog for their region? He wondered who was responsible for this inverted symbolism. The brave, adventurous, independent people of Andalusia represented by a whiny, ill tempered, over-fluffed excuse for a dog? Catalonians at least had the sheep dog. Goofy, but better than this tabletop ornament.

As an adopted Andalusian, he felt less true attachment to the choices made by the native population. Yes, it was most assuredly an awful symbolic choice, but thankfully, it was not his burden to bear.

For a brief evil-twin moment, Lanning contemplated granting the imprisoned dog's whining wish by cutting it loose. He balanced both the potential entertainment value versus the simple silence of stopping its irritating sniveling. True to his gentler nature, he simply chose to ignore it. He moved on to a familiar grassy rise behind the gathered crowd.

Begun twenty years back, following the harrowing fifteen years of royally decreed Torquemada terror, the local folks of Algeciras had managed to steal back a piece of their political independence. The Plaza de Paloma, former home of the Inquisition's local gallows, was benignly re-branded as "Speakers Corner."

The free space evolved from the previous moribund tradition granting every condemned victim a final say moments prior to their own execution. During this penultimate 'free time' the victim chose from a tragic dessert menu of terminal options. They might confess their crimes – a poetic, pleading, last gasp at a hoped-for reprieve through desperate contrition; or rampage against the 'man.' The pro-totypical 'rampage' option decried the consistently true draconian injustice inflicted upon their innocence by an evil, overzealous religious despot. For many, who knew their claims fell on not only deaf ears, but a debased collection of sadistically ghoulish voyeurs, they simply used the time to bid either a fond or defiant adieu to existence. Any of the optional choices held zero risk of retribution beyond the preordained finality of the victim's circumstance.

After a regrettably long life the despot, Torquemada, ultimately passed onto the fiery bowels of Hades to await the arrival of his soul-mates – Hitler and Stalin among others. Woefully, his apparatus of evil lived on, diminished only slightly by region. The Algeciras townsfolk determined that their time to grab back a piece of their independence had arrived at least in one corner of their domain.

The plaza, yet again rebranded some years ago as Rincon de Revelle, stood as the solitary spot in all of Andalucía designated as a free zone for the willing. It retained the free speech while terminating the more egregious practice of human extinction. Definite progress!

Anyone fervent, bold and, potentially foolhardy enough to risk all, had permission to speak their full and true mind to whomever might choose to listen. Rincon de Revelle welcomed even the intellectually incoherent to risk their fate at the hands of whomever passed for their peers. All who gathered on any side of the event collectively stood exempt from any sort of royal retribution. However, like a modern-day base jumper, they were advised to proceed at their own risk.

Loyola called back to Lanning once more before being absorbed by the crowd, "Really not coming?"

"I've seen this go sideways. I'm fine over here, but you enjoy."

Lanning staked out a spot that met his safety criteria.

"Looks friendly enough to me," said Loyola.

"Not always, Lieutenant!"

His curiosity now piqued; Loyola slid back over to Lanning's spot. "And?" he prodded.

"About twelve years ago," Lanning began. "Revelle, yep, square's name is his, don't remember his surname. Anyway, he'd been a former extended stay guest of the Inquisition; twenty years in the Toledo prison. Somehow, he evaded burning, hanging and disemboweling."

"Lucky guy," flipped Loyola.

"Matter of perspective. They convicted him for being a Jew. He claimed otherwise. It was a drizzly Saturday morning in November. My father and I were headed home from the docks, carrying our fresh caught sea bass for dinner. Like you, we heard the crowd and veered over to check it out. On the podium, poised and ready, stood the self-titled, local legend, El Afortunado – the Lucky One. A pillowy, middle-aged man with a voluminous white Santa beard and matching shoulder-length hair. My father, who had grown up with Alfredo, his real name, said he'd been growing that thing for his entire forty-five years.

"El Afortunado served as the square's regular warm-up act and de facto master of ceremonies. He performed his magic tricks in between the day's more passionate podium visitors. At our birthday parties he'd pull a veritable potpourri of unexpected items out of that beard - birds, prosciutto, a lute! One time, with some effort, he yanked out a camel head. Scared the crap out of Lorenzo. How do you do that? Naturally, we all loved El Afortunado, and never questioned the power of his greatness."

"Alfredo to Afortunado. Branding is everything," Loyola nodded.

"On this day *Alfredo*," Lanning decided to spite Loyola's take and re-brand him, "is getting ready to perform his 'mystery from the beard' act when we heard shouting from the back of the crowd. Aggressively irate before he even started talking, Revelle pushed his way to the front. 'Out of my fucking way, Santa. I'm here to speak my truth,' he commanded, wrenching Alfredo off the podium by his beard. On its way down the beard offloaded a loaf of my mother's ciabatta.

"Don't know how Alfredo got hold of it, but Revelle paused,

slightly baffled. He picked up the bread and ripped off a sizable chunk to gnaw on. He used the remainder to beat *El Afortunado* over the back before tossing the rest into the crowd. Humiliated, Alfredo melted into the crowd."

Loyola realized it was a rather lengthy tale and took a seat on a nearby rock.

"The last angry man launched into his protracted truth, goading the already perturbed gathered crowd of onlookers. 'I have been mercilessly abandoned by your contemptible God. I claim the right of trial by tribunal. The Catholic Church acts as God's representative on earth, yet failed to keep me safe from the Devil! My baptism was a sacred contract between me and God. By taking twenty years from my one and only life, the Church and your GOD failed to keep our contract. God must pay the ultimate price for forsaking me. I will sue your precious church!'"

"Not that it mattered, but that could not have gone well for him," said Loyola.

"Oh, it gets way worse. 'Fuck you, heretic!' came the instantaneous eruption from the crowd. Pieces of my mother's crusty ciabatta zoomed back onto the podium. A woman standing next to my father grabbed our dinner and hurled it end over end towards Revelle. Numerous cries of blasphemy and heresy, along with profanity, made landfall on Revelle's ears."

"It was clear even to my twelve-year-old ears the man rippled with conviction. Still, he had to know that was coming, right?"

"Why? When someone swims in righteous indignation there's no space for reflection. Only passion!" said Loyola the soldier.

"He had to know it would provoke a reaction."

"Think of the courage it took to step up there in the first place. Same as holding the banner ahead of an attacking force. Bravery overcomes consequences!" declared Loyola.

"That's a load of camel dung. Did Achilles hold the banner, did Genghis Kahn? If the banner holder gets all that bravery credit, why aren't the best warriors ever holding one? Because no one in their right mind wants the *honor* of collecting the first spear through the heart. That's why!"

"Well, I had a neighbor who tried suing God when a lightning bolt struck his house, wiping out his prized goat herd," added Loyola.

"How'd that work out?"

"Not well either, but it was a bold move nevertheless."

With a look of disdain, Lanning continued. "You realize that even at Speaker's Corner, the crown has ears and eyes. People watching this carriage wreck covered their ears for plausible deniability."

"Revelle screamed back as good as he got. 'Fuck you hypocrites! The devil is real. I was a wrongly accused innocent man. Who defends the innocent if not God? Who is responsible for upholding the ultimate truth, if not God?'"

"The crowd grew rowdier by the second. My father feared for our safety. We moved to the back of the assembly where I spotted El Afortunado. He stood glaring at Revelle." Lanning pointed as if it was at that exact moment, "Just there on that small rise where the midget slept, I watched as he began wrestling with his magic beard. I'm not sure who, if anyone else, was watching. After a struggle, he withdrew a fully loaded San Marcos Marc II crossbow from his beard."

That caught Loyola's full attention. "Holy shit, a Marc II! That is a formidable weapon. It's one shot deadly."

"Kind of the point of it, right? Moving on, El Afortunado sighted then triggered his arrow with one smooth practiced motion. Sure of its destiny, he instantly replaced the bow somewhere inside his cavernous facial hair, and skulked away. The gathered fell suddenly silent. The arrow had found a straight, unobstructed path over the smoldering crowd, directly into the surprised left eye of he formerly breathing Revelle in mid-rant."

El Afortunado vanished from Algeciras that same day. Still can't believe I was the only one who saw. If my father had noticed, he never said a word to me. Members of the crowd now directed their common outrage in defense of Revelle's right to speak. Many of them scattered about town, fruitlessly hunting for the unseen killer. There were no reprisals and no formal investigation. Ever."

"Yeah, not a surprising ending. Of course, today, the Marc IV is even more lethal," said Loyola.

Lanning looked sideways at Loyola, sensing the man had missed the entire point of the story altogether. Reluctantly, both men inched closer to the hubbub.

A mixed crowd of thirty or so fellow Andalusians, were merrily engaged in tormenting a pint-sized, slightly bent, gray-haired woman tenuously elevated on a triple stacked pile of wooden orange crates.

"In one of the darkest nights for the soul of humanity, I bring news from the indomitable forces of free will." She fanned her pointed index finger across the crowd. "YOU, all of YOU, have been denied!" She passionately thundered away with a grandiose moral authority that belied her fragile frame.

"Huh? What is all that gobbledygook?" shouted a scruffy, bearded man in the front.

"Yeah, dumb it down for Rosario. He's a fisherman," said the man standing next to Rosario, elbowing his buddy in the ribs.

"Are we talking about fisherman's rights? My husband's a fisherman!" yelled a woman from the back of the crowd.

"We know Elyse. He's standing right here!" answered the man next to Rosario.

"Rosario? You lazy bastard. Why aren't you at work?" scolded his wife.

"Quiet! Rude townsfolk!! Let her speak," Loyola roared with a commanding voice from the back of the gathering.

After a thankful nod tilted Loyola's way, the woman continued. Lanning slapped his forehead in disbelief. "Ssshhh," he muttered to Loyola, who ignored him.

"My friends, the powers that be..." Her eyes, along with a double head bob, pointed up towards the palace. "Are keeping all of **US** locked out! Locked out of opportunity, locked out of freedom, locked out of independence. We remain locked out of the bountiful future **WE** have a God-given right to seek!"

"She ain't from around here, or she'd be more careful, even at Speaker's Corner!" cautioned the Squirrel & Mutton's lone representative Doris. "We shouldn't be listening to this," she declared to no one in particular while symbolically wiping her hands on her squirrel-stained burlap dress.

"I ain't *seekin'* much except a free ale or two and some decent mutton from you know where!"

Lanning couldn't tell where the comedian was standing, but joined everyone else in laughing.

"Laugh if you want. I bring news that is far from a laughing matter. I bring liberation, I bring a reconstruction of the known universe. It will change, shudder, and collapse the very ground beneath our feet."

"Are you a woman of the enigmatic arts perhaps?" chimed in Loyola again despite Lanning's disapproval.

"What the heck does that mean?" asked Rosario.

"He wants to know if she's a witch," answered Elyse.

At this point the Bichon freed itself from the sleeping midget's tenuous grip. It scooted between the assembly, barking and growling its way up to the orange crates. The diminutive, growling pooch then faced the crowd, assuming the attack posture of a dog three times its size.

"Reggie!" said the gray-haired woman, "Lie down!"

The dog complied, laying suddenly quiet and still.

"Sorry, he's protective."

"Speak your mind, woman. We're listening," said Loyola, turning to make sure the crowd remained cooperative.

"There is no bewitched mystery to the truth, friends. Only fear from hiding it. We are being lied to. Every day. This earth we stand upon, this universe we are a part of, is not what we have been led to believe. Awaken Algeciras!"

"Oh my God. Get on with it, woman," cried another frustrated stout man gnawing on a roasted turkey leg.

"Spit it out woman," shouted yet another anonymous member of a rapidly devolving, irritable throng.

"We are in one of the darkest nights of the soul of humanity," she repeated.

"We know, we know. It's dark, it's dismal, and...perhaps only You can bring the light?" spat out a cynical woman from the back of the crowd.

"Madam, is this about Jesus? Are you a priest for some new sect perhaps?" continued the Loyola.

"I did say that. Sorry, lost my place," She fumbled with papers in her dress pocket, then mumbled through the previous statements to herself, "let's see...um...dark night...um...locked out...opportunity.. um soul of humanity...um.."

"For shit sakes, wench, come prepared," Rosario mocked.

"Right. Here I am." She resumed her roll, "Prepare to be liberated.

You are about to possess a knowledge few have; see a truth only few do. Once learned, you will leave the uninformed behind. For you will have traveled beyond the edge, metaphorically of course. Or is it? Is the edge of the known universe real or imagined?"

"Oh no," thought Lanning remembering a moment from his past.

"Losing patience back here," implored a back row voice. "Cut to the chase on the 'big news' – I've got to slaughter a goat this afternoon before dark so."

Lanning recognized the unmistakable booming voice. Contigo stood a head taller than the five people around him. Both men acknowledged the other's presence without needing to nod.

Recognizing the crowds growing impatience, the woman finally cut to the chase.

"The earth," she pointed downward before arrhythmically stomping her foot like a novice square dancer for emphasis. "My friends, this very earth that we share as one, is not a two-dimensional plane, any more than each of you exists as a one-dimensional cave drawing. It is something entirely different. It is infinite, like each one of us. Our world, this world, my friends, is... round. Yes! This is neither fantasy nor witchcraft. It is the truth of science. Round. All of us stand on the round ground of a sphere, a bubble of blue and green floating in a heavenly firmament!"

The woman waited; a gap worthy of Minister Goodman's finest. She nodded. She held silent, awaiting the repercussions for shattering each person's existing reality. The wait seemed a tad longer than expected, but no matter. Her confidence remained unshaken. After all, the news was indeed shocking and breathtaking simultaneously. A lot to process for the simple folk of Algeciras. She attributed the lengthening, really deafening silence at that point, to each witness of this revealed truth recalculating their lives all at once. The shock and awe connected to such a gargantuan displacement of their own universe would be truly breathtaking. She nodded. She waited.

Growing a little weary of keeping the nod going, she singled out the fisherman, Rosario. His eyes darted about the crowd, his head on a swivel searching for something. Probably compassion, she thought to herself. The sudden surge of life's altered meaning, his personal universe unraveling, a cold loneliness overtaking his former reality. She felt for him and the others surrounding him. They locked eyes for a moment. She silently messaged him a glance of assurance, empathy and comfort. He scanned the assembled once again before summoning his thoughts to share with the assembled. "At last, a man with courage," she thought.

Rosario raised his hand slowly above his head, palm facing forward, "Nah," he said throwing his arm forward to wipe away, in one gesture, the ludicrousness of this crazy woman's false truth.

"What a letdown," added Rosario's pal Oscar.

"I gave up tasting beer at the Squirrel & Mutton for this load of crap?" piled on another.

"What if it is? It's Algeciras. Why do I care?" dismissed another.

The crowd disbursed with a collective, groaning disappointment. People broke away either in small, grumbling groups, or simply wandered off in disgruntled solitude. Like ordering a fantastic dessert, taking your first anticipated bite, and having it taste like burnt sawdust.

A few stragglers remained behind, including Lanning and Loyola.

"You small minded, sewer rats! Any of you idiots ever heard of fucking Aristotle? Galileo, Copernicus?" shouted the now wide-awake dwarf. "My wife delivers you world-changing truth, and you dismiss it like she's some indigent beggar groveling for scraps at your doorstep?"

Lanning and Loyola watched as the man continued to "bay at the moon" while re-leashing Reggie and helping his wife down from the wobbly crates. They made quite a cute couple, she, only a head taller than he.

"Go back to your caves. We'll let you know when they invent FIRE! Incurious idiots!"

"Well," began a well-dressed fortyish gentleman. He raised an ebony cane adorned by a pewter collar.

"Madam, I believe this actually makes some bit of sense to me. For which I stand grateful."

If Loyola had suddenly traveled twenty years into the future, then miraculously landed back at this very spot, he could've been this man. Wavy blonde hair, a goatee, and an ostrich feathered hat completed the stranger's look. Definitely not a local.

Standing behind and slightly off to the right side of the man was an expressionless, dark-skinned man a head taller than anyone else present. He had jet black hair tied behind him in a mid-back length ponytail.

"One person! What a desert we have landed in my love," exclaimed the loyal husband.

He reached up to kiss his wife on the cheek before turning back to the stranger.

"You sir, have resuscitated my bleak outlook of humanity, at least for the moment, here in this outpost of the intellectually moribund."

"Take heart, stranger, I see some truth as well," added Loyola.

Turning to the older man, Loyola asked, "You look familiar. Perhaps we have met? Madrid?"

"Uh, look in the mirror much? He's you, twenty years hence," said Lanning, flashing an ironic smile.

"Juan Sebastian Elcano, Señor Elcano to you, sir," he replied with a shallow bow.

"Lieutenant Ignatius Loyola, and my smart-ass comrade, Captain

Lanning Delaford."

"I find truth in this as well, little man, and always have," Lanning added. "But other than some logistical navigation relief, and the fleeting joy of decent debate, I don't see the bother of it."

"My size is as one-dimensional as your brain, Señor."

"Half your size yet twice as clever. He betters you in the blink of an eye," chortled Loyola.

"Apologies, sir." Lanning bowed.

"None of you graceful idiots want to ask any questions about the earth?" chimed in the woman.

"The crown insists on a flat earth, madam," said Lanning.

"My very point, sir. Of course they do. The power of the truth ultimately overwhelms the tyranny of the empowered."

"Not soon enough for my taste! However, I'd take caution," quipped Lanning.

"The earth, sir, is a sphere. That is simply scientific fact," affirmed the woman.

"An irrefutable fact!" chimed in her husband.

"Thanks, honey." She bent to kiss him on the cheek before rising to continue. "I suggest you boys recapture the power over your own destiny instead of actively harming yourself and those around you."

"I suddenly feel well-schooled on the future!" said Loyola.

"I will say, no one I know has yet fallen off the edge of the world. But these things do not concern me at present," said Lanning, growing impatient to be on his way.

"Small minds, like light winds, can never create giant waves."

The tall man had spoken up from behind Elcano. His voice was soft yet convicted.

Loyola and Lanning turned to look at the mysterious man.

"It seems this is your day to receive an abundance of free advice,

Captain," said Loyola.

"My pardon, gentlemen, for the offense," said Elcano.

"None seriously taken. May we be introduced to your associate?" asked Lanning.

"Uh, Nantucket is less my associate, more my slave by agreement," fumbled Elcano.

"I am no man's slave," said Nantucket.

"I won him in a contentious card game during my last streak of good fortune some months ago in Cordoba. Not quite sure from where he comes."

Neither Lanning nor Loyola could withhold their disdainful expressions.

"I do not approve of enslaving other men."

"Nor do I," echoed Loyola.

"I am no man's slave," pronounced Nantucket.

"Please do not get the wrong impression. I am no slaver. I believe him to be a kind of medicine man, or spiritualist lured from the New World by my despicable opponent in a competitive game of Primero. The man simply threw him into a growing pot, betting his flush against my full chorus of Kings."

Elcano's demeanor grew visibly defensive about his characterization of Nantucket as his property in the worst sense of the term. He sheepishly took a step back from the small gathering.

"I took him with the intention of freeing him immediately. However..."

Lanning figured this was the moment to exploit Elcano's claim. "Well then sir, why not make this that very moment you planned?"

"Yes, here and now!" piled on Loyola.

"I do have engagement elsewhere, so it is not inconvenient to do as you say. Luck being fleeting, as mine most certainly was," Elcano squirmed, fidgeting with his cane. He unscrewed its pewter top, held it to his mouth and took a deep gulp of whatever he had stored there.

"Join me in some fortitude, my friends?"

"A bit early in the day for me, Sir, but thank you," said Lanning.

Loyola begged off with a head shake as Elcano took another fortifying gulp from his cane.

"Yes! I say YES to your proposal," exclaimed Elcano, screwing the top back onto his cane.

"Besides, I certainly have plenty to deal with at this very moment. I do owe the crown a tidy sum. Failed investment outside of Cordoba. Housing development...but interest rates..." he muttered to no one in particular.

"And so, Nantucket, my worthy traveling companion, quiet man of mystery, consider yourself now a free soul in the New World! Go forth unfettered!"

"Not so much the new world?" said Loyola.

"To him it is," answered Elcano.

"Perhaps your world is very new compared to mine. At least all of you act new!"

"Ha! He's got a valid point! Plus, a wry sense of humor that I like," said Lanning.

Elcano turned back to the wife and husband who'd triggered the sharp left turn his life had taken. He bowed gracefully.

"Madam, I thank you for the powerful lessons learned. I am fortunately or unfortunately destined to prove the pragmatic certainty of your argument. With that, I must take my leave."

Elcano turned to face his traveling companion for these last several months. He clutched the Indian warmly by the shoulders and spoke genuinely to him.

"Nantucket, my new friend, may good fortune smile upon you on the journey ahead. I do believe we shall meet again in sunnier times!"

"We must head off as well. Be mindful in Algeciras, you two," cautioned Lanning to the diminutive couple.

"Appreciate the suggestion. We are headed elsewhere as well," said the old woman.

The couple gathered their things, stuffed them in two large backpacks, and headed off towards the quay, their yappy bichon in tow.

"Shit, we've lost a ton of time with all of this." Lanning prepared to resume his rapid track toward the palace.

Nantucket stood stiffly upright as he watched Elcano recede on his own path forward.

"Good luck to you as well, sir. Congratulations on your newfound freedom," Lanning said, turning to go.

"I shall come with you," declared the Indian resolutely.

Lanning had struck out at pace with Loyola following close behind. Hearing Nantucket, Loyola turned to look back while Lanning simply ignored the man.

"He's definitely talking to you," said Loyola.

Lanning kept up his pace without turning around.

Nantucket followed the two men.

"He's behind us, keeping pace," said Loyola.

"Why?" said Lanning.

"Uh, we can stop and ask him," said Loyola.

Lanning again picked up his speed.

"That's not going to matter. He's following YOU. I'm only an interested observer."

"What makes you so certain it's me?" Lanning stole a quick glance behind them. "Nah. It's definitely you."

"You can't prove that," said Loyola.

"Exactly *my* point. I've got no time for a tag-along. Offer him instruction on the joys of freedom, or point him in the direction of adventure, or opportunity, or God, or whatever. I don't care. I'll see you at the palace."

"Fine. I will do my best." Loyola turned around to meet up with Nantucket.

Exasperated, Lanning shifted into a light jog and rapidly moved out of range. He glanced more than once over his shoulder to gauge the scene unfolding behind him. Loyola had turned and stopped in his tracks. On his next glance, he observed the two men standing in the middle of the road. Their conversation appeared overly brief to Lanning, who saw Nantucket turn back in the direction of town. Loyola remained in the middle of the road, hands on hips. Lanning thought he heard Loyola's distinctive voice loudly screaming the word, "TAXI" repeatedly. He laughed to himself and doubled his pace to the palace.

"Where are the taxis?" Loyola threw his arms in the air and bayed to no one in particular.

"This is Algeciras, not Madrid, pal. We're the bottom rung of the Hapsburg Empire. Oops, one second." Rory Garza clutched his stomach, leaned left, placed both hands on his bent knees, and released a small puddle of vomit onto the street. After a quick shooter of sea air, he continued the conversation as if nothing had occurred.

"If you must find transportation. You're welcome to follow me over to the pub to meet Algeciras' finest."

Keeping a respectable, healthful, distance between them, Loyola tracked Rory over to the Squirrel & Mutton.

---— Chapter 9 ——

PROVE IT!

"Not true, and I'm gonna prove it!"

Nine-year-old Lanning Delaford made the rebellious declaration at his brother Felipe's seventh birthday party. El Afortunado had magically pulled a scaled flour and water map of the known world from his beard. The offending map's shape, as are many items of a flat nature – square.

"Knock yourself out kid, but nobody of salt cares. In this town, there are things of larger concern than the shape of the rock we stand on. Besides, it IS…" Here El Afortunado paused for emphasis, "flat as your mom's ciabatta."

"She's NOT my MOTHER!"

The guy had a real way with children, but birthday entertainment options being limited, the magic beard overruled demeanor. His side comments to Lanning flew far over the gaggle of younger partygoers, while the attending adults uncomfortably smirked. Humiliated, Lanning streaked into the house.

It had been a rocky couple years for the boy. Since Gonzalo had rescued him, he'd had to cope with complete life upheaval. At seven he had to adjust to a new family, learn a foreign language, all while integrating himself into a new life and culture. A steep mountain to climb for any moderately adjusted adult. For a single digit-aged child, it appeared insurmountable at times. This was one of those times.

Despite not knowing the nature of his heritage, Lanning wanted to maintain his individuality by staying true to it. He also desperately wished to fit into his new surroundings. The struggle too often yanked him in opposing directions. Compassionate to the conflict roiling inside

Lanning, but locked out of the boys' deepest feelings, Gonzalo offered his guidance as best he could.

"First off, his real name is Alfredo, so there's that." He had hoped to coax a smile from Lanning. "Second, you can be both at the same time," he said to the stoic boy.

"It's round. Anything else is stupid!"

Gonzalo watched as his advice bounced cleanly off Lanning's frustration.

"We all come at problems according to our starting point. You may be right, in which case time will provide the truth. Try and keep some space for the truth to emerge."

"How am I supposed to do that?"

Gonzalo tried to come up with an example to match a nine-year old's experience. For the past year, he had been instructing Lanning on protecting himself with a sword. The boy was quite talented. "Which is more deadly: a waving sword or an opinion?"

Lanning scrunched his face to ponder the question. "What if it's the King's opinion?"

Gonzalo nodded in appreciation of the precocious answer.

"Hmph! I didn't expect that sharp of an answer. Clearly you have thought more deeply about the answer than I anticipated. I'll think harder myself next time." Gonzalo scrunched his face, took a slow inhale, tapped the boy on the knee gently, and slowly sat down next to him. "Can you be nine for a moment, so I might recite the fatherly things I'm supposed to?"

Gonzalo watched as Lanning's eyes welled again. Not the desired impact.

"You are not wrong, Lanning. You are blessed with experiencing things others have never and will likely never see. You've been in a shipwreck at sea, witnessed and survived death. Now you stand in a foreign land with people who aren't your own. I owe you the truth at all times."

"I can still cry though…"

"If it helps, why not. Does it?" Gonzalo wanted to understand and help his adopted son on the rocky path he had already traveled, as well as the road ahead.

The welling overloaded Lanning's eyes as a slow stream of tears bubbled down his cheeks. "I don't know. Sometimes?"

"I was thinking maybe we'd wait a bit for the cry, but now I can see that this is the exact right moment. You chose well."

Lanning rolled his shoulders, trying to process the cascade of emotions racing through his body, tightening his belly, clenching his jaw, and reddening his eyes.

"Let me take a guess about what's going on. You can kinda nod if any of these strike a chord for you. I'm betting you've got a bowlful of anger, piled on top of frustration, sadness, and emptiness, combined with an indeterminate picture of your future?"

Lanning could not process all of Gonzalo's summation, especially that whole last part. His eyes flooded with more tears. Gonzalo pulled the boy close for a comforting hug.

"Things will get better." Gonzalo offered some simpler solace.

Lanning let his anger loose, "You don't know that!"

"You're right again. I suppose they could get much worse. That is another option. But in my experience, we adjust. You will figure out enough, you will experience something that explains and even answers questions inside of you. Wisdom sits in places. If you visit enough places, you will find answers."

"You're not my dad. You don't know."

"Two absolutely valid, yet unrelated statements. I am not your dad. You are not my son, yet I have grown to love you as if you were.

As to *knowing* that is not yet proven or disproven. I might be wiser than you think, or I might be another village idiot. Like Alfredo even!"

That brought a smile to Lanning through his tears. The recognition from Gonzalo that he agreed with Lanning's bottom line assessment had struck home. Alfredo was not a razor-sharp intellect. His beard was truly amazing, but that didn't mean he had a corner on all available knowledge. He did know some things, but not all things well. Both at the same time.

Gonzalo let loose his hug to face the boy directly, "Now how about some flat as hell ciabatta!"

Chapter 10

BEAR THE PAIN TO GET THE GAIN

"Please accept my profuse apologies, your highness. My behavior was inexcusable."

Royal sycophant Viceroy Roderick Gagnez slinked into the room offering himself up for Prince Ferdinand's retribution. Employment opportunities being what they were in Algeciras, he willingly bent the knee to maintain his minor dominion plus the favor of Spain's newly installed foreign rulers. No bar was too low for him to slide under.

Gagnez' shrewd coyote instinct for personal survival was not lost on Ferdinand. However, since he was a royal, but mostly powerless to decree anything substantial, toying with Gagnez had become his only satisfactory recourse. Non-toxic fun for a teenage Prince, is still joyous.

"We, (insert royal pause for affect) do not appre-see-ate your discordant actions. You remain a pig! However," (insert an extended royal pause to enhance pedant discomfort) "Here," the Prince tossed in a royal yawn for giggles before continuing, "we shall consider overlooking the misstep on this singular occasion. What have you brought us?"

Gagnez, the master thespian, swallowed hard. 'Kiss my righteous wide Spanish ass, you pretentious, teenage brat-scallion Austrian invader!' His inside voice longed for liberation. Locked in his overcrowded basement collection of retorts, it had nowhere to go but the echo chamber of Gagnez' own head. Like a self-flagellating monk who turned disruption of the flesh into humility before God, Gagnez had his own practice. His bastardized version of piety conveniently altered the beneficiary of the inflicted pain from God to...well...him. 'Who else is there,' he assured himself. This personal alchemy absorbed all manner of extraneous humiliations, insults, or royal flagellations, only to magically reconstitute them as appeasement bouquets for the assailant.

Reaching to a tabletop behind him, he grabbed a rectangular tin plate covered with a fringed gold cloth. Gagnez had carefully prepared his presentation and the story behind it.

"Strudel! I am aware of Highness' love for the traditional dessert and had…"

"Most excellent!" said the Prince, cutting him off mid-grovel. "You're dismissed."

The prince quickly left the room, followed by his servant, who snatched the plate from Gagnez' hands.

'Poof! I am still magic!' said his satisfied inner voice. Although he did not get to deliver his well-rehearsed apology in full, the mission had been accomplished.

Like many, Gagnez held the interloping new monarchy in contempt. Had Ferdinand and Isabella not been such short-sighted, reproductively impotent rulers, Spain would not be subject to the invading hordes of foreign rulers and aristocratic pretenders.

Gagnez held firm to a mantra that carried him through each and every conflict riddled day - *A pox on all on all of them! Twice!*

Ironically, it karmically paved the way for his own future retirement plans. Within three short years, as a result of his own leisure travel across the fifty-mile stretch to Tangier, Roderick Gagnez would wither, shrivel and mercifully expire as an oozing lump of unrecognizable flesh riddled with the very pox he wished upon all comers.

Following his performance grovel, Gagnez made his way to a less populated area of the palace. He entered a large room overlooking the corduroy lines of palace grape vineyards covering the sloped hills that descended into the valley surrounding Algeciras.

Without a knock, the large oak door to Gagnez' office gave way to the newly minted Minister of Finance. Angelo Goodman, a meticulously coiffed, Flemish native, blew into the private study. He appeared irritated. Gagnez felt instantly behind in the conversation Goodman had already begun in his head.

"We're in the business of making money! Commerce! The great gods of wealth push us towards the promised land of liquidity. We must explore, push boundaries, perpetually invest in the unknown. We discover the unknown to own it, thereby controlling the future!"

"I'm not following your Eminence," replied Gagnez.

"This shit must end. You will make that happen."

Goodman spoke with unquestioned authority. Brown nose not yet wiped clean from his previous engagement, Gagnez sprang into a command performance of sycophancy.

"Yes, of course, Minister. How may I be of service?"

"That little cock-driven pissant has lost his way. He suffers, we all suffer."

Not yet on the page with the Minister, Gagnez treaded water as best he could. "No doubt, Minister. There is definite suffering, and loss?" he said tentatively.

"Of course, we are all losing. That's obvious. For the good of the empire and mankind, we must force the issue, change the game. We must return to our mission. Exploration wins the day."

"Explore where? All is here, is it not? We have a wealthy kingdom rimmed by the edges of the world."

"Idiot – The world is not edged!" Goodman unleashed his frustration. "Besides, that is not the seminal issue we face. Spain is broke! Worse, it is in unfathomable debt. The world awaits us, abundant and unending, yet we go nowhere. Even if it is flat, let whoever must fall off the fucking edge exploring the possibilities of progress, get to it without delay. We cannot stop at imagined boundaries. Treasure must be forged from the wilderness of the undiscovered. Find me men willing to breathe in the dust! One MONTH! He has not been out of his suite for one entire month! The nation lies immobile, at the whim of a teenager's penis!"

Goodman was practically foaming with anger and frustration. Gagnez figured the best way to get along was to let him freely express.

"True. I have not seen his Majesty in quite some time, but..."

"We can no longer tolerate a King, nee Emperor."

"He's an Emperor? When did that happen?" asked Gagnez.

"Keep up, Viceroy," Goodman scolded, "Yes, Emperor. Whomever set up this unholy inherited monarchy structure without so much as a simple exam required, should be castrated by acclamation. The boy will simply not stop fucking that rag of an aging whore long enough to perform his fiduciary duties."

"So, we are to form a plan. I understand, Minister. I can help."

"Moron, do not speak. You have nothing. You *are* nothing. I have the plan. I have written it down to avoid any confusion. YOU will execute the objective. How you do this, I leave to your discretion. Simply put - get it done."

The Minister did not need to tag a threat onto his command. His look of contempt and sustained tone of irritation made the consequences of failure perfectly clear.

THUD.

The table-shaking weight of the sack of funds dropped on Gagnez' desk had captured his complete attention. The irritable Minister next placed a folded piece of paper beneath the bag. Delivering a final glare, Goodman vacated the room, not bothering to shut the door behind him. Gagnez reviewed the note, opened the bag, lifted his eyebrows, and let a Cheshire cat smirk cruise across his hummus-starved face.

Gagnez scribbled a quick note, then summoned a page to deliver it to the palace kitchen. Two hours later, taking up position on a narrow tile-lined balcony, the Viceroy reached behind an oversized Roman pot holding a six-foot Italian cypress tree. He grabbed the end of a heavily braided rope. With more effort than it should've taken, he tossed the loose end over the balustrade onto the ground some twenty-five feet below. Huffing and puffing from the effort, the human bowling ball took up a casual lean against the outside wall. He pulled his precious Dutch-made clay pipe from his pocket, packed down its tobacco, lit a flame, and inhaled deeply. Alternating puffs with anxiety-cleansing breaths, he waited fifteen minutes before taking another peek over the side at the empty rope. A lone figure emerged from the vines.

"Is this truly necessary?"

Gagnez blew a dense trail of smoke over the balcony. The large pot lurched, signaling the weight now dangling from the end of the rope. Message successfully sent.

"I'm not a damn baboon. This is the last time."

Gagnez smiled as he overheard the grumbling climber's moans.

Five minutes later, an exhausted outstretched hand gripped the top of the stone balustrade followed by another. The irritated, weary Marco Bellini pulled himself onto the balcony. The Viceroy greeted him with yet another puff of wafting pipe smoke.

"You look like a damn Turk. All you need is the turban," said an out-of-breath Bellini.

Gagnez took another draw before calmly sizing up the man standing in front of him. "Smoking refreshes the weary man and awakens a drowsy brain. With your recent actions, you'd do well to take it up."

"That's my last trip up your *secret* rope. I work in the palace. We can meet in the kitchen over grog and ciabatta."

"Sure thing miscreant. I, am the Viceroy, you are the scum bag. I may be the only one that knows your tragic backstory, but *we* do not *hang out* together. **Ever.** You will climb this rope, or end up hanging from one whenever I say."

Bellini boiled. He knew a short reach down to the dagger concealed in his right boot could end the conversation in a heartbeat, but… Perhaps at some point, but not today. He grimaced and held his tongue.

Both men heard the creak of a door closing simultaneously. Each glared at the other, waiting for someone to make the obvious move to investigate.

"Right," said Bellini. "I'll go."

He fast-walked to the doorway, leading to the second-story hallway. Cautiously pulling back the thick oak door, he scanned the area. Nothing. He noticed that the table next to the doorway had a light residue of flour in the shape of hand. He wiped it clean with his own hand before returning to Gagnez.

"Nothing to worry about. Probably a random servant," said Bellini.

"Never hurts to be cautious."

Relieved, Gagnez moved onto his agenda. "Is everything set?"

"As per our agreement."

"There's no margin for error."

"I've doubled our odds. It cost a bit more, but, as you've said, no margin for error."

Gagnez reached into his desk drawer, and withdrew a canvas pouch.

"I need your absolute certainty it will be handled."

"You don't trust my word?"

"Why would I tie my success to your word?"

Gagnez wrote another note and handed it over to Bellini. *Take this and follow the instructions.* Bellini read it.

"Not a chance."

"I understand the hesitation. Think of it as a service to the crown. The greater good."

"That's a laugh, coming from you."

"We serve others best when we serve ourselves."

Bellini flashed him a look of revulsion.

"And how will I be served, you toadying jackass?"

"Fine. There will be a bonus in it for you at the end of the day."

A disdainful Bellini swept the pouch off the desk and headed for the doorway.

"Not that way."

Bellini stomped back to the balcony and grabbed the rope. Straddling the rail, before descending, he gave Gagnez a contemptuous glare, a middle finger and two words:

"Fuck you!"

He disappeared in an instant, belaying down the wall. Gagnez relit his pipe for a long drag and a short smirk.

At the crack of dawn, Bellini scraped himself together and made his way to a small inlet near the iconic Rock of Gibraltar.

Chapter 11
JUST SO

Lanning continued his forced march towards the palace, wondering how things had had gotten so suddenly complicated. His chest tightened from building anxiety. The unexpected brush with death at the hands of kamikaze assailants now seemed light years removed from his avalanche of a day.

"Run the bastard through," Lanning said to himself, thinking how Gonzalo would've handled Espinosa's extortion. At least to start off, before offering a more peaceful alternative for Lanning. What would my real father have said? For all I know, thought Lanning, my real father was a cowardly wimp who ended up as fish food at the bottom of the great ocean.

Lanning recalled nothing about the circumstances of his birth. So many other questions hovered unanswered in his mind, plagued by the permanent fog bank he had to navigate on a daily basis. Most days he pushed through it like an airplane on autopilot. Take off, poke through into the sunshine, then worry about the landing later in the evening. Today's calamitous events changed the weather inside his brain. Cloudy conditions had shifted to a nightmarish gale force storm warning. The storm had stirred up his lifelong dilemma, at least as lifelong as twenty-seven can be.

The brush with death had awakened the multitude of questions he had held down for so long. The vast origin vacuum that existed within him carried consequences he was only beginning to sort out.

Delaford sounded French, he thought. Am I French? Do I have a sister, a brother, friends, relatives? Did I have a dog? Better not have been a damn bichon. He had only blurred visions of his father, none of his mother, or his birthplace. Did anyone miss him? Was he loved? Maybe I will never get to see the whole picture, he thought sadly.

He started to regret not peering over his own edge to find any answers. Dealing with the obstacles of fitting in had displaced his drive to learn who he was. Looking for answers often had felt so pointless. A few simple questions to Gonzalo or Molly, and his life could be re-defined in one revealing moment of verifiable truth. Discovering whatever lay in that darkness was both frightening, and at rare times, compelling.

"Did *anyone* ever search for me?" he asked aloud in frustration as the road turned outside the city gates.

"I don't know you well enough yet to tell," answered the dashing Lieutenant trotting up behind him on the road.

Loyola looked thoroughly self-satisfied. He was mounted on an innocuous brown mare, while holding the reins of a compact grey Andalusian with his right hand. All was not well for the royal dandy, he sported a skanky piece of bloodied rag dangling from his right nostril.

"I see you met the locals," said Lanning.

"Renting a horse required a larger deposit than I thought."

Lanning simply nodded figuring what was coming next.

"I saw these two beauties tied up outside the Rat & Mole."

"The Squirrel & Mutton," corrected Lanning.

"As you please. I thought to myself, why not a quick borrow? Who leaves a horse tied up like that?"

"Everyone." said Lanning.

"But I encountered no squires." Loyola dabbed his nose.

"We're not really a *squire* community. And then?"

"He got the drop on me, obviously. Otherwise, it would've gone quite differently, I can assure you!"

"Yes, but YOU were actually the horse thief," summarized Lanning needlessly.

"That is one interpretation. We eventually settled on a fair rental price and a few pints of something they're calling beer. Absolutely foul."

"Well, thank you. I'm not going to complain too much about a free ride! What about your new friend Nantucket?"

Lanning grabbed the reins from Loyola easily, swinging himself up on the rental mare.

"He'll be just fine. I will see him later," answered Loyola.

"I knew you two would get along."

Lanning put his self-discovery on hold for the moment, and gave his horse a nudge. Both riders moved forward up the road. Given his previous trip, Lanning kept his head on a swivel. Once they crossed the palace gate to enter the grounds, he let out a relieved exhale, and headed for the kitchen to meet up with Molly. Loyola continued along the main path, confident that a regal reception befitting his station awaited. They agreed to meet later and head back to the L'Aquila together.

Tying his horse up to a nearby oak tree, Lanning skipped steps down to the kitchen and burst through the door.

"I'm back!"

Looking around the empty kitchen he picked up a small piece of his mother's ciabatta to nibble on.

"Molly? Your favorite adopted son is here...Hellooo?"

He heard the sound of his mother weeping. Lanning swept over to the large oak and iron hinged door of the meat locker. He pulled it open and found his mother sitting on a stool, wiping her eyes with her floury apron.

"Took you long enough," she said, looking up.

"What's happened?"

"You're late. We've got to get upstairs." Molly rose from her seat, pushed her hair back, and grabbed Lanning by the hand.

"Molly, tell me." Lanning froze on the first step. "Mom!"

"I promise we'll talk about it, but not this minute. You've got somewhere to be. Uh, I did say to look presentable."

Lanning shrugged. "This is my look. Trust me, it works. Besides you're the only one complaining."

"I love you, but why do you need to be so disheveled?"

"Other people who love me don't care how I dress."

"Friends tell friends the truth. Find some."

Lanning pondered this. "I have friends..."

"Oh, hurry up."

Molly hit the stairway with surprising swiftness. Lanning scooted after her.

"Molly please," Lanning said. "I've had a miserable tortuous day, so don't pick on me. Why do I know this is all about Bellini."

She ignored him and continued up the stairway. They emerged onto the main level of the palace. The massive three-walled, taupe colored room opened up onto a terracotta tiled terrace overlooking the expansive grounds. Lanning moved toward the terrace.

"Wait here," demanded Molly. "And don't touch anything."

Lanning moved to take a seat on one of the couches lining the walls.

"Don't sit! In fact, no moving, period. At all! I'll be right back. Tuck in that wrinkled mess of a shirt!"

Six massive, brass votive ceiling lamps hung symmetrical distances from each other all the way out onto the terrace. Lanning knew it overlooked the Hapsburgs' royal tennis court. He stood stock still, reviewing his appearance in a handy floor length gilded mirror. It hung next to a painted wooden relief depicting Saint Peter clutching a six-foot tall cross. Taking poetic license with the historical timeline, Peter looked dashing modeling the latest in Florentine fashion. A self-conscious comparison creeped into Lanning as he tried to smooth out his shirt before his mother reappeared.

She arrived tailed by Angelo Goodman, Minister of Finance. As before, Goodman appeared garbed like a dandy in his tragically hip Italian threads— a dark doublet with fashion-forward pink sleeves. He wore a coordinated black velvet hat with a turned-up brim covering his tousled chin-length brown hair. His look would not resurface until the Rock n Roll British Invasion of the mid-1960s. The crow's feet around his eyes belied the self-conscious attempt at youthful hipness. Lanning figured he was ten years older than any age he might admit to. As opposed to Gagnez, he appeared a model of mannered decorum.

"Just so…" came the Minister's first words along with an extended open hand.

Molly noticed a touch of flour on the Minister's doublet, no doubt from where they had exchanged a brief hug prior to meeting Lanning.

"Pardon me, Minister, I seem to have slightly dusted you!" She used a corner of her apron to remove the white powder.

"Who doesn't love your mom?"

"Happy to hear that, your Lordship," replied Lanning.

Goodman glanced back at Molly for a brief moment. "We won't worry about other things right now, will we."

Switching back to Lanning he pushed ahead. "Just so…Not quite a lord; not yet anyway," he mused with feigned humility. "Simply a minister. A grand title as well, that I have earned through hard work and education."

"Yes, Minister, I'm sure," replied Lanning.

Lanning's mood took a steep turn away from nervous anticipation.

He banked straight into annoyance dusted with a dash of distrust. Lanning reviewed their exchange. Goodman had done nothing to overtly reveal a hidden agenda, yet there it was: a sense of duplicity. Feeling pressed for time and solutions, he dismissed his sentiment as a byproduct of his day of upheaval.

"Just so...You are a hard worker too. Am I right, son?" asked Goodman.

"As the Minister knows, I have been of some use to the prince," Lanning said.

"It seems the prince has requested I find more opportunities for you."

'There it is at last. He's been forced into doing something he was reluctant to do. The prince to my rescue!' thought Lanning.

"I'm honored..."

"Just so..."

"I..." Lanning began, before Molly tapped his forearm.

"We greatly appreciate the prince's kindness," Molly interjected.

"Just so..."

"How may I serve Minister?" Lanning asked.

"Lady Beaufort," came the reply.

A blank look fell over both Molly and Lanning as they awaited further elaboration.

"Our young King has a concubine of some surplus maturity to instruct him in..."

Lanning deduced *surplus maturity* as diplomatic code for hoary. Goodman held a tactful pause while he waited for Molly and Lanning to *board* his train of thought.

"Yes, of course," said Molly after a moment. "We understand. Don't we, son?"

"Aaannnd...?" Lanning wondered where this was headed.

"She has a daughter," added Goodman.

Finally, he arrived at the heart of the matter. Lanning recalled the beautiful woman he spied that morning on the very terrace they now stood on. 'Oh, *she* was the King's concubine.' He did not agree that she looked mature in the manner described. He had figured their ages were the same. Perhaps he might be a year or two younger. He guessed the morning light had played tricks on his eyes.

Now he pictured her kid. Lanning did not have much use for children. In truth, he had spent zero time around what he considered untrained animals. Was he about to be forced into wasting his time corralling an irritating, whiny, self-soiling toddler? Maybe the child was already walking, and wanted tennis lessons? That wouldn't be so bad. The kid had to be more coordinated than the Prince, and then there would be more money! He desperately needed an influx of cash. Even if it meant he would have to immediately hand it over to that pig Espinosa.

With a half-bow, beneath a forced smile Lanning said, "How may I serve the little Lady Beaufort? I am happy to help, but my business has me sailing with the morning tide for a single night in Tangier. Perhaps the following day would be more amenable for all?"

Not knowing his current perilous financial situation, Molly shot Lanning a motherly *death stare.*

"I understand you are quite the Tangier expert. Yes?" the Minister asked.

"I'm sure that's a matter of opinion, although, I am quite familiar with certain aspects of the city."

"Perfect!" The Minister broke into a wide satisfied smile. Apparently, a considerable weight had been craned off his shoulders and spot-welded to Lanning's.

"We shall deliver the daughter to your dock promptly at the

morning tide. She will enjoy an adventurous day of shopping, with you as her able guide! The crown thanks you for your service. Trust that you shall be well compensated. Accept this as a small down payment for your upcoming efforts."

Goodman reached into his stylish cloak and handed Lanning a small but weighty pouch. Not bothering to wait for a reply, he disappeared back into the palace.

"Seriously?" groaned Lanning.

"She's a child. They are easily entertained," Molly said.

"What the hell am I supposed to do with one of those things?" he whined.

"It's one day! Let Shafi watch her. He loves kids. He loved you when you were one of 'those' things. Felipe will be helpful too," advised Molly before whispering, "I can hear that jingle!"

They smiled conspiratorially. Lanning could tell by the pouch's weight it would greatly help his cause.

"I know you're right," he admitted. "But Shafi would bore the poor kid to tears. Felipe hates kids more than I do. It's on me, as always!"

"Keep your voice down. Ears are everywhere! All I ask is you keep her from drowning!"

"God, I didn't even think about that." Mockingly he added, "I've got it, I'll lash her to the mast for safety."

"She's not Odysseus, son! All you need to do is keep her in your cabin for the crossing."

Lanning stared in commiseration with the hanging wood relief of Saint Peter up on the cross.

"Fantastic couple of days coming up," he said.

"Find your gratitude, located right next to that pouch in your pocket! You will thank me eventually."

"While you wait for that tell me why you were in the meat locker weeping, when I walked in?"

"Nothing serious. The pressures of the job. You had better get going. Your brother must be waiting on you."

"Flip has plenty to occupy him on the boat. What the hell is going on?"

"I can handle him," said Molly nervously wringing her hands together.

"That prick Bellini. What's he done? I've got my own issues with him as well."

"You too?" exclaimed Molly.

Lanning struck a serious tone. "I will deal with him when I get back from Tangier. On both our accounts."

"Please leave it alone."

"We're definitely not done with this." Lanning bent down and kissed his adopted mother on the forehead. "I love you Mol."

"See you in a couple days. Watch out for your brother."

"Why? He's a chronic pain in the ass!" Lanning joked as he headed back down the stairs through the kitchen.

Letting out a deep sigh, Molly burrowed down on a nearby couch. An expression of concern overtook the smile she had displayed for Lanning's benefit. She had heard enough to suspect Gagnez and Bellini were plotting something else besides skimming a bit of money off the castle vendors.

Chapter 12

AND ANOTHER THING

Lanning trotted his borrowed mount back through the wisteria-covered pergola leading to the palace gates. The horse held an easy gait on the gentle downhill back to Algeciras. As the pouch jingled in his pocket, Lanning began to run through a multitude of phobic scenarios triggered by the presence of a small child onboard his rented tar baby, the L'Aquila.

"Stay put for one minute kid…" Then he'd turn his back for a split second before hearing a small splash over the port gunnel. A peek over the rail to reveal a lone dorsal fin rolling down into the deep. No splash, no scream, no kid…

One random scenario like that would result in Lanning's hanging, disembowelment, or both. He pondered an escape into the depths of the dark African continent fifty kilometers across the strait, but hiding held no promise for success either. If the world only had four corners, the Hapsburgs would surely send emissaries to every option. If the earth proved to be a sphere, as he had always believed, then he would eventually run back to where he came from. Again, no joy. While contemplating his tenuous fate a voice jogged him back to reality.

"How about a ride back?"

The voice sounded familiar, but he couldn't quite figure out where it was coming from.

"Up here, dickhead!"

Lanning pulled back on the reins, and stopped his horse. It couldn't be Loyola. Peering into the palace entrance on his way out, he had seen him holding a brimming glass of wine and whooping it up with the royals. Besides, he had his own ride.

"Loser! Over here," the voice called out.

Now Lanning knew who it was. Next came the simple matter of locating him. He scanned the grounds behind him as his horse took a few steps forward.

"Flip!" Lanning yelled. "Quit screwing around. Do you want a ride back or not?"

He spotted his brother clinging, with his bare hands, one hundred feet up on the rocky bluff that held the palace grounds.

"Are you nuts?" Lanning trotted his horse to the base of the bluff.

Felipe shouted down while continuing his rapid assault on the face.

"Relax. Give me a couple more minutes to make the top."

Lanning marveled at the speed his brother raced up the rock wall. Hand, foot, lift, grab, reach, grab, lift, pull, grip, until finally his younger sibling scrambled over the top of the wall to stand on flat ground. Within a few minutes, Felipe Cortez came strolling through the arbor at the palace entrance.

"Hey güey, thanks for waiting. Kind of tired."

Felipe reached for Lanning's hand and swung himself onto the horse behind his brother.

"Got water? Super thirsty. Come to think of it, super hungry too." he said.

"I know a spot." Lanning kicked his horse, and off they went down the hill towards town. "I don't understand the reason you take those risks," Lanning chided. "Seems needless."

"Okay, Mom! Which one of us will climb the mast in a storm? You? Not a prayer," replied Felipe.

"True, but that would be a necessary risk, and we have lines for safety. Cliffs are crazy."

"It's training, so when the time comes, I'm ready. Plus, it's sport!"

"Bullfighting is sport, futbol is sport. No one does that, but you."

"I'm a trend setter. I think it'll be really popular someday. Don't you do anything strictly for fun?"

That dig penetrated, but Lanning chose to place it in his TBD cave for future consideration. He gazed ahead looking for something in particular. "Ah! At last!"

Along the side of the road stood a two-wheeled wooden food cart. It rested beneath a tattered burlap canopy supported by four poles. Sitting in the artificial shade on a wooden crate slept its beret-wearing vendor, Esteban Del Pozo.

"Morning Esteban. You weren't here earlier, were you?" asked Lanning.

"The older I get, the later I start my day. Why?" asked Esteban.

"No reason." Lanning decided against recounting his mornings nightmare.

"I thought all old people got up at dawn," smirked Felipe. "You know, to savor those last hours before the final nap."

"Where'd you read that? Oh, apologies, you probably can't read," countered Esteban.

"Come on gramps, don't you wanna make every minute count for something?"

Esteban simply glared back at Felipe and held up a middle finger.

"Nothing better to do with your damn day than to irritate a fruit vendor?"

"Well, this morning I watched an argument between my brother and the asshole who owns us."

"At least buy something!" said Esteban.

"He doesn't own us; he owns the boat. What's fresh today?" Lanning asked.

"Same as every day for the past thirty years. Nuts, nectarines, and oranges," said the merchant, re-tuning his jumbled fruit display.

Felipe had already snagged a nectarine to quench his thirst. Lanning pointed to a bag of pinenuts and dropped a coin in the vendor's outstretched hand.

"Did you dance today?" Esteban looked at both men.

"Was there music?" asked Felipe checking his brother for a similar response to the absurd question.

"No time for that," said Lanning flatly.

"I did," said Esteban, returning to his seat in the shade. "Same as every day for the past twenty years."

Now understanding his point, Lanning nodded. "Lucky you."

He climbed back onto the loaner horse.

Felipe reaching for Lanning's hand. "Is that old-guy code for getting laid?" he asked as Lanning pulled him onto the horse.

"It's a good thing you're the best sailor on the docks, because the rest of you..."

"YOU DITCHED ME?!" Ignatius Loyola, sporting a new, regally plumed hat shouted, in mock anger, as his galloping horse came to a full stop at the fruit cart.

Like a finely tuned gymnast, Loyola dismounted in one smooth, hands-free motion as his horse came to a rolling stop. He landed in front of the pile of nectarines. Before speaking, he looked around as if expecting either a perfect ten from the judges, or at least sufficient plaudits from the crowd.

"You're a damn General. No one's worried about your welfare," answered Lanning.

"Nectarines?! I LOVE nectarines. Fruit of the gods," Loyola pronounced.

"Sir, may I?"

"This is a man who knows the joy of the Lord!" said Esteban.

Loyola let out a belly laugh. "Definitely never been accused of that before, friend. I have nothing against the Lord! As a soldier, I have hastened many a man's journey to his presence, but cannot truly say my joy is related to him directly."

"Time to go, featherhead," mocked Lanning gesturing at Loyola's hat.

"Gift from the Prince."

"More likely re-gifted," came the reply.

"Envy does not become you, Captain. No matter, our borrowed mounts are now overdue."

Not waiting for a response, Loyola nudged his horse into a leisurely canter. Feeling a slight tinge of remorse over his behavior, Felipe turned back to offer polite farewells to Esteban. The awaiting middle finger, coupled with a doff of Esteban's faded crimson beret, signaled his apology had been sardonically accepted.

Within an hour they were dockside. Lanning found his crew loafing about the deck of the L'Aquila, sluggishly preparing it for the next day's journey. The brothers had deposited Loyola back at the Squirrel & Mutton for a night of repulsive food and noxious ale. He'd surely pay the true price of his lodgings by hanging over the side at dawn.

A sudden realization gripped Lanning as he walked up the gangway. "FUCK!"

"What?" asked Felipe.

"Bad enough that this day caved in on me, now I'm working on tomorrow which hasn't even happened yet!"

"Gagnez..." Lanning's voice trailed off in thought.

He had completely forgotten about delivering Gagnez his prized shipment of hummus which, he now knew, lay nestled somewhere at the bottom of the Gibraltar strait.

"Flip, we're off at dawn with the tide. Have her ready."

Felipe had walked over to the main mast and stood huddled with Shafi.

"We're one short, brother."

"One short of what?" asked Lanning.

"It's Rory," said Lorenzo, "My dad scared the shit out of him, plus the bump on his head, and the vomiting."

"He was vomiting?" Lanning asked.

"Pretty much non-stop. I'm gonna say mostly the vomiting changed his mind," added Lorenzo.

"I sent him home," added Shafi.

"He **lives** on the boat," Lanning said, shrugging his shoulders.

"Probably went to the Squirrel & Mutton to sleep it off. It's the reason that place always reeks," said Lorenzo.

"Well, it's on one of you to replace him!" commanded Lanning.

Felipe shot back, "Look around. You think I don't have enough to do getting this scow ready to sail? That's on you…Captain!"

Felipe turned to his pre-sail chore list, leaving Lanning to deal with the last-minute dilemma.

"Damn it!" Lanning straddled the gunnel and hopped back onto the dock.

Exhausted and aggravated he headed up Avenida Virgen del Carmen towards the center of town. His mind a bouncing blend of disjointed thoughts, Lanning whip-kicked a phantom soccer ball up the street.

"Nice to see you again, Midget."

Without hesitating Lanning drew his sword. In a lightning-quick swoop, he had the sword tip poised beneath the hairless chin of one of the twins.

"Not playing around right now big fella. Too much to handle and too long of a damn day. Would you prefer to run along or drop your life here in the street? Choose quickly." Lanning tapped his foot to emphasize the point.

"Whoa, easy pal. I'm simply saying 'hello' to a new friend."

"Which one are you? Lonzo or Hector?" asked Lanning without moving his sword.

The man raised his open hands above shoulder level. "Lonzo's home tending to the kids. Truly, I was only saying hello."

"I'm not overreacting, Hector given our recent history." Lanning sheathed his weapon.

"Understood. But you've got to admit times are tight. Enjoy your night," said Hector, walking away.

As Lanning walked on, an unorthodox solution to his immediate problem occurred to him.

"Hector! Hold up," he yelled. "Do you enjoy boating?"

Chapter 13

ANOTHER PERFECT DAY IN PARADISE

A razor-thin beam of sunlight stung the corner of Lanning's eye, abruptly terminating a night of fitful sleep. Still foggy, he braced for the day. Against an early morning cyan sky, he checked the horizon for any tipoffs of favorable sailing weather. Gently floating white puffs in the distance indicated the day's wind outlook. He silently prayed for a heavy dose of westerlies. Generated from the uncharted western edge of the earth, a healthy dose of westerlies powered a sail like a turbo blast from an F16. Nature's booster rocket could double the speed of the L'Aquila's channel crossing to Tangier. Halving his day put a creased smile on his face. Lanning crossed his fingers while squinting to the horizon. Nothing to see meant a longer day at sea, and a slow pull relying on the normal currents.

Despite his wishful thinking, Lanning knew "nothing to see" when he saw it. "Long day coming," he concluded. More sailcloth in the rigging meant more time with an unwanted passenger. Make that passengers, counting the insufferable Lieutenant Loyola. Breakfasting on a day-old piece of his mother's ciabatta, Lanning felt an impending dread.

There's an idea floating about that the universe bends towards justice. Lanning's stepfather, a kind but impatient man, often told his adopted son, 'Expect mud, wear boots.' For Gonzalo, nothing bent without you bending it.

Lanning pulled his boots on, grabbed another piece of ciabatta, and headed out the door towards the quay. Rounding the corner from Calle Teniente Maroto onto Avenida Virgin del Carmen, he ran straight into one of the Viceroy's uniformed guards. Lanning stopped short of this unexpected roadblock.

The man's uniform was regal Spanish. Gagnez demanded that his men be well dressed representatives of the crown. He was clad in thigh-high white stockings, over-puffed yellow and red striped bloomers, nicely paired with a white linen shirt beneath a matching yellow and red doublet. His garb was topped off with a simple soldiers Morion helmet— light metal with a comb along the top and the iconic upturned brim. Turn a hot water kettle upside down, and you too can be part of the Spanish palace guard. The man held a lethal halberd spear, a weapon economically designed as both an axe and a spear. Given the users expertise, and sufficient time, the halberd insured any assailant was both speared and disemboweled with a minimal number of precision swipes.

"Good morning to you, Señor Delaford," came the polite greeting.

"Uh, good morning to you, sir," Lanning stammered out his first words of the still new day. "A bit off your normal route, I suspect?"

"I have orders from the Viceroy," said the man, extending the business end of his halberd towards Lanning.

"How do you choose which side of that thing to use? Is it simply a comfort deal?" Lanning attempted to disarm the man with sarcasm. The man remained expressionless. Taking advantage of what looked like a standing coma, Lanning brushed the weapon aside, intending to carry on with his day undeterred.

The man withdrew the weapon. Slowly a thought appeared on his face. "You are to accompany me. Actually, I am to accompany YOU, since I am the soldier. The Viceroy would like a word."

"So you've mentioned."

"Please, follow me," he repeated.

Mostly a polite fellow, thought Lanning. Only doing his job. Given how long it must have taken to put on the uniform, he probably got up earlier than I did this morning. Or perhaps he worked the night shift and would've preferred to be home right now cozying up to his pet owl, or rat, or even his wife. Knowing he could not afford the time it would take to traipse over to Gagnez estate and still sail with the tide, he attempted to negotiate with the emissary.

"Of course." Lanning began slowly planning to work his way around the issue diplomatically. "Sir," he said with an overabundance of placating, "if you wouldn't mind, please inform the Viceroy that while a chat on any other morning would be fine, today is crazy busy for me. Let him know I will return this evening with his shipment. I plan on delivering it personally to him before he lays head to pillow. That should suffice."

Lanning bowed politely and took the next step on his journey towards the L'Aquila.

"I don't think so," answered the soldier, blocking his path. "First, I can't possibly remember all of that mumbo jumbo, but mostly, I don't care."

"You're an emissary. That implies a certain latitude in understanding, doesn't it?"

"I'm a soldier with orders."

The soldier stood fixed in place, combo death stick at the ready.

"It's a simple message. I can try and make it easier if that helps," offered Lanning.

"These are your problems. Not mine," said the man, "Would you prefer to walk or, I can wake you up when we get there?"

Lanning was seconds away from losing his cool when he heard a familiar voice behind him.

"Hey Cap, is this little guy bothering you?"

"Actually, yes."

Hector, to whom virtually everyone was a "little guy," covered the gap between himself and the soldier with a single step. His arrival at the unprepared guards position heralded by a single roundhouse punch. The clean blow to the unprotected chin of the soon to be dormant man lifted him a full foot off the picturesque cobblestone street. In a renaissance moment, the soldier lay face up, limbs splayed. A newly minted *street angel*. Hector gathered up the man's spear and helmet, then leaned the unconscious man up against a convenient stone wall. He placed the tea kettle and stick of doom beside what looked like the soldier's peaceful, post-morning, coffee naptime.

"Quite a nice job, Hector," Lanning said.

"Can't leave a clutter for the next person."

Lanning realized the potential mess the well-meaning Hector had created. He pushed it back to number fifty-seven on his to-do list, determining he would deal with the fallout post-Tangier.

"Yeah," he exhaled, "we're good."

Arriving at the quay, Lanning could see the L'Aquila poised and ready for sail. He also saw something unexpected. Stoic and still, next to the bow line stood Nantucket. Felipe, seeing the giant accompanying his brother, then the stranger at the bow looked confused. Felipe waved them over to the gangway.

"As far as I can guess, he's been there all night. Hasn't said a word," said Felipe. "I figured he was your new recruit, but now, maybe not?"

Lanning felt equally mystified. Had Loyola acquired a new traveling partner? That would mean an additional fare for the crossing. He had no time to figure it out as a carriage from the palace pulled up dockside. Gulping down his dread, Lanning reluctantly prepared to greet his burden for the day.

"My Captain! I am arrived."

Self-heralding from the quay railing, the hyper-energetic Sir

Ignatius Loyola fanned his feathered hat in the light breeze now making its way in from the west.

"Perfect," Lanning mumbled as he approached the carriage. All of his problems had arrived at once. He took a moment of peace to watch the gently oblivious rocking of the L'Aquila, before a sudden whiff of night jasmine puzzled him.

The coachman dismounted from his top perch. He grabbed a set of steps hooked to the running board and placed them by the carriage door. Lanning strategically took a knee by the bottom step. He figured the child would be less intimidated meeting someone its own height, rather than a looming adult. They could then establish their rapport for the day's journey.

"Unexpected yet lovely. Shall I be treated to such exceptional service all day?"

"You?" He felt baffled.

"Filippa Beaufort," she said. "Don't let the dress fool you. I can take care of myself."

He stammered, "I, I, I,"

"You, you, you have a stutter? Don't be embarrassed. I am tolerant."

"Uh, no." Lanning managed a brief smile and recovered his wits. "Pardon milady, I'm confused. You are meant to be an added chaperone for the child. My mistake."

Filippa cut him off. "Child? What child? I am the sole passenger."

"Minister Goodman said the **daughter** of the King's friend, er girlfriend, ah consort,"

"My mother. 'Concubine' works," Filippa replied unapologetically.

Lanning rebooted his brain to fit around the new concept.

"That's YOUR mother? No judgment," he added a second too late.

"Uh huh…" She drew out the sardonic reply. "In case you were curious, I have not a clue who my father may be. Probably royalty of some strain, since those are the only circles my mother runs in."

Lanning fumbled his way along. "Of course. Didn't mean that in a weird way at all. I meant, that it doesn't matter at all to me. Unless it might to you, but I'm guessing not?"

"I've moved on." Filippa staked her ground, which was considerably higher than where Lanning happened to be standing.

"Allow me to graciously welcome you aboard Señorita. Beauty needs no provenance." Loyola had slyly stepped over to offer his hand to Filippa.

"A gentleman, at last!" said Filippa.

Lanning stared crosswise at Loyola and motioned to Nantucket.

"Pardon, sir, but I'm sure you've got something *else* requiring your immediate attention."

"Nonsense. Our new friend is well sorted. We cannot ask the lovely Lady Beaufort to wait, can we?"

Loyola escorted Lady Beaufort to the L'Aquila gangway. They were met on the other side by an equally gracious Felipe, who assisted her onto the foredeck. The coachmen followed the lady, lugging a larger than expected trunk onboard. Lanning took note of the size before tossing it off as another symbol of privilege. Even though he found himself abandoned, standing alone by the palace coach, and left to swallow a public embarrassment, the day's prospects had taken a profoundly positive turn. With a renewed sense of optimism, Lanning hopped over the nearest gunnel and shouted the order to ready the ship for castoff.

Both Hector and Nantucket had remained on the dock, awaiting direction.

"Bro, where's your game? That was a zero!" whispered Felipe.

"Psshh," he waved Felipe off. "Caught off-guard is all, and snaked by the dandy. Besides, she's a royal. Not really a royal, but..."

Felipe took two fingers and pointed to his eyes then at Filippa. He shrugged his shoulders, embarrassed for his brother. "Zero!" he mouthed, holding his thumb and index finger in a symbolic zero.

"Which one of those two is our replacement for Rory? That mountain or the Indian?" asked Felipe.

"Hector! Come on board, big guy," shouted Lanning before turning to Loyola. "Uh, is your new friend coming?"

Hector lumbered up the gangway, the ship creaking as the giant man stepped onto the L'Aquila's deck. Loyola excused himself from the lady with a courtly bow, and hopped over to Lanning.

"Of course, he's coming. And why not? He's a free man," said Loyola as he motioned the man on board.

"You will be paying his passage?"

"If need be, Captain."

"Need be," he answered.

Loyola welcomed Nantucket with a handshake as he walked him over to the main mast.

"Hold up, sailor," ordered Felipe. "There's a couple things every sailor needs to know."

"Like what?"

Hector was wearing a green scarf wrapped around his bald head. Felipe snatched it off and tossed it overboard.

"What the hell, tiny man!"

"Never wear green on a boat! Never. It makes it seek land. Two, no whistling!"

Hector formed his lips to whistle, only managing to deliver air and spit. "See, I can't whistle anyway."

"Good. Don't learn. Whistling challenges the wind itself, and challenging the wind is begging for a storm. No whistling!"

"Is that it?"

Lorenzo, Shafi, Rodrigo and Lanning were enjoying the hazing Felipe was laying on their new crewman.

"Most important,"

"More than whistling?"

"Yes! NEVER, EVER under any circumstances say the word 'rabbit' while your feet touch the deck of a ship."

Hector's face went blank. "Huh? What's wrong with 'raaa...'"

Felipe cut him off. "Don't say it." Felipe held up his index finger for emphasis and shook his head.

Hector nodded. Satisfied with his new charge, Felipe nodded, grabbed Hector's hand, and shook it.

"Welcome aboard, sailor. Grab that line on the foredeck and pre- pare to let loose."

Hector froze trying to sort out Felipe's order. Next, he tried a helpless glance at Lanning for translation. Felipe watched the interac- tion. He glared at Lanning; his displeasure plainly displayed through the middle finger on his right hand.

Stern-faced, Felipe shot back to Hector, "ME AND ONLY ME. See that rope attached to the dock up there? Go untie it, hold it, then wait until I say *let go*! Simple, right?"

Lanning tossed Hector a wink to break the tension.

"Easy peazy!" said Hector as he marched up to the foredeck.

"Really?" Felipe hopped down to the deck next to his brother.

"Don't let his size intimidate you." Lanning gave Felipe an elbow nudge. "Best I could do on short notice. Work with it!"

Seeing that everyone was now onboard and situated, Lanning issued the first order of the day.

"Prepare to cast off. Felipe has the bridge."

Between the two brothers, Felipe was the true sailor. Lanning's first and best claim to seamanship lay in his cast iron stomach. Regardless of how nauseating the conditions – twenty-foot seas boosted by a howling cross-wind chaser, following a luncheon of deep-fried mackerel—they were no match for Lanning's resilient inner ear. He enforced a strict zero tolerance policy for deck-top vomit on board the L'Aquila. Anyone afflicted with a queasy stomach had to wear the bucket until completing their purge. As Lanning saw it, the pragmatics of his policy outweighed the occasional need for passenger empathy. The ship was a rental, after all. Given the tenuous nature of his relationship with the disagreeable Oscar Espinosa, less wear and tear on the ship would make regaining his weighty security deposit at the end of each season a better bet.

For his part of the brotherly arrangement, *Captain* Lanning focused on the business end. Anything to make a buck between Algeciras and Tangier fell under Lanning's dominion—cargo, passenger, or whatever else he could think of. Although his seamanship knowledge paled in comparison to Felipe's, his younger brother was not a leader of men. His character enjoyed the challenge of the sea, but not the burdens of obligation and accountability. Those he left for big bro.

"Shall we stand here for the journey, or do you have somewhere more comfortable?" Lady Beaufort said.

"Cast off!" shouted Felipe from the bridge.

Filippa Beaufort stood shoulder to shoulder next to the main mast with her new pal Loyola.

"Apologies, of course Miss Beaufort," answered Lanning realizing he had shirked his host responsibility.

"Lady Beaufort will do," she smirked.

"LADY Beaufort," Lanning said. "You and your new friend may

find it more comfortable back on the stern. Not much in the way of wind this morning. It could be a four-to-five-hour journey across to Tangier."

"Very well, but where shall Doug stay?" said Beaufort.

"Who's Doug?" asked Lanning.

"STOP!" screamed Beaufort. "You've left him in the carriage!?"

"There's a baby in the carriage? I thought you said there was no infant?"

Lanning motioned to Felipe to maintain the lines. The stern line had already been cast off. Fortunately, not comprehending the term "cast off," Hector maintained his grip on the bow line.

"Hold fast!" yelled Felipe to Hector.

"Sure," said Hector looking confused.

"Good job sailor," yelled Lanning back. "Now pull us in. And do not let go."

Lanning pantomimed hand over hand pulling of the rope. Hector remained frozen.

"Pull us in!" repeated Lanning.

He waited.

"Good lad!" said Felipe chuckling to himself. "Make taut the rope," he added.

Sporting a blank look, he remained still.

"Pull us back to the dock," Felipe said pantomiming the action as Lanning had done.

"Sure thing."

He obediently pulled the L'Aquila closer to the dock and held her there. Lanning once again leapt over the gunnel onto the deck and hustled back to the still parked carriage. He opened the door to find a three-foot-tall cage containing a fully alert bird of prey.

"It's a bird!" Lanning shouted down to Lady Beaufort.

"It's Doug! Bring him down."

"Please?" said Lanning sarcastically.

The bird was beautiful—a dark blue-grey body with pale under-parts sporting narrow dark blue stripes. Doug had what looked like a black yarmulke covering the top of his head with matching mous-tache-type markings below his jet-black eyes. The dagger hook on the end of his beak looked as lethal as a halberd. Its razor-sharp point magnified as the bird menacingly swiveled its face directly in line with Lanning's.

"No way am I reaching in there!"

"It has a handle," yelled Beaufort.

"Oh," mumbled the relieved Lanning spotting the handle, "Time to go...Doug."

He grudgingly reached for the cage. As he pulled it out of the carriage the rattling shook open the cage door. Sensing freedom, Doug launched himself through the door like a guided missile. Several loud shrieks 'KEE, KEE, KEE' heralded his joy. His wings spread to their four feet span as Doug made a low Phantom jet pass over Lanning's head. Lanning dropped the cage and hit the ground in a head-covering tuck. Doug made two passes around the boat and the carriage before settling on top of the L'Aquila's main mast.

"Nice work Captain," said Loyola.

The bird had assumed a sniper's pose surveilling the horizon.

"Is Doug hungry?" asked Lanning.

"He's always hungry," answered Lady Beaufort smirking, "DOUG!" she shouted.

The bird ignored the shout from below. Nantucket suddenly came to life. He turned his brightened gaze to the top of the mast. From his crouched position Lanning heard a similar series of high-pitched, successive sounds.

"KEE, KEE, KEE!"

The sound came not from the falcon, but from the stoic Indian. Doug peered down from his perch and cocked his head.

A peregrine falcon can track prey at the speed of a Formula I race car. They can track a mouse from a mile away while flying 180 miles per hour. Humans have roughly 30,000 cones (the cells that allow us to see light and color)—the family of Doug-like birds have over one MILLION of those. Vision to a peregrine falcon is a constant 4K Imax 3D-affair.

Nantucket let loose with another fusillade, "KEE, KEE, KEE."

The bird glided off its perch and corkscrewed down, passing around the mast before landing gracefully on Nantucket's extended left arm.

"We understand each other," said Nantucket.

"I have never seen anything like that," said Lady Beaufort.

"DOUG, here!" Lady Beaufort said, extending her arm.

With a nod from Nantucket, Doug lightly floated onto his owner's arm.

"What other surprising talents do you have?" asked Lanning, coming over the gunnel with the empty cage.

"Thank you, Captain," Lady Beaufort said.

Lanning placed the cage on a nearby barrel lashed to the deck. He held the door open. Lady Beaufort took two steps with the falcon before ushering him in. Obediently Doug returned to his perch.

"That's a thing I haven't seen," said Lanning in amazement.

"Because you have not seen a thing, does not mean the thing cannot be seen," said Nantucket.

"You need to get out more!" quipped Loyola. "A beautiful specimen of peregrine falcon, madam," added Loyola, embodying his role as bon vivant suckup.

"Feel free to take your two pals and go there, Milady." Lanning pointed up to the raised area accessed by an inset ladder behind the main sail.

"Thank you, sir. I am familiar with stern, bow, port and starboard," said Lady Beaufort.

"Now?" Felipe confirmed with Lanning, who nodded.

"CAST OFF!" yelled Felipe.

"Hector, you can let go of that line now," Lanning said to the bewildered giant on the bow. The raw recruit waited for the Felipe nod, which he got.

The bow dock line slid slowly off the boat, dropping into the water next to the receding dock. All twenty meters of the L'Aquila drifted gently away from the quay as the crew raised the square main sail in concert with the two lateen fore and aft sheets.

They carried no cargo for this trip although the boat had plenty of space for it. The sails luffed gently in the light breeze that slowly carried the L'Aquila on its course towards Tangier.

"We *will* be traveling faster than this, right?" begged Loyola.

"Doubtful. I'm happy we're carrying nothing other than the two of you, er, the three of you."

"And Doug," interjected Loyola deadpan.

Lanning ignored Loyola. "Things often change when we clear the harbor."

A single figure raced down the quay. Despite the receding pace of the L'Aquila, the man never broke stride or hesitated as he approached the lip of the dock. With an Olympic athlete's skill, and a dancer's grace that belied his size and age, the man, legs bicycling in midair, propelled himself off the end of the dock. He caught the starboard rail at the maximum extension of his outstretched arms, and boosted himself over the rail. Safely onboard, he bent at the waist, grabbed his knees and took a baker's dozen of rasping breaths.

"Phew...too damn slow," he said to no one in particular.

The man turned to face the surprised assemblage.

"I hope it's not an imposition, but I needed a ride to Tangier. You're headed over there, right?"

Lanning sized up the unexpected guest. The entrance surprised him but considering recent events, not the need for a sudden lift.

"Good morning, Contigo."

RENAISSANCE BOATER CERTIFICATION COURSE PART I

Bigger, faster, stronger. How did sea captain's tasked with navigating the greatest barrier to civilization's expansion, conquer the challenges? Bigger, faster, and stronger boats had to be the answer. Exploration forced constant, fantastically risky, "all-in" gamblers innovations on the men and occasional women who pursued the unknown.

Ship construction in 1519 had become a burgeoning and evolving industry. There were a few hard and fast rules—boat must float, boat must be waterproof...sort of, boats needed propulsion, and lots of it. Shipbuilders confronted a constant barrage of curve balls.

Wood may float, but it does not truly enjoy water as a primary choice of lifestyle. To this day, heavy seas, wind, and rain stress any modern ship made of metal or futuristic composites. Caravels like the L'Aquila creaked, moaned, and shimmied on the calmest of sailing days cruising on the vast ocean. Add to that very basic frailty the baker's assortment of vermin and pestilence, and you have the makings of a floating purgatory. Rats, mice, lice, roaches, and bedbugs were ubiquitous on every ship. Can't overlook shipworms either. These gifted bivalve mollusks used their mini shells to rasp and bore their way through a boat's hull, progressively undermining the seaworthiness of the entire vessel. To eradicate them one would first have to find them. All of them! No one had to look very hard, because they were everywhere.

Survival at sea had a timer on it. It became a race against pestilence, seaworthiness, and the elements, plus the very nature of sailors. Perhaps this was the reason recreational boating took so long to become popular.

No wonder "faster" became a dominating design feature to reckon with when designing a vessel. Beating the ticking clock of survival on the water translated to riches in a variety of ways. Speed depended on maximum use of sail dragging a boat through water. The linchpin for accomplishing greater speed lay in the uneasy marriage between mast height and depth of keel. More mast equaled more sail; more sail equaled more speed. Not exactly a magic computation, but definitely a perplexing mathematical challenge for the boat-building industry. Consequences for poor job performance were rarely paid for by the builder, unless they happened to be on the same field trip.

The maximum length mast that a boat can carry is greatly determined by the righting potential of the boat. Simply described, how much lean can it take before flipping over and ending a sailing day on a very bad note. A ship's ability to remain upright in the arduous elements of wind and waves lay in the size of its mast. The righting moment (which is a good thing) is affected by the width of the boat, the weight and length of the keel, and placement of the ballast (how low the weight on the keel). Once a boat starts to list (lean over) the weight of the mast now has a vested interest in finishing the job. The ship must have a counterbalance to right itself. The greater the length of the keel and the lower the actual weight is carried on the keel, the taller a mast can be.

This concludes the Renaissance boating certification course.

⇥ Chapter 14 ⇤
BREW HOUNDS

The Queen of Sheba had recently been modified to address the pivotal force of the big three. Speed created the greatest advantage for those choosing the Barbary coast profession of piracy. As Machiavelli once said, speed kills, but only in the appropriate circumstance. Despite a Formula 1 race car traveling at excessively high speeds, you would not choose it to run errands around town. It certainly can't hold a trunk full of groceries, since it has a trunk full of engine. Trade-offs do matter.

The redesigned Queen now had the necessary speed to track down and overcome the L'Aquila or any other merchant traveling through its preferred kill zone. However, like anything else in life, the Queen also had a lurking weakness. Self-awareness makes us aware of both our strengths and our weaknesses. We may not be able to truly do anything about them, but at least the awareness can make it possible to protect against too many self-inflicted consequences. No self-awareness creates a haphazard life lived at a perpetual surprise party.

As the L'Aquila passengers and crew settled in for their day's journey, concealed in a sheltered inlet on the far side of the landmark rock of Gibraltar, another captain gave a similar order to cast off.

The Queen of Sheba launched on its southward journey across the strait. Like the L'Aquila, its hold was empty.

Feeling the west wind, Longshort held a broad reach on a starboard tack. Even with the scant breeze, the Queen easily made six knots of headway.

"Today is a good day. I can feel it," pronounced the captain.

"A bit early to tell if you're askin' for feedback on that, Captain," offered Longshort, keeping his eyes on the mainsail.

The captain's brow furrowed into an instant scowl.

"Why turn my optimism into a steaming heap of camel dung first thing in the morning?"

"I'm a pragmatist." Longshort shrugged.

"You're a flagon-half-empty guy, is what you are. I refuse to let that ruin my sunny outlook. Not today. Hold your course and think of something nice to say next time I *don't* ask for commentary!"

With that, the captain bounded off the bridge heading for the bow. A fresh morning breeze off the Mediterranean would renew the sense of hope and opportunity the Fearless One had awakened with that morning.

Destemido groused at a rail-thin crewman with black curly hair emerging from the ships hold.

"Name!?"

"Baptiste, sir."

"The hold is empty, correct?"

"Yes, Captain. I believe we offloaded everything last night. Ummm, would you mind hanging on a quick second?"

"'I believe?' Did I hear you correctly?"

A wrong word, a failure to comply, an error in judgment, or even something as innocuous as a poorly chosen word might be the difference between a crewman's next meal or no meal - ever again. The consequences for disappointing this captain could be severe. The suddenly panicky sailor kneeled by the cargo hatch. He craned his neck into the dark hole to take a second look for his own personal safety.

"Take all the time you need, crewman."

Not sure how to read the captain's tone of voice, the petrified sailor jumped down into the hold to make certain he had reported correctly. He had not. In the far corner of the dark hold rested a lone barrel most likely filled to the brim with Moroccan hummus. "Dammit," he thought. Poking his head back through the hold, he reported in.

But before he uttered a single word, the captain had surmised the update.

"Hummus?"

"Uh-huh," answered the shrinking sailor.

"Please tell me there is no more than one vat. I really don't care how much damn paprika they throw in it anymore."

"Just the one, sir. Guess we missed it."

As the sailor prepared for the worst, the breeze off the Med fortuitously picked up, reminding Destemido of the optimism imagined in the early dawn hours.

"So be it." Destemido said.

Personal catastrophe averted. The man quickly dropped back into the hold, remaining there until the captain moved off to the bow.

Daytime raids were considered far too risky for privateers striving to make a decent living along the Strait of Gibraltar. Ships could spy any threat appearing on the horizon with more than enough time to protect themselves. Salvation options included more sail to increase speed, a hasty return to port, loading cannons for battle, daring the brigands to attack, or simply reaching their destination before they were overtaken.

Travel distance between virtually any port along the Andalusian coast and Tangiers added up to fifty miles. A skosh less from Algeciras. Common travel time took three to four hours. The deep blanket of darkness consistently prevailed as option of choice for your medium-brained privateer. But not today. According to the big brain in Captain Destemido, the recently completed redesign of the Queen of Sheba had changed the game in a profound way. A daytime way. The Queen now held twice the sheets of any similar boat, plus its new shallower draft meant less drag. Less drag equaled more speed. Destemido knew speed killed. It tipped the odds overwhelmingly in favor of the Queen of Sheba.

"Just now, two points off the starboard bow," came the call from the bow mate.

Destemido extended a spyglass and peered over the bow through the oncoming spray. Sure enough, the L'Aquila sheets lazily fluttered in the weak wind. Destemido instantly calculated an intercept course. The Queen would strike them well before they made landfall in either direction.

"Longshort!" came the bellow from the bow, "Is that our ship?"

"Aye, sir. The hounds are on the scent!"

Longshort had made the same calculation, and adjusted his course anticipating the captain's orders. The Queen deepened her reach angle, filled her sails, and picked up another knot of killing speed. Smiling, Destemido headed back to the stern.

"I love a rallying hunt. Gives the crew purpose. I recall your father and I," began Longshort.

"Yes, you recall a time in the meadows when you and dear father were leading a pack of thirty English trained bloodhounds, plus thirty bluebloods – perhaps a king or two—all bearing down on a single, frightened, little red-tailed fox you flushed from its formerly hidden lair for no good reason. The mist hanging thick on the field, half of the hounds losing their way, forcing all to rely on you and *my special dad* to find victory for the slaughtering horde and win the day."

"I wasn't going to say any of that, but..."

Destemido cut him off again. "Please, no more father tales. What's with the heavy fox-hunting metaphors today anyway? We're in Spain, on a boat, I don't see the connection."

"To hunt is everything. Hunting transcends time and place. It

is man's primordial right. Before domesticated animals, before shepherds, before ranchers, before the first farmers raised crops - before
man became lax, spineless, and indifferent to his own survival - the
hunt defined existence. Well before wine softened our resolve, survival
was our only quest."

"You're anti-fruit of the vine? Wine is good. I think you're too
wound up today. Now, there's even some new swill I tasted last weekend at the Squirrel and Musk," said Destemido.

Longshort knew the captain was having some fun at his expense.

"Beer? You're talking about beer. Far better than ale if you ask
me..." volunteered a random crewmember tending to the stern sheets.

Longshort glared a look of death at the crewmember, who immediately threaded a rope through his hands and Tarzan'd down to the
deck without looking back.

"Fine...Beer," Longshort resumed, "Where was I?"

"You were talking about the hunt, despite my best attempt to get
you to stop," said the captain.

"Of course. Without the hunt, humanity could not survive and
flourish. It is the seminal, crucial component of primitive and modern
society too often dismissed as evil. The wolf and the fox uphold both
metaphorical and literal meaning in our world. Yes, sir, the hunt! I
live for it."

"Is that the tale you were about to tell me, or will there be more?"
asked Destemido.

"Noooo. That's simply the truth of creation. I was about to tell
you of a battle 25 years ago when..."

"You do realize, Longshort, there are better days ahead as well
as behind?"

"Of course, but valuable lessons for better days often lie in
yesterdays."

Destemido shrugged, then pointed to the sail on the horizon.

"Right, the hunt at hand!" Longshort said.

"Keep her reaching for the wind, my friend. I can't say I'm thrilled about this, but I do agree a hunt is a hunt."

The captain headed down the ladder and amidship to contemplate the actions to come.

For both Destemido and Lanning, it was all about the Pillars of Hercules.

On labor number ten of the twelve he signed up for, Hercules needed to steal a herd of mythically colossal cattle from the very badass, two-headed-four-legged descendant of the snake-haired gorgon sister, Medusa. As Greek gods eschew traditional forms of birth, Lord Geryon had simply emerged from Medusa's recently decapitated body, courtesy of the swift blade of Perseus. Hercules was contracted to bring Geryon's prized herd back to Eurystheus, the curmudgeonly, self-esteem challenged King of Argo.

While on his way to heist the cattle, Hercules ran smack into a giant unforeseen roadblock. The Atlas mountain range had rudely blocked the fastest route from the Mediterranean to his final destination on the Andalusian west coast. Could he have climbed over it? Sure. Could he have added a couple scenic days to the trip and simply walked around it? Certainly. But he was Hercules—the universe's strongest demi-god.

Making use of his birthright, Hercules simply split the whole damn range into two parts: the Rock of Gibraltar on the Andalusian side, and its mythological twin sister, Jebel Musa, on the Moroccan side. The iconic Pillars of Hercules were born. Courtesy of the world's strongest man, humanity would now enjoy a new n: between two previously unconnected bodies of wate

Since mythological times, all tourist bureaus

new development as the slightly intimidating *Edge of Oblivion*; a certified no fly-zone for fear of probable extinction. There was one small caveat attached to the pillars. Like a piece of Greek Pita, the earth was deemed a flat plane with an infinite abyssal ledge leading to oblivion. *Doom* in mythological Greece translated as a direct pass to the home of the Greek god in charge of oblivion, Hades. Hercules, and those who came after, considered his remodeled pillars the last way-station before Chez Hades.

As the L'Aquila cleared the Algeciras Bay headlands on its southwest tack, Felipe and Lanning caught site of pillar number one. It loomed large in their rear-view mirror at roughly eight o'clock. They knew that a clear view of the Rock of Gibraltar often signaled the start of the most challenging section of the passage. They'd find out in a hurry what kind of day it might be, once the prevailing funneling west winds got an open free shot at their little caravel.

It may have started the day as a gentle chillaxing breeze wafting over the sunny beaches in the Azores, but a radical personality shift could occur. Once the gentle wind drifted into the narrow passage between two of the world's largest continents, the games began in earnest. The close proximity of the two continents compressed and funneled that breeze into an often-ferocious gale-force wind capable of destroying even the stoutest vessel traveling at the wrong moment at the wrong angle on the wrong day. Crossing the bay, however, was always easier than making one's way either straight into or out of the channel onto the vast dispassionate ocean of mystery.

Direct combat with frenetic nature was much worse than a passing skirmish on the route to Tangiers. Navigating across the narrow strait still presented a host of obstacles, however brief the battle. Aside from the blast of wind, ferocious currents moved from the ocean into the more petite Mediterranean Sea. Add rapidly shifting extreme tides possessing the subtle, yet unrelenting force to push any vessel far off its intended course to that mix, and a short day would become a nightmare.

So far on this day, the west winds emerging from the shadow of the bay were light and steady. Seemed like the L'Aquila had a smooth, straightforward day of sailing ahead of it. Experienced pilots like Felipe hoped for the best, but always prepared for the worst. After hundreds of crossings, he had a learned to recognize coastline markers and read the weather with precision. He could estimate the depth of the water by observing the color of the sea—deep blue equaled safe; light blue equaled not much depth, but a sandy, brown bottom meant *shouldn't be here*. By keeping a sighting on both pillars, Felipe managed the delicate balance between wind angle and course direction. Every crossing tested his ability, dancing the wafer-thin distances between perfection, disaster, uneventful, and "uh oh."

Chapter 15
UH OH

Shafi finally succumbed to the nagging feeling of a full bladder. Turning around, he discreetly relieved himself over the stern rail. Enjoying the momentary relief, his gaze drifted to the horizon. In the distance he caught faint sight of a sail directly astern of the L'Aquila.

Before taking his shift at the wheel as a standard part of his navigation duties, Lorenzo took a brief head turn to align their course against Gibraltar.

"Hmmm," Shafi murmured.

Lorenzo caught the utterance mid-turn. He quickly mirrored Shafi's gaze, arriving at a slightly different conclusion.

"Shit!"

"Might be nothing," suggested Shafi.

"Don't think so, Uncle," countered Lorenzo.

"Take a breath."

"I took several."

"You might be right. Probably not good." Shafi continued squinting hoping to magically improve his vision.

"You!" Lorenzo shouted at Hector.

Trying to hold down his nausea, Hector was barely keeping himself upright by the stern gunnel.

"Me?" He gulped down the vomit erupting in his mouth.

"Go get the captain! Now!"

Deep breathing, he walked slowly over to the ladder.

"New guy! Put a skip in your step," urged Lorenzo.

Hector double-timed it down the ladder, then giant-stepped to the bow. The two brothers were discussing the wind, course, and attractiveness of Lady Beaufort.

"I hadn't noticed."

"Loyola has!" laughed Felipe.

"Excuse me," Hector tried to interject. Neither brother paid attention. He tried again to no avail. He let loose a piercing whistle.

Felipe turned in outrage. "You whistled? You whistled on my ship!"

"Sorry, but you ignored me. Both of you." Hector exhibited little remorse.

"Goddamn it," Felipe continued.

"What is it, Hector?" Lanning appeared less tweaked. Preferring not to carry on with Felipe's hazing routine. Hector pointed up to the bridge, where Lorenzo motioned for them to come up.

"That guy, the one waving back there said for me to come get you, so I am."

"That's Lorenzo," said Lanning.

Lorenzo had escalated his waving. He shifted his motion to a frantic point back towards Gibraltar. Lanning and Felipe followed the gaze of their shipmates at the stern.

"Shit," said Felipe.

"Yeah, that's not good," Lanning added.

Both men jumped down from the bow and beelined for the stern of the boat, racing by both Loyola and Lady Beaufort in the process.

"Everything ok, Captain?" asked Loyola.

"Stay put!" said Lanning over his shoulder.

The full black sails of the Queen of Sheba billowed up against the stark blue horizon. Everyone on the bridge knew from the angle of its track the implied intention.

"Maybe not awful," offered Shafi.

"If you'd get a pair of damn glasses, you would not be saying that," scolded Lorenzo.

"He's right, Uncle. There's no question."

Lanning kept his gaze glued to the horizon.

"What does it matter if he has glasses or not?" asked Loyola as he climbed up to the stern.

"We're not talking about glasses, we're talking about those sails on the horizon line," Lanning said.

"I don't need them," groused Shafi.

"He does, but thinks they make him look weak. We need more cloth in the wind," said Felipe.

"Those sails are miles away," said Loyola.

"Not for long," said Felipe.

"Not a good thing," said Loyola.

"Welcome to the world as is," said Lanning.

"Probably two hours or so, unless..." Felipe had some ideas rumbling around his head.

Shafi fumbled around in his pockets, finally finding the ancient pair of scrunched-up metal thread loop glasses he never admitted to having. He threw the looping string over his head and placed the slit bridge lenses over his nose. The fullness of their predicament now rushed into focus.

"I make it two and a half! Unless you keep sitting on your ass instead of adding sheets to the wind Felipe!"

"Ah, Shafi has arrived!" said Lorenzo.

Loyola leaned against the stern gunnel, placing his hand in some of Hector's vomit. He wiped his hand against the rail as he peered to get a better view of the boat behind them.

"Why do we think this is a bad thing? Maybe they're simply compatriots headed for Tangiers, as we are."

Lorenzo, laser-focused on keeping the sails taut with wind,

commented to no one and everyone, "He's almost as funny as me, in a completely uninformed and shut-the-hell-up sort of way."

"Seems like our courses are similar yet different. Hardly proof of anything to my military eye," surmised Loyola ignoring the insult.

"Riiiight. I'll leave that to you, brother." Felipe jumped down onto the main deck.

Lanning had also heard enough *expertise* from the Lieutenant.

"Featherhead, the reason you can *see* them better now is because they are *getting closer to us,* which means they are *faster!* Two, their course is slightly different than ours because it's called an *intercept course*—meaning sharpen your blade and prepare yourself. Now step off and let us do our work."

"Contigo!"

Lanning shouted down to the man he was sure did not take this change of events lightly.

"I've been down in your mess area. A very poor selection."

Contigo held the L'Aquila's largest meat clever in one hand and an ax in the other.

"We've got a bit of time. No need to hold your weapons at this point," advised Lanning.

"Can we outrun them?" asked Contigo.

Lanning eyed the situation yet again. He glanced fore and aft, assessed the wind, taking in all the conditions, plus the distance back to Algeciras versus maintaining course to Tangier.

"More likely they'll catch us short of Tangier. We'll need some luck. Loyola over there, is a trained soldier, a lieutenant, so he must know how to fight. That beast of a man," he pointed at Hector, "well, he's a beast. I don't know how good an actual fighter he is, but he's an oak tree. I can handle my sword. I'd prefer to avoid conflict, but if they are set on boarding us, can I count on you to organize these folks?"

"Understood."

"Thank you."

"This is why I hate boats." Contigo walked off toward Loyola.

Lanning thought of the irony from Contigo. I, myself, prefer boats to damn wagons chased by men on horses, he said to himself. Why doesn't he also hate wagons? Lady Beaufort skimmed by the ax-toting Contigo towards Lanning. Her demeanor remained calm, even though she had noted the increased intensity aboard ship.

"I can see all is not well today."

"Milady is correct. Rest assured you will be safe. However, at a point I'm going to suggest you head down into the hold for your own safety."

"I can see the sails. I know how to handle myself. While I appreciate your concerns, my safety is my own to protect. And I will."

Lanning contemplated several responses ranging from chivalrous and courtly to full-tilt Ahab.

"Are you going to stand there silent, or respond?"

"Milady," he began patronizingly.

"We can dispense with the bullshit chivalry at this point."

"I don't believe it will come to that. If you're comfortable with a sword, have at it. I'd still prefer you remain below, at least to start. No sense in creating a provocation with a woman on board. More of a royal than a woman, if you know what I mean."

"Agreeable. No offense taken. Doug seems fine up on the mast. May I leave him, or do you want him caged?"

"Leave him. I like the look! Take about half an hour more on deck."

Filippa gave a tight smile and moved off towards Contigo and Loyola, who were gathered at the base of the main mast. Felipe had enlisted Hector to assist him in raising a larger foresail. Hector's wingspan held up the sail against his body like someone trying to measure a new dress for fit. Felipe wove the lines through the sail's grommets, and the two hoisted it up foremast.

"Captain, they're hanging more cloth," said Longshort, still at the wheel of the Sheba.

"Won't help," answered Destemido shaking out the spyglass to take yet another look at their prey. "Fifteen or twenty minutes more or less won't matter. I'll take the wheel. Prepare the men."

"Aye, Captain," answered Longshort. He jumped down the ladder to the main deck and assembled the crew.

Destemido took the brief alone time to choose a best course of action against the likely defenseless vessel now under an hour away. No point in extreme violence if that could be avoided. He knew that while a healthy amount of dread existed in the slow but steady pursuit they had undertaken, it would not be enough for a quick surrender. Broad daylight diminished the fear factor of fire, and the surprise element was also blown. Threats thrown across ten meters of ocean would likely not lead to a quick resolution, either. After sifting through these options, Destemido knew what had to be done.

"Longshort!" he bellowed.

The first mate released the assembly of ten men on the main deck and bounced back up to the stern bridge.

"Captain?"

"Only one certain path for swift victory," announced Destemido.

"I agree completely," said Longshort.

"You agree completely?"

Destemido looked at his friend sideways like a German Shepherd puzzling over a bone.

"Really, you're surprised. You don't recall the very first thing during your first battle?" asked Longshort.

"As a cabin boy?" asked Destemido.

"There's a reason the English turned tail so quickly," Longshort recalled.

"Cannons. Lots of cannons," said Destemido.

"That was the second thing! We blew them up second," Longshort said.

"Huh. You're right. That is where I got that idea."

"I've got the exact man for the job," said Longshort.

Chapter 16

FRONTIER LIVING

"Dammit!" said Felipe on his return to the bridge.

"Dammit!" Lanning echoed.

"It's the wind," Felipe concluded.

"It's the current," countered Lanning.

The L'Aquila had moved into the center of the strait, where the merging forces of nature argued incessantly. A beautiful beach day in the Canaries played quite a different tune in the strait.

"They're definitely moving faster than we are." Another unnecessary observation from Loyola leaning against the bridge ladder.

"It's a caravel like us...how can it be that much faster?" Lanning said ruminating out loud to no one in particular.

"Something is different. I can't put my finger on it either," said Felipe.

"How long?" asked Contigo twirling his meat cleaver.

"Imminent. Maybe half an hour. Dammit! We're short of Tangier. I need to talk with you two," said Lanning.

He hopped off the bridge onto the main deck and motioned Loyola and Contigo to huddle up.

"Pirates want cargo, which we don't have."

"We must stand and fight," Loyola said with a soldier's authority.

"Agreed, except we are likely outnumbered," said Lanning.

"There are other options besides the sword," offered Shafi, approaching the trio.

"Ahh, mysterious old man comment. Someone always says some obtuse thing like that. What's wrong with the obvious? Stand and fight. Simple, clear, and truthful."

Loyola had spent most of his life as a man of battle—a professional soldier who resolved most conflicts with the weapons in his hand. As a schooled Berber apothecary, Shafi had spent his life searching for veiled solutions to the afflictions that cursed the frailty of the human body. A fisherman by trade, he understood the need for patience. Rarely were solutions as simple as slicing through a man's gut with the point of a steel blade.

"No mud, no lotus," Shafi answered back.

"An old man riddle, now?" Loyola was getting exasperated.

"It's philosophy; it's a deeper meaning. You have to think about it," said Lanning.

"Appears we have insufficient time to think on that today, Captain."

"Uncle, I appreciate the advice," said Lanning to avoid further discord.

"I too believe we need to prepare for the worst," added Contigo.

"Agreed," said Lanning. "They won't be expecting us to fight, so we do have some surprise on our side. But I'd still rather not take that route if it's avoidable."

"In my experience, mercenaries commonly take the easiest route to the prize." said Contigo.

"I agree with...you're a butcher, though, right?" said Loyola. Contigo nodded.

"Seems, the war-savvy *butcher* and I agree," emphasized Loyola. "Surely an unexpected aggression will shake their resolve."

"Yoo-hoo, warriors! Not so keen on dying for a Tuesday day trip to Tangier up here," yodeled Lorenzo from the bridge.

Loyola turned toward Lorenzo, but addressed himself to everyone in a bellowing voice.

"All men are sentenced to death before the cord has been cut.

Many of us are going to die in most unpleasant ways. Whimpering is not the way I plan on exiting this world! Nor should you, simply because fate has added one more unexpected chance of death to the already lethal lineup of options. Follow me into destiny, and we shall not fail!"

"Very inspiring, but I've got plans tomorrow," insisted Lorenzo. "I'd rather die playing tennis, or bathing my children, or over a pint and a squirrel with my friends, or how about fucking anything but a sword sliding through my gut! This is a paycheck for me, not a career. I'm about to graduate!" countered the fearfully agitated Lorenzo.

"No one is going to die needlessly today," said Lanning.

"When they approach, we will keep the distance between us manageable to avoid boarding. However, if I am killed, you will surrender to avoid any further bloodshed. We must all protect Lady Beaufort from harm."

"Oh, for god's sake. We talked about this. I can protect myself, thank you!" the voice echoed up from the ship's hold.

"Brother!" yelled Felipe from the bridge.

"Can it wait?" asked Lanning.

"Definitely not."

Felipe was pointing to the dead middle of the strait, "See it?"

"See what?" yelled Lanning.

"Get your ass up here, now!"

Lanning excused himself from the group and hopped up the ladder.

"How about now?" said Felipe pointing.

"Got it! Holy shit!"

Lanning grabbed Lorenzo by the shoulders and leaned in.

"Lorenzo?"

"Unless that gung-ho, glory-horny aristocrat gets us in some apocalyptic melee," answered the terrified Lorenzo. "No joke, you gotta keep that guy in check!"

Lanning knew it was his responsibility to make the choice for all souls aboard the L'Aquila, despite any of his personal unresolved dilemmas.

One breath at a time. He recalled his adoptive father's advice during what became their very last conversation. As Gonzalo packed his duffel for a lengthy sea voyage, fifteen-year-old Lanning watched from the bedside.

"Son," Gonzalo began, "the gap between what you desire of this world, and what the world desires of you, is the frontier. Your frontier."

"Okay," answered the puzzled teenager. "Why are you telling me this now? Is that supposed to help me figure out what I'm supposed to do?"

"No. That will simply appear at some point. I'm telling you now, because things happen in life. Now, if a thing happens, we will have had this conversation."

"So, will you be telling this to Felipe too?"

"Not today. This is more of a personal compass conversation. For you. At some point if there's a 'thing,' you will explain it to Felipe," said Gonzalo, who had moved to sit on the bed.

"If I don't know what we're talking about, how can I explain it to him?"

Gonzalo had a premonition that the voyage he was about to embark on might be longer than anticipated. He wanted to give the boy tools for tougher times.

"I take your point, but let's not get sidetracked. You are about to become a man. If I'm not here, my hope is these words will help you find your way."

"But I haven't asked about any of this. Do I need to get a job?

Support mom and Felipe? I can be a fisherman, or join the army, but what if I'm not supposed to do that?"

"This is not about getting a job. It's bigger than that. Besides, remember, what you do does not define who you are. You are studied. You can read and you can write. You have a moral compass. You have character, and understand the truth when you hear it. You can discern a good man from a charlatan. I have taught you to handle yourself in battle. Although you may not fully understand all of this now, you do understand the effort it took to accomplish these things? Yes?"

"Yes sir," said Lanning not comprehending great gulps of Gonzalo's observations.

"Your compass," Gonzalo touched his index finger to the boy's temple, "in here, is the sum of all that. It is your guide to the frontier to come."

"How do I know when I'm there?" asked the boy.

"The moment when you overhear yourself and the world simultaneously."

Lanning felt thoroughly mystified.

Gonzalo watched the blank look on Lanning's face and realized his message would probably get lost in the muddle of a teenage brain.

"You're not wrong. This is a lot to take in."

"I hear the world?" asked Lanning cherry-picking one graspable literal piece.

"Probably too tough a concept. Sorry, son. Put it this way. When you feel jumbled and maybe faced with something that appears insurmountable; when the mountain looks too big to climb, that's when you climb it anyway."

"Okay," came the boy's response. He simply wanted the conversation to end.

"Excellent. The rest you will figure out in your own time.

And Lanning," he gently gripped boy's shoulder, "You are unique. Your place is different from mine or your mother's, or your brother. Understand?"

Nope.

He did not comprehend hardly any of it. He filed it away for as long as he could, until the actual "thing" happened to Gonzalo. Even then, he never truly reflected on the message, until the moment currently confronting him.

This is my frontier, he surmised. Let's run down the checklist—insurmountable ominous feeling, check! Chaotic conflicting choices, check! Feeling a foreboding sense of dread tinged with a spark of teetering hope...? He acknowledged Gonzalo's description of the frontier. Nightmarish scenario. But he was still breathing, still thinking, and there was no option but to take a breath, followed by a step. He'd puke up his guts later if there was time.

Lanning did not disagree with Loyola's observation. He also knew Loyola was not the ideal messenger to deliver the undeniable truth of the human condition. The world had a final outcome designated for all living things. Despite might or right, strength of mind, depth of spirit, personal resolve, or simple chance of fate, our final truth lay in the certainty of life's unavoidable, absolute finality. The fear comes from not being able to choose our own preferred ending. Imagining our end is mostly unimaginable until it isn't. Since it is so difficult to imagine, we deceive ourselves to think it won't happen. Accurately forecasting the end remains a rarity for anyone but the suicidally inclined, or the designated banner holder racing ahead from the pole position of an attacking army. Those guys have to know they're toast.

Of course, he also knew Loyola to be a glory-seeking, arrogant elitist, intoxicated by the call of false glory. Lanning, like Shafi, believed there was another option. More importantly, he knew what it was.

Chapter 17

TAKE THE FIRST LEFT

"Phew! I feel sooo much better. What is up, L'Aquila!"

A fully renewed Rory sprung from the hold of the ship into the throng of activity onboard the L'Aquila.

"I thought he went home," Lanning said.

"I am home," answered Rory.

"Morning! You missed a couple things."

"What's up, Zo!"

"We're being pursued by mercenaries on our way to Tangier. They most likely outnumber us, I'm guessing three to one, and, except for one glory junkie with a hero complex, our outlook is grim. Along with the rest of us, fate has dealt you the short straw, my friend."

"Do I have time for a snack? Got that nasty after-vomit taste in my mouth."

Lanning ignored the dazed crewman to catch Contigo's attention.

"I've got another man for you." Turning to Rory, "That big guy holding the meat cleaver wants a word."

"Was that Lorenzo being mister negative, or is this truly my final hour on earth?"

"Bit of both. The odds are long," Lanning thumbed Rory towards Contigo.

Feeling like a ping pong ball, Lanning headed back to the bow. Shafi stared wistfully at the port of Tangier in the distance.

"We're not going to make that, Uncle."

"The secret of victory is to make your enemy contemplate defeat," counseled Shafi.

"I'm working on it."

"Highly unusual to be attacked during daylight hours. Hubris, no?"

"This captain is either myopically arrogant or boldly confident. Meaning they've surely gauged the move," Lanning said, leaning down on the bow railing.

"I don't see any panic on your face."

"Then you should definitely put your glasses back on."

"Panic, an alarm for the unanticipated. The hubris of having control over the uncontrollable, life. Bewilderment is the preferred option. It contains a dose of suitable humility."

"You sound like Gonzalo! I need a month to figure out what you're talking about. Let's say I'm bewildered, if it plays better for you."

"Panic is the dead-end street that spins back upon itself in an endless spiral of paralysis. Far better to be perplexed than overwhelmed with anxiety and fear over an uncontrollable loss of power over a powerless situation. I advise leaving space for curiosity and resolution…"

"Get your sword, Uncle, then take care of Lorenzo. That's my resolution for you."

Lanning searched for Filippa and found her near the ships hold.

"Did you mean what you said earlier about the dress?" Lanning figured his best approach was to stay focused.

"Absolutely."

Lanning observed her natural confidence. Without even considering her beauty, he was drawn to her. For him, chemistry had always been a two-way feeling. He tried to convince himself she felt the same way about him. Felipe's teasing that he had no game bubbled up in his brain, undermining his nerve. None of that mattered at this moment regardless of his nerve or Filippa's. Unhappily, any of that would take a deep sideline for quite a while, if ever.

"Good, there are some things in my cabin. Can you find your way?"

"Yes, I can. And I do get your meaning. Thank you," she said.

She turned to make for Lanning's cabin. Lorenzo piloted the L'Aquila closer to the middle of the strait. The wind had picked up at least four knots coming from the west. Taking advantage of the strength of the wind allowed him to hold a tighter starboard close reach into the strength of the wind. Three hours after they'd left Algeciras, the two boats were now within one mile of each other.

Lanning, Contigo, and Loyola conferred by the main mast to review the strategy. Hector, relaxed but poised, leaned against the port side by the forward mast. The sword tucked in his waistband looked like a buck knife relative to his massive size. Positioned in front of the main mast stoically stood Nantucket. He held a single piece of anchor line cut from the end of the anchor chain. Rory crouched against the port side gunnel amidship, clutching both a sword and single shot pistol. Shafi had positioned himself on the bridge next to Lorenzo, who remained focused on holding their course. Tangier appeared closer and closer yet, still miles in the distance.

"We're good to go, Captain. How many men do you think we're up against?" asked Loyola.

"More," answered Lanning flatly.

"Count us, plus one," said a sailor, suddenly emerging from the cabin below the stern deck brandishing a sword.

"Who's this then?" asked Contigo.

"It's the only way to keep her safe if everything goes sideways," said Lanning.

Chapter 18

SIDEWAYS

"Surprise is overrated!"

Framed by bow spray, adrenaline flowing, Destemido stood poised on the bow of the fast-moving Queen of Sheba.

"Won't be needing this anymore." Destemido pitched a spyglass up in the air.

Longshort, temporarily away from the tiller, caught the flying spyglass and collapsed it in one smooth motion. The Queen had finally moved into hailing distance of the L'Aquila. It's crew of twenty eagerly waited for the order to board.

"Looks like a skeleton crew. Shouldn't be much to contend with. We ready?"

"On the stern halyard, Captain," said Longshort with a head tilt.

Destemido spotted the small, stout sailor crouched low and partially hidden by the sails. He held a line of rope originating from the center mast along with a cutlass.

"On your order," continued Longshort.

"Match their reach, prepare for boarding," ordered Destemido.

Longshort echoed the command, and moved to the main deck. The Queen of Sheba deep leaned against the rising wind, picking up another two knots while skipping across the whitecapped water. Twenty poised men lining the starboard gunnels pulled kerchiefs from necks over noses, awaiting the word.

The single passenger onboard the Queen abruptly interrupted. "You'll be leaving me out of this shit show, Captain."

"Obviously," Longshort said answering for Destemido, who simply displayed a scowl. "We know the arrangement. Kindly keep yourself below until we..."

Destemido cut him off, "Stay the fuck below unless I tell you to show your disagreeable face." The man did not cower, but disappeared, nonetheless.

"Prepare for boarding," shouted Longshort.

The two ships drew closer, the L'Aquila now a shrinking two hundred yards ahead. Destemido yelled from the bow.

"Drop your colors!"

There was no panicking scramble aboard the L'Aquila. Lanning appeared calm and thoroughly non-plussed by the encroaching conflict.

"Someone is yelling at us, Captain," said Loyola, who cupped his ear straining to hear. Lanning waved him.

"Drop your colors!" Destemido repeated.

Lanning moved to the stern bridge. He cupped his ear as if attempting to make out the hail from the approaching ship. He stood huddled with Shafi, Lorenzo, and an approaching Loyola.

"Did he say, 'up yours?'" asked Lanning cynically.

"Doubt that," said Lorenzo, keeping his eyes forward.

"He seems angry," observed Loyola.

"More likely battle rage; psyched up," said Shafi.

"He's waving up at our mast," said Lorenzo.

Lanning pointed up at the mast, then signaled back by pointing to his ears. He then extended his arms and shrugged his shoulders. The international symbol for "can't hear a fucking word you're saying."

"How long do you plan to keep this up? We may be able to outrun them," said Lorenzo glancing back.

"Not hardly, and as long as we need to. Fall off the wind a bit on my mark," commanded Lanning.

The Sheba closed the gap to one hundred yards apart. Once again Destemido shouted at them off the bow.

"Lower your colors and prepare to be boarded!"

Aboard the L'Aquila, little doubt about the message remained. Lanning held the stern rail and replied.

"No thanks, but do enjoy the rest of your day!"

Destemido looked down at Longshort, bemused.

"You heard that, right?" said Destemido.

"Unexpected, but original," Longshort said, with a slight smile. "Shall we simply stay with the plan?"

"So much for the easy way. Bring us along their port side, and let's be quick about it."

Lanning watched as the Queen tightened its course against the wind, increasing speed by another knot.

"Port side, for sure, brother," said Felipe. "That's not going to work for us."

"Got something in mind," Lanning said calmly.

The two ships were less than a boat-length apart. The Queen began to angle towards the port side of the L'Aquila.

"Lanning?" Lorenzo's nerves were fraying.

"Not yet. Haaaannnnggg... onnn."

Lanning waited, gauging the perfect convergence of elements—wind, current, the position of the two boats. Holding off until...

"Lower your damn colors!"

Lanning was counting on Destemido's escalating frustration.

"As you can plainly see, we are not flying colors, sir. We are a pleasure cruise to Tangier."

Lanning turned his head towards Lorenzo whispering, "Mark!"

Lorenzo did not move; he had lost his bearing while transfixed nervously watching the two ships moving closer together.

"Lorenzo! MARK! I said MARK, on my mark...do it now!"

Reawakened, Lorenzo relaxed his grip on the wheel. No longer held in force by Lorenzo's iron grip, the wheel whipped itself back to neutral in a counterclockwise spin that would have ripped the arm off a mountain gorilla. The boat came to an instantaneous stop on the surface of the ocean. Everyone onboard save Lanning, Felipe and Lorenzo, who had planned on the effect, crashed to the deck. Felipe, who was in the rigging, clung to the mainsail halyard and watched as the Queen of Sheba blew ten boat lengths past the L'Aquila in a matter of seconds.

"Wahoo! Brother, that was a beautiful thing..." Felipe whooped from the rigging.

"Resume close reach and move us to the middle," commanded Lanning, bracing himself against the stern rail. It's not over yet."

Lanning raced towards the bow. He passed the befuddled Loyola, Contigo, and Filippa who were slowly pulling themselves back to upright.

"Sailing can be fun, right guys?" he called as he sprinted past them.

Lanning knew he had bought them some time, but not freedom from peril.

"I like this captain," said Longshort. "He has spirit!"

"I want you on the wheel now! Bring us about. I've had enough games."

Longshort moved the sailor manning the wheel off to the side, and spun the wheel to bring the Sheba into a wide downwind course reversal. They would easily recapture their position against the L'Aquila, and put a rapid end to the tactics of the slower vessel.

Shouting from the bow of the L'Aquila, Lanning tried yet again to avert conflict.

"We've got no cargo. Trust me sir, we're not worth your effort."

Destemido stood firm on the Queen's bow. Arms bent at the elbows, he returned the signaled the international symbol for "can't hear what the fuck you're saying, and don't give a damn!"

Now running with the wind, The Queen closed the distance between the ships at twice the clip. They approached head-on along the L'Aquila's starboard side. Longshort moved his kerchiefed mercenaries to the port side. The single lone sailor holding the main mast halyard held his crouch on the upper bridge deck.

"Contigo, prepare for battle," said Lanning.

Loyola drew his sword, and like Contigo, moved over to the starboard side of the boat. Contigo motioned the others to reposition, facing the starboard side of the ship.

"I don't think I'm up for this, Uncle," said a shrinking Lorenzo.

"We're never truly ready for this, son. You'll be fine."

Shafi fumbled with his glasses, before opting to let them drop against his chest. Lanning headed amidship.

"Heave to, and life will be simpler," yelled Destemido, rapidly approaching and within easy and obvious earshot of everyone on both vessels. Both Longshort and Destemido needed to clearly identify the opponent's captain before launching the attack.

Filippa tracked Lanning to the starboard gunnel.

"Captain, Doug can help."

"What does that mean? What can he do?"

"He can attack on command," she declared.

"No shit? That's epic. Can you choose who he strikes and when?"

"He'll strike the closest perceived opportunity, but I can't be sure of the who, only the when. It's a hand command."

"Hold him ready and wait for it. Now, please stay off the gunnels and hold by the tiller with Shafi."

Filippa grabbed the cage and headed up to the bridge.

Lanning extended himself over the starboard rail, "Sir, this is your last chance to call off the unwanted visit. We are peaceful, but not without means."

The ships were within twenty feet of each other as Longshort looked at the sailor concealed on the stern deck. Figuring the signal had been given, the sailor released from his blind. Extending his cutlass, he swung out from the Queen. Like a legendary flying Wallenda, he emerged from behind the mainsail in a graceful deadly arc across the gap between the two ships straight for Lanning.

All eyes and bodies on the L'Aquila froze in surprise. All except Hector, who had been doubled over streaming vomit when he caught sight of the crouched sailor a moment before takeoff. The flying assailant in a perfectly timed motion let loose of the rope. His deadly weapon was poised to cut Lanning in half lengthwise with one blow.

He dropped out of the air about ten feet overhead. To his great astonishment, the giant hands of Hector plucked him from his appointed destiny. Stopping the man's forward momentum, Hector gripped him head-high for a split second, and then threw the assailant down on the deck of the L'Aquila with the force of a Steinway piano free falling from ten floors up. As he leaned over to complete his vomit stream, he stomped on the man's chest and crushed it with a single blow. The invader lay dead, covered in a pool of vomit. Hector picked up the man's cutlass and looked towards Lanning.

"Hector! Damn!" said Lanning.

"Prepare to attack," ordered Longshort from the Queen's starboard railing.

Lanning angled his gaze abaft. Catching the signal, Filippa, opened the cage, and gave the hand signal to Doug.

The freed raptor lit out in full predator mode. He made a straight-line run, striking Longshort at fifty plus miles an hour. The impact lifted the unwary senior mercenary two feet off the deck before pancaking him flat on his back, impaled by Doug's razor-sharp talons viciously shanked deep into his neck. A gush of pulsing deep red blood streamed over the stricken man, freezing the Queen's horrified crew in their tracks.

Taking advantage of the moment Loyola and Contigo rushed to the rail, poised to head off the boarding maneuver. Contigo brandished his meat cleaver, plus the cutlass he had snagged from Hector.

Destemido, in horror over the fate of his mentor and friend, prepared to give the order to board when he caught sight of Contigo. His eyes widened. Contigo met the gaze, staring back at Destemido, then wincing at the carnage he had witnessed on the deck of the Queen.

"HOLD!" shouted Destemido.

Lanning took the frozen moment to execute his plan of action. He ran up to the bridge shouting at both Lorenzo and Felipe:

"NOW NOW NOW!"

Lorenzo heeled the L'Aquila sharply to port. Felipe, along with Rory and a woozy Hector, pulled the mainsail and foresail halyards taut harnessing the maximum force of the rising wind. The ship swiftly reacted, leaping forward at triple speed even before the sails had filled. Felipe moved up to the bow to help Lorenzo focus on holding the correct course, waving his arms left or right.

Together the crew had managed to lock the imperiled L'Aquila square in the center of the powerful hidden current that ran through the narrow strait of Gibraltar.

"What just happened?" asked a mystified Loyola.

"Fucking seamanship!" answered Felipe as he moved to check the rigging.

"There is a westbound current that occasionally runs the length of the strait. That, plus the wind, adds as much as eight knots to our travel. We caught them flat -footed, and now, no doubt, tending to their wounded," Lanning answered.

"Holy shit, that bird is your PET? It did some gruesome damage," commented Rory as he tied down a halyard.

"They still could've boarded us. They'll turn and give chase," said the battle-savvy Contigo.

"Filippa, can you recall Doug before they kill him?" Lanning asked.

Filippa's confidence appeared shaken. Then they both heard a sound. On the foredeck, Nantucket stood, hands cupped around his mouth, calling into the wind.

"Keee, kee, kee, keeee!"

The dark speck against the blue sky grew larger and larger. Gliding in on outstretched wings, Doug made a graceful spiral before settling on Nantucket's waiting arm.

"Thank you!" exclaimed Filippa. She ran to grab the cage.

"No need. You can trust me," said Nantucket, waving her off.

Doug bowed his head to receive Nantucket's gentle stroke. Filippa took note of Doug's behavior with this stranger.

"It seems that I do," she said.

"The time for true trust is when doubt lies in your mind," he advised.

Filippa was caught off-guard, "Yes, I suppose that is true."

Lanning turned to see the Queen of Sheba making its own tight turn into the channel. The race was on again.

"We are far from out of the woods. Felipe," he yelled. "We still need some magic, brother!"

Chapter 19

SLIP SLIDIN'

Success, like interpretive dance, is more often an exercise in trust tempered by fate. The best plans fail miserably at times. No matter how much we try to conjure a controllable future, with the certainty of an Einstein calculation, the universe always holds an unseen water balloon.

The magic of a life well-lived occurs in the liminal space between cataclysmic disaster and subjective success. We all contend with unpredictable variations thrown at us by a disaffected universe with a wickedly morbid sense of humor. Euphoria and despair, exaltation and desolation, triumph and misery, stand together like a family of biblical twins.

Now with only himself to rely on, Destemido could fare no better, no worse, and certainly no different than the dispassionate odds forecast.

Scrambling down to the wounded Longshort, Destemido grabbed the closest sailor and ripped off his kerchief. He cradled Longshort's head in a crooked elbow before tightly wrapping the scarf around his friend's shredded neck. But trying to staunch the bleeding proved futile.

"You're not going to die from this," Destemido lied.

"I think I might," Longshort croaked.

The blood-saturated scarf confirmed the outcome.

Longshort eked out a few more words, "You saw him?"

"I did. It *was* him. You can share all your stories with me after we catch and kill those bastards," said Destemido.

Longshort nodded and reached for Destemido's hand, but never made the connection.

"Come about and chase those bastards down!" commanded Destemido as he stood.

The Queen made a rapid full course reversal. The wind kicked into its sails as the boat leapt forward. They slid into the current, giving instantaneous chase. With its shallower draft, and despite its deadly head start, they would catch the L'Aquila within twenty minutes.

The furious, vengeful captain stomped back to the bow. Not a single crew member felt emboldened enough to approach him.

At a loss without his lifelong companion, yet somehow buoyed by the finality of the loss, Destemido calmed himself as Longshort would have counseled. He took the time afforded to conjure another option for success, then gathered his crew, hoping to avoid any further unscheduled balloons.

Once again, the Queen sheared in on the L'Aquila. As Destemido prepared for battle, the low-slung buildings of Tangier, perched on the western entrance of the strait, moved into view.

"Hey!" yelled Lanning from the stern railing. "I told you we carry no cargo."

Destemido stood stone-faced.

"Why waste blood on a battle that has no victory?"

Again, Destemido offered no response only ruthless resolve. Lanning's words had also been heard by the mercenary crew of the Queen. A sheepish representative for the crew made his way up to the bow. Coincidentally, he and the captain had shared an encounter only that morning.

"Sir, the crew," began the anxious crewman.

Without hesitation, Destemido turned the man sideways to the L'Aquila, withdrew his sword, and ran him straight through the abdomen. Holding the dying man upright, he slowly withdrew his sword. The captain then discarded the lifeless form to the deck.

"Anyone else?" he bellowed down to the deck. "Prepare to board!"

"Holy shit!" said Lorenzo.

The two ships continued drawing closer together. The L'Aquila had to play for time to reach safe harbor. Lanning caught sight of two ships leaving the port at Tangier, heading out into the strait.

"I can see better opportunities for you than a tourist ship, Captain," Lanning shouted.

"Soon you will be dead, and your ship will be mine. That will be prize enough."

"Is this really a wise choice of occupation? Why not find legitimate career options better suited to your talents? Pirating's a lifestyle riddled with stress, and unnecessary risk. You can do better."

"Taunting him? That's your strategy?" said a Loyola. "Fuck 'em, let the battle begin!"

"He's trying to save you for another battle on another day," said Shafi.

Nantucket walked up to the stern bridge with Doug perched on his left shoulder. Loyola began positioning the crew to repel the coming attack. The two ships drew close enough in the channel to see the Queen angle port to starboard side. Closing in. Lanning knew his options were becoming increasingly limited.

"I've got a deal for you, Captain," he said.

Destemido considered the circumstance confronting him. His crew, while obediently holding battle positions on the port side, was surely dubious. Destemido realized fear alone would not keep them in alignment for long. Longshort would surely have opted for the path of least resistance. The threat of defeat had bowed his adversary. The closer they drew to Tangier; the less time was not in their favor. He too had seen the ships embarking from the harbor.

"State your offer," Destemido said.

"I am happy to procure some bit of cargo for you from Tangier, in exchange for our continued passage. Tomorrow upon departure, we can meet along the same route and exchange goods as payment. Do you have a shopping list?"

"We will send you a list, but I require a good faith gesture," answered Destemido.

"State your terms."

The two boats had drifted side by side. All parties had a clear view of each vessel and its occupants. Destemido noticed two particular crewmembers onboard the L'Aquila. They had caught his eye for two distinctly differing reasons.

"We require a guest. Someone to relax with us on a brief overnight visit. While you shop the souk, we will entertain a crewmember of our choice."

Lanning's quick glance caught Filippa staring over the rail. Slyly he motioned Loyola to nudge her away from the starboard gunnel.

Contigo saw the movement and stepped into the gap where she had been standing. Squinting for sharper vision, he peered across at the captain standing on the bow of the Queen.

Without hesitation, "Her," Destemido pointed at Filippa slinking away with Loyola. "We'd like the woman."

Panic spread through Lanning's brain. How could this captain so easily distinguish the well-disguised Filippa?

"Hah! Perhaps you've been on the water far too long, my friend. There are no women on board today," said Lanning cavalierly. "I, though not the fairer sex, offer myself as your honored guest."

"The woman, or your lives. Prepare to be boarded."

"Wait!" Contigo interrupted the sparring match. "I am certain the captain would not mind if I accepted the kind invitation."

Contigo stepped back from the rail and made his way to the

bridge. Filippa, feeling both terrified and relieved, stopped cold in her tracks at the sudden change. Although he knew Contigo's particular skillset made him an ideal candidate, the responsibility of command weighed on Lanning.

"Can't let you do that," he whispered to Contigo.

"Yeah, you can," he whispered. "It'll be fine. I feel very confident about this."

Destemido, in a surprising reversal, agreed without argument. "Heave to," he said.

"Contigo, we can't be certain of your safety," said Lanning.

Nantucket stepped between the two men.

"Let go of certainty. Its opposite is not uncertainty, but openness, curiosity, and a willingness to embrace the unknown."

"Oh my god, there's two of them?" Lorenzo looked over at Shafi.

"We cannot, should not trust this pirate!" pronounced the battle-ready Loyola.

"Your word is your bond then, sir," said Lanning.

"As is yours," replied Destemido.

"We can offer a wide variety of goods at some value from Tangier. Hummus – an amazing blend of chickpeas,"

"Absolutely not!"

"I happen to know the premier source for..."

"Hell no!" insisted Destemido. "In fact, to show our good faith I will bless you with hummus. BAPISTE!"

At the ready, the allegedly eviscerated sailor magically appeared on deck somehow raised from the dead.

"But he's...you ran him through?" exclaimed the surprised Lorenzo.

"I may be a brigand, but I am not without a moral compass. Why kill a perfectly innocent man unnecessarily if the mission does not require it?"

Although there was truly nothing amusing about their circumstances, Lanning could not help but give a nod of admiration.

"I see that we are all clever men," Lanning said.

"We are certainly all cunning," Destemido replied. "Sailor!" he
bellowed, "Take that cursed crap out of the hold and send it over the
side when we tie up."

"Heave to and prepare the lines," said Felipe to his trepidatious
crew. "Hector, not you!"

Felipe still feared for his brother's life. He felt better stationing
the giant near Lanning for safeguarding. The two ships drew closer
together. Soon lines were exchanged and made fast on each deck.
Contigo had kept a sharp gaze on Destemido throughout the process.
Loyola stood at the ready by his new comrade, right hand poised on
his sword hilt.

The two ships now lay lashed together, rocking in the waves as
one uneasy vessel. Baptiste handed the barrel of hummus over the
Queen's gunnel as Contigo made his goodbyes.

"Thank you, sir! You will be rewarded," said a grateful Filippa.

"No fear my friend. We will be back for you tomorrow with the
afternoon tide," said Lanning as he gripped Contigo's ample forearm
with both his hands.

Loyola gave him a soldiers inclined head emblematic of his respect
for Contigo's bravery and self-sacrifice.

"I have your list. Are you sure about these items? I can suggest
better," said Lanning.

"Tomorrow on the mid-day tide," answered Destemido as he
watched the butcher cross between the boats.

"Cast off," said Felipe.

The lines let loose, and the two ships steadily drifted apart. Sails filled with wind, the L'Aquila turned to port and headed into the Tangier harbor. Destemido slowly walked up to Contigo.

"You've changed," Contigo whispered.

"It's not what you may think, Dad."

Chapter 20

THE ART OF TIPPING — PART II

Back in the fall of 1494, Marco Bellini had wrangled himself a well-paid spot as the head chef at Restaurante Balzi Rossi, named after the Don's long-dead older brother. Situated in the red-hot border town of Ventimiglia, *The Lamb Shack,* as it was affectionately known by the locals, was owned by Don Burducci, and poorly managed by one of his feckless, perpetually inebriated nephews, Matteo Rossi. Over the course of his six-month tenure, Bellini had parlayed his skillsets as both a chef and lethal extortionist into a sizable nest egg. His gains were acquired directly at the expense of the Don's own tithe derived from restaurant profits. Bellini bought all the food, maintained the payroll, and managed the receipts. Anything correlated to cash passed through Bellini's active hands. Matteo was only obliged to greet the customers, guzzle down the house chianti, bed the widows, and do fuck-all for large parts of every week.

It was in this quaint town on the bleeding edge of the French-Italian war that Bellini's festering past intersected with his plans for the future.

The war had begun during the spring of 1494, amidst a jumble of competing political and economic self-interests. Spain had continued to focus on its love affair with slave trading, indigenous native slaughtering, and the over-hyped rogue explorer Chris Columbus. Meanwhile, Italy and France had tried to settle their differences over more mundane sundry items wrapped up in a tossed salad of popes, aristocrats, and naturally, money. Surely something also related to buffalo mozzarella versus camembert, or some other dubious cause.

The peaceful, commerce-driven Republic of Genoa had fallen

victim to the first invading hordes of ill-mannered Frenchmen. For those poor dredges saddled with defending the Italian frontier zones, the war shape shifted common folks lives upside down and inside out. As always, the chaos of war represented opportunity for the opportunists. To Don Burducci, committed lifetime opportunist and expert pearl diver, the world was his oyster.

Prior to his posting at Balzi Rossi young Bellini, bound and obligated by debt for his postgraduate two years of service, had set about his student loan repayment plan to the Don. In exchange for room and board, personal training, plus a minor, ridiculously, insultingly tiny stipend, Bellini performed a never-ending series of temp jobs applying his unique skillset.

The onset of war had crushed the retail clothing segment of the Genovese economy. Val Fauci, owner of Fauci-Wearables, a custom lambskin coat shop, found himself unable to pay some of his supplier's bills. While most were compassionate, offering extended terms, or barter for payment, one was not.

After a few months of impatience, the Don sent Bellini on an early morning visit to the diminutive Señor Fauci. True to form, Marco retrieved both the overdue payments, some unused skins, and a few stylish new coats—size Marco. He accomplished all of this before his first cappuccino of the day. Sadly, Val Fauci did not make his weekly bocce game or anything else. Ever.

Comparable work continued over the succeeding two years, spiced up on occasion by the odd sous-chef assignment at one of Don Burducci's restaurants in the Genovese province. Nicknamed by the Don, Coltello da Cuoco—The Chef's Knife—Bellini generated quite the reputation for prowess with the blade inside, and more definitively, outside of the kitchen. Confronting his apportioned finger every day progressively salted his disposition. It remained an endless, visceral reminder of the slights and unappreciative attitude he had suffered at the hand of Boss Peaches. In Bellini's eyes, he remained inequitably, usuriously compensated. Never known as a generous soul, the Don did afford Marco the life-altering opportunity to forge his way far beyond the slaughterhouse. One might argue that Bellini's growing bitterness had questionable merit. How long until a debt of obligation or gratitude is truly paid? However, for a young man of unquenchable ambition patience devours dreams.

Bellini bided his time as best he could.

As the calendar closed in on the Christmas holiday season, the ongoing war ebbed to a convenient lull. Don Burducci decided to take advantage of a tentative cease-fire to tour his various opportunity zones and collect overdue tithes. He announced travel plans weeks ahead, giving his toadies time to gather their sacks of tribute.

Burducci owned a custom-built carriage designed for extended travels. Most ordinary on face, yet well-appointed as befit his wealth, the coach concealed a host of cleverly disguised hiding places for his collections. Any opportunistic brigands hoping to score a trove of cash would be sorely disappointed. As luck would have it, young Bellini's final task in service to the Don, six months earlier, included picking up the carriage and delivering the final payment to the artisan. Bellini completed the final carriage inspection himself. That meant no one beside himself and the Don knew the whereabouts of the trove of secret compartments. The master craftsman never made another one like it, nor was he seen at the local bocce tournament again. Ever.

By the time the Don showed up in Ventimiglia, his weighted carriage scraped a razor thin line above the road. The Don had been forced to improvise another halter for the additional horsepower needed to pull the carriage from point to point.

Fat, happy, and famished, the Don showed up for his scheduled dinner at the Lamb Shack ready to enjoy a sumptuous meal, on the house. He would dine, then collect his final tithe before heading home to Genoa. The Shack was crowded with locals. As it happened, there was also a table of French officers on holiday leave from their duties at the front. They had no quarrel with the border town locals of Ventimiglia.

"Uncle!" exclaimed his inebriated nephew. "At last! Welcome. Welcome back!"

Already three Chianti bottles deep into his evening, Matteo fawned on his blood relative and benefactor.

"Wine! Bring wine for the Don."

"Not just yet nephew. Where is El Coltello?"

Burducci pushed past Matteo into the kitchen, where Bellini leaned over a large stew pot.

"There he is! Come, greet your Don." Burducci opened his arms wide, awaiting the obligatory patron hug.

"Fuck yourself in the ass you festering corpuscle of greed. Die slowly," Bellini thought while staring into his stew pot.

"Good to see you, Don Burducci. Wine?" Bellini painted a smile on his face, and grudgingly walked over to give the Don an embrace.

"Why does everyone want me to drink wine? Alright, I'll have one, provided my nephew hasn't finished off the cellar yet!"

"Please make yourself comfortable. Get set to enjoy your meal."

"We will talk later," declared the Don.

It was not a question. The Don never asked.

"We will talk after dinner," Bellini agreed.

Burducci made his way back into the dining room. He was seated at a round table with a basket of bread and a glass of chianti. The French soldiers seated in the middle of the room were creating a disturbance hassling the waiter.

"What will WE 'ave? Do you not know what you 'ave to offer?" said the soldier. "Water? You offer us water? No wine? We are French. Wine is our water. You, there! Large man!"

He called over to the Don, who had taken a sip of his wine while sitting patiently awaiting his meal. The Don was feeling expansive that evening. His coffers were bursting, and his excursion virtually completed. He took no offense at the rudeness of the French soldier. He chalked it up to simple cultural dyspepsia.

"What can I do for you, Lieutenant?"

"But I am a captain. 'Ow could I a-fford zee outrageous pricing of such a place at an an-feary-or rahnk? No mat-tere. You seem a lo-cal, what deesh duz one ordar 'ere?"

"Naturally I recommend the lamb!"

"We shall 'ave it! Merci, sir."

The soldiers returned to their newly delivered glasses of wine. Matteo placed a healthy serving of braised lamb shank swimming in a rich red wine tomato broth in front of the Don. The seven-hour braise rested on a feather bed of pillowy polenta. The Don inhaled the hearty aroma, slurped his wine, and dug in. Ten minutes later, the Frenchmen received the identical meal.

The captain's comrade scooped a bite into his mouth, then immediately spit it back into the bowl. He pushed his chair back from the table.

"Terreebe! 'Orrible. Zees eez not lamb? I cannot possibly eat zees. Eat iz an insult to my country!"

Witnessing his comrade, the captain spooned his own bite before following suit.

"Zees eez not gigot a la culliere! I demand to see ze chef."

Matteo rushed over to the table, trying to calm the situation. The Don looked up from his empty bowl. He surveyed the behavior and shook his head with disdain.

"What?" bellowed the captain. "You have somesing to say to me? You who recommen-dead zis swill!"

"Monsieur, you do not speak to this man in such a manner."

Matteo attempted to tamp down the brewing conflict.

"I speak to whomever I like, 'owever I like."

Bellini heard the discord filling the dining room and peeked out from the door separating the two rooms. A slight smirk passed quickly across his face, and he retreated into the kitchen.

The Don rose from his table, sauce-stained napkin still tucked into his shirt, and approached the captain.

"If you don't like the food, if you don't like the wine, if you don't like the waiter, if you don't like anything else, kindly leave. I will pay your bill. Either way, I've *'erd'* enough from the two of you, so choose quickly."

"Salud! No one speaks to me zis way!"

The captain and his colleague gathered their things and headed for the door.

"We will meet again, Monsieur. I assure you."

"Look forward to it," answered the Don.

As the Frenchmen exited Bellini emerged from the kitchen and approached the Don's table.

"The French, they are all bastards."

"To each his own," responded the Don with uncharacteristic calm.

"You let them off so easy?"

"I'm heading back tomorrow. I don't need any headaches. Grab my useless nephew's tithe and bring it around back to the carriage."

Bellini nodded, and passed Matteo on his way back through the kitchen.

"Was he angry? I thought he was going to kill those two on the spot. Did he like the dinner?"

"Shut up and hand me his damn money."

Matteo sloshed his way to the back office. Breathing a sigh of relief, he grabbed a fat canvas bag stashed under his desk. Finally done for the night, he handed the bag over to Marco, then sat down and put his forehead on his desktop. Marco tossed his apron on the floor and slung another bag over his shoulder, holding the tithe in his left hand. Leaving out the back door, he met the Don by the carriage.

"I'll take it from here," he said, grabbing the bag.

"But where is monsieur headed so soon? No time for a digestif?"

The French captain and his mate appeared, swords drawn. The Don stood unflinching. He knew his secret weapon stood undaunted beside him. El Coltello would easily cut these brigands to shreds. All the Don needed was to keep them occupied for a moment, stand back, and let Bellini pounce.

"Gentlemen, this is a very bad idea for you," he warned.

"Two Frenchmen against one fat old man 'olding a large bag of money? Au contrare, I sink iz a pretty good idea."

The Don, bracing his left hand against the carriage turned to his secret weapon.

"Do you think it's a good idea, Marco?" he asked facetiously.

Burducci suddenly felt the quick burning sensation of whetstone sharpened steel slicing through his wrist. Watching his own hand fall to the ground, his eyes grew wide in the realization of the betrayal. Bellini waggled his shorn little finger in the Don's shocked face.

"It's always easier when they don't expect it...Peaches!"

Bellini coldly passed his chef's knife through the Don's chest, cleanly severing his aorta. Don Burducci fell to the ground, eyes open wide, bleeding his life onto an empty street. Bellini handed the pouch the Don had been clutching over to the captain.

"This concludes our business together. I'll take that border pass now."

Chapter 21

STREET WISE

The crew of the L'Aquila let loose a collective sigh of relief. Taking the port fork on the ocean road, they made a beeline for the capricious port of Tangier. Not a soul, save Lanning, turned to track the direction of the departing mercenaries.

As Lanning watched the Queen disappear against the horizon, he felt the guilt soaking into his conscience.

"YES, still alive," roared Lorenzo, clutching his forehead in relief.

"Phew! Brother, how in hell did we escape that shit storm?" reveled Felipe.

"A battle not fought is a battle not won. I live to fight another day!" True to his swagger, Loyola was honorable and blow-hardy in equal measure.

Whether a Catholic, a Jew, a Buddhist, or some random Barbarian of imprecise origin the trouble with guilt lies in its weight.

Filippa bore the weight of Contigo's sacrifice too. She looked shaken. "What will happen to him? He likely saved my honor!"

"Likely your life!" declared Lorenzo.

"Twice in a week, I thought I was dead. Twice in ONE week! What are the odds? Thank you, Jesus!"

"Rory, what are you on about?" asked Lanning.

"It's ours!" Rory had his hand elbow-deep in the vat of hummus.

As the L'Aquila approached the Tangier quay, Felipe stood at the tiller. On signal, Rory went to the foremast and dropped the jib. The ship slid into the harbor on its inertia no longer needing sails to dock. Shafi had dropped down to the main deck as well.

"Shafi?" asked Lanning as he moved off the bridge.

Shafi reached into the vat of hummus for a taste. He nodded his head. "Unmistakable."

"The Antonietta! It was them," exclaimed Rory.

Lanning sidled up to the vat and dipped in as well. Although he knew instantly by the smooth consistency, the true tell was the color. The pale rouge tint came from a subtle artisanal introduction of smoked paprika and cayenne mixed into the creamy blend.

"Bastards! We had them! We had them," he howled.

Loyola, gathering his things, smirked, "Perhaps true. But only in the sense that they had us tightly gripped by our own collective balls."

The truth stung Lanning's pride. Loyola could see that the humor had wounded his new friend. He tried to soften the blow while bringing him back to the moment at hand.

"My Captain, you did amazing getting all, save one, to safety. Having faced the threat of death together, we are now bonded as men, and will remain so until the end of time."

"Despite your death wish," offered Lorenzo as he coiled a mainsail halyard.

"That's poetic, but I see what you are intending. I have left a man at risk. A man I have stood with in battle as well," said Lanning.

"I would be more than happy to chase down retribution at your side. However, my path leads in a different direction."

Shafi stood in front of both men. "Revenge is a never-ending journey."

Loyola countered. "You don't like happy endings, parable-afflicted old timer? Nothing wrong with a bit of sweet revenge."

"You are young. Life's meanings will eventually catch up to you."

Shafi moved on with his tasks, leaving the two men to their final goodbyes.

"More woo-woo language," mocked Loyola. "How do you

decipher all that every day? Exhausting."

"I was raised with that in my ear. For me, it's just Tuesday."

The L'Aquila gently glided up to the quay. Hector, still suffering from seasickness, leaped off the bow a good ten feet from the dock. Grateful to be on dry land, he celebrated with a few final dry heaves before standing upright. Rory threw him the bow rope and told him to hold onto it. Lorenzo and Rory followed Hector onto the dock and secured the boat. The three men embraced in collective relief as Hector dry-heaved once more to seal the deal.

"Honestly, have never seen a human being hurl so many times," said Felipe shaking his head.

Feeling as if the crossing from Algeciras drained ten years off his life, Shafi informed Lanning it had taken six hours. Weirdly, for all that had transpired, only two hours more than usual had passed. The summer sun would not set in Tangier until half past eight, leaving another seven hours of daylight for Lanning to take care of pressing issues. First, he would say his farewells to Loyola and Nantucket, then get Filippa situated before heading into the medina.

Felipe, Rory, Lorenzo and Shafi got the boat in order. Hector lay down on the wooden dock and fell into a nausea-free sleep. Loyola placed what few things he had into a leather satchel. Nantucket gently tucked Doug into his cage.

"Gents, should you require passage back by tomorrow, we will be leaving with the tide. You're always welcome. If not, I wish you a safe onward journey," Lanning said.

"We do not travel together. I have other plans and, as you know, I am due in Pamplona within two months," said Loyola.

"That's a surprise. I assumed you two were..."

"Your path is now my path," pronounced Nantucket.

Lanning shook his head. "Is it though? Because I see a real

problem there."

"I have chosen."

"Yes, but it's not entirely up to you now, is it? We need an agreement between the two of us. This is not a unilateral decision."

"Your language is strange to me."

"You meant *conveniently strange*, right? Seems as if you see things as you wish them, not as they are. I'm going back to Algeciras tomorrow, after we face off with the mercenaries again, grab Contigo, and ...the rest of whatever occurs gets sorted out."

"Our stories are now connected."

Nantucket headed for the bridge.

"Nothing like the mystery of a new friend. You're welcome!" said Loyola, chuckling.

Looking more the lady, Filippa appeared on deck after changing out of Lanning's clothing.

"Milady," Loyola extended a courtly bow, "I take my leave. I wish good fortune for you, and a straight line of luck for all your days ahead. Should you find yourself in Madrid, I will look forward to encountering you at court."

"May the Lord grant you safe passage and good fortune, wherever you may roam."

"Kind of you. While we do not speak very much, I do believe He has a special eye trained upon me!" Loyola pointed a thumb in the air.

"Be prepared for a winding road, my friend. Life can change in an instant," counseled Shafi.

"Thank you, old sailor, mystic man! Farewell!"

Donning his plumed hat, Loyola zipped off into the teeming streets of Tangier. Only a few months later, Loyola would find himself stumbling down an unmarked road towards the destiny he never saw coming.

Chapter 22

SCREW BRIDGES

"Shopping?"

"You don't mind if Doug stays, right?" said Filippa, ignoring Lanning's snark.

"I guess having the energy to shop seems a tad trivial, compared to a life or death near-miss."

"Maybe *YOU* need a nap, but life goes on. Can I get someone to go with me?"

Lanning looked over at his compatriots, none of whom appeared eager to assist.

"Zo, can you at least keep an eye on Doug?" requested Lanning.

"Not really. I was planning on heading down the street to the Howling Cricket. Gotta rehearse my graduation performance."

"Rory?"

"Gonna catch some winks, then show Hector how to vomit proper."

"Doug will be with me."

Nantucket bowed graciously towards Filippa.

"A man among lads!" said Filippa.

"I will accompany you, as long as you accompany me on my tasks as well."

"Agreed. Shall we?"

The two ventured out into the crowded medina while maintaining a respectful distance apart. The paths they walked meandered as whimsically as an afternoon breeze. Despite appearing as a couple, neither wanted to give anyone the wrong impression. Tangiers winding narrow streets were inhabited by a river of cross-cultural diversity, it's headwaters having multiple origins from deep within the African continent to Bohemia and Europe. Europeans made the easiest marks. They stood out like a black dress at a white wedding. Not only because of their pale skin color, but their clothing, and their snow-globe bubble of personal entitlement. Filippa's stride carried the full measure of the latter. Neither was aware of the two pairs of eyes observing them from a distance.

Tangier chronicled its considerable history back over twelve thousand years. The Carthaginian Empire dropped anchor on the Phoenicians back in the 5th century B.C. followed by the Greeks. The long enduring Berbers had named the city "Tingis" for the daughter of the Hercules' grandpa titan Atlas. The lady Tingis married the son of renowned swimmer and ocean enthusiast Poseidon. A strong lineage from which to grow its value as a seaport of strategic value. With apparently no greater thought than the extra donut tossed into a "baker's dozen," ownership of the city passed seamlessly from one draconian host to the next miserable despotic regime. The day-old donut served the Phoenicians, Romans, Vandals, and even the legendary Visigoths, before finally joining, temporarily, Morocco in the 11th century A.D.

Despite its rocky past as an unwanted stepson, Tangier retained a rabid independent dignity, lightly concealed beneath a Vichy-esque candy-coated exterior. However, on some occasions that coating showed up thinner than advertised.

During Lanning's timeslot, Tangier jockeyed between the benign possession and tenuous moodiness of two possessive Kings—either Manuel of Portugal or the youngster Charles I of Spain. During this extended fall weekend, Spain held the high card.

The flag that wafted over the city held zero sway to the locals. They remained inured to the whims of nationality, but not so for the tourists. While the Spanish-flagged L'Aquila was more than welcome in port on this blustery day, the Queen of Sheba was not as fortunate. It meant that Lorenzo could easily secure a stand-up slot at the Howling Cricket, while another notorious barfly had a much harder time receiving decent service at the same bar.

It was at this moment when Lanning and Filippa passed by the swinging beach wood doors of the Howling Cricket.

"And stay the hell out!" roared an unseen baritone.

A small torpedo-shaped man dressed in Spanish finery abruptly catapulted through the Howling Cricket's doorway. The man landed in a crumbled heap at Filippa's feet. Lanning quickly kneeled down and attempted to help the scuffed-up stranger to his feet.

"Hands off the merchandise, Pilgrim. I don't need any damn help."

"More the wiser am I," cracked Lanning.

Lanning and Filippa prepared to carry on when the man's feathered hat, first cousin to the recently departed Loyola's, lofted like an errant frisbee onto the ground. Filippa reached down to make the grab.

"Yours?" she said, dusting it off.

"Bastardos!" he shouted into the bar with a raised fist.

Brushing off toe to head, he moved grumpily over to Filippa and managed the slightest, tilt of chivalry.

He curtly squeezed out his name with a gravel-filled voice, "Ferdinand Magellan," before being overwhelmed by six rabid sneezes coupled with a wheezy cough. Catching his breath, he said begrudgingly, "Thank you for my damn hat."

As Magellan extended his hand to accept the hat. The stoutly built man gave another series of sneezes, followed by a wheeze-riddled inhale. Lanning wondered. He puzzled if the gentleman had some sort of dangerous communicable affliction. Perhaps he and Filippa would be better off creating a wider buffer zone. He did not physically appear sickly; in fact, his physique was exactly the opposite. Still, he had not heard such a caliginous sound of potential doom since the Algeciras plague of twenty years past.

"Are you ill, sir? Because you sound like shit!"

"Piss off, tourist! I've got unfinished business inside."

Magellan turned to pick up his sword from the ground. A triple X-sized Berber with a shaved head and devil-pointed beard burst through the double doors, heading straight for Magellan, swinging a scimitar. Unarmed, and with his back turned, Lanning knew Magellan would be cut down in a split second. Filippa glared at Lanning with a silent "do something" message as he drew his sword from its sheath.

A loud, high-pitched screech of metal on metal signaled Lanning's blade meeting the scimitar at its apex. Using all his strength, he kept his sword pinned to the curvature of the attacker's knife-edge. Sliding down the curve, it screamed like nails on a chalkboard. Realizing his European foil was ridiculously overmatched, Lanning only figured on delaying the onslaught for a moment. With the deftness of a baseball player eluding the tag sliding into second base, Lanning kept his sword arm raised while hook-sliding into the oncoming Moroccan. His legs crossed the ankles of the large man, upending the unsuspecting assailant in a split second of airborne surprise.

Taking advantage of Lanning's intercession, Magellan grabbed his larger saber and planted it on the neck of the bewildered beast at his feet. The point only nicked enough of the man's skin to communicate a clear message.

"Over a damn beer? All I wanted was decent service!"

"No Portuguese allowed," grumbled the compromised man.

"Idiot! I fly the Spanish flag now."

"You are Portuguese."

A loud jingling from down the street caught everyone's attention. Sauntering down the street, sporting his three-armed motley hat and jingle bell pointed shoes, came Lorenzo.

"Well, well, what happened here?"

"Who is this fool?" asked Magellan.

Lanning took umbrage at Magellan's caustic tone.

"He is no fool."

"At least not officially!" interjected Lorenzo.

"Lorenzo, meet Ferdinand Magellan."

"Are you here for the two o'clock show?" asked the Berber, strangely disconnected from the point at his throat.

"I am hoping to get a spot."

"Imbecile! Don't go in there. This man just tried to kill me," said Magellan, straightening out his clothing with his other hand.

"No offense sir, but I hardly know you. Perhaps you deserved it. Random violence in Tangier is a rarity in my experience," Lorenzo said.

"Are you Portuguese?" asked the Berber.

"Of course not."

"See Jeff. He works behind the bar. Tell him I cleared you," said the Berber.

"Sure you want to go in there, Lorenzo?" asked Lanning.

"Gotta get the work in, pal. Jeff, you say?"

"What a gigantic collection of morons I've stumbled across," said Magellan as he withdrew his point from the Berber's neck.

Still red faced with anger, the man cautiously rose and viewed the two-armed men semi-circled around him.

"Feel lucky, and get the fuck out of my sight," said Magellan.

His hubris told him he could re-engage them as a whirling dervish of death. Self-preservation advised him to reconsider his options. After all, was it worth it over a beer? No one liked their beer anyway. The Berber wisely chose withdrawal. Once the giant disappeared into the doorway, the two men sheathed their weapons.

"Though you have questionable taste in friends, I owe you a greater debt than I can repay," said the humbled Magellan.

"You certainly do," chimed in Filippa. "You were a dead man until --"

"Don't like to see an unfair fight, is all," interrupted Lanning.

They walked down the street together into the teeming medina, Magellan once again hit the sneeze button.

"Sure you're not sick?"

Magellan shook his head.

"It's a LOT of sneezing. You really do *sound* sick," said Filippa.

"I'm a man of the sea. Land does not agree with my constitution. Neither does that short-sighted Portuguese killjoy Manuel. No vision, no vision at all," grumped Magellan completing yet another round of sneezes.

"You blaspheme the King of Portugal?" questioned Lanning.

"I'm not talking out of my ass, son. All the real money is in the Moluccas. People are so enamored with gold. Oh, the Aztecs have gold, the Inca's have gold. We must have gold, as if..."

"Gold is pretty much the standard measure of wealth," argued Lanning.

"Commodities! Commodities are the future. Gold is a fleeting metal used for other things. What are those other things? What do people truly need?"

"Gold," answered Filippa cynically.

"I'm surrounded by feeble, small-minded pissants!"

"Hey now, I just saved your life!" said Lanning.

"Doesn't mean you're a visionary. No one realizes it's all about spice. The future my friends is spice!"

"Like oregano?" Filippa said incredulously.

"People thought the Iron Age was big. *'Check me out, I can make a spearhead!'* Losers! Spices are going to blow the metal spearhead back to the Middle Ages. Unlike that shit-heel Manuel, your carpet-bagger Austrian King, and his Belgian bankers, at least have a handle on the future."

"You got money from the Emperor."

"I simply promised him the land grab he was after anyway. It's all about screwing the Portuguese for him, uh, them."

"But **you** are Portuguese!" Filippa said.

"I'm a man of the world. He gets what he wants. And, as for me, I'm bound for the Moluccas. Frankincense, myrrh, white pepper, nutmeg, cassia, cloves..."

Filippa looked mystified. "This all about cooking? What do you even put myrrh on? Fish? I don't get it."

"I can see that. Think medicines, essential oils. Never mind. You are too limited. I leave for Cadiz in the morning, then the open ocean, followed shortly thereafter by untold wealth, power, and immortality."

"Moluccas are a long way from here," said Lanning.

"Not so long as people think."

"There's a way around the edge?" wondered Filippa.

Magellan turned to Lanning with an exasperated expression.

"Oh, for shit sakes! One of those?"

"Apparently," answered Lanning.

"What is so terrifying about the future? If it's not the damn clerics, it's the insecure monarchy."

"How can you be so brazenly political?"

"Everything is political. Don't you realize that? Besides we're in Tangier. I have my ships and my crew, the money is spent. What could go wrong at this late date!"

Filippa hated the constraints, pomposity, hypocrisy, and self-ag-grandizing indulgence of the royals she had been surrounded by her whole life. She found herself silently in agreement with both arrogant men in front of her.

"Doubt remains the law of the land until proven otherwise," she argued with only half-hearted conviction.

Magellan emphasized his point by gracefully waving his arms one direction before flowing back to center.

"Ever heard of Christopher Columbus? There and back...again. Yes, an insufferable boob, but neither he, nor his ships, fell off your *edge* of the world. Hermy Cortes ring a bell for you? Another one of the explorer-class insufferables, and another obsessive gold-digger. However, that glory hound somehow managed to NOT fall off your edge of the world!" snapped Magellan.

"Perhaps they did not venture far enough! 'And after these things, I saw four angels standing on **four corners** of the earth, holding the four winds of the earth, that the wind should not blow on the earth, nor on the sea, nor on any tree.'"

Filippa quoted the bible as she crossed her arms in indignation.

"Middle Age drivel. The good book is a fun read, but it's another tool of the aristocracy holding you down. It's the Renaissance, for god's sake! Read a science book."

Lanning thought he sensed a stubbornness to Filippa's argu-ment which undermined her façade of deep conviction. He found his attention wandering from engaging her point of view to the shallower pursuit of baser impulses. He couldn't help his physical attraction to her.

"Even if you were correct, which you are quite obviously NOT, it matters not! As long as I hit the Moluccas, become the Spice King, and gain fortune before I hit the great abyss you speak of...Who. The. Fuck. Cares!"

Magellan concluded Filippa to be a gigantic waste of his dwindling time. "You can't talk to crazy," he thought.

Swiveling to Lanning, he said, "Kid, consider joining me. Take the plunge. It's a generous offer, plus payback for saving my life. You, me, five ships, couple hundred other guys in close quarters..."

"I've got my own ship, and Filippa has made a fair point: you never do know what is truly out there."

"I do. The road to riches, and I'm offering you a lift." The overconfident explorer sounded like a 16th century PT Barnum.

Lanning had felt the nagging tug of the unknown since he was a child. His life had been constructed on top of the shaky foundation of the unknown, or at best the murkiness of the mostly unknown. The weightless feeling of ditching a life with too many questions, responsibilities, obligations, and detritus held a compelling attraction.

Why shouldn't he ditch a destiny randomly created for him? He had never truly belonged. A simple accident of fate had knocked him off whatever path of destiny he had been traveling on. How could he be certain this was not the exact moment of chaos that Gonzalo had hoped to prepare him for? His escape hatch appeared before him as a short-tempered, allergenic, opportunistic prospector masquerading as a heroic explorer on a mission to change the world.

Lanning felt suddenly off balance. "When do you sail?" he asked.

"Evening tide. But..."

Magellan hesitated as he looked at clouds taking form on the western horizon.

"But what?" asked Filippa following his gaze westward.

"Mares tails and mackerel scales!"

"You think?" questioned Lanning.

"Maybe. Keep a sharp eye," Magellan added.

Old sailor adages abound in conversations between fellow travelers. The classic "red sky at night, sailors delight" refers to the presence of a high air pressure system. Most weather systems in the northern hemisphere approach from the western sky. As the sun sets, its light shines through much more of the lower atmosphere, which contains dust, salt, smoke, and other particles. These particles scatter some of the shorter wavelengths of light, leaving only the longer wavelengths—the oranges and reds. High pressure means good weather; low pressure means not so good weather. A mackerel sky alludes to cirrocumulus clouds which precede a warm front. Warm front means winds, clouds, and lots and lots of rain. A very non-delightful sight for sailors. Mare's tails tell the wise sailors to adjust their sails.

As Lanning pondered his answer, Shafi passed them on the narrow walkway of the central medina.

"Heading over to catch Lorenzo at the Howling Jackal," announced Shafi. "You coming?"

"Cricket," corrected Lanning. "Have you seen the weather, Uncle?"

Shafi looked skyward. "Planning on sleeping late tomorrow, Captain?"

Thinking this was a good time to confer with Shafi about things other than weather, Lanning looked over at Filippa and Magellan.

"I'll catch up to you."

Filippa and Magellan continued their sojourn down the main artery of the medina. Shafi and Lanning stepped off to the side, where they were immersed in the mélange of exotic aromas wafting out of the open-door spice shop next to them. Cinnamon, turmeric, ginger, cumin, coriander, white pepper, and paprika filled their noses and tantalized their empty stomachs.

"That smell is making me hungry for tagine," said Shafi. "You do know who that is, right?"

"You know Magellan?"

"Not personally, but he's a very well-known guy. Heard he made a deal with the Emperor."

"He's invited me along. Which is tempting."

"Of course it is. Generally, I've found if one does not know to which port he is sailing, no wind is favorable."

"What's wrong with not knowing? Why do I need to know? Magellan has this pretty well mapped out."

"Hmmm. Do you know about the blind men and the elephant?"

"Since I'm about to find out, can you make it quick?"

"A group of blind monks heard that a strange animal, called an elephant, had been brought to their village. None of them were aware of the exotic animal's shape or form. Out of curiosity, the group's leader said: 'We must inspect and learn the true nature of this mysterious creature. We will use our heightened sense of touch to discover its truth.' So, they sought it out. When they found it, each man groped about encountering a different aspect as they moved around it. The first monk, whose hand landed on the trunk, said, 'This being is like a thick snake.' To another man whose hand reached up to its ear, it seemed like a kind of fantastical fan. The third blind man, whose hands were upon its front leg, said, 'this beast is an unending pillar like a tree-trunk stretching to the heavens.' Yet another man in the group who placed his hand upon the elephants' side said this elephant beast, 'is a great unscalable wall.' Another who felt along its tail, described it as an unbraided rope of infinite tensile strength. Finally, the last blind man ran his hands along the beast's ivory tusks. To his reckoning, the elephant was hard, smooth, and as deadly as a spear.

"So you see," summarized Shafi.

"The inexpressible nature of truth. One man's knowing is another's mystery. Truth is subjective, there is no totality of truth."

Shafi let out a hearty laugh, before nodding in acknowledgment of Lanning's maturity.

"Your father would be proud. You can see, I have no right answers for you son. And yes, I've seen the line of clouds to the west."

Lanning slumped against the wall. For a happy millisecond, he pondered ditching his life by signing on to Magellan's quest to become the global spice czar. However, he knew the difference between true choice and a convenient back door slide into the lure of the unknown. Letting his own fears, expectations and insecurities govern life's options had "cowardly, cheese-brained sucker" written all over it. While Lanning laid claim to many irritating traits—arrogance, convicted wise ass, bull-headed know-it-all—he was neither an opportunist nor a quitter. His inner conflict arose over more legitimate, weighty concerns. The safety of his crew facing what would most certainly be a stormy crossing had to be balanced against his word to Contigo. He would not desert a man who had saved his life only a few days ago.

"We can't stay in port and leave Contigo to...whatever. I gave my word!"

"Your word to a pirate? Hardly morally binding. They know there's a storm brewing. They're probably already heading for a safe harbor. Your friend will turn up somewhere, at some point."

"Maybe, but..."

Lanning questioned his own statement. The "but" gnawed at him. He parted ways with Shafi, and raced to catch up with Filippa and Magellan down Hummus Alley.

Chapter 23

I CAN DO IT BY MYSELF

Despite the haphazard meandering nature of the medina streets, Lanning knew the way to Hummus Alley by heart. He let his feet navigate while re-gripping his personal compass. Trying to synthesize Shafi's sound advice proved a troubling task. He turned right off the Rue de la Marine to round the Hummus Alley corner marked by Yassini's—Tangier's most renowned weaver. A collection of multicolored robes, pillowcases, and blankets hung from the awning of the bustling little shop.

He detected a bit of commotion in the shop, but chalked it up to haggling. He shuffled on passing the next doorway without looking up. It was cluttered hanging and clanging pewter pots, carved wooden canes in large metal buckets, and a host of other flotsam and jetsam from years past. This shop marked the end of retail, and the beginning of Tangiers top hummus vendors. Each one proffered their own unique blend of chickpea delights.

Ordinarily this long narrow alleyway was a quiet respite from the cacophonous vendors swarming the main thoroughfare of the medina. Not so this day. A sudden eruption from behind startled Lanning. "Haggling must've taken a darker turn," he presumed as the voices ramped up in intensity and spilled out into the tight quartered alleyway.

"Alone in the medina with your good looks?"

The voice was a hoarse, grisly, baritone devoid charm.

"Oh, she means to meet someone special!"

The second suitor made the first suitor sound like a crooning Frank Sinatra. He melded a chirping squirrel with chalk on a blackboard.

"We just want to have a coffee. Hahahahaha."

The third guy at least had sounded plausible. Lanning figured they were hassling some unfortunate woman who had wandered a little far from her escort. Although he felt completely content with his interventions for the day, his conscience decided to make sure nothing too untoward went down.

"Not about to happen for you dickwads!" the woman shouted emphatically, followed by another large commotion. A man involuntarily rolled out of the doorway of Yassini's, his head wrapped like a burrito in a stunning cobalt-blue Toureg djellaba.

"That's your color loser."

Filippa raced out of the shop, rounding the corner directly into the collection hanging pewter pots. Lanning knew he was unalterably engaged in yet another non-volunteer event. She was being chased by two men who were drawing knives from their waistbands. Lanning pulled his sword.

With practiced ease, Filippa grabbed a beautifully hand-carved thuya cane from one of the buckets by the door. Thuya is a biblical conifer from the cedar family, a fairly hard wood growing only in the forests of the Atlas Mountains. The same ones that Hercules relocated those many eons ago.

Before springing into action, Lanning paused a moment to admire Filippa's exceptional prowess in parrying the first attacker's blade with a hard right swing of her elephant head cane. The cane's return trip to center caught the attacker directly under the jawline. The crack, echoing down the small alleyway, brought several neighboring hummus vendors to their doorways. Unfortunately, the cane's age showed immediately, cracking in half after the blow to the jaw.

Filippa picked up the man's blade lying at his side. Two to go: the recovered blue djellaba victim and his pal. Lanning waited no longer. Sword in hand, he sprang into action.

His first swipe sliced a neat line through the second attacker's midline. It took the man a split moment to realize his injury as a thin line of blood oozed from his belly. The ooze preceded a gush of gore. One assailant already down on the ground, not yet cognizant of his upcoming dental work, the third man squared off against Lanning, waving his ten-inch junior scimitar.

"I'd reconsider, friend," offered Lanning graciously. "I can be kind, but I believe that moment has passed you by."

"You don't know me, pilgrim," answered the attacker.

"That's okay with me. I don't have time to meet new people today..."

The man lunged for Lanning, who had anticipated the charge. He matador-stepped sideways as the now-unbalanced Moroccan clumsily slid by him. A swift kick in the ass provided by Lanning propelled the stumbling attacker further down the alleyway towards the hummus vendors.

"Sir, your invitation to be my friend has been summarily refused. Either collect your colleagues and move along, or..."

"Too much talking!"

Once again, the attacker mounted a ferocious charge. Reaching up to the collection of hanging pots, Filippa snagged a lovely medieval Portuguese crock with matching lid. Her elegantly timed combo bash caught the man on the back of his head, ringing his proverbial inner bell. Staggered for a moment, his anger hit the redline. He turned back to Filippa, prepared to fillet her with his blade.

Catching the opening created by the man's shift in focus, Lanning moved forward. With the precision of an orthopedic surgeon, he sliced the knife from the man's hand with one downward stroke of his foil. More accurately, the man's hand, was liberated from his arm. Still gripping the scimitar, it landed with a dull thud on the ground. The attacker only briefly paused to notice his loss before making a renewed frenzied charge towards Lanning. Having little choice, Lanning extended his blade, separating the man from his life directly through the heart.

"Time to go," Lanning said, wiping the blood off his blade on the man's pants.

"Understatement."

Grabbing Filippa by the arm, Lanning turned back up the alleyway toward Yassini's. Filippa's gaze shifted enough to catch the dazed squirrel attacker hurtling toward them from behind. In one reflexive action, she whisked the knife still in her right hand. It struck the squirrel square in the plate. The man, now wearing a blood-soaked broach, dropped to his death.

"You have skills!"

Filippa shrugged her shoulders in mock embarrassment.

They walked at pace towards the L'Aquila.

"What happened to Magellan?" asked Lanning.

"He took off. Something about the weather and delays, onward and upward, blah blah blah."

"The pressures of exploration. However, I agree with the sentiment."

"Not that I'm unappreciative, but I had it handled."

"Absolutely. You easily had those three hulking serial rapists in the palm of your hand."

"I've told you I can handle myself."

"Never have I seen such deft use of both cane and cookware! I need to stop at the Howling Cricket. I recommend you go ahead to the ship."

"You might need my protection. Besides, why not just stay the night in port and leave at first light?" asked Filippa.

Lanning gave her an incredulous glare.

"One dead, two on the critical list. We'll find a safe inlet and set anchor."

They fast walked down Rue de Liberté turning, onto Rue de la Kasbah to reach the Howling Cricket's doorway. Hearing laughter, Lanning figured Lorenzo's act had hit its stride. They entered cautiously, wary of the Berber security guard who might be holding a grudge.

Chapter 24

NEED I SAY MORE

Lanning prodded Filippa forward toward the Howling Cricket doorway.

"You stick *your* head in there. Given the day so far, I see no point in unnecessarily tempting fate."

Filippa gingerly peeked in.

"You don't die when you're old, you just feel shitty the whole time. This aches, that hurts, why am I coughing, I can't piss in a straight line anymore, I don't want sex! Oh my god, is that part of it?"

She turned back towards Lanning with a smile on her face.

"Lorenzo's on-stage wearing harlequin, talking about getting old."

"He's done. Wave him over."

Felipe, Rory, and Shafi walked out of the pub, shielding their eyes from the sun.

"Where's Lorenzo?" asked Lanning.

"Coming," said Felipe. "I didn't see him crack a smile the entire time. Did he?"

"It's complicated humor...subtle," said Rory.

Nantucket and Lorenzo emerged, engaged in an animated conversation.

"You have to understand idiomatic expressions. It's a contextual conceit related to the current set of cultural norms."

"I said 'subtle'..."

Lorenzo nodded. He was doing his best to break down the nature of his humor. Nantucket wasn't budging.

"I understood the references."

"I don't think so. If you truly understood the insights, you'd be laughing."

"Nantucket laughs when things are funny."

This evoked an instantaneous roar of laughter from the other three crewmen before Lanning interrupted.

"Who's with Doug?"

Nantucket said, "Hector is standing guard."

"We need to get to the boat and weigh anchor NOW!"

They canned the conversation and hop-stepped it back to the L'Aquila. As the crew roused Hector from a deep slumber on the dock, everyone noticed the changing weather. In minutes, Hector threw off the bowline. The boat drifted away from the dock in sight, yet out of reach, of a large contingent of locals marching down the quay with summary judgment on their minds. Their fury being stronger than their constitution, they watched their intended prey recede into the bay. The disappointed crowd grumpily disbursed back into the medina.

Satisfied they had avoided another confrontation on a day riddled with them, Lanning set about figuring out an anchorage to wait out the coming weather. He entered his cabin to sort out their options in quiet. Filippa appeared at the door.

"You can come on in. It's fine."

Filippa sat on her knees atop Lanning's bunk. She was about to change her clothes to clean up from the day's episode.

"Forgive me. You go ahead." Lanning chivalrously averted his eyes.

"Don't be such a prude."

"No, Milady."

"Really? Back to 'milady? I can't figure out if that's a lame move or simply lame."

"Lame? Offense taken. I made my 'move' in the alley back there."

"Ah, yes, that move. Then knock off with that dismissive phrase, 'milady.' It's counter-productive."

"Not intended. It's manners and respect."

"From an ownership perspective."

"I'm showing my proper gentleman behavior. Not effective?"

"I've seen all the moves, so maybe, in this moment, try for something more authentic."

"Pretty much think you've got a healthy sample of my authentic by now."

"Besides, we are not in court, and I'm not a courtesan, at any rate. That's my mother."

"Yeah, wouldn't want to bring your mother in here."

Filippa struggled trying to reach behind her head to unclasp her blouse. "Would you help me with this? The clasp in the back."

In the close quarters of his cabin, Lanning had remained six feet apart from Filippa. Now he moved closer to help.

"I will leave you to it."

"Why? I'm positive you've seen a woman change clothes. Unclasping does not constitute a betrothal. I am not suddenly YOURS, neither are you my exclusive. Unless..." she pondered for brief moment, "Have we reached the zenith of your moves?"

The surprise on Lanning's face made Filippa smile wryly. Not difficult to sort out her intentions, Lanning felt both relieved and transparently enamored.

"So....we are having a moment. You, me, this moment."

"It's enough about the moment," she said.

Filippa approached Lanning and slowly draped her arms around his neck. She leaned in with a tantalizing brush against his lips, before pulling back with a smile. Lanning reciprocated by running his hand down her curving body. The abrupt knock on the door startled him, more than Filippa.

"Captain, a word."

Felipe's voice was unmistakable. Lanning released his embrace moving to the door.

"Uh…"

He shrugged his shoulders at Filippa, holding up one index finger. Exiting his quarters, he faced his brother.

"A word?" he mocked, "When have you ever said that before?"

"When have you ever had a woman in your quarters before? Didn't think you'd want me to barging in."

"Fair point. What's up?"

Felipe pointed up and over the bow. An ominous gathering of cumulus clouds loomed on the western horizon.

* * *

Sharing the same moment in a different spot, Destemido stood on the bridge of the Queen. Watching the western sky and the shifting profile of the strait he observed Contigo lean against the stern transom, taking in the same sight in silence.

"Amazing, right Captain?"

Longshort's unctuous second mate, a legume of a man, with matching angular face and nervous, gummy smile, had declared his presence on the bridge.

"What is it you're talking about?" Destemido asked.

"The Queen. She performed better than we expected!"

VanMeter, a head-to-toe tattooed Dutchman, had blown up the captain's contemplative moment. Destemido glared back in silence.

"Bad time?" VanMeter asked baring his gums.

The man carried his entire allotted quantity of hair in his eyebrows. Extending a full two inches into the airspace, they edged his eye sockets before heading south to frame his entire face down to the pronounced Dutch cheekbones.

"You tell me," said Destemido, directing their gaze to the horizon.

As second mate, VanMeter stood next in line. That responsibility terrified him. Mostly because he knew that "sailing master" was a considerable distance away from his expertise wheelhouse.

"In case you missed it, Longshot bled out on the deck."

VanMeter gulped. His brain was petrified by the realization of his limitations. His sailing expertise came from designing flat bottom, flat water, canal boats in Delft, a backwater village outside of Amsterdam. Essentially floating buses, his boats had no keel, and were about as seaworthy as a bathtub duckie. Longshort had recruited him as a raw visionary project; someone with potential who needed mentorship. Longshort had hoped to mold him into his eventual replacement. Someday down a long road, maybe, but absolutely, positively not this day.

"Uh...well, sir. I agree with you."

"I haven't said anything to agree or disagree with."

Keenly aware of Destemido's nasty temperament, the man tried one more waffling answer.

"I guess I advise cut and run. She's fast enough to get to a safe harbor, unless you believe it's a squall, in which case we cut through it. The crew trusts your judgment."

"He doesn't know shit about shit," Contigo chimed in.

"Is that true, sailor? Do you not know shit about shit?"

"I know she's a fast ship, Captain. You said there's a storm coming, so there must be a storm coming."

"Whatever did Longshort see in you?"

Resisting the urge to dispose of another crewman in frustration, Destemido ordered the man to set a course for their safe harbor on the Algeciras side of the strait.

"What about your agreement with the L'Aquila?" Contigo reminded.

"I imagine they'll make the same calculation we have and run for cover. Besides, you're in no danger from me."

"But *they* don't know that!"

Destemido smirked at the thought of his counterpart's anxiety over Contigo's indeterminate fate.

As the Queen came about to make its way towards the Spanish mainland, a strong swirling wind emanating from the east picked up speed.

Cumulus clouds swept up their stratus cousins, folding them into a line of rising danger. The whitecaps multiplied in a heartbeat. They stretched out in all directions to surround the bouncing Queen.

"Now a good time to take a leak?" asked Contigo.

"I'd secure yourself first. You'll piss your pants soon enough anyway," counseled Destemido.

Chapter 25

ROAD TRIPS IN THE GOLDEN AGE

FALL 1494

After his final dinner service at The Lamb Shack, Bellini knew the best opportunity for a long-term future demanded a hasty skedaddle from both his recent past and his native country. Deducing that an Italian in France given the present hostilities also had limited options, he veered his newly acquired, horse-drawn treasure chest away from any city centers. Clinging to the Mediterranean coast, he crossed the border into Catalonia above Barcelona.

Other than picking up dynamite recipes for slow-roasted chicken thighs, plus another for braised short ribs in ancho chili sauce, Marco transited Spain in an economical three weeks. He had contemplated the alluring southern coast as his final destination, but the ongoing Spanish Inquisition dissuaded him. No sense tempting the randomness of fate. Hearing about a thriving restaurant scene, and a benign monarchy driven by capitalism over religious insanity, he set course for Lisbon, the hipster capital of Portugal.

The capital finally in sight on the horizon line, Bellini double-whipped his horses, craving a night's sleep in an actual hotel bed. The thrill of his custom coach had entirely worn thin over the extended, bumping, backroads journey across the continent. Exhausted yet energized by his final destination, he failed to notice the two riders who emerged from a dense stand of cinnamon-colored trees. The Portuguese called these low standing broad leaf evergreens *strawberry* trees. Their fruit, which in polite circles appeared as kissing cousins to the strawberry, looked more like a pair of angry, red, old man balls. Eaten raw, these berries could induce a spontaneous dry heave. Whatever one thought of the appearance and taste, the fruit did distill into quite a lovely and regionally popular brandy called aguardiente de medronhos.

The trees grew rather thickly and lined the main roadway into Lisbon.

At a gallop, the two riders soon caught up with the fast-moving carriage. Bellini only noticed them in his peripheral vision at the very last moment, giving him no time to contemplate a defensive action. One rather stocky rider lurched ahead, drawing even with the lead horse. He deftly grabbed the bridle of the horse on the left. This brought the entire scene to a halt. Bellini slid his right hand to his ever-present stiletto parked in his belt. For the moment, he chose to remain passive.

"Greetings, Señor. Why such a hurry?"

The second rider, a wiry older man, appeared on the right side of the coach. He extended his pistol twelve inches away from Bellini's cheekbone.

Even though Bellini spoke no Portuguese, he did have a working command of Spanish, and a deep knowledge of the international language spoken by a cocked pistol.

"Welcome to Portugal?" He quipped cynically.

"Ah, you are Iberian?" The thickly built, muscled man spoke perfect Spanish. He took over the conversation while his partner dismounted his Appaloosa to commence a slow walk around the carriage.

"You are probably wondering why we have stopped you. Yes?"

"I assumed you were bandits who noticed a well-to-do traveler alone on the road, and who wished to improve their fortunes. Yes?" Bellini expected his sarcasm to prickle the man, hopefully forcing him into an incautious act of temper.

Unfazed, the man merely chuckled as he withdrew his foil from its scabbard.

"I can certainly see where you might leap to that conclusion, friend." He lightly placed the point of his sword on Bellini's right wrist. "I will thank you to remove your hand from that well-crafted stiletto blade I see in your waistband. We'd like to keep the day as pleasant as the weather."

Bellini was having some trouble tracking both his adversaries. He'd lost sight of the other brigand, but felt the carriage rocking a bit from behind.

"Allow me to introduce myself, I am Contigo Sousa, a Lieutenant of the King's guard. To be on the safe side, why don't you take that blade out with the first two fingers of your LEFT hand. No thumb, please. You can simply drop it on the ground."

"Am I under arrest for some infraction, Lieutenant?"

"Tigo! Got something."

Bellini realized the other man had found one of the multitudes of secret compartments in the carriage, but held his composure.

"A gentleman must take precautions. Is that a crime, sir?"

"I am sure you will be surprised to learn that we have seen a rise in smuggling and thievery along this very road. We stop you for your own protection. Kindly step down from your coach and join us."

Bellini parsed his way through any options he could think of while cautiously climbing down from the carriage seat. Zero. That was the total he came up with in figuring a way out of the present jam. Contigo knew by instinct that the gentleman standing uneasily before him was neither an innocent traveler, nor from the Iberian Peninsula. By the time both men arrived at the back of the carriage they had each taken a full measure of the circumstance and contemplated the options for resolution.

Three giant bags of coins greeted the two antagonists. Contigo knelt to open one of the bags and examine its contents.

"Ah...you must have traveled a very long way. Much further than

I had imagined, although when I examine the excellent ITALIAN workmanship of your carriage more closely..."

"Yes, I am Italian. Given my concern about your intentions, I chose not to reveal this fact. However, these funds are legally tendered to me from business dealings in Italy. You have no right to them."

Contigo's sinewy compadre moved to yet another compartment beneath the carriage. The sound of two more weighty sacks of coins dropping to the ground shook Bellini. Knowing he had no way out other than a weaponless fight with two able assailants, his frustration erupted.

"I will not be robbed of my life's work by thieves under the guise of the King's law."

"I sense this is not actually YOUR life's work. However, neither is it ours."

Bellini suddenly brightened at the turn in his prospects.

"We shall, I think, need to confiscate these sacks for the present. I am confident that you have access to more reserves. After we investigate these Italian coins, you may claim your funds from the palace exchequer no less than one week from today. If they are not smuggled funds, you shall be reunited. Until then, carry on and enjoy your journey to Lisbon."

"I may truly leave, you say, yet you keep my means of support. Seems unjust."

"We can be gracious," offered the older man.

"Quite right, Longshort. Point taken!"

Longshort reached into one of the confiscated bags, withdrew a handful of coins and handed them to Bellini, who pocketed the token gesture.

Followed by both men, Bellini slow walked back to the front of his carriage. He kneeled to pick up the stiletto.

"Please leave the blade where it lies, sir. Apologies, occupational caution on my part. No disrespect intended."

Bellini leered at Contigo. Burning his image into memory along with his comrade.

"One week to the exchequer. I have your word on it?" Bellini saw no reason to trust either man.

"Provided the funds are clean. You have my word. Buon viaggio amico mio."

As Bellini shook the reins, he spied Contigo neatly flip the stiletto into the open window of the departing carriage. The perfect Italian farewell had disarmed him. He needed no further proof that he had dramatically under-estimated the man. He would do better next time.

Considerably poorer, yet unharmed, Bellini found a stylish hotel in the heart of Lisbon's trendy Bairo Alto district to gather his wits. Visiting the exchequer after a week's time posed a level of danger he wisely chose to contemplate before attempting. He was still in possession of a reasonable amount of the Don's tithes and in no immediate danger. Lisbon truly offered a multitude of options for a man of Bellini's skillsets.

The Corpo Santo hotel occupied a toney corner on the hottest shopping street in bustling Golden Age Lisbon. As fortune would have it, only three doors down from his temporary digs sat the prestigious Restaurant Tavares. RT's was, hands down, the finest restaurant in town. Frequented and revered by those who needed to be seen, plus all those who wanted to say they were there, seeing them, while also being seen. Nightly patrons were comprised of legions of sycophantic aristocracy, visiting bourgeoisie, masquerading wannabes, and a tasteful smattering of random royals opting for a night away from a palace in transition.

The recent roadside events required Bellini to refuel his embargoed stockpile of appropriated funding. He was more than prepared for the challenge. Knives in hand, he coolly dropped in on Tavares, following an early morning espresso. Flashing his best Italian chef accent, Marco easily arranged a parlay with the two owners.

The inseparable Tavares twins, Alia, and Enrico, always on the prowl for innovation, patiently listened to Bellini tap dance his way through his kitchen resume. Opposite pinkies extended, the twins sipped on their own espressos. Enrico was by far the more emotionally demonstrative twin. Their faces had familial similarities; dark eyes, wavy black hair, protracted aquiline noses ending at their chins. Enrico's overlapping chin triplet overwhelmed Alia's well-toned single. The corpulent, flamboyant, Enrico adored his two-minute-older sister. He deferred to her on all matters of restaurant business. His expertise proved more symbolically aligned to his well-fed profile.

Along with an unfailing palate, Enrico was also a committed numerologist. Bellini sized up Alia's passions as revealed by the elegant designer silk tunic and bejeweled rings weighing down both her hands. She happily deferred RT's classic menu construction to Enrico.

"When were you born?" inquired Enrico, pencil in hand.

Bellini was taken off-guard. Not able to come up with a spontaneous lie, and not understanding the nature of the question, he uncharacteristically, hesitantly, told the truth.

"Eighth of March, um...1473."

"He has to work out the thing," explained Alia.

"What is the thing?"

"I am determining your angel number. Are you a risk to us, do you have skills, are you reliable, creative, trustworthy, plus the rest."

"You can ask me questions."

"He doesn't work that way."

"It's science. Science is truth."

"Depending," said Bellini.

Enrico looked up at Bellini before making his notations. Paper being a valuable commodity, Enrico scratched his computations on the tablecloth in front of him.

"You *can* trust me," Bellini lied.

Enrico ignored him and continued to scratch out his calculations on the table.

"He looks trustworthy enough to me, and attractive in an urban vigilante sort of way. Can we move it along, brother?"

Of course, Alia had other things to do. She had suffered through her brother's process many times before, and knew she had to endure it along with the designated victim. Her wry comment generated an unintended consequence.

Bellini thought he had uncovered another aspect to Alia's profile which he could possibly exploit. He smiled slyly back at her. Alia, all business, ignored the undertone.

Enrico said, "Well, hmmm. A '*One*' means the angels are trying to calm and reassure you. Although there is some confusion in your actions."

Bellini struggled with an uncontrollable outcome. "What did he mean by actions?" he thought. "What can this possibly reveal about me?"

"Using qualities of the One—foresight and the adequacy of self-judgement—you can always keep your goal in sight."

"That's good?"

Bellini looked to Enrico, who continued to ignore him caught up in his interpretive roll. He glanced at Alia, hoping for a lifeline.

"Is that good?"

"Not a clue, sorry," she said.

"The Four in the message of heaven predicts big problems in your personal life. Career obsession is a time bomb."

"I'm lost."

"That's got to be a good thing. Obsessed with career works in our favor, right?" suggested Alia.

"The *Seven* means that you have trouble seeing the difference between your abilities and your duties. But the Three says you are doing everything right, without doing everything that you could do."

"Perhaps this is not a good fit for me."

Bellini looked to extricate himself from the walls he felt closing in.

"No, no. Try not to overreact." Alia thrummed her fingers on the table, signaling Enrico to quicken the pace.

"His life path cycles do look promising if a bit muddy. He adapts to any situation, yet sometimes lacks the anchors to stop at the right moment..."

A solution dawned on Bellini. "Pardon me, but may I simply cook for you? By all means continue the calculations, or whatever it is you are doing. Allow me to focus on the kitchen."

"An excellent suggestion!" applauded Alia.

Enrico nodded. "Yes, why not!"

They gave him one hour in the kitchen to prepare a meal of his choosing.

"Wow me," said Alia, raising her right eyebrow.

"Your very best," said Enrico.

Once he left the room, the twins exchanged wondering looks.

"Mediocre at best, if his numbers are anywhere near correct," predicted Enrico.

"Why did you waste so much of our time if that's how you feel?"

"Science, sister. Had to do the science. You can't argue with it."

Shaking off the doppelgangers and festering paranoia, Bellini found his way into the kitchen. Foraging through the ingredient stocks, he opted for a classic Italian dish. The very one that cost him a fingertip - La Genovese. He made a ziti pasta by hand, braised the beef quickly, and improvised the remaining simple ingredients.

Exactly one hour later, cunning as always, Bellini sheepishly placed a bowl of pasta in front of each twin with a candy-coated apology wrapped in humility.

"I apologize for the hasty nature of the meal, but I did my best in the time allotted."

Knowing full well the delight of the dish was self-evident he added, "If I had a bit more time…"

"Ssshhh…" Alia put up her hand.

The luscious rich scent of onions, beef, and wine had intoxicated Enrico, who had already shoved a forkful into his mouth.

"Oh damn! Can you make more of this? Tonight?"

"Easy brother," cautioned Alia.

"Taste it.," Enrico insisted.

Alia scooped a small taste that melted onto her palate. She looked at Enrico, mouthing the word 'science' with a question mark.

"Yes, tonight would be excellent."

"I'm flattered," said the chef, "however, perhaps tomorrow is better. I do have expenses. We should first discuss the pay scale."

"Sir, there is no problem that money cannot solve," responded Alia, waving off his hesitation.

"Agreed," said Bellini.

The gleeful owners shook hands with each other, ecstatic in the knowledge that they had just scored the next great thing for Restaurant Tavares. Bellini departed, leaving the two to contemplate their good fortune.

Content that he had secured a modicum of stability in a new city, and with a healthy pouch of bonus payment in hand, Bellini paid his hotel bill one month in advance. He had negotiated a day to take care of personal business before coming to work.

Bellini spent the day disposing of his former home, along with its two horses. He removed the remaining pouches of tribute from their undiscovered hidden compartments.

The following day, while eying him warily, the two existing Tavares chefs reluctantly greeted their newest comrade. Bellini knew he'd have to prove himself worthy in their eyes. He kept his distance from the current crew, focusing on a sizeable batch of La Genovese for that evening's meal. As Lisbon's busiest dining spot, RTs boasted multiple table turns each and every night.

Enrico preened about the gold-walled, decadently mirrored dining room placing small sample bowls of Bellini's dish on every table. The vat of La Genovese vaporized before the second table turn. Guests clamored for more, only to be devastated by the news of an empty bowl. The dish became legendary in one night. Enrico reveled, genuflecting at six-second intervals over his good fortune. He repeatedly tapped a gold framed parchment letter hanging on the wall by the door to the kitchen. An equally thrilled Alia had her hands, full counting the receipts while handling the overflowing clamor for follow on reservations.

One short month, later the celebrated Bellini elevated his stature to become the latest celebrity toast of the town.

"Manuel is coming tonight! The King! Holy Jesus!"

Brandishing a royal scroll dropped off by the palace herald, Alia ran about the nearly empty restaurant announcing the news.

"Sister, relax. It *is* much overdue. Recall we have sent three to-go vats of Le Genovese over to the damn palace, so yeah."

"For the King!" emphasized Alia.

"For free! We should raise our prices tonight!" countered Enrico, munching on a sugar doughnut.

"That is *my* decision. Do we tell Marco?" asked Alia nervously.

"Of course, we do. Not that *that* icicle would care. Nothing shakes him. Still can't shake the feeling I've missed something about him."

"He is pretty opaque. Maybe all he cares about is the dish."

"Doubtful. Numbers don't lie," answered Enrico.

"That's not what you said a month ago!"

"Well...maybe. Right now, let's hope the King's tastebuds don't break us!"

Enrico walked over to the entrance to tap on his gold framed good-fortune totem, as Bellini strolled through the doorway.

"What is in there, and why you are always tapping on it?"

"He doesn't know about the kingdom?" Enrico hunched his shoulders at Alia.

"Someday we'll all get there. 'Honey flows and milk abounds' – says so right here!" Enrico pointed to a passage in Latin on the encased, tattered, but well-preserved parchment.

"I don't know Latin, but I do know a standard bible reference," replied Bellini, unphased by the portrayal of religious piety from the twins. Religion dominated everyone's lives; some, for piety's sake, but most courtesans for economic advantage.

"No, no, no," Alia said, "I read your cynicism."

"Prester John is the real deal. A holy ruler of a hidden Kingdom, not merely some heavenly bible reference."

In the twelfth century, a mysterious series of letters circulated around Europe. Written by a Christian king known as Prester John, the letters told of a magical, peaceful, kingdom free from crime, and vice, where "honey flows in our land and milk everywhere abounds." He detailed a land where rivers ran filled with gold. The news, however, was not all grand.

Prester John had called for aid from Christian European armies claiming his land was besieged by infidels and barbarians after its spoils. In case gold filled rivers were not inspiration enough to compel a rescue mission, Prester John also let it be known his realm hosted the legendary Fountain of Youth. The Happiest Place on Earth, plus eternal life were hard to argue against defending. Surely, inspired by protecting religious freedoms everywhere, plus the odd pot of gold, European monarchs launched numerous missions, over many decades, with the goal of rescuing both King and kingdom.

"We're not ginning up reservations with piety. It's for real Marco," Alia added. "And the King is a big believer, so when he shows up tonight for dinner if you doubt it, hold your tongue."

Bellini held up his hands in mock surrender. "Got it. Well, well, the King?" He showed no demonstrative level of enthusiasm upon hearing their headline news.

Alia provided enough excitement for everyone. "You heard that correctly, Manuel himself showing up TO-NIGHT! Ce soir, este noche, questa sera, hac nocte. That's Latin."

"Well, in that case, I will create something special for him."

"Why? He loves the Genovese. Why mess with success?"

"Absolutely!" Enrico echoed her.

"How much time do we have?" asked Bellini.

"You tell us. Make it memorable, is all we ask!" said Enrico.

"You've got until eight pm. It's the goddamn King!" Alia repeated.

Bellini smirked on his way into the kitchen. His ambitions far surpassed the current job. Set on maximizing the opportunity at hand, he chose to create a new hybrid dish from his experiences in Italy, Spain, and now Portugal. He called it Frango em Pepitoria. Languidly braised chicken thighs covered in a luscious saffron, cinnamon, garlic, and brandy picada almond sauce. With calculation worthy of Descartes, Bellini selected Lisbon's favorite brandy, aguardiente de medronhos, as his secret dream ingredient.

"Heavenly! Here."

Enrico swooned over the forkful of richness washing over his palate before offering a bite to his sister.

"Cannot. Too much anxiety."

Alia dashed about the empty restaurant, attentive to a litany of details. She placed small bamboo centerpieces on each table. The King had received a mini-grove of bamboo in a single pot as a coronation gift from visiting Danish dignitary Ingman Green.

Denmark had maintained its sovereignty at the time because of its isolated geographic location. Too far north, and too damn cold to bother with conquering. Ingman burned considerable time futilely trying to build trade relations between Portugal and Denmark. No one caught the sly smile on Ingman's face masking his frustrated contempt as he handed over the somewhat unusual gift. "I suggest your majesty find a place in your garden for this unique plant. Water it well." After bowing his way out of the room Ingman returned to Copenhagen within the month.

Rumor had it that Manuel had fallen in love with the stuff; amazed at its prodigious growth. The newbie King had ordered his gardeners to spread the joy about his royal gardens. That was six months prior to dinner at Restaurant Tavares.

The gifted bamboo that spread about the royal gardens was of a freakishly exceptional strain which grew at a rate of three feet for each and every 24 hours. The horrified royal gardeners watched this mutant strain launch skyward at two inches per hour. Like the Spanish Armada sweeping the seas clean of all comers, the invasive plant overran and consumed virtually all other plants in the garden.

After a few months of behind the rake struggles, the King finally noticed the destruction of his once-proud gardens. During a particularly janky game of lawn bowling with the royal exchequer, Manuel tripped over a piece of aggressive bamboo which had evaded all defense and reared its head directly in the King's follow-through on his finishing ball.

"Firebomb that shit. I hate it!" he roared to the assembled onlookers.

Alia had no way of knowing this. To her, centerpieces were part of everything appearing perfect prior to the monarch's arrival. She had held the doors of RTs closed until the King arrived. No early seating on this night. Amused by all the preparations, Bellini leaned against the front desk, his white apron pressed and pristine.

"You're not going to tap the letter for good luck tonight, Enrico?" he mocked.

"Very funny. No luck needed with tonight's dish. You have topped yourself chef!"

A powerful double knock on the restaurant door caught the immediate attention of both twins.

"I'll get it. Go find something to do!" Alia nervously commanded.

Opening the door, she encountered two of the King's most trusted security guards. Bellini recognized Contigo immediately. Before being spotted, he jetted into the kitchen.

"Your pardon," Contigo offered, graciously bowing. "Here to check the dining room before the King's entrance."

"Of course." Alia stepped aside.

Contigo and his companion quickly split up and moved about the dining room, checking under tables, behind drapes, before ultimately pushing through a door into the kitchen. Bellini had strategically made himself scarce.

"Well enough. Thank you for your cooperation," said Contigo. "Ummm," he pointed to the bamboo centerpieces. "I don't quite get the joke."

"What do you mean? What joke?"

"The King absolutely hates that stuff."

Alia flew into an instant panic. "But I got it from the King's very gardeners! They were ecstatic! I thought…"

"They hate it more than he does!"

Contigo now stood at the doorway, motioning the all-clear sign to the parade of coaches lined up outside of the restaurant. On cue, carriage doors opened in unison as a league of eager guests streamed towards the door.

"Shit!" Alia muttered to herself, knowing it was too late to do anything about it.

"What?" Enrico had wandered by and heard his sister. "Shit, you said shit. What shit?"

"Doesn't matter. Forget it. Here they come. Smile!"

Preceded by his fluffed, festooned, and bejeweled entourage, the newly crowned twenty-six-year-old King Manuel I casually strolled into the restaurant the embodiment of golden age cool. Fueled by his ambition for greatness, Manuel wielded his power with the ease of birthright spiced with a hipster cool. Life was his oyster for a brief moment on history's timeline, and he knew it.

Once through the doorway, the young King turned up the swagger making his royal way to the center table. Manuel grabbed the bamboo centerpiece, extending his arm with the pot as if holding out a bag of recently collected cow dung.

"Uh NO!"

Maurizio Entrada, the King's head groveler, and most recently appointed Minister of Foreign Affairs, obediently snapped the pot from the King's hand. He passed it down the reluctant entourage conveyor belt back to the front door, where it was drop-kicked onto the street.

Alia held her breath, fearing further repercussions.

"Welcome, Highness," she said with a bow. She held one eye on the King, the other on the remaining table settings which so far remained untouched.

Enrico realized the meaning of the previous 'oh shit' moment. He offered his greetings by way of a deeper bow than his sister's, no small feat for the corpulent brother.

"So, my friends, what's for dinner? We are ravenous."

"You're going to be wowed!" answered a relieved Enrico.

"Oh, by the way, we brought along a plus one."

The King motioned to his attendants. Like a curtain opening, they parted, revealing a plain, blanched skin, sour, bulimic young woman weighted down by a gothic overkill, black velvet dress. Shuffling her feet towards the table, she demurely sat next to the King.

"Move down a bit more, would you mind dear? We need more space."

Manuel waved her back. She continued scooting her chair along the table. By the time the King stopped waving his hand she had reached the far end of the table, where she received a royal thumbs-up.

"Meet Isabella of Aragon. Life altered since her first husband, tragically, died. Poor choice, dear," he quipped to Isabella. "Most likely she's the politically correct choice for Queen. Provided we get the contracts worked out, of course. Sex be damned for expedience, I suppose."

Isabella's expression did not betray her opinion of the arrogant monarch. Knowing the King's hatred of bamboo, she had watched with surreptitious amusement as the centerpiece migrated out the front door. Thanks, Mom and Dad, for dishing me off to this jack ass, she thought.

The entourage issued a courtesy titter parade at Manuel's weak daggers hurled at Isabella's expense. Alia bristled at the caustic treatment of another woman, but kept her thoughts to herself. She was simply thankful the monarch had not noticed the remaining bamboo decorations. She added a place setting for the heir apparent to Ferdinand & Isabella, the Catholic Kings of Spain.

Alia opened her arms wide, "Welcome to Tavares! Prepare to feast!"

The royal entourage scattered itself about the restaurant, all eagerly anticipating a meal to remember. Witnessing the unanticipated crowd Enrico, rushed to the kitchen in a panic.

"They're all eating. Everyone! Have we got enough?"

Unfazed, Bellini revealed tray upon tray of his newly created dish, ready to be served.

"You see," he cracked, "luck has nothing to do with preparation!"

Chapter 26
ELEPHANTS

The earth plays host to roughly 45,000 storms each day.

To even the most battle-scarred seaman of the day, the unfurling scope of one storm to the next occurred as a slowly revealed murder mystery. Clues were numerous, but so were possible twists. A ray of random sunshine peeking through a closing cloud deck might engender misplaced hope or, increasing dread. Wind is wind, rain is rain, waves are still waves; at least until their force level surpasses any in previous experience. Blasting wind and waves, when powerful enough, or when floating out of position, will fracture and pulverize any hull.

Neither crew from the Queen of Sheba or the L'Aquila had the slightest foreknowledge that the dispassionate maelstrom now forming off their bowsprits was coming for all of them.

"Humph, just a little drizzle," said Lorenzo as he manned the L'Aquila wheel.

A shifting wind hand-delivered a light drizzle to the formerly peaceful Gibraltar Strait. Proving they had a depraved sense of humor along with a healthy dose of misanthropy, the weather gods interspersed a few scattered false hope luminous rays of *god light* to torment their victims.

"We can outrun this little sprinkle." noted VanMeter at the Queen's tiller.

"Always looks worse than it is. Right?" asked Hector, searching for any shoulder to lean on.

Both veteran captains noted the change, and each exhaled with wavering conviction. Even without the benefit of a gps storm-scope, they knew better.

The sprinkling soon gave way to its storm featurette sequel. Despite being miles apart, a circling wind of increased velocity enveloped the two boats. From the victim's vantage point, the wind spawned from all directions at once. Shifting texture from scattered whitecaps to an intensifying, psychotic disarray, the ocean too became victim number one to the driving forces of nature. Whitewater waves emerged from all points. They collided and banged off each other, spawning intensifying confusion. All of these forces made navigating a true path to anywhere a Sisyphean task. A quilted mass of multiplying darkened cumulus clouds crowded the sky. Each cloud rolled onto the next compressing then knitting themselves together in an impenetrable blanket of peril.

A fully realized, ambitious storm cloud can warehouse up to five hundred thousand tons of water weighing upwards of one billion pounds. An African elephant can weigh fourteen thousand pounds before dinner. A Boeing 787 Dreamliner weighs in at five hundred and fifty-five thousand pounds. Pick your poison. Should either one of those land on a human being they would become an instant, flesh-flavored, flatbread. Through the power of meteorological magic, the daunting truth of epic storms meant that at any one time, suspended in midair, hung seventy-one thousand African elephants, or ten fully loaded Dreamliners.

Both crews could see that the darkening sky had turned into bumper to bumper, water laden, fully fed elephants. Yet even that would not have been so overwhelming if the *fetch* hadn't added to the incoming misery bath.

Rodrigo, suffering from a bursting bladder and a budding case of Moroccan dysentery, had picked that moment to park himself in the L'Aquila's jardine. This sixteenth-century open-air toilet hung gingerly over the port side of the boat, suspended by a ragged set of guide ropes.

Despite the increasingly rolling seas the desperate Rodrigo had managed to cautiously negotiate himself over the port side gunnel, onto the rocking seat. He held a piece of pitch-covered rope with which to clean himself post event.

Bad timing for Rodrigo.

The *fetch* makes for a good day, a challenging day, or possibly the end of days. The strength of the wind: how long it has been blowing, and the distance over open water it has been blowing, define the fetch. As these variables increase, so does the size of the waves. The wind had been blowing for quite some time. Waves correspondingly increased in size by the moment: five, ten, fifteen, twenty, and more. Each time the L'Aquila entered a trough between giants, it settled with a gruesome cracking sound imperiling the very old bones of Señor Espinosa's rental boat. The Queen suffered along with the L'Aquila.

As Rodrigo settled in, a rogue mountain of water swept over the L'Aquila from the starboard side. It whipped over the rails, slamming the boat into a deep port side lean. The rush of water entombed Rodrigo, sweeping him away to eternity. Nantucket, his arms encompassing the mast, witnessed the poor man's unscheduled departure. He bowed his head for a moment, then affirmed his grip on the mast and rope securing him to Doug's cage.

"We need to furl the sails!" yelled Felipe to Lanning.

The wind and water whipped over and around the boat, mercilessly slinging it haphazardly from one position to the next. The sails were acting as an involuntary tow line attached to the whims of the maelstrom.

Lanning knew the level of danger that meant for his brother. He realized everyone's survival relied on them, leaving no other option.

"How do I help?" Felipe had made his way over to Lanning at the base of the mast.

"You're not going to say, 'it's too dangerous, brother'?"

"It's too dangerous, brother," Lanning parroted.

"Not feelin' the love." Felipe tried to lighten the dread for both of them.

They gripped arms briefly before Lanning tied a rope around Felipe's waist. He secured the other end to the base of the mast before turning to the giant man lashed to the bird cage.

"Nantucket. It's my brother's life. Hold the hell out of this line."

"I'll need slack too," cautioned Felipe.

The waves continued to pound the L'Aquila. They rocked the caravel from all directions as the gyrating wind pushed and pulled them through the chaotic seas. Nantucket realized Doug's cage posed an unnecessary inhibitor to protecting Felipe. He untied the rope from his waist, freeing the cage, which was immediately on the move with each tilt of the ship. Unable to maintain his balance, Doug caromed off the sides of his cage.

Filippa screamed across the deck from Lanning's cabin doorway. "Let him go! Let him go!"

Nantucket too realized the best option for the falcon was freedom.

"He knows where to go," declared Nantucket, calmly opening the cage door.

Doug shot out the cage like a ballistic missile. The falcon soared high and away at light speed. He never looked back. Filippa marked the moment with a nod before shutting the cabin door.

Felipe leaped up the mast's rope ladder as if climbing the cliff by the palace. The speed of his hands and feet working as one well-practiced machine had him reach the top in seconds.

"Uncle!" yelled Lanning towards the bridge, "Take the helm and hold her into the wind. Lorenzo, foremast now!"

Lorenzo jumped off the bridge, bracing himself against the

cascading waves with whatever he could find for stability. He made the foremast as Lanning untied the jib lines. Lorenzo caught and furled the dropping sail best he could. A gust of wind filled and furrowed the collapsing canvas, whacking Lorenzo hard to the deck. Lanning raised him up as they both scrambled to lash the sail in place against the boom before the next rush of water. Without the jib, the boat quickly lost a good piece of its lurching, swirling momentum. It now hung briefly, sheltered from the wind, stalled in a deep trough between cresting waves that appeared double the mast height or more.

Felipe, at the top of the mast, withdrew his knife set to cut the lines holding up the mainsail. He watched a towering swell rapidly approaching the boat from the port side. The wave's frothing crest matched his eye level. The force of the wind increased in unison with the oncoming wave. He knew with a broadside hit, the L'Aquila would be instantly swamped, then capsized.

The two brothers caught each other's gaze, both dreading a fatal outcome. Looking towards the tiller Lanning felt confident he had made the right choice. The picture of calm in the eye of the storm, Shafi simply nodded, first to Lanning, then up to Felipe. A hint of a smile lit up his eyes, reassuring Lanning in the midst of the chaos, at least for a moment. Holding the wheel firmly with his right hand, the old Berber displayed a pedagogic calm. He half-raised his palm facing up towards Felipe. The gesture was not a wave. Felipe understood its meaning. Although he desperately wanted to cut the lines and slide down, he waited.

The ship was being pelted with rain, an intensifying wind, and a wall of bombarding spray; so much water it was impossible to tell fresh from salt, spit from tears.

"Jesus, man! Cut and run!" yelled a panicked Lorenzo to Felipe.

"Don't lose your shit, Zo. He *has* to wait," answered Lanning, wiping his eyes in vain.

The L'Aquila began an ominous sideways crawl up the face of the incoming swell. As the angle became more acute, the stress against the boat's keel intensified. Every loud crack of wood felt like the doorbell of doom.

"NOW!" yelled Shafi, dropping his hand.

Felipe cut the ropes as fifty knots of wind ensnared the mainsail. The loose canvas billowed out over the starboard side of the boat like a bedsheet pinned to a clothesline in a hurricane. In one frozen moment of disaster ballet, Shafi spun the wheel starboard, flipping the rudder to match both the gust and the sail. Like a surfer carving a perfect cutback off the shoulder of a rolling wave, the L'Aquila gracefully arced down the face of the enormous swell, escaping oblivion for at least another moment.

Felipe miraculously clung to the mast, avoiding the twin threats of tangling or falling. He breathed a quick sigh before heading down to the deck. The main sail now dangled halfway over the starboard side of the boat. The boat's momentum had carried it straight across the next swell, where they were greeted by an oncoming wind. The billowed main sail now an easy target of this opposite-direction blast. The formerly dead sail rose up to sweep across the deck, matching the speed of the wind. The sail's force snapped an unprepared Felipe off the mast, pocketing him inside its center before collapsing over the port side and being by the rushing waters of the chaotic sea.

"MAN OVERBOARD! All hands port side!!!" screamed Lanning.

He rushed to the rail. Hector met him at the gunnel, clutching Lanning to prevent him from leaping down to his brother.

Unfazed, Nantucket turned to the rail, set his feet, bent his knees, and began pulling on the mainsail rope. Expressionless, the Indian worked hand over hand, steady and smooth. Fortunately, Felipe was not tangled up in lines and canvas. Rather, he found himself folded dead center like pulled pork in an Algeciras taco.

His wits gathered, Lanning used all his to strength to help Nantucket heave from the rail. Hector pulled on the sail, folding it onto the deck as fast as he could. The rope moved, the sail moved, and Shafi kept the boat headed straight into the wind.

"Hurry the fuck up. I'm drowning down here!" Felipe had scratched his way out of the folds, gulping for air. He hung onto the rope as Lanning strained to reach his brother's outstretched arm.

Amidst the mayhem on the deck, Shafi noticed something he couldn't quite decipher on the upcoming horizon. He repeatedly rubbed the blur from his eyes, believing it to be an apparition. Since he knew no one was watching him, but mostly to prove to himself it was real, he put his glasses on, trying to fathom the vision. It appeared briefly, only to disappear between the rolling seas. Whatever it was, the task at hand demanded his focus. Ignoring what might be, he concentrated by fighting the resistance on the wheel to maintain their heading as best he could.

Nantucket's massive arm reached over the rail to grab Felipe before finally hauling him onto the deck.

"Worse than my worst nightmare!" coughed Felipe.

"Don't be such a baby. You needed a bath anyway," said his deeply relieved big brother.

"You two good? Because..." Lorenzo stood pointing to the horizon of menacing seas.

"Back to work," said Felipe.

Lanning bear-hugged his brother before moving onto the next brimming catastrophe. He wobbled up to the tiller where Shafi had his sights glued to the upcoming horizon.

"What?"

"Wait for it," said the Berber.

Lanning followed his gaze to eleven o'clock, one point off the bow.

"Just there! See it?"

Lanning thought he saw a black dot appear then disappear behind another looming swell. The L'Aquila, stripped of most of its speed, remained pointed into the wind. They navigated over the oncoming swells which, in Shafi's mind, had lost a scintilla of their ferocity.

"Paaatience..." Shafi extended the word.

A long, loud, rumble of erupting thunder echoed across the ocean scape. Nantucket froze on the deck, and redirected his gaze to the horizon.

"Thunder is shit. Waves are way worse," pronounced Hector.

"Thunder never travels alone. And there are worse things than water hitting a boat," said Nantucket with certainty.

"Nothing could be worse," Hector insisted.

In the Team Physics footrace of the elements, the speed of light thoroughly demolishes the speed of sound. It is not close. Thunder accepts its job as a courtly herald signaling the impending arrival of the main event.

Shafi felt his beard trying to leave his face, followed by the hair on his arms rising to attention. The sudden wave of static electricity swept unseen through the air. He looked at Lanning and pointed a thumb skyward.

A bone-cracking sound of electricity birthing erupted half a moment later. Emanating from nowhere, yet existing everywhere, a biblically brimstone span of branch lightening spread psychotically over the entire breadth of the sky.

"HOLY SHIT!"

Hector dove for the deck as the driving wind whipped the ocean into yet another frenzy.

"Neniigo," uttered Nantucket to himself.

"Oh my god!" Filippa emerged from her cabin, braced for end of days.

"Get down!" Hector yelled to Filippa.

"That's terrifying!" Lanning's head swiveled, absorbing the sky on fire.

"There it is again." Shafi nudged Lanning and pointed as the L'Aquila crested another wave.

Lanning followed Shafi's finger to the horizon line.

"Someone's in the water!"

Chapter 27

DAMN THAT FALCON

"We have to outrun this."

"The first decision made in the face of an approaching storm returns the greatest consequence." The sage advice from immortal Viking Lars Holmgren, gone missing back when men with oars ruled the seas.

Destemido glared sideways at ferryboat artisan, woefully over-matched first mate, Jan VanMeter. He deeply missed Longshort, yet cursed him for a mistimed demise. The deeper tragedy of his untimely death had resulted in very real consequences.

"Now you're convicted?" said an incredulous Destemido.

Jan stood still, reviewing in his mind the multiple cataclysmic outcomes if the Queen did not make an immediate escape.

"I thought a lot about it," he blurted out, "We need to run as fast as fucking possible."

Destemido had seen the look of abject fear in many men's eyes before. However, the pirate was usually the one generating it. Not this time.

"Make for the nearest shore in any direction."

Unhappily, destiny was already set on an irreversible course. VanMeter's sum total seafaring experience evolved from a few blustery, rainy days navigating the Delft canals every February. He had not a clue on open sea storm strategies, other than canal-driven common sense. Neither did the overmatched ferry driver have a gaggle of weekend sailors hanging out after the weekly *wet Wednesday* race to shoot the shit over best storm-running tactics.

Whitecaps unfurled, banging into the ship from all sides as

VanMeter scanned the horizon, trying to make a decision. The sky closed down from every cardinal direction. Running at the fastest possible speed angle for sail and boat seemed the first best choice. The Queen's speed across the water was her greatest asset.

An inconvenient five hundred and sixty years before the great-great-grandchild of VanMeter's third cousin, thrice removed, founded the Algeciras Yacht Club, Van Meter had to reason out the best choice to make before the oncoming tempest entombed the Queen. There's a time for barbeque and a time for speed. At some point, time simply runs out.

VanMeter called out the order, "Rig for beam reach. Full cloth!"

While running for cover may seem like the preferred choice, the greatest danger lies in being caught in a storm close to shore with zero room to maneuver. Rocks and shoals along the Gibraltar coastline were littered with the remains of poor choices. The less intuitive strategy of sailing away from the storm's path, keeping plenty of open ocean around the boat, took a bit more foresight, experience, and courage than the first mate had on hand.

Contigo suffered the terror of the unknown. He had felt that way only once before in years past. While intellectually marveling at the forces of nature in play, the sheer terror of survival felt overwhelming. Taking Destemido's advice, he lashed himself to the nearest gunnel on the rear deck to remain in sight of both captain and first mate.

The Queen navigated into the absolute worst sailing position possible. While excellent for speed, VanMeter's hastily chosen strategy exposed the ship to the struggle of overcoming the onslaught of forming waves at the exact wrong angle. True to its design, the ship flew through the ocean at breakneck speed. They made amazing progress initially. The Queen pointed towards the Tangier coastline on a direct route; the caravel skipping handily over the building waves.

Six-then ten-footers posed only minor obstacles to the little flying boat. Geometry can be an unforgiving bitch. Calculating angles, elements, physical stress forces, plus unknown, unplanned variables, overwhelm the best sailors. VanMeter was hardly best of breed. At a rapidly approaching point, it became simply too much for his 16th century inland waterway knowledge base.

The game changed when the wave height surpassed fifteen feet. At eighteen feet, both Destemido and VanMeter, who handled the tiller, noticed the Queen back-skidding while climbing up the wave faces. As the next monster twenty-foot wave hit the boat from a ninety-degree angle, the men locked eyes. Speed, as a combat strategy for the intensifying storm, was definitely the fool's choice.

Contigo knew fear when he witnessed it.

"What?" he shouted through the wind and driving rain.

"We've got time," shouted VanMeter, gritting his jaw.

Also knowing bullshit when he heard it, Contigo ran through his options.

Water rule of thumb: one cubic meter of ocean water (1000 liters, or 264 gallons) weighs in at an even 1000 kilograms, a little over one ton (a tad more than a 1967 VW bug). The storm waves doubled in size every half hour. Even though no one on board the Queen held an advanced Renaissance math degree, dread does not require a slide rule. Looking at an approaching ten-meter wave that might break against the Queen's port side hull translated into over four hundred tons of water. That translated into a well-stocked car lot of more than 450 VW beetles, walloping the wooden deck of the remodeled caravel.

Naturally, zero souls onboard the Queen had any foreknowledge of the trend-setting, 1960s gas-conscious VW beetle. However, they all understood the concept of splintering tar-covered wood, a catastrophic rollover in rising ocean swells, and a grizzly death by drowning.

Destemido hurled VanMeter aside with a violent kick to the man's legs.

"ENOUGH!"

VanMeter crumbled to the deck. Destemido quickly released the pressure against the tiller. The wheel spun rapidly clockwise, allowing the Queen to fall off its perilous beam reach tack. Gaining back some control, the captain tried to point the bow perpendicular to a wave rushing up on the port side gunnel of the compromised caravel.

The wave crested, spilling a cascade of water over the deck, and washing away anything not tied down.

The falling lip, more than ninety feet across, enveloped the entire length of the Queen in a crush of frothing sea water. The massive blast of water inundated the ship with metaphorical Volkswagens hurled at all angles against the overmatched boat. Wood railings snapped like dry twigs, lashed lines tied in all manner of sea knot from Flemish loop to Marlow braid ripped away like an untied shoelace. The unabated surge of angry ocean cascaded into open crevices over the ship's decks, filling any available space with salt water. Crewmen bounced off all sides of the ship, mangling bones, impaling some on splintered shards of railings and decking. The curled-up ball of Jan VanMeter, with nothing to hold onto save his own balls, was swept from the Queen's top deck, and the world in general by a single riptide moment. His body rag-dolled over the cracking starboard rail by the chest crushing pressure of over two thousand pounds of water. He left a wife, a ten-year-old daughter, and an equally tattooed younger brother back home in distant, dreary, land-locked Delft.

The blow absorbed by the initial wave proved a mortal one. Destemido knew it. So did Contigo. In the interim between an oncoming final death blow, the Queen's single passenger scrambled up on deck, escaping the flooded cargo hold. Pale, besotted from being force-fed gallons of unwanted sea water, Marco Bellini tenuously staggered to his feet. He searched for some path to survival when he spotted Contigo lashed at the rail.

"Fuck you!" yelled Bellini.

Contigo unlashed himself.

"Death blow?" asked Destemido, seeing the fire in Contigo's eyes.

"To an unarmed man? Think better of me."

Contigo hopped down to the main deck. Catching sight of a yet another oncoming swell, Destemido held the wheel. He desperately tried to hold a course straight into the wave. Bellini watched as Contigo tried to make his way over to him.

"Fuck you!" Bellini repeated.

Contigo stopped, and looked back at the man. "In that case, feel free to pick your own way to die." He turned back to the stern.

"Figured you were going to kill me."

"Still might..."

Determined to find a way out of the disaster, Bellini followed Contigo back to the stern. As the two men climbed up to the wheel, the Queen started its journey up the face of a thirty-foot monster. Destemido felt the boat slipping halfway up the face.

The quick-thinking captain grabbed the rope Contigo had used to lash himself to the railing. He wove it around the inside spokes of the tiller, then around his own waist. He tossed the remaining slack over to the two men. "Tie yourselves together. Jump when I tell you."

"Jump?" screeched Bellini, white with fear.

Contigo simply thumb-pointed over the rail at the roiling ocean. Destemido spun the wooden dowel holding the wheel to its mount. He yanked it off its post as the Queen began its death slide down the face of the wave.

"JUMP!!!"

Chapter 28
ICE

FALL 1494 RESTAURANT TAVARES (AFTER DINNER)

Despite his larcenous and violent past, Bellini had zero clue about the events set to overtake him. He had proudly placed the wafting saffron-scented Frango em Pepitoria down in front of the famished, fledgling King of Portugal.

While the King celebrated the epicurean delight by applauding the chef, his dour date had already sucked down a first forkful. A gasp of joy escaped her grip, as she quickly arranged her next bite without waiting on the monarch. Definitely a royal rules faux pas which in ordinary moments, might have drawn a rebuke, or at minimum a brow raise from the King. This moment took off in an entirely unforecasted direction, leaving royal manners far behind.

With the monarch's first bite, forkfuls launched across the restaurant. The sounds of utter joy reverberated as each diner tasted the exquisite mingle of Bellini's creation. Some gulped, while others savored each bite. The twins watched over it all with a surreal happiness, confident this event would convert to bountiful times ahead.

Anaphylactic shock is nothing to mess around with. Had the medical community tracked the Golden Age statistics, they would show zero survivors based on zero existing remedies and zero existing knowledge. People usually responded with religious explanations or other hypotheses:

Damn, he's dead.

Yeah, she turned red, swollen, then stopped breathing altogether.

The Lord must have needed him, ASAP.

God works in mysterious ways.

I'm sure as hell not eating that!

When certain people, such as the King of Portugal, are exposed to a food they are allergic to, like almonds, it triggers an overzealous autonomic immune response. The body assumes a hyperdrive Defcon One posture in its attempt to combat the invading enemy. The Autonomic Defense Force (ADF) floods the system with a sustained barrage of counter-measure chemicals. The unintended consequence of this reaction is often funeral arrangements for the very victim intended for salvation. Death is most often preceded by a host of ominous symptoms: hives, vomiting, diarrhea, rapid pulse, weak pulse, cramps, or dizziness. In Manuel's case, a wheezing constricted throat which appeared as choking, but more aptly described as royal suffocation.

Instantly, the room echoed with the sound of forks dropping to the floor. The writhing King also fell to the floor, not to pick up an errant fork, but to gasp for his rapidly diminishing air. The entourage sat frozen in a DaVinci portrait of tragic ineptitude. All in the restaurant, save one, fell victim to the limitations of Golden Age emergency medical care, such as it was.

"What have you done?" Enrico glared at Bellini.

"Why?" Alia asked in a panic, witnessing their sovereign struggling for life.

Bellini stood shaking his head in denial, equally horrified at the unfolding tragedy. Isabella, perhaps foretelling a poorly matched bridal couple, remained calmly in her seat, even managing to slide one more unseen forkful of the Frango em pepitoria into her mouth. The King's ministers, all recent appointments to their jobs during the transition period from Manuel's cousin John, read the tea leaves of death and hit the panic button. Listening to Enrico accuse Bellini, they ordered the chef seized immediately.

Contigo obliged. He grabbed Bellini around the waist, removed his apron with a single tug, then held the chef's arms behind his back.

"We meet again, sir!" he said to Bellini.

"Someone do something!" cried Alia, kneeling down to the struggling King.

"There is nothing to be done. It is God's will. Hallelujah!" Isabella pronounced with a tinge of glee.

"Total bullshit! Let me through!"

Forty-six-year-old legendary explorer, Bartolomeu Dias had accepted the dinner invitation of the new King only a few hours earlier. He hoped to discuss yet another proposed journey to the horn of Africa, which he had discovered and named Cape of Storms back in his heyday. He had little patience for the arrogant new King, but the upkeep on his winter home in Lisbon, summer home in Porto, and the appetites of his twenty-three hungry Lusitano horses, was crushing him. Embracing his 'B' list status, he swallowed his pride and rode over to Tavares, hoping to pitch the monarch on his newest adventure.

Manuel writhed on the terrazzo floor, his eyes had bugged out, and his face turned imminent death blue.

"It's something he ate, not the Lord God calling his damn number. I need..."

Dias looked around the room, searching for something. He caught site of Bellini's waist, which without his apron revealed the ever-present stiletto stuck in his belt.

"There! You! That man has a blade. Give it to me," he ordered Contigo.

No one doubted the allegiance to the crown and the heroic stature of Portugal's most famed explorer. To the gasps of all assembled. Contigo reached for the blade. Alia raced over to Contigo. She grabbed the stiletto and ran it over to Dias who was kneeling over the fading King.

"Apologies Majesty, little sting coming!"

Despite Manuel's eyes bugging out, Dias rapidly but precisely made an incision in the front of Manuel's neck. The well-used stiletto cleanly sliced through the cartilage above the clavicle, sinking its tip gently into the King's windpipe.

The King grabbed a breath of air. His eyes grew even larger in blessed relief.

"We need something to hold this open, or he'll die!" exhorted.

"Bamboo!" barked Alia, reaching for the centerpiece on a nearby table.

"Absolutely forbidden! The King detests bamboo," declared the Minister of Finance, stepping between Alia and Dias spreading his arms.

"You, sir, are an idiot. Move, or I will stab your genitalia with this stiletto."

Dias displayed the weapon, and the Minister instantly hopped aside. Alia grabbed a lengthy piece of the tubing snapping it in half before handing it over.

Having experienced a similar predicament in the arid coastal zone of southern Africa, Dias cautiously placed the bamboo cut end into the incision. The pin-drop stillness in the room gave way as everyone heard the King's first breath emerge through his new improvised airway.

"It's a miracle. God's will," flatly pronounced the disappointed Isabella.

"Nothing of the kind, madam. During my travels I happened to witness a native Chief choking on a piece of sugar cane near the Horn of Africa."

Shouts of huzzah, plus a loud round of applause, doused Restaurant Tavares, with a palpable multi-level relief. Dias completed the job by wrapping the King's neck in a collection of aristocratic scarves and bandanas. After resting on the floor for another thirty minutes the King slowly returned to function, albeit with a bamboo straw extending ingloriously from his neck. Awake, aware, and regally angry, the King motioned for his men to take Bellini into custody.

In this particular case, Bellini knew he was unequivocally innocent of any deliberate foul play. He was simply a victim of the King's undiagnosed allergy to almonds. As the throng of royal entourage departed Tavares, Alia noticed one person who did not.

Chapter 29

DISCOVER THIS PAL...

Somewhere in the vast archipelago of human behaviors floating inside the human brain exists a moral compass. For most, it floats illuminated above the islands in plain sight. Although perhaps dusty, in slight disrepair, or somewhat dimmed by underuse, it remains substantially useful and accessible. Marco Bellini fell into the category of "not most people." Marco's compass lay covered in vines and banished to an untracked, isolated, bat guano cavern in the deepest recesses of his island group. Overcoming the obstacles in reaching it required a machete, pith helmet, a Windex-soaked rag to kick it back into working order, and the conviction to begin the task. His incapacitating fear cock-blocked a clear path to any noble, honest, or selfless act. He lacked the skillset to navigate through any obstacle other than self-preservation. This narrow lane left no room for sympathy, remorse, regret, or accountability. His conceit continued to blur any other options. It remained the reason why, in his stony hubris, it mattered not one iota who became roadkill to his survival.

Bellini stewed in the palace lockup for the two weeks it took King Manuel I to heal enough to conduct a kangaroo court. Given the word of mouth spreading through Lisbon's social circles, Restaurant Tavares remained strategically closed. Alia and Enrico spent the two weeks in a perpetual, sleepless panic over the ramifications in coming within a bamboo straws-length of offing the country's new monarch.

Contigo, special forces chief, visited the restaurant several times during those two weeks. He probed the twins on their hiring of Bellini, inquiring about his credentials and background.

Alia had a jumble of thoughts rolling around her brain, chief among them *survival*.

Enrico launched into a mind-numbing dissertation on numerology and interpretation which uninterrupted, would have outlasted the sunlight. After three espressos, more than an hour of patience, and simple self-preservation, Contigo finally called it quits.

"Can you please sum this all up for me?"

"Arrogance and discontent," Enrico blurted out.

"At? From? Because?" Contigo tried to force a definitive thought from Enrico.

Enrico wavered for another moment, struggling to arrive at some conclusion. "Plus, something I could never put my finger on. I did always suspect something. Right, Alia?"

Enrico shook his head. All of it confirmed that Contigo's initial gut reaction upon his first encounter with Bellini many months previous, had rung true.

Bellini stewed in the palace prison waiting for the opportunity to exonerate himself.

"Looks very bad for you, my friend. Anything you'd like to share?"

Contigo had paid Bellini a visit. His only visitor.

"Fuck you."

"Nice share, but not very helpful to your cause."

"I'm innocent of this whole business. I'm a chef, not a murderer."

"It doesn't look that way from this side of the bars. By the way, you never did pick up your bags from the exchequer. Forgot?"

Contigo thought the sarcasm might shake loose some truth via anger. Bellini crossed his arms, raised his middle finger and remained silent.

"Have it your way."

Within the hour a retinue of three guards released Bellini from his cell, and escorted him upstairs to the kangaroo court in session.

Neck dashingly wrapped in a white scarf, the King sat on his throne. Still brooding over her fiancée's miraculous salvation, the dour Isabella, sweaty and weighed down by a designer horse blanket of black velvet, sat nearby, observing the proceedings.

"Thank you, sire. You shall live to see the wisdom of your generosity!"

On bended knee, Bartolomeu Dias thanked the King for returning the favor of one life saved for another. Manuel had granted the funds and approval for his journey around the horn of Africa, making only one royal demand of the expedition.

"And you *will* find the sacred kingdom of Prester John to the benefit of all."

"I swear on my life, sire, I will not fail."

"Of course, of course," Manuel said. "Let's keep it moving."

Many of the Restaurant Tavares eyewitnesses stood on tiptoe, anticipating some righteous retribution.

"Herald, read the charges," commanded the King.

"Marco Bellini is accused of the premeditated and willful poisoning of the rightful and newly crowned King of Portugal, Manuel I."

The King's face went from approval to a querulous disdain.

"Why does that include 'newly crowned'? What's that got to do with anything? Newly crowned, recently crowned, I HAVE THE CROWN. I am THE KING. PERIOD. He tried to poison me. AGAIN."

The poor herald looked askance around the room.

"Apologies Sire, I did not write this, I merely read it. I have no answer."

"Who wrote this drivel?"

The King scanned the room.

The herald searched for someone to step up and claim

accountability. The odds of someone claiming accountability were only slightly better than spotting a unicorn grazing on bamboo in the palace gardens. Fearing for his own neck, the young man improvised.

"Uh, Sire, perhaps I misread it?" he offered sheepishly.

"You request a royal do-over! Granted."

"Marco Bellini is accused of premeditated and willful poisoning of the rightful King of Portugal, Manuel I?"

"Exactly!"

Even though his life hung by a thin filament of inopportune anaphylaxis Bellini's survival instinct remained undiminished. He focused solely on a means to escape the fire storm in front of him.

"I am surrounded by morons and egotists," Bellini defiantly muttered under his breath.

He was mostly correct. It was the perfect crowd for his planned defense.

"I was a pawn; Jews did this," he said.

"Jews? What?"

Startled out of her oblivion, Isabella junior, who had been trying to disappear inside her deep cushioned royal chair in the corner of the room bolted upright. Any defamation of Jews rang the Inquisition happy bell for the daughter of the religious whackos sitting on the Spanish throne, wreaking havoc and genocide on the Jews of Spain. She instantly rose.

"Absolutely right!" Isabella proclaimed.

"What on earth do the Jews have to do with this?" Manuel felt the room begin to spin.

"Jews connive, Jews plot. It is common knowledge," Isabella added.

As Bellini had hoped, an ally had emerged, no less an ally than the daughter of Spain. The hook had sunk in. He only had to work the reel.

"What is this ludicrous idea?" The King threw up his hands. "Hold your tongue woman!"

"That's the Jew right there! Why not ask him?"

Heads turned as all eyes followed Bellini's pointing across the room.

"To whom do you refer sir?" the King asked.

"Uh oh, not good..." thought Contigo.

Those pesky Visigoths, who definitely got around, built São Jorge Castle in 480 A.D. They majestically perched it atop Lisbon's highest namesake hill as a symbol of their empiric strength—location, location, location! Sounded good right up until the Moors throttled, then mercilessly crushed them out of existence. Not particularly fans of the Visigoth aesthetic, the Moors set to work on a major remodel, completing significant upgrades and modifications during their 11th century stay. Since no one wants to be the last invader stuck holding the scepter when the original homeowners return, the Moors created a series of hidden passageways designed for rapid escape in the event of a besieged castle.

As Sao Jorge grew, so did Lisbon. Below the castle's highly defensible placement, the burgeoning city spread out in all cardinal directions.

Contigo assessed his odds in determining whether to fight or flee. He quickly deduced his last grain of salvation sand was briskly spiraling down the hourglass.

As the head of Manuel's security force, he had spent hours mentally cataloging every known and unknown passageway throughout the castle. Contigo now stealthily slid to the back of the packed throne room. Save his oldest friend, Longshort, who watched the moment with grave concern, Contigo managed to remain unnoticed.

His right hand moved across a row of books. He yanked on a copy of John Lydgate's barnburner romance novel, *Complaint of the Black*

Knight. Pulling on the spine triggered a rotating set of shelves that silently turned, revealing a pitch-dark void. Contigo leaped into the darkness. A steep, mold-slick, brick channel caught him. In an instant, he launched on a high-speed slide through the narrow Moorish-dug tunnel. Although scraping his sides along the snaking path, his exit was completed in a matter of minutes. Bumped, bruised, but intact he emerged from a dense pile of dried conifer needles at the base of the castle hill. Free for the moment, he sprinted home to warn his only daughter of the impending danger headed their way.

Chapter 30
I WILL IF YOU WILL

At Sea

The tempest took a brief, atmospheric, coffee break. Drawing a line through the seas with his arm, Lanning had kept his eyes glued to the survivor's last position. Felipe, recovered and at the wheel, navigated the L'Aquila between the falling swells according to Lanning's track. Not knowing their cardinal direction became subordinate to surviving the perilous conditions.

Fortunately, their course took them downwind of the storm. None of that prevented a steady stream of nausea for Hector, and healthy amount of doubt from Lorenzo's cynical birthright.

"They're drowned by now. Why bother?"

"That's dark, Zo. If it were you?" Lanning countered.

"Death comes for everyone in time."

The sounds of Hector's retching cut through the constant wind and rain.

"Couldn't have said it better, Hector!" Lanning dismissed Lorenzo. "Uncle! Can you please give something to Hector to help him."

Shafi pulled a ratty, apparently decades-old piece of raw ginger from somewhere on his person and shook it in the air. "I've offered."

"No chance, that is disgusting," gagged Hector.

Shafi threw his hands in the air, "We've been down this road the other day. If you…"

"THERE!! Three! I see THREE over there!" Filippa shouted leaning against the rail pointing. "Starboard."

"Look at you, using sailor language," called Felipe down from the tiller.

"I'm a quick study."

As the L'Aquila forded the waves, three bobbing heads came into view.

"Zo! Grab a line," Felipe ordered.

"They're alive!" Lorenzo now ran to the port side gunnel with a length of rope.

"One shot at this. We're not about to turn around," said Felipe.

"Ready! Someone grab my waist."

Nantucket ran over to Lorenzo and lashed a line around both their waists.

"HOLY SHIT!" Lorenzo's face turned whiter than it already was.

"Agreed," answered Lanning.

Lorenzo hesitated throwing the line. "Must I? Really?"

"Do it!" Lanning commanded.

Filippa also recognized two of the three people in the water. "Shit!"

"It's the right thing to do, son." Shafi pulled a curved knife from his belt and headed for the rail. "Hector get over here!"

Hector wiped his mouth, and met up at the rail.

"Last chance." Lorenzo spun the rope in the air, preparing to let loose.

"Do it!" Felipe commanded.

A perfect shot. All three waterlogged people lunged then grabbed the rope. The L'Aquila hit a giant swell, dragging the survivors along with them. Nantucket and Lorenzo began a rapid, steady pull on the rope. The three sucked in gallons of water as they were dragged through the ocean swells. They banged hard against the L'Aquila's starboard water line. Hector threw another rope over the side. The biggest of the three drowned rats caught hold of it. Hector easily pulled the one man to safety.

"Welcome aboard, Contigo! Promise kept." Lanning had jumped off the stern deck to greet the stocky survivor. The other two men were hoisted aboard along with their flotation device. The cracked remnants of the wheel all that was left of the Queen of Sheba.

"Introductions?" Lanning looked at Contigo.

"Well, we both know this gentleman!"

"Marco Bellini? What the hell?" Lanning looked dumbfounded.

"Never mind this scoundrel, I'd like you to meet my kid!"

"Your kid?!"

"Long story," said Contigo.

At that moment a twenty-five-foot bombing wave struck the stern side of the L'Aquila. The cascade of water bowled over the boat, flinging everyone to the deck like so many bowling pins exploding on a perfect strike. Coffee break over!

Hector scraped himself up from the deck, grabbing both Destemido and Bellini by their collars. "What do we do with these, Captain?"

Lanning looked back over to Contigo, who tilted his head towards Bellini.

"Drop the left hand and stuff the right hand in the cargo hold. Everyone lash yourself to the ship as best you can. Filippa, get back in the cabin."

"Hell no!"

Filippa rushed up to Lanning and Felipe.

"My future is your future, Captains!" She tied herself to the two brothers and held on for her life.

"Edge of the world, here we come! Right, brother!" Felipe held the wheel firmly in his grip, guiding them through the unrelenting storm.

Wave after wave pelted the L'Aquila, leaving just enough time for a gasp of breath between each subsequent swell. Exhausted bodies clutched on to anything near them for stability. With Rodrigo vanished, Hector and Nantucket manned the port and starboard side lines. Shafi lashed himself to a capstan on the main deck, where he relayed and translated Felipe's orders to the two novice sailors. *'Luff the mainsail,' 'reef the jib'* became *'untie that line and let it slide through your hands', 'pick up that rope and pull with all your might.'*

Survival was the priority. Steering for a safe port would have been a futile and dangerous risk. As he navigated the storm, Felipe's eyes seemingly darted in all directions at once on guard for rogue waves, cloud bursts, or worse, the unknown.

Hour upon drenching hour passed with no relief. Lorenzo tied a substantial length of rope to his waist, allowing him to roam the main deck. He alternated spelling Hector or Nantucket, depending on who needed the break. Despite his larger size, Hector's stomach upset proved more taxing on his abilities. Fatigue soon overwhelmed him. Nantucket, however, proved tireless. Though willowy lean, Lorenzo matched Nantucket for stamina. His experience matched the Indian's pure strength.

"You are a beast, Lorenzo!" Shafi applauded his efforts.

"Tell my father!"

"If you survive."

"I will, if you will."

"Oh...my...god...what...manner of devil or god is that?" Hector, exhausted and perpetually terrified for hours on end, dropped the line he had been clutching and pointed up to the mast head.

"The Great Spirit has come to bring us home." An exhausted Nantucket let loose his line, taking a knee in reverence.

Both brothers gazed up. Leaping blue tongues of light skipped about the air above the boat in a display of frenetic madness. The luminous blue hues continued to splay out in all directions at once, like sprites dancing centered around the iron sheathed top of the L'Aquila's mast.

"It must be the end of times. We have surely reached the edge of existence," Filippa folded her hands in the prayer position. She too took a knee, mirroring Nantucket.

The blue sprites leaped about without the sound or crackling that accompanies the fierceness of lightening.

Lorenzo looked around, waited another moment to be sure, then also took a knee.

"If our journey in this world must end, so be it. We shall go no further! Praise unto her who redeems us and shepherds us. For she is the one, the true, the..."

"Not the right moment, you clown," said Felipe.

Lorenzo looked miffed as Lanning, Felipe, and Shafi all shared a glance, a wink, and a smile.

"What?" asked Filippa rising. "I smell bullshit. Out with what you know, so we don't continue to make fools of ourselves."

"Black magic?" asked Hector.

"St Elmo's fire!" Lanning said with a Cheshire cat grin.

"It's a good thing," Felipe added.

"A very good thing!" Shafi agreed.

St Elmo's fire was named for Saint Erasmus, the patron saint of sailors. Storms that generate a great deal of friction create powerful electrical fields that extend down from the clouds (where the elephants live) to the ground. This charged air has the power to break up molecules of water into their sub-atomic parts—electrons—creating plasma. Naturally, the four sailors knew none of this science, but they did understand that this was a positive sign.

"I've never seen it, but it's supposed to mean the worst has ended!" Lanning attempted to calm the crew.

"Everyone's multi-flavored end of times moments can wait for another day," concluded Lorenzo.

The tongues of light subsided. Feeling a sense of relief, the crew let down their guard. As if the storm had been waiting for such an unguarded moment, a series of three giant swells swamped the boat from the stern.

"TIE IN!" yelled Lanning.

The next two hours of tempest wiped out any optimism gained from the St. Elmo's phenomenon. Each crew member reached deeper into their tapped well of endurance. After so many hours of unrelenting battle, all save Felipe collapsed from exhaustion and stress.

At some point an exhausted Felipe simply fainted. He had ordered all sails furled to take advantage of the driving current which had gripped the boat. One moment he was awake holding course, the next his body collapsed. He lay folded onto the deck with one hand still clutching the wheel.

The waves continued pounding against the hull. Luckily, the current had dragged them along a favorable path. Each swell hitting the stern drove the worn and weary L'Aquila further and further out onto the Great Sea.

Sometime during the final hours of the night, sliding towards the wee hours of the morning, the sky poured out its full complement of elephants.

Chapter 31

AFTERMATH

As *the stone-grey cloud cover* dissipated, the haze of a super-saturated nightmare dissolved into a bluing sky. The white-capped ocean inhaled deeply, taking a minute to calm itself down. Out in the middle of the boundless ocean bobbed the resilient, storm-weary L'Aquila. The black-pitch-covered caravel rocked uneasily while the prevailing current dragged it along like another random piece of floating seaweed. The shredded lateen foresail hung from its mast, sporadically fluttering with a fading breeze from an unknown compass point. The mainsail, another blob of haphazardly rolled canvas, lay drooping onto the deck, barely tied to its boom.

The early morning light revealed all manner of bodies strewn across the deck. Most splayed about lashed by ropes to sagged rigging, fallen ballast barrels, deck latches, the masts, and gunnels. Lanning and Filippa were coupled together. Nantucket simply sat upright tied to an empty bird cage, while Lorenzo lay enmeshed in a Gordian knot of tar-covered rope tied to the ship's forward capstan. More hours passed as the sun rose warm and healing in the calm skies.

"YES!"

Clothed head to toe in his red, yellow, and black harlequin doublet with matching jodhpurs, Lorenzo had gradually floated up to consciousness. His hands trolled up and down his body, pausing for the essential inventory before reveling in his personal salvation.

"YES!" he repeated.

Fear had momentarily kept him from breaking the seal on his eyes until confirmation that life still coursed through his body. Knowing he lived triggered a shift from simple existence to the business of survival.

Bracing himself for the worst, he decided on a dual course of action. "I will open my eyes then sit up in an epic flourish of heroic courage."

Lorenzo had figured his words were spoken only within the confines of his mind. The familiar laugh echoing around him told him differently.

"All out loud, I take it?"

Lanning stood over his friend holding his nose.

"Oh, one hundred percent. For better or worse, I feel like I know a whole different part of you."

"Definitely your good fortune, for I am quite wonderful!" Lorenzo quickly began to free himself from his self-inflicted bondage.

"Phew!" Lanning fanned his hand in front of his nose.

"I reek, don't I?"

"Extraordinarily! Don't be embarrassed about..." offered Lanning backing away.

"Embarrassed? Not in the least. I am alive, WE are alive! More than I could have hoped for." He took a moment to inhale himself deeply and wince. "Woohoo! Hell yes, I reek of piss!" he pronounced unabashedly. "Piss is life and I, my friend, am fully full of piss!"

Lanning flashed a smile at his best friend who was wrestling with the tangle.

"You've got to get out of that outfit! Can you get yourself free, or do you need a blade?"

"Eventually," he answered. "I don't understand how I tied myself up like this."

"A perfect metaphor for your mind - confused, but amazing in short spurts," chuckled Lanning.

"Any idea where we are?" Lorenzo asked.

"This is the Age of Discovery, lad. We get to figure that out for ourselves!" said Shafi while sorting out the sail cloth strewn about the deck.

"Not helpful, Uncle," scolded Lanning.

"Truly, not!" added Felipe.

Lorenzo was making progress, but still struggled. "Was I the lone straggler?"

"Certainly the most amusing," answered Felipe, trying to reclaim some of Lorenzo's loose ropes. "Whoo, way too foul. I'll let these dry out for a while." He, too, fanned his nose and moved off.

"Yes, I know," dismissed Lorenzo.

Squinting his eyes against the emerging sun, Shafi looked up at the sky. "Spectacular and a most welcome sight!"

"HEADS UP!" The shout came from the doorway of the captain's quarters. Filippa had emerged just in time.

"SHIT!" Shafi shielded himself just in time to receive a fifteen-pound steelhead salmon falling out of the sky onto his broad bent back.

"That's a bad omen!" yelled Hector hovering by the mainsail boom.

"It's a salmon!" said Lanning plainly.

"Good hunter," stoically proclaimed Nantucket as he squeezed the sea water from his shirt onto the sodden deck of the L'Aquila.

"Doug is alive!" Filippa was overjoyed to celebrate the return of her falcon. She watched the bird gently waft down from high above the mast to neatly glide onto his perch inside the open bird cage.

"Touching scene."

All heads turned towards the cargo hold as Destemido, the last minute guest aboard the L'Aquila, climbed up onto the deck. Destemido was followed by Contigo.

"Damn! You survived. My bad!" Lanning responded to Destemido's sarcastic comment.

The pirate strutted over to the foredeck to confront Lanning.

"I am commandeering this vessel."

An audible gurgle reached the ears of everyone in proximity. Realizing it originated from his own stomach, the pirate gulped down air as a counter-measure. The hesitation undermined the intended force in his declaration.

"Not because I want to..." Gag, cough, inhale.

"Uh, but because you *have to*?" suggested a bemused Lanning.

Gag, cough, rasping inhale. Destemido raised a hand signaling the answer was forthcoming. That was followed by a groan-gag combination as the pirate tried to suppress the vomit. The gathering crew watched the struggling brigand.

Almost freed from his self-imposed prison, Lorenzo filled the pause. "But, because we need you to?"

Destemido surrendered to one final dry heave followed by a stream of vomit projected onto his boots. He wiped his mouth on his sleeve before finally finishing his thought.

"It's obvious we are all going to either die, or eat each other, before we see land again."

"Gross *and* dark," said Lorenzo.

Lanning stepped in to abbreviate the conversation. "Appreciate the offer, but we're all good. Contigo, you doing alright?"

Lanning was concerned about his friend, who looked equally sallow. Contigo flashed a thumbs-up wiping some remnant vomit from his chin. Even the stoutest sailors could succumb to uneven seas. Regardless of station or calling, no one was impervious to upset when it happened. Destemido continued retching on the deck, seriously undermining the gravitas needed for any successful takeover.

"What now, Captain?" Filippa asked the question everyone wanted answered.

"How about I grill this up?" Shafi held the fish by its tail.

Hector scoffed, "This entire boat already reeks of dead fish and hurl. I can't eat that."

True enough. Even if the fish had dropped from heaven like some cruel biblical joke, the nauseating stench of rotting fish hung over the L'Aquila like a lingering fog bank.

"Well Hector, you know where to find the only other option," said Shafi.

Hector's expression turned from disdain to glum as he descended the ladder into the hold.

Finally freed from bondage Lorenzo stood. "Well, I'm starving, and I love fish. Food is the first order of survival."

"Actually, changing those clothes is the first order of our survival." Filippa held her nose as she walked by him.

"Into what?"

"Anything else."

She continued over to the cage and reached her arm inside. Doug hopped onto her forearm.

Felipe trolled the deck, gathering ropes, checking hatches, and placing things back in order. Aside from a pitying glance or two, everyone ignored the folded pirate dry-heaving on the foredeck.

Lanning approached Contigo. "Where's Bellini?"

"Bound and gagged in the bilge, as he should be. The better question was Filippa's. Where are we, and what happens next?"

"Something always happens next," Shafi quipped as he roasted his fish on a makeshift grill next to the main mast.

Nantucket, who had barely spoken over the past days, scanned the horizon. He watched as the clouds in the far distance lifted and dissolved. A silence draped over all things.

"Wisdom sits in places," he said to himself.

Privacy on a boat is not a given. It is granted by the generosity and humility of those who travel together. In this case, Nantucket's comment was not private.

"Do you know this place?" asked Lorenzo, coiling his urine-soaked ropes to dry out in the sun.

"I've heard that expression before!" said Lanning.

Chapter 32
TAKE A BREATH

The savory smell of grilled salmon mingled with a potpourri of scents hovering over the L'Aquila: a bouquet of saturated pine, rancid bilge water, rotting bore worms, wet burlap, plus random puddles of vomit accented by a hint of dried urine. Lanning had grabbed a small piece of salmon before retiring to his cabin for a moment of thoughtful solitude.

Lucky to be alive was no longer the most pressing sentiment shared by the surviving crew. Aside from the two new passengers, Destemido and Bellini, Lanning had no idea where upon the great vast sea they were floating, or how far from land and rescue they were. He knew the current had dragged them to the west and south, but not how far or how fast. What about food and fresh water? How long did they have to solve these hurdles? Spending its time transiting by line of sight between the comfort of Algeciras and Tangier, the L'Aquila carried no navigation instruments of value. Dead reckoning with no landmarks and only the sun, moon, and stars to guide them, would be challenging.

"Any land will do, brother!"

Felipe stuck his head into the cabin.

"Agreed. See what you can do."

Felipe shut the door. Shafi opened it less than a minute later.

"This is not your fault."

"I know. Wait, someone said it was my fault?"

"Not really. I am being reassuring."

"That's not reassuring."

"I thought it was."

"Didn't actually play that way for me, Uncle."

"No need to apologize," Shafi replied.

"That was sarcasm, not an apology. Feel free to leave."

"What matters most is how you walk through the fire." Shafi bowed his head and left.

An immediate knock on the door followed.

"What?" said an increasingly irritated Lanning.

"I didn't whistle." The huge head and shoulders filled up the space with innocence.

"No one's blaming *you*, Hector."

"Didn't say 'rabbit' either."

"Stop worrying. You're in the clear with me."

Hector looked relieved as he was set to close the door. Lanning sensed the interruptions were not done.

"Who else is out there?"

Lorenzo leaped around Hector, still wearing his sodden jester jodhpurs.

"Pal, you've got to find a way out of this shit before we start eating each other. After all..."

"Happy to be alive? Shouldn't your joy have lasted a bit longer?"

"Positively still good to be alive, but what good is delaying a painful death by starvation, being eaten alive by my fellow man, or falling off the lurking edge of the world?"

"You're too smart for that."

"Says who? I'm as susceptible to the mundane fears of man as anyone else confronted with their own mortality. Plus, the bad omen of the fish from heaven."

"You ate it. How can you eat a bad omen?"

Confronted by the hypocrisy of his actions, Lorenzo simply dismissed it.

"Hungry."

"Everyone's outside the door now, right?"

"Yep."

"For god's sake. I can't make everyone happy. I'm not tequila! Tell them to go away. I need a minute."

Distress etched on his face; Lorenzo stormed out. "No one takes me seriously, when I'm serious!"

Lanning enjoyed a whole two minutes of solitude.

"You needn't be the hero," Filippa peeked her head through the door.

"I am the captain." He waved her in.

"That's different than a hero." She shut the door.

"Barricade that damn door, please?"

Filippa looked around the cabin for something to hold the door closed. Lanning made his way over to her. She turned to put her back to the door. Reaching around her, he twisted a small block of wood positioned over the doorframe. The end of it extended down to cover six inches of the door wedging it closed. Filippa wrapped her arms around Lanning, who matched her embrace with his own.

They kissed. A long, languid, passionate kiss that took both of them far away from the reality of the moment. Slowly they made their way over to the only bunk of any comfort onboard the L'Aquila. Moving into each other, they lost themselves in a surreal bubble of time. Granted a very short time. Lanning felt overtaken by his own emotional roller coaster. A desperation for an escape from his fears made him vulnerable. That vulnerability clutched Filippa close.

His inner voice, quieted for all too brief a time, re-emerged to harass him. 'I feel affection...wait, what? What am I saying? She's not a cat or a dog, or my favorite horse. I lust for her. Oh shit, that's an even more ridiculous thought. Completely insulting and lame. 'I feel lust for you. No one says that. Why do I have no game with this woman? Everything in my head sounds adolescent. I love you? Ugh, way, way too soon. Attracted? Obviously, we're in bed together. Why say anything? Yes, that's the answer. Say nothing, thereby actually saying everything.

"HEY!"

Lanning was startled by Filippa snapping her fingers in his face.

"Over here!" She cradled his face in her hands, "Having a good time in there?" She tapped on his head.

"You heard me?"

"Of course not, but I can tell. You vaporized on me."

"Sorry. I was trying to sort out my feelings for you."

"You have feelings for me? So soon. That's nice."

"You don't have any for...I'm trying to say the right thing."

Filippa waved him off. They pulled apart.

"We're in the middle of an unknown ocean, with a crippled ship. The odds of a long relationship are pretty minimal. How about we don't worry so much about that for now? This is not the right time for any 'moves' or whatever you've got going on in your head."

"All fair points. But..."

"But what? Don't be so fucking careful. I'm not a porcelain doll..."

She paused to take stock of Lanning, "wait...I'm not your first?"

"Funny, I was about to say the same thing to you." Lanning matched her tone.

"Uh huh." Filippa appeared to know better.

"Maybe I'm your first seagoing man?" Lanning said with a note of pride.

"Maybe, and I'm your first courtesan?"

"Hah!" he teased. "Absolutely not. I mean Algeciras is a small town, but I do get around a bit."

"Oh yeah, I can tell."

Lanning's mind drifted off for a moment as he noticed her scent had filled the room. He opted to ignore her last flippant retort. "Mmmm...night jasmine. Even after a storm."

"What's that?"

"How can you still smell like night jasmine?" He threw his arms up in the air.

She smiled.

"You're right. There are bigger things to be concerned about." Lanning realized he had to deal with the larger crisis looming for all aboard.

"What's up with you and confrontation?" she asked.

"Nothing," he said defensively. "I've had days of nothing but confrontation. I'm all about confrontation. How can you even suggest..."

She cut him off, "Not what I meant. You avoid confronting your own dangers. Your own unknown."

"How about at sea **yesterday**? How about that unknown?"

He had no stomach for another level of conflict on top of simple survival.

"Beyond yes. One hundred percent awesome. I did not say you could not *handle* a conflict. There's a difference between rising to a challenge and challenging yourself to rise."

"I think Shafi is affecting everyone on board. Is that your best post-love making conversation?"

While he didn't enjoy this conversation; he could not deny its truth. On reflection, he had been frozen in an endless loop of repetitive behavior: take an order, fill an order, get paid, repeat same. That loop had kept him safe by avoidance.

"There is more to life than hummus!" He blurted out.

"No doubt. And?" Filippa began to pull herself back together.

"Just echoing you. With a bit of, um, flourish!" Lanning declared.

"Delaying the unknown doesn't help alleviate the frustration of inaction."

"Is there some question coming?" he asked.

"I'm sure there is. I don't know your questions. It only seems to me that you are either not asking, or don't want to answer them."

Holy shit, he thought, she had wormed her way into his brain. She probably knew even more than she let on.

"Do I constantly talk out loud? How are you so inside my head?"

"I've seen you wrestle with yourself. It's not magic. Believe me, I understand. I have spent a ridiculous portion of my life waiting or even expecting a rescue that has never come."

"Fuck the journey, Filippa. I want answers."

Filippa raised herself up onto her elbows and leaned against the inside wall of the bunk space. "Fuck the journey! Amen, Captain!" She kissed him on the cheek.

"Strangely all this just brought my father, whom I can't remember much of at all, to mind."

"That makes both of us. I will never know my father," Filippa replied.

Lanning waited a beat before continuing, "We don't truly know each other much at all, do we?"

"I think we do. A bit."

"I'd like to know you more, and I hope we have that time."

"Me too."

"We could be out here for quite some time to come. I need to get back to it." Lanning got up to head out the door. "We can talk about all this inside stuff later, yes?"

Filippa nodded.

Chapter 33

HOODS & SCIMITARS

According to the hard and fast made-up rules of the sea, the captain shouldered the burden of consequences. It was easy when it was easy, which it had been anything but over the past three days. Lanning, being a fair-minded soul, offered his crew along with reluctant guests a voice in what course of action they should take. He called an all-hands meeting. Despite his own contempt, he included Bellini.

"We need to talk about our options," Lanning began.

"It's considered more of a predicament, than a situation, by definition."

"Lorenzo, seriously?"

Bellini leaned against the port side gunnel mostly disinterested, yet fully content to throw shade on the entire assemblage. "It's fairly simple. We are all dead."

"You first!" Contigo replied.

"Felipe and I have calculated our stores. We have a single barrel of fresh water which is not great, but!"

"Hummus! We've got a shit ton of hummus," added Felipe.

"Hummus will save us," said Shafi calmly. "My father ate nothing else, and lived until one hundred and twenty-two."

"From that shit? Impossible!" said Destemido.

Hummus was one of the first true superfoods. It contained nutrients – vitamins, fiber, citrus, and oils, that pushed the Mediterranean retirement age past one hundred. One cup contains over four hundred calories. They might get thirsty, but they would not die from lack of nutrition. Hummus would sustain them for weeks, maybe even months, without any other food source.

Felipe continued the damage assessment. "Our sail is in tatters and our mast needs repair."

"I'm less seasick."

"Ginger," Shafi deadpanned.

"That's great news, Hector," said Lanning, flipping a thumbs-up.

"I can figure out a dead reckoning course from sighting the sun and the stars," Felipe said confidently.

Three days at sea were packed with repairs, assessment of provisions, along with rationing calculations. Mercifully, they were calm days with a consistent, non-threatening breeze coming from what the brothers concluded as the northwest. Each day, Felipe, Lanning, and Destemido begrudgingly cooperated to determine their ambling course, based on the position of the sun, moon, the north star, and their combined sailor acumen.

Filippa and Lanning spent the nights together. Their pillow talk was interrupted one morning by a commotion on deck.

"SHIP! I see a ship!"

Felipe banged on the door, "You need to get out here!"

Fiddling with his glasses, the unmistakable glint on the horizon had caught Shafi's attention. The billowing sails glowed with golden rays of sunlight. The illuminated ship's hull was visible from miles away.

"Definitely has us spotted," noted Felipe.

"Coming this way for certain. I suggest we prepare to defend ourselves." Destemido took a command stance as Lanning emerged to make his way up to the wheel. Filippa followed a moment later.

"Easy does it, Captain. You're barely qualified as a guest."

Filippa had her first chance to take a close look at their former adversary. They exchanged a touch too long a glance before the pirate looked away. Maybe they were both distracted by the sudden chaotic, metal-on-wood cacophony emerging from the hold.

"Someone wants some fresh air," said Lorenzo.

"Hector, bring him up."

"I can do it."

Nantucket peered down into the hold. "You stop now." When the noise continued, he simply jumped down. Everyone heard one singular thud, then the banging stopped. The site of Marco Bellini soaring out of the hold stunned the crew. They watched as he crashed landed on the deck in a befuddled heap.

The shaken, disheveled man managed to sit up, and unruffle himself while trying to reconnect with his dignity. "Fuck all of you. Especially you!" He pointed at Destemido.

Other than witnessing his rescue in the midst of the tempest, Lorenzo had no clue who the grungy man on the deck might be. Still, he couldn't help but make a shrewd observation. "Unless you did a header into the hummus, you've got vomit pretty much everywhere."

"Gee, I figured he'd be most upset with me," said Contigo.

"We are going to talk about the history between you two," said Lanning.

"We will."

"We can't outrun anyone in our condition." Felipe addressed the overriding truth bearing down on them by the minute. He had a fixed gaze on the approaching ship.

Lanning had no time to address anything else. "Señor Bellini, you can either enjoy the fresh sea air and stay silent, or enjoy an open-water swim. Up to you."

Bellini realized that he was at a severely compromised disadvantage. Silence served him equally well.

Felipe shaded his eyes and peered ahead. "It's a beast of a ship, brother!"

"Where is your long lens?" Destemido leaned against the port side gunnel, shielding his eyes from the reflecting sun. "That ship means us harm. I'm sure of it."

"Gone with the storm, I'm afraid," answered Lorenzo.

"There are always alternatives." Lanning feared the pirate was correct.

Felipe bobbed his head between both captains. "Gotta go with the pirate, brother."

An incredulous Lanning stared down his little adoptive brother. "Seriously? My own brother?"

"No doubt, that is one big-ass ship," Lorenzo chimed in.

"First, it's a galleon, so the better description is 'deadly massive.'" Destemido began to shake his head. "Yep, damn it. Far more important, it's got cannons. I can see them from here. At the very least, falconets."

"What the heck is a falconet?" asked a perplexed Hector.

"Your eyes are amazing! I can't see that from here." Glasses dangling from his neck, Shafi squinted to confirm the sighting.

"You can't see shit regardless of how far away anything is," Felipe shot back.

Contigo looked sideways at Destemido. "How do you know so much about this?"

"Most likely they're slavers. I'd go below if I were you, Indian."

"Nantucket does not hide. I stand my ground," replied the oak tree.

"Not against fifty slavers you won't. Sometimes the smarter move is to hide. Isn't that right, Contigo?" said Destemido.

Contigo glared at Destemido.

"Have to agree again," said Felipe, shrugging.

"You have wisdom that did not show itself in our previous

engagement," added Shafi.

"You sir, are no SIR!" Filippa stepped forward, looking directly at Destemido.

Destemido scolded Lanning, "Control your woman."

Filippa laughed. "That's a false conviction. As you could see through me, I see you just as clearly."

Contigo moved closer to Destemido, and took the same defensive stance he had witnessed only days before during the battle on the wagon.

"She's right!" Contigo answered.

"Impossible!" Bellini broke his silence.

Contigo and Destemido exchanged an unspoken conversation calculating any remaining options to escape the truth.

"Truth is truth." Destemido removed the bandana wrapped around her unfurling jet-black hair.

"Because of that bastard, I had to abandon my Día!" Contigo pointed at Bellini.

"Your daughter?" said Lanning. "What the hell?"

"There are girl pirates?" asked Hector. "This trip can't get any worse."

"Lots of family drama I see, but perhaps not the best time to seek restorative justice," Lorenzo summarized.

A flash of light, followed by a booming noise, announced an incoming cannon shot that splashed down far short of the L'Aquila.

"That's definitely a falconet. They have limited range," said Destemido.

"Uh-huh. Thank you for that expertise." Lanning turned to Contigo. "Do I need to put all this together on my own, or can you help out? Your daughter is a corsair AND a weapons expert?" Lanning had some of the pieces assembled in his mind, but was missing a few nuggets. He stopped himself. "Never mind, for now. Can we raise any sail, Felipe?"

"Not enough to matter."

"If it's to be a fight, I'm ready," said Hector.

"That's ridiculous. They've sent us a message," Lanning said.

"So, you speak 'pirate' then?" Lorenzo turned to Lanning, then to Destemido. "She speaks fucking pirate! How lucky for us we saved your ass from drowning!"

Destemido managed a chuckle while rewrapping her bandana. "I guess that's true!"

"They'd like us to remain in place while they come alongside," said Lanning.

"See, everyone can speak *pirate*! I'd say we've got half an hour, maybe more," said Destemido to Lanning.

Given the pressing storm and limited privacy aboard the Queen, Destemido and Contigo had managed only the briefest of moments previously to swap questions about their paths. Both had borne an empty space for each other for ten years.

"Contigo?" said Lanning.

"It's not anything I expected. I had to leave Portugal to save her," he answered.

"Not what I expected either. You left me in the care of Longshort. Thank God I had Alia Tavares too, and the King," Destemido said.

"As in The KING of Portugal?" Lorenzo exclaimed.

"I am a privateer in the service of King Manuel." Destemido looked over to Lanning. "That scorpion down there is the cause of our separation."

Bellini realized his compromised position and tried to make the best of it. "True, you are not a wanted man. If I neglected to pass on that information, you have my apologies. It's just that there was no advantage to sharing that little truth with you. Until now." Bellini stood up to dust himself off.

Contigo turned to Lanning. "Do I need your permission to beat the living hell out of this man?"

"Can you do it in less than a minute? Because we have more pressing issues."

"I am on the crown's business! You cannot touch me," Bellini said.

"Which crown?" asked Lorenzo.

"Does that matter at sea?" Felipe asked.

"He had a letter from Viceroy Gagnez," interjected Destemido.

"To what effect?" asked Lanning.

"Passage to Tangier in pursuit of you, and of course the Lady. Her." She pointed to Filippa.

"What's she got to do with anything?"

"Idiot! SHE is actually *everything*. Not you and your ridiculous ferry service," Bellini was frustrated having to negotiate with expendable idiots.

BOOM! The sound echoed around the ship much louder than before. The shot splashed down quite a distance away.

"Cannon!" Hector looked petrified.

"A falconet. At least according to the she-pirate," said Lorenzo.

"I hate this damn ocean. This is what I get for trying to help out my brother with extra dough." Hector took a minute to handle his regrets for taking what he thought was an easy money day job. "Gonna cost more than you promised for this, but I will fight!"

"Steady. We have alternatives."

Lanning had no idea what those alternatives might be. Not knowing anything about the oncoming galleon, or where on the great ocean they had found themselves left him at a loss for ideas. He hoped something would occur to him before they were overtaken.

"Sometimes our fate is simply our fate." Shafi had moved closer to Lanning. The Berber saw the struggling young man and tried to comfort him.

"It was not supposed to go this way, Uncle. Still, I'm not done," said Lanning.

"Neither am I. But I am prepared to shift my balance in order to stay standing," said Shafi.

"That whole ship looks golden in this light." Contigo squinted into the sun.

"Unless you idiots are expecting Prester 'fucking' John to be on that boat, I suggest putting up some sort of fight." Having staved off an unwanted swim, Bellini felt free to castigate his captors.

Shafi replied, "I know this legend."

"King Manuel was a huge believer in that fairytale," Contigo chimed in. "How about we use Bellini as a human shield instead?"

Something sparked in Lanning. He stared at Shafi, before moving to Filippa. "Have you heard of this legend?"

"Of course. I can't say if it's true or not, but many people believe it."

Lorenzo felt helpless. "What damn difference does any of this make now? Religion never saves anyone. You have to save yourself. Are we just going to sit here and float? Maybe I should put my pee-stained working clothes back on and entertain them to death?"

"We can do both!" Spurred by a crystalizing idea, Lanning sprang into action. "Felipe, do we have repair paste in the hold? You know, what we use to repair leaks?"

"If it didn't float away in the storm. I'll check." Felipe jumped down into the hold of the boat.

"Found it!" he shouted from below.

Lanning's eyes widened as another idea hit him. "Wait! Bring up that chest we tossed down there too."

He turned to Filippa apologetically. "We're going to need your chest of clothing."

"The one you gave me a shit ton of grief for?"

"I think I understand now why you brought all of that." He and Filippa exchanged a look derived from the many nights they had spent together.

"Sorry, but we're going to make a mess of it."

"How can I help?" Destemido understood exactly what Lanning had in mind.

"Nantucket is the one," said Lanning.

Nantucket looked mystified as he suddenly became the center of attention.

A double cannon shot with splashes erupting two hundred yards from the L'Aquila heralded the coming showdown.

"Got it all!" announced Felipe, emerging from the hold.

"Raise the white flag, brother."

Lanning opened the chest, revealing an ample collection of luxurious silk and velvet dresses.

"Perfect!" said Destemido.

Bellini said, "There's no point to anything you're scheming. We're all dead."

Lanning nodded to Hector who calmly walked over and cold-cocked Bellini with a three-hour right hander. He then carried the limp body down to the hold.

―――― Chapter 34 ――――
TRIBAL

As shadows on the deck grew long with the falling afternoon sun, a massively timbered, triple-masted galleon sporting two dozen—yep, they were falconets—pulled even with the diminutive L'Aquila. More than fifty Barbary corsairs milled about its decks, lackadaisically peering over their gunnels at the vastly overmatched little boat. A blood-red flag holding a single white crescent moon nestling a five-pointed white star inside its curve fluttered off the top of the stern mast.

"Hellooo? Anybody around?"

All appeared quiet on the L'Aquila.

The diminutive, round man with a hunchback called glibly across the narrow gap between the two boats. Below his oversized beige turban, he wore pitch black Arabic robes. The lines on his face were deep and craggy, aside his large fishhook nose. His precision groomed, salt and pepper beard culminated in a perfect isosceles point. Despite his unenticing appearance, the older man projected an air of old-world elegance.

"No need to be shy."

Nantucket, hooded, and clothed head to toe in the improvised velvet attire from Filippa's trunk, emerged on deck. Two slashes of white repair paste painted beneath his eyes, together with his imposing stature, gave pause to the privateers on the galleon. They swooped to the rails pointing and murmuring.

"Pardon me, holiness." Lanning, in matching fashion, appeared from his cabin. "I will handle this."

"Greetings, Captain. You have fired on our ship," Lanning said.

"Captain is so formal. I'm actually an Admiral. However, you may address me as Sinan."

"Admiral, we are simple pilgrims."

"Pilgrims?" Sinan replied dubiously. "I see. Well, *Father*, that was hardly an attack. More akin to a neighborhood shout-out: 'Hey friend, hold up.' Definitely not a 'stop or we will destroy' you signal. If we had '*fired*'..." The captain used air quotes to emphasize his facetious tone. "You and your boat would be breadcrumbs, and *we*, would not be having this cordial conversation."

Destemido, also sporting Filippa's clothing, moved closer to Lanning. She whispered, "That's Sinan, the Jew! NOT a gentleman by any stretch. We are all in deep jeopardy."

"Well, we have stopped to '*chat*' as you *requested*, although I do believe that is not your true intent. Your ship seems dressed for mightier things than *tea* with a neighbor. And you, my '*brother*,' do not seem as benign as your demeanor," Lanning said.

"Well, that's certainly a mouthful of presumptions. I see by the condition of your vessel you might be in need. We offer you basic hospitality – food, water, good company. Perhaps that would help to change your mind about us?"

"As I've said, we are gentle pilgrims. Emissaries of his highness, Prester John," Lanning knew he was pressing their luck, but maintained as straight a face as possible.

"Prester John? Really, *the* Prester John? That is a revelation. First impressions can be so misleading."

Sinan waved his hand. The air instantly filled with lines flying across the narrowing divide between the two ships and slapping down on the L'Aquila's barren deck.

"I will come to you. I know people get tense around things like this. I promise you have nothing to be overly concerned about. Give me a minute and I'll be right over."

Sinan removed himself from the rail and headed down to the main deck of his ship.

Feeling he had already betrayed their ruse, but knowing they had zero options Lanning simply opened his arms wide in the universal hospitality gesture. Contigo, Destemido, Hector, Felipe, Lorenzo and Shafi gathered around Lanning and Nantucket. Each of them had disguised themselves to varying degrees of success with Filippa's clothing.

"Not too late to make a stand, maybe?" suggested Felipe weakly.

"Provided we'd all prefer a quick trip to the afterlife!" snapped Lorenzo.

"Something will occur. All we need is patience." Shafi looked calmly at each face, hoping to infuse a dose of hope.

Felipe said, "Patience? Uncle, they're boarding our boat in ten seconds!"

"Sinan is an untethered, psychopathic mercenary for the Ottomans. That being said, I do agree with the Berber. Something will occur. It must," Destemido said.

"Occur? Imprisonment, torture, death plus all the things in between those horrible things?" Lorenzo said.

"It's a matter of being ready for the moment when it arises," counseled Contigo.

Lanning waved off the noise. "We are set on a course, so we will stick with it. Up or down."

The disguised crew of the L'Aquila gathered on the deck to receive the Barbary coast Admiral. Although his reputation apparently loomed large in pirate circles, the man was a whisper above a hobbit in size. His head drooped along with his rounded shoulders. He scaled the gunnel of his own ship, then stepped across the gap onto the L'Aquila's rail before using his hands to lower himself down onto the deck.

The next man leaped over both rails, landing with a deck-shaking stomp. Filippa and Lanning gasped. The *huge* skinhead, wearing a matching devil's pointed beard hanging between his dagger ears stood silently next to the Admiral. He kept a tight grip on the scimitar wedged into his waistband. Glancing at Lanning, the former bouncer of the Howling Cricket gave a wink of recognition.

Contigo caught the exchange. Gripping his own blade concealed beneath his robes, Contigo raised an eyebrow towards Lanning. Lanning waved him off with a hand gesture coupled and a subtle "absolutely not" glance.

"Well then, let's get acquainted." Sinan took up position next to a barrel of hummus. He lifted the lid and pulled out a fingerful to taste.

"So, I see they have made a stop in Tangier recently. Curious."

He shut the lid, then struggled to perch himself on top of the barrel. Lanning noticed that Sinan had a disturbing habit of murmuring to himself. Like he was engaged in conversation with both sides of his brain at the same time. He leaned in to determine whether the man was speaking to him or to himself.

"So, who are you? Druids? 'There are druids at sea'? You're druids?"

Lanning hadn't clue one about druids. He decided his best defense was to ignore the reference entirely.

"I'm sorry, was that question for me?"

"Obviously. You are druids?"

"Apologies. We are pilgrims. Simple, peaceful pilgrims."

"Ah, pilgrims."

"*They're pilgrims, also at sea,*" Sinan repeated aloud to himself. "Alright, pilgrims. *Pilgrims should know where they're headed.*"

"Again, are you asking a question?" Lanning knew he was testing the man's patience, but he needed time to ferret out his intentions.

"We were caught in a storm," Lanning offered.

"I saw the storm," he said to himself. "That was stupid. Pilgrims should not be in a storm, let alone at sea without proper sailors to ferry them."

While the parties spoke, the former bouncer had placed a full barrel of fresh water, plus another filled with oranges and lemons, on the deck next to the main mast. Tin cups appeared as the weary crew eagerly sated their thirst.

"Very kind of you, Admiral," said Lanning.

Sinan got up to grab an orange from the barrel. "Sinan, please," he said. "Respect and honor are due all men, is it not?"

"And women!" Filippa added.

Destemido listened, standing against the nearest gunnel.

"A liberated *pilgrim* woman? Haven't encountered that before. Novel: not sure I like it." Sinan looked bemused then annoyed.

"You prefer for us to trust you?" asked Lanning.

"Oy." Sinan groaned and searched for a place to sit down. "My back sucks. Some days are worse than others."

The bouncer retrieved a three-legged stool from the galleon and placed it behind the Admiral.

"Such a good hire," Sinan said to the Berber before continuing, "Where were we, pilgrim? Oh yes, trust. I have done nothing to undermine your trust. Yet, you expect me to trust *you*. Why? What have *you* done to earn *my* trust? Who is truly trustworthy?"

"That's a false equivalent. You have the cannons," countered Lorenzo.

Sinan appeared ready to lay his true agenda on the table.

"Hah! On that you are correct. My good fortune, I suppose. However, all of you have already violated our mutual trust. As we all know, there is not a *pilgrim* among you. Which also means although highly creative, you are certainly NOT in the service of Prester John.

Sadly, my trust in you has already been violated. I, on the other hand, have done nothing other than display respect and honor towards you."

Destemido chimed in, "Your reputation speaks differently."

"My reputation? That's marketing. Who's going to be afraid of a bent-over, old man? To my grandchildren, I'm the gentle beloved soul who brings them gifts from strange foreign places."

Destemido stepped forward. "We are not children. Sinan the Terrible, Sinan the Assassin, Sinan the Slayer."

"The Slayer? Hadn't heard that one. Pretty good though, no? How about Sinan the Great Jew?"

"Not really out there, no," answered Destemido.

"Your reputation appears more steeped in dishonor than nobility Admiral. Sadly, we are at the mercy of wherever the truth lies," Lanning said.

"So, you are." Sinan slowly rose from his stool. He continued peeling his orange as he walked over to the starboard rail.

Tossing the peels into the ocean, he said, "All of this has been a wonderful chat. However, I am a man of duty. As such, I am mindful of my obligations, commitments, and loyalties. Such are the constraints which guide the latitude of my behaviors. Now you mock *pilgrims* present a challenge. The unexpected is always a challenge."

"Cut the shit!" A voice erupted from the hold. Bellini had slipped his gag.

"I speak treachery fluently," Bellini bellowed. "Why not cut to the chase and knock off the theatrics?"

Sinan motioned and the Berber jumped into the hold. A moment later Bellini was ejected from below. He bounced out into a familiar heap on the deck.

"God damnit! I can walk up the fucking ladder."

"Ahhh another pious pilgrim? Maybe a tad light on the piety?"

Bellini brushed himself off and continued, "You seem like a shrewd man familiar with many forms of larceny."

"Go on," prompted Sinan.

Contigo calmly walked over to Bellini and clocked him with a vicious right cross sending him back to the ground.

Wiping his bloody mouth on his sleeve, Bellini burst out, "You do know they're lying."

"I am aware."

Lanning stayed the course, "We are pilgrims, Admiral. This man...

"Is not important," Sinan agreed with Lanning. "You may be pilgrims, but you may not be in the service of Prester John."

"You can't know that," replied Lanning indignantly.

"Oh, but I can, and I do. I serve Prester John."

A great silence overtook the assemblage. Nantucket, astonishingly burst out laughing. Lanning wondered what had made him react in such an uncharacteristic manner. Perhaps he had misunderstood the language?

"Strange sense of humor from your heathen," said Sinan.

"He knows bullshit when he hears it," Bellini offered.

"Many things are true. It's only the vantage point of the disbeliever that inhibits the truth finding the light," said Sinan.

"Holy shit, he sounds like Shafi! What is that supposed to mean?" Felipe looked incredulous.

"You sir, are a slaver!" accused Destemido, "Slavers are not in the service of God."

"I wrestle with that conundrum constantly. Your deceit is evident as well. If you are a woman, you should dress like one."

Unmasked, Destemido froze.

"There are no saviors, no heroes, no solace for a life poorly chosen, or unluckily ended. There are only consequences," Bellini continued.

Sinan now dropped all pretense of hospitality to assume his true posture. "This has been an unexpected diversion. Days at sea can become so tedious. Thank you all for the distraction. However, it's well past lunch, I'm starting to get hangry and truthfully, a bit bored. We will take your ship in tow to a port where you will be disbanded and processed."

At that, Shafi burst forward sword in hand and lunged at Sinan.

"AAAHHHH!" He screamed, crumbling to the deck grabbing at his left leg.

The Berber threw his own secreted blade, catching Shafi in the muscle of his upper thigh. Before running over to Shafi, Lanning glared at the bodyguard, mouthing, "I saved your life."

"Now we are even," responded the man quietly. Lanning realized the bodyguard could have easily lodged the blade into Shafi's heart.

Contigo lurched forward, hand on the hilt of his blade. "Would a Great Jew imprison his own?"

"Who is Jewish? You?"

"And," pointing to Destemido, "my daughter."

Sinan looked both up and down. "Nah..." He dismissed Contigo with a wave.

"It's true, he is Jewish," said Lanning.

"I knew it!" exclaimed Bellini.

"Come closer," demanded Sinan. "Show me!"

"What? Now?"

"Show me!"

Contigo pulled out the waist of his pants as Sinan looked down into the 'hold'.

"Praise God! Jews! Both are welcome aboard the Actium."

"I was hoping for more generosity," urged Contigo, pointing at the full complement of the L'Aquila.

"Feel free to hope. The offer stands as given." Sinan headed back to the Actium.

Chapter 35

EDGING

Sixteenth century sea battles often played out like a beer-infused, weekend dart competition at the Squirrel & Mutton, in a hurricane, with moving targets. If you had enough darts, despite the wind, something was bound to find its target eventually. Naturally, lethal cannon balls hurling about in all directions had more dire consequences than a random dart in the ass.

Firing cannons and falconets demanded speedy, line-of-sight reckoning in quick order. The best strategy lay in proximity. Get as tight as you could to the adversary, launch a shit ton of ordinance, then hope something found something to crack, smash, disable, or detonate. Follow that up by hooking some lines, boarding your prey, and getting bloody.

Sinan the Simply Horrible and his galleon had been towing the L'Aquila for one whole day. Even though Contigo and his daughter had been invited over to the Actium as guests, they had refused on principle. Their fate now rested completely at the mercy of their captor and his unknown destination. Perhaps they were headed for the legendary kingdom of Prester John, but most likely not.

"Somebody else is coming," Hector mumbled over his shoulder.

Three ships had appeared against the horizon, all with full sails angled on a hard and fast port beam reach. They were headed directly for the L'Aquila and the Actium. Hector, who had exhausted Shafi's supply of ginger, was once again vomiting over the aft rail when he spied them.

"Slavery really isn't so bad if you know how to work the system." Bellini offered some unsolicited advice to Nantucket.

"I have been a slave and a prisoner. I prefer being a free man."

"So, you plan on dying fairly soon once we get wherever we're going. Poor strategy." Bellini shook his head and walked away.

"Somebody else is coming!" Hector yelled. Felipe rushed to the tiller.

"Where? There! I see them!" Felipe said.

Lanning rushed to the bow of the tethered L'Aquila, which was trailing twenty yards astern of its jailor. He yelled across the gap. "Sinan! Sinan my friend!"

The bouncer leaned over the stern rail. "He's having his tea, *pilgrim.*"

Lorenzo pointed to the bridge of the Actium, where Sinan had emerged extending his telescoping spyglass.

"Oh, they are definitely going to catch us. See that spray blowing off the lead ship's bow? That's speed," Destemido shaded her eyes from the sun.

"I'll trust your eyes over mine. Good or bad?" Shafi added.

"This is the something!" Filippa appeared hopeful.

The L'Aquila suddenly lost all of its momentum, falling dead calm in the water.

"What's happened?" asked Contigo.

"They've cut the line," Felipe said.

"YES! Freedom!" exclaimed Lorenzo.

"I don't think that is such a good thing." Lanning furrowed his brow.

"My friends!" Sinan shouted down from his bridge.

"Friends don't sell human beings, you bastard," Lorenzo shouted across the widening divide.

"Perhaps. Sadly, our time together grows suddenly shorter."

Lanning offered his facetious reply, "Those three ships got you scared?"

"There are four," corrected Destemido.

Hector turned momentarily to Destemido. "Oh sorry, she's right. There's another one!" He pointed to the horizon.

Lanning continued his sarcasm. "Perhaps some friends coming to lend a hand. What's the rush?"

"In this case, my business elsewhere must take precedence over making new friends," Sinan said, then shrugged.

"I thought you enjoyed the distraction of spontaneous adventure at sea?"

"Oh, I do. I have a fantastic distraction in mind. Not so much for you; more designed for our approaching company."

Sinan turned to his first officer, a willowy senior sailor with a mass of twisted, ropey hair that resembled a well-used deck mop.

"Roll out your guns, lay the foremast first, then rake her amidship on the up roll!"

The mate relayed the command down to the main deck, triggering a bustle of activity among the crew.

The Actium pulled further away with each moment as the four ships bore down from the east.

"He means to blow us out of the water and make an escape." Destemido stated the obvious.

"Shit, she truly does speak pirate," said Lorenzo.

"I see five ships now. Gotta be either Spain or Portugal, right?" Felipe sounded hopeful.

"Maybe." Lanning was preoccupied. "More pressing matter, brother. Can you change our course? Like right now?"

Lanning already knew the answer. Still, he had to ask.

Reminiscent of their first encounter with Sinan, both crews heard the distant cannon fire and watched as a splash appeared one hundred yards behind the drifting L'Aquila.

"Admiral," Lanning shouted across, "I'm sure they'd just like a friendly chat."

"Who can that possibly be?" asked Filippa.

"Does it matter if we're cornflakes in another minute," said Lorenzo.

Lanning looked at both Filippa and Nantucket, and pointed at Doug's cage, then towards the Actium.

"It worked before," Destemido added.

"Sorry about Longshort," Contigo said to his daughter. "He was a loyal friend."

"To both of us."

"I recommend you reconsider your options, Admiral!" Lanning shouted to the retreating galleon.

"It's a matter of perspective. As the Ottomans say, 'Peace be upon you.'"

Nantucket had opened Doug's cage, perched him on his extended forearm and screeched to him in a language only they understood. Doug exploded off the perch, reaching full velocity with two flaps of his powerful wings. The predator took a flat line across the gap separating the two ships.

BOOM! Splash.

Another cannon blast, even closer this time. The shot landed next to the L'Aquila.

BOOM!

Once more, the next splash landed between the two boats.

"Trading one death merchant for the next. Dead either way." Bellini sat down on the deck, yielding to his fate.

Doug headed directly for Sinan. With a surprising catlike reaction, the Admiral hit the deck. Talons already poised, Doug made a split-second course correction ramming straight into the neck of the deck mop. A screech and an abbreviated scream ended the man's life. The falcon had shredded his throat leaving a mass of spurting blood pouring onto the Actium's deck. The bird shot back up into the sky like a missile heading for orbit.

BOOM!

BOOM!

Two more cannon blasts with splashes dropped on both the starboard and port side of the Actium. Sinan remained non-plussed by the sudden barbarity of the scene.

"Full sail, prepare to fire," he commanded calmly.

After a brief pause to absorb the carnage, the Actium crew renewed its activity. Additional sails were hoisted, as the cannon doors on the starboard side of the ship raised. The firing crew nosed the falconets through their openings, aimed directly at the helpless L'Aquila.

"Son, this isn't the way I saw it. I'm sorry." Shafi limped his way over to Lanning, and placed a fatherly arm around him.,

Lanning returned the hug and scanned for Filippa. She caught his eye as well. Life happens in a brief flash. Joy, sorrow, anguish, some more joy, a dose of anxiety, dread, laughter, tears, regret, denial, acceptance, love, belonging, despair, hope, resignation, terror, peace. Maybe we have the capacity to experience all emotions simultaneously, or maybe none at all.

Lanning observed himself from an altitude he had never reached previously. His outward expression turned to astonishment as his clarity of so many things came into focus. His feelings of incompleteness —he had let life happen to him for so long, he had failed to act on his own behalf, masking that inaction with his action for others. Well, hold on, that's not a bad thing, selfless is still a redeemable quality. Figuring imminent demise not the ideal moment to argue with himself, he moved ahead on his list. He understood his feelings for Filippa were much stronger than he anticipated. Too late.

"Fuck!" said Lorenzo.

"Fuck!" echoed Felipe.

"We are in a thin space!" Nantucket stood in the center of the L'Aquila's main deck. He appeared strangely serene and unmoved by the circumstances.

"Acceptance," Lanning thought to himself. "So that's what pure peace at the end looks like." Nantucket's peace somehow compounded his irritation with himself. "Damn it! I spent my time worrying about becoming, and never fucking became!" He wished for that calm in himself and all aboard.

A broad smile appeared on Nantucket's face he stretched out his arm and waited for Doug to return. Lanning took another look around at his comrades, another look at the Actium readying its barrage, and one final search for Filippa's gaze.

The water roiled between the L'Aquila and the Actium. They braced for the **FIRE** command which erupted from the mouth of Sinan the Murdering Bastard. In the split moment between the command and the cannon fire, the water around the Actium suddenly detonated. A great geyser lifted thousands of gallons of sea water, obliterating their view of the galleon.

"Oh my god, what manner of hell is that!" Lorenzo pointed across the water.

Six gigantic spinning creatures rose from the great ocean in a blurring mass of black and white upheaval. Water shot off their bodies, spraying the starboard side of the Actium just as the cannon fired from Sinan's command. The sea dragons knocked the ship into a full starboard lean, and altered the point-blank cannonball, kill-shot trajectory.

The cannonballs took a simple elevator ride straight up, followed by the return trip. They landed with an innocuous splash between the two boats.

The violent collision between beast and boat sent the Actium's stupefied crew airborne. Some of the mercenary souls struck the ships rigging, causing instantaneous decapitations. The lucky ones only suffered shattered bones. Ten of the cannon crew were crushed under the weight of their flipped, skidding, cannons. A dozen sailors working on the rigging catapulted overboard hitting the roiling ocean with all manner of inadvertent acrobatics. Many were sucked beneath the water, falling prey to the undertow created by the relentless creatures pummeling the Actium.

Shafi observed the upheaval from the relative calm of the L'Aquila. 'Not unfamiliar,' he thought.

Three more beasts from the deep emerged on the port side of the boat, with another laying hard up against the Actium's bow. Two more arose between the receding L'Aquila and the Actium. Perhaps the largest and most terrifying beast exploded out of the water, in a gyrating fit. Its gaping jaws revealing row upon row of razor-sharp teeth. Soaring out of the water as if propelled by a rocket, the beast landed itself with a crushing thud onto foredeck of the Actium. The ship splintered under the weight, and manic energy of the infuriated beast.

"Well, their day went certainly went to shit in a hurry!" Lorenzo said.

"Something definitely occurred!" said Felipe.

"I'm never, ever, ever leaving land again." Hector could not take his eyes off the carnage being inflicted on the Actium.

Shafi switched his gaze to the rapidly approaching vessels. "The only question remains, who are they?"

Cannon fire from the five ships reached the range of danger. Lanning spun to respond to the new imminent threat.

"It's not the only question, but, I agree, the most pressing," Filippa said.

Two of the massive creatures torpedoed through the water to collide against the Actium's starboard side. The ship shivered as the blow cracked the foremast and splintered the main mast. Beneath the water, an expanding hairline crack appeared in the galleon's keel.

Sinan stood stock-still on the bridge bereft of options against their otherworldly foe.

The crippled ship's cracking deck boards sent a deafening echo heard across the gap between the two ships. Adding to the maelstrom, a whistling sound strafed over the L'Aquila. A cannonball looking for parking found its new home amidship on the Actium. Like birds leaving before an earthquake, the giant creatures abruptly disappeared from view. The ocean eerily returned to a dead calm.

Sinan looked up to the heavens in disbelief, perhaps trusting in his faith in God to intervene and save him. Somehow, Lanning seemed to know what was coming. He stared across at Shafi, who had caught his gaze with the slightest nod. Gripping tightly to the starboard rail as if trying to squeeze something out of memory and into consciousness, he momentarily lost his bearings.

Chapter 36

HOLDING IT DOWN

"Dad, let's go up to the bow!"

The angularly handsome man in his mid-thirties wiped the early morning sleep from his eyes. He had reached for a small leather notebook off the single shelf in their one bed cabin. Vital and in his prime, he had the intrepid look of someone with his eye on the horizon, and a long unpaved roadway stretched out ahead.

He rolled out of bed, journal in hand, and kneeled to speak at eye level with his son.

"Sounds good to me. Let me finish my diary entry first, then I'll meet you up there."

The boy nodded and reached for the door.

"Lanning," said his father, "hold on tight up there. Wouldn't want you taking an unscheduled swim before we get to the Caribbean!"

Some distance away from father and son, the same leaden skies greeted two men as they woke surrounded by the cold chill of dawn. "At least the seas are relatively calm," thought Gonzalo Cortez. Gnawing on a piece of dried salted cod, he finished setting bait on six lines before tossing them over the rail of the single sail chaloupe.

"I see what you're doing," said his bearded companion.

"I'm holding it down."

"You are, by far, the worst fisherman I've ever known."

"Said the Berber pharmacist with questionable vision. Nausea is part of the game. I fish for family, not for passion."

"I have offered to give you something, but I know you prefer recreational puking."

"I'd rather hurl than eat that crappy ginger root you're pushing.

So for the hundredth time, no thanks."

"It's painful to watch."

"Stay home," Gonzalo said.

"I don't want to leave my godson without at least a passable father figure."

Gonzalo smiled as he leaned back over the rail, and untangled some lines before re-positioning them once again. He let out a resonating belch, punctuating by vomiting into the ocean.

"It's always the cod," deadpanned Shafi.

They passed the next few hours in comfortable brotherly silence. The boat bobbed, Gonzalo juggled his vomit bubble, and they took turns monitoring the lines.

"I hate the waiting. Who sincerely loves all this silence besides nuns and the dead?"

"I like it," said Shafi. "You know, for reflection, pondering one's existence. Apologies, I forgot *thinking* makes you nauseous."

The two men were startled by a thundering explosion. A mushroom cloud with a glowing red epicenter extended across the horizon line.

"I make it maybe two miles?"

"Shafi, put up the sail!"

"We've got lines in the water!" Gonzalo raced around the deck, scooping all of them up at once.

"PUT UP THE SAIL!" he repeated.

At the mast in an instant, Shafi hoisted the single lateen sail with five strong pulls. He raced to the tiller to angle the little chaloupe for maximum wind. They aimed for the spot of the explosion. Two hours later, the first signs of debris appeared: pieces of ships decking laced with rope fragments, a mass of shredded canvas riddled with burn marks, and more.

Gonzalo surveyed the debris. "Whatever happened came quick.

Maybe a powder magazine?"

"Awful. I feel ill."

Shafi did look sick at the sight of mangled body parts floating off to oblivion on the prevailing current.

"I prefer an unexpected, instantaneous death, as opposed to the lingering horror of the damn plague!" Gonzalo said.

"If it's the one written for me, I will take the lessons imparted."

"Uh huh. So poetic, but complete crap. At least these poor souls went quick. When death comes for me, I'd prefer it not dick around. Take my ass and move along."

They had drifted into the center of a massive debris field.

"Must have been huge!"

Gonzalo felt mesmerized, absorbing the number of floating fragments from what was a galleon of considerable size. Railings, mast fragments, deck boards, some clothing, plus more gruesomeness covered the water. Shafi pointed aft towards an almost intact piece of the ship's bow.

Shafi blinked, trying to sharpen his vision. He peered over the chaloupe's transom.

"Over there!" he said.

"I see it too!"

Each man pulled an oar from the deck, and paddled through the grisly scene.

"It's a kid!" exclaimed Gonzalo. "That bow is almost intact. It must have shot off the boat from the explosion. Get me a bit closer so I can reach in there."

Gonzalo stretched his frame over the bow, trying to make a grab for the child.

"He can't be much older than Felipe!" said Shafi, easing them closer.

Tucked inside the half-floating, iron rimmed bow was a small boy in shredded clothing. His body was dusted in black soot.

"Daaad?" the semi-conscious boy mumbled.

"English!" Shafi said.

The men abruptly turned their heads as, without warning, the water around them erupted in turbulence. Two successive geysers of water shot twenty feet into the air. Emerging from the deep came two, slick black bodies, each the size of a King's carrack.

"Got him!" Gonzalo reached across the divide to snatch the boy. He laid him on the deck of the chaloupe.

"You're fine. Stay put!" Satisfied the kid wasn't going anywhere, Gonzalo raced for his paddle.

"Sea beasts! Could they have done all this?"

Shafi speculated on the destructive power of the two creatures now floating on the surface of the ocean.

"No need to find out. Paddle!"

"They're watching us," Shafi said. The beasts floated motionless on top of the water.

"They look curious."

"In *your* mind!" Gonzalo doubled his paddling speed.

The two creatures rotated sideways in the water, revealing two white oval patches behind their eyes. The patches connected to their white bellies. Neither made a move to follow the boat. Both silently held position as if only monitoring the rescue.

"Gonzalo, watch them. They're either curious or maybe..."

"Hungry," added Gonzalo, still paddling.

Shafi turned back to his mate and urged, "Take a quick look, you'll see."

Gonzalo turned, but the creatures had vanished.

"Now it's worse. Where are they?" he said.

The beasts did not return. The two men paddled clear of the debris field, raised their sail, and headed back to Algeciras with their catch and survivor intact.

—— Chapter 37 ——

HELL YEAH

A shock wave of wind hit Lanning, knocking him out of his momentary lapse. He locked gazes with the doomed Admiral Sinan an eighth note before the universe played his overdue exit music. The magnitude of the blast turned the formerly imposing vessel of war into a billowing cloud of sawdust. Splintered wood and flying shards rained down on the empty spot where the galleon had floated only a moment before. A cannonball had landed inside the powder room of the Actium, igniting its entire store of gunpowder in a single blast of extinction.

"Contigo?" Destemido looked around her, suddenly aware her father was not on board.

"In the water!" Shafi pointed into the roiling water, alive with gigantic sea creatures.

"Dad!"

"He's got someone by the neck," Shafi hopped over to the rail. "Bellini!"

Lorenzo yelled over the rail, "Drown him!"

"Incoming!" Felipe tossed a rope over the side.

Bellini had been watching with delight as the Actium experienced its karmic retribution. His spot against the starboard rail afforded a bird's eye view of the maelstrom. It seemed safe enough until a random wave from the blast detonated against the L'Aquila. It lifted and tilted the caravel in exactly the wrong direction for Bellini's well-being. His double mobius twist over the rail went unnoticed by everyone. Everyone except Contigo.

"Fuck me," thought Contigo. Surely letting this man drown equated to justice served. "Why risk my life to save this despicable remorseless man?" He knew no one aboard the L'Aquila would take issue if that was the choice. Yet, over the rail he went.

The water roiling with sea monsters, Contigo swam hard through the whitecaps towards the floundering Bellini.

"Come to finish the job?" Bellini managed to spit words in between his gasps and gags.

"Yes, but not in the way you'd prefer."

Contigo wrapped a thick forearm around Bellini's chest. He spotted the line Felipe had tossed over the side, and dragged Bellini back towards the L'Aquila. As Contigo side-stroked his way fifty feet from the boat, the surface of the ocean transformed yet again. He stroked through the glassy water, not a ripple between him and the L'Aquila.

"Keep it coming, big guy. You're almost here," said Felipe.

Lorenzo shook his head. "I'd have left him to fate."

"Stop," Nantucket said quietly, putting his hands up facing Contigo.

Even before noticing Nantucket's signal, Contigo had stopped swimming. He hung fixed in position treading water.

A single creature emerged from the depths of the ocean. Jet black skin covered the top of its mammoth body. It seamlessly joined the equally smooth, brilliant white skin that wrapped from belly to jawline. The enormous being defied gravity. Effortlessly floating atop the water, light as a cork, it had positioned itself mid-path between the two men and the L'Aquila.

"Yes," said Nantucket quietly.

The beast approached the two swimmers. Actually, the one swimmer and his clinging human remora.

"They look like giant fish. Monster fish! Dragon fish!" said Lorenzo.

"It's big enough to swallow them whole!" Hector said. "Throw something to distract it!"

SPLASH!

All heads turned as Lanning swam through the debris field, heading directly for the two men.

The creature also continued its path straight for the two men. Contigo counted down his remaining living moments, lamenting the time he had missed with his daughter at the hands of the man clinging to his back. Why not simply toss Bellini into the demon's sawtooth jaws, then swim away? Justice delivered.

"HEY!" Lanning began shouting at the great beast. He splashed as much water as he could to distract it. His efforts were fruitless. Instead, yet another creature emerged from the deep directly behind Lanning.

"It's going to be fine." Shafi couldn't have been calmer.

"You don't know that," answered Filippa.

"But I do."

As Contigo prepared to whipsaw Bellini into that day's afternoon snack, the creature froze three feet from them. It floated, suspended.

"Smells like the back of your wagon," Bellini said.

The beast maintained a fixed distance from them, impervious to the ocean current Contigo fought against. It was a standoff. The only sound emanating from the creature a deep breath as if a chorus of fifty had inhaled in unison. Contigo felt himself tiring. Lanning, trailed by the second beast, had kept swimming, and finally linked up with Contigo.

"Now you're dead too. This was pointless," said Contigo.

"I don't think it is, but stay put." Lanning slowly swam towards the creature.

The beast rotated sideways, tracking the approaching swimmer. A giant white patch which, at first glance, Lanning thought to be its eye appeared. He then caught sight of its sky-blue eye. The blue oval was the same size as a cow's eye, and located on the lower left end of the white patch. It blinked once, then twice. Lanning felt a presence he had not expected. He heard a clicking noise which followed each blink. The other beast had quietly moved next to the first one. Both pivoted, observing the three men floating before them. A burst of crackling whistles and clicks were exchanged.

"That one is staring at us!" said Contigo.

"Stop looking at it. It knows we are helpless prey."

"That's how *you* think, Bellini."

"Quiet!" whispered Lanning.

In Contigo's mind, the creature had intentionally stopped to take their measure and determine their intentions. Contigo, the trained soldier, held his fear in check, heeding Lanning's advice.

Although its eye looked bloodshot, Lanning did not sense a threat. Both animals now focused exclusively on Lanning.

"Contigo," Lanning whispered, keeping his gaze locking on the beasts, "swim for the boat. Slowly."

With Bellini in tow, Contigo quietly stroked for the L'Aquila.

One blink, two clicks, one whistle, and Lanning watched the fantastical animal open its jaw ever so slightly.

"Are you two smiling at me?" Lanning puzzled out loud.

"Smacking its lips, more likely. I hope it's quick," Bellini whispered to Contigo.

"Shut the hell up, you ungrateful sludge; he just saved both of us."

"He's safe." Shafi exhaled a knowing sigh from the deck.

"He's still in the water, and so are the beasts." Filippa felt confused over Shafi's confidence.

"It's not his first time."

Contigo and Bellini made it to the boat, and grabbed the line

Felipe tossed over the side. With Hector's help, they hauled the two men on deck. Once Lanning saw the rescue, he offered a smile and a nod of thanks to the two creatures.

"If you two don't mind, I'm going to head over there now." Lanning began a slow backstroke to the L'Aquila. Holding eye contact with them, he retreated from the scene.

The two animals swiveled to watch him go. They neither moved forward nor backward, simply observed from a distance. Once they saw Lanning had made the boat, and without a ripple, the beasts slid into the deep beneath them.

Only after he had a firm grip on the line did Lanning take in the full calamitous fate of the Actium. The mass of splintered wood floating nearby represented all that remained of their former captors.

As Nantucket pulled up the rope holding Lanning, everyone aboard heard a voice shouting from the fast-approaching fleet of ships.

"You're welcome!"

Chapter 38

THE JOY OF DIALECTICS

It was impossible to mistake the graveled voice shouting down from the rail of the lead ship. Magellan sidled his barque, The Trinidad, next to the wounded L'Aquila. He surveyed the sad shape of Lanning's boat.

"You are braver than I to have undertaken such a lengthy voyage on this piece of dung, my boy."

"It's a rental. I'm getting my money's worth. Your timing was fortuitous, but I had the situation well in hand," answered Lanning.

"Welcome, grumpy friend!" Filippa made her way back over to Lanning.

"Ahhh the lovely Filippa. I see you have not fallen off the edge and slipped into the abyss...YET!"

"Thankfully neither have you, Captain!"

Destemido and Contigo huddled and hugged, overwhelmed with sheer exhaustion. Lanning interpreted that as both relief and restoration of hope for father and daughter. Lorenzo and Felipe exchanged man hugs, delighting in the revelation that a cannon blast had not abruptly ended their lives. Head bowed, Shafi rested on a barrelhead, quietly decoding the deeper meaning within, and how all of this melded into his mindful path through life. Hector exhibited genuine joy over their narrow escape from disaster. Nantucket remained unreadable. Bellini took the prize for most unlikely response. He wept.

"Feeling those feelings?" Filippa had observed Lanning from behind.

"Sorting."

"Uh...how about joy? We *are* rescued, after all."

"But is it?"

"About to die, versus not dying? For me, that defines rescue. By any stretch..."

Lanning interrupted, "Sure, but kind of simplistic. I was *rescued* when I was seven. Now here I am, getting *rescued* yet again."

"And that's a bad thing? I don't understand."

"I'm going for the full range. It's my deal. I treat conflicted thoughts and feelings as a positive. Feel free to join in." Lanning forced a half-smile to appease Filippa.

"I feel terrific about the joy of rescue, so..."

"I think it's a longer event horizon to review before calling it an actual 'rescue' is all I'm saying." He drew air quotes around the word.

Felipe patted him on the back, "Great time to get your head out of your ass! This is not the time to ponder your existence. Find happy."

He added a quick hug before assisting the oncoming galleon in securing a line between Magellan's barque and the L'Aquila.

"Your brother is a wise man." Filippa continued, "Stop being such a downer. Take a personal minute."

Filippa left to celebrate with Nantucket and Doug.

Lanning followed, and reached an arm around Filippa by way of apology. They both leaned back against the bridge rail to soak in the relief.

Contigo approached Bellini, mystified at his reaction.

"Not what I expected from you. What are you scheming?"

"To what end? I am undone," said Bellini, wiping his face clean of tears. The man seemed shrunken.

"You," insisted Contigo, "will return to Lisbon with my daughter and me to clear our names. Then you can be *undone*."

"You're under no threat from Lisbon, Father. More important for him to clear Lanning's mother of any wrongdoing," corrected Destemido.

Overhearing the last bit of conversation, Lanning jumped down onto the deck.

"Felipe!" Lanning called.

"Molly? What have you done?" Lanning's anger zoomed from zero to one hundred.

Felipe grabbed the man by the throat. "Talk!"

Destemido revealed the truth she had learned from Bellini when he boarded the Queen. "He and Gagnez had Molly accused of embezzling funds from the palace vendors."

"But why?" asked Lanning.

"It was an exchange," Bellini admitted.

"For what?" Felipe tightened his grip.

"A killing. He's a hired assassin," answered Destemido.

"To kill me?" said Lanning.

Felipe loosened his grip so Bellini could respond.

Bellini chuckled a bit while rubbing his neck. "You dumbass; you're meaningless. Life happens far above either of us."

Filippa stopped in her tracks to do the math. "Me. It was me."

"You are smarter than he looks," added Bellini.

"Perhaps I can answer that a bit better." Magellan had dropped onto the L'Aquila to observe the commotion from close up.

"How do *you* make sense of this?" asked Lanning.

"Economics. I tried to explain this to you in Tangiers."

Lanning remained confused. Still, he was half a length ahead of everyone else in comprehending things. Everyone except Shafi.

"We are a tool." Shafi was finishing an orange he had peeled. "A means to an end. To be disposed of like the rind of this orange." He tossed it overboard.

Magellan continued, "Life in the modern world revolves around money. Who has it, who needs it, and who controls it. I may be a soldier and an explorer, but above all I'm a pragmatist."

"What a joke," spat Bellini.

"Something amuses you?" Magellan asked.

Bellini mocked Magellan. "A Portuguese soldier flying the Spanish flag? You are a mercenary, just like me. Your ambition is for hire from the highest bidder."

"Evidently not quite as deviant as you. My work is in service to something_the crown, the republic, humanity."

"This has less to do with me, than with my mother," reasoned Filippa.

"Sharp thinker when you want to be. The newly minted Emperor has been overly occupied with *your* mother. Orgasm over affairs of state."

"Minister Goodman? That goddamn money guy!" exclaimed Lanning with a stark epiphany.

Magellan summarized, "Belgian creditors need to keep their coffers filled, Spain must pay its debts, and the world of opportunity keeps expanding. Personally, I couldn't care less, since explorers are the beneficiary of that avarice."

"My mother..." Lanning interjected.

"Your mother is fallout," Filippa finished his sentence. "My mother fucking that wimpy ass, boy-king created all of this." Filippa appeared both outraged and contemptuous.

"Turning of the wheel. It occurred long before your mother. It's the way of things," Shafi said. "There are those of us who hope to live in simplicity. Food on the table, comfortable shoes, shelter, and peace. There are those whose lives of duty and obligation concuss against that dream."

"They didn't cover any of this in school. How are we supposed to know?" Lorenzo chimed in.

"You're not," answered Destemido. "You pick your spot and own it. Take the rest as it comes."

"Says the gratuitously violent she-pirate!" Lorenzo summarized.

"Dutch, Belgian, Italian, Andalusian—nationality has no padlock on greed or power." Shafi shook his head.

"First things first. We've got to kill *this* fucker." Felipe gripped Bellini once again by the neck, "then go back to kill Gagnez, and whomever else is responsible."

"We wouldn't last six seconds. There's another way." Lanning looked towards Magellan.

At that moment, a giant hand reached over the rail of the L'Aquila. Hector saw it first. He reached over the side to haul in the waterlogged, bald-headed Berber who collapsed onto the deck.

"Rot my guts!" Magellan recognized the bouncer from Tangier.

Shafi threw himself between the two men, "Wait!"

"Scoundrel!" said Magellan, ripping his sword from its scabbard.

"No, let him through," gasped the Berber. "I'm out of fight."

The Berber bowed his head. Seeing him lying in a pool of submission took all the air out of Magellan's retribution balloon.

"I can't rapier a defenseless victim. Get up and defend yourself."

Filippa moved between the two men alongside Shafi. "He has yielded, sir. Let him be."

"Or?" Magellan made a weak show of indignance, but his fuse had burned out. He had already decided to spare the Berber.

"Or take some other form of compensation for your reparation," suggested Shafi with outstretched arms.

"Hold on," Felipe interrupted, still holding Bellini securely by the throat, "We're not finished here."

"This will be handled in a minute, then we can decide about him," said Magellan.

"Who put you in charge?" asked Contigo, also impatient to determine Bellini's fate.

"It's the law of the sea. He has the larger fleet," answered Destemido.

"She's right," added Lanning.

"Fuck! Be quick, god-damnit," said Felipe slamming Bellini down on the deck.

"Speak more of this compensation," Magellan said to Shafi.

Filippa chimed in, "What of value can he offer to you in exchange for, I guess..."

"His miserable, contemptible life? That's the tradeoff? He was going to whip me!" Lorenzo felt outraged.

Lanning pointed to Shafi's knife wound, as Shafi nodded.

"Why, that is an excellent idea," exclaimed Magellan. "I have some ideas on that. Are you handy in other ways besides simple brutality?"

"I play a pretty decent oud," answered the Berber.

"What is an oud?" asked Filippa.

"It's the Moroccan version of a lute, only twangier," said Destemido.

The assembled glared at Destemido, the unexpected Ethnomusicologist in their midst.

"I had a crewman that played the lute so, I know a bit about the oud," said Destemido sheepishly.

"No true man plays a lute," declared Magellan, "nor do men require music at sea."

"You have a lot of thoughts around male behavior that I don't think are accurate," declared Filippa.

"That's what I thought as well, but turns out it has its moments. Broke up the monotony," added Destemido.

"An oud played well is not twangy. If I had one, I could show you. Of course, I can make one."

"You are a cobbler? That is a skill. Can never have enough decent carpenters on a long journey." Magellan sounded enthusiastic.

"Well, it's more of a hobby than a real career choice. *Henchman* obviously pays quite a bit more."

"Then you'd rather be thrown overboard?"

"Not if that is my only choice."

"How will I know if you are competent or more fit for fish food?"

"He can repair the L'Aquila," suggested Lanning. "That will serve both our needs."

"Superb. I will assess your skills before guaranteeing your safety onboard the Trinidad. Agreed?" Magellan extended his hand.

The Berber rose to his feet, two heads taller than Magellan, one head taller than even Nantucket.

"Deal." His hand entombed Magellan's.

As the two men completed their handshake, a sudden, dramatic shift in the weather occurred. An ice-cold wind descended from the heavens. It swirled down like an invisible tornado, engulfing the collected fleet.

The five boats of Magellan's fleet plus the wounded L'Aquila, found themselves confronted with yet another unnatural chain of events.

"What madness is this?" exclaimed Magellan.

Chapter 39

TRUTH IS A PATHLESS LAND

"Nantucket?"

Juan Sebastian Elcano, navigator to Magellan's fleet peered down over the rail of the bridge high above the L'Aquila's deck. His former companion had not been difficult to spot, given his size.

Nantucket barely acknowledged Elcano's existence. "A nod? Nothing more?"

Nantucket had moved to the prow of the L'Aquila. He had barely turned his head towards his former friend before facing back to the open sea.

Lanning saw Elcano leaning over the rail of the Trinidad, equally unnerved by this sudden change in the stoic man's demeanor.

Conjuring an image of Shakespeare's Prospero summoning the gods, Nantucket raised both arms up to the heavens.

"No idea. I'm as dumbfounded as you," Elcano shouted down to Lanning.

For no discernable meteorological reason, a phantom wind rose from nowhere to swirl about the fleet.

"He looks possessed," said Felipe, gingerly backing away.

"Maybe a bit squiffy?" offered Hector.

"I'd happily settle for drunk. This is something well north of that," said Lorenzo.

Not sure what to think, Hector slowly approached Nantucket.

"Hey friend, what'cha doin'?"

"The time is upon us," Nantucket answered without turning.

"Uh...He says the 'the time is upon us.'"

"I don't like the sound of that." Magellan placed a hand on the hilt of his sword.

"Tell him no, it's not," replied Lorenzo.

"He is doing this somehow!" declared Bellini.

"Impossible!" Felipe continued his slow retreat.

"God is mightier than nature." Shafi appeared in reverence of Nantucket.

"Captain, give us the word. We will stop this now." Contigo and Destemido had both drawn their weapons, ready to move on Nantucket.

Aside from the few sailors cowering below decks, most of Magellan's two-hundred-seventy crewman packed the rails of their vessels. Some screamed for mercy, others lamented that the edge of the world had been breached, while still others stood gape-mouthed. An expressive few lay prostrate on the decks, resigned to their fate at the hands of some heathen demon. One man perched on the rail, one eye squinting, and aimed a Mark IV crossbow at the events below.

"How many times can I possibly be this close to fucking dying? I'd be better off doing it myself." Bellini headed for the bow.

"WAIT!" urged Filippa. "We need to trust him." Her eyes pleaded with Lanning.

"Because you accept death as your savior? Not this guy, and not now. I've got plans," Magellan said.

Nantucket perceived Filippa trying to head off Magellan's assault. He turned to face the deck, arms relaxed at his side.

"Oh! That is simply not natural at all," said Lorenzo seeing Nantucket's face.

The entire front of his body, head to toe, glowed white, as if dipped in powdered sugar. The man stood coated in a healthy dusting of tiny snow crystals.

"HOLD, EVERYONE!" commanded Lanning. He gripped the

hilt of his blade and pulled it slowly from its scabbard.

The icy circling wind had slowly shifted to a following breeze that towed the fleet into a wall of shimmering fog.

"I will handle it."

Filippa caught Lanning's sword arm. With an imperceptible shake of her head, she dissuaded his attack on Nantucket.

Magellan took a stance next to Contigo, Destemido, and Bellini.

"You had better hurry, son. One clean swipe of your blade ought to do the job."

Appraising his last several weeks of life read like an abridged version of Canterbury tales, a series of seemingly disconnected tales woven into an extended roller-coaster of calamity, salvation, directly followed by calamity and salvation, and now, careening back to calamity.

His mind spun, thinking, "This must all be connected somehow. Right, Dad? Either Dad?" He reached for an all-knowing voice in his head, one wise soul to interpret the events and deliver a usable answer. The silence told him he had come up empty. He viewed the chaos encircling him.

Filippa remained the calmest person in the maelstrom. Nantucket had been a quiet mystery for the entirety of his time on the L'Aquila. He did have a mystical sensibility. That might just have been some front-loaded bias, simply because he was from another land. He did speak with birds, or at least Doug. He had a dry sense of humor and a healthy understanding of humanity from an outsider's perspective. Could the same man be a demon, taking all of them down a fast track to oblivion? Why didn't he see this coming?

"No one saw this coming, son," Shafi whispered in his ear.

"*Sometimes it's just you and a choice.*" Gonzalo's words made a last-minute appearance in his mind.

"You're right!" Lanning exclaimed.

He bolted five steps towards Nantucket with his sword extended.

At the last minute he turned to face the universe as it was, gathered before him.

"Felipe, take the tiller. If we're going for a ride, we might as well cooperate."

"What??!" Magellan screamed in disbelief.

Bellini exploited the moment. With a single blow, he knocked Magellan to the ground, grabbed his sword, and charged Lanning.

"NOW!" yelled Bellini, swinging the sword. "You fucking, useless coward!"

Wielding his blade on an angle Bellini felt certain he'd caught an unprepared Lanning with a killing blow.

Lanning had not been surprised. He parryied the thrust with practiced ease. Bellini's anger and frustration – two emotions he had always manipulated to his advantage in battle, undercut his skills. He attacked without a clear strategy. Lanning did not want to kill the man, but realized it was his only course of action until he saw Shafi.

The old man had grabbed the hatch covering the cargo hold. He bolted across the deck and swung it at Bellini from behind. Reading the look of surprise in Lanning's eyes, Bellini sensed the threat. He caught the danger in his peripheral vision a moment earlier than Shafi intended. Bellini rotated his hips towards the attacker. His blade followed suit, slicing horizontally through the air at the same time the hatch caught him in the jaw. Despite the blow, Bellini's blade cut Shafi cleanly across his mid-section, as both men crumbled to the deck.

"NO!" Filippa rushed to Shafi.

Bellini stirred once more, ready to strike. Lanning heard a familiar whistling sound from long ago pierce the air. The arrow caught Bellini through the palm of his blade hand, and pinned him to the deck. Lanning traced the arrows path, scanning the starboard rail on

Magellan's flagship. The man with the flowing beard gave a nod to Lanning before disappearing from the railing.

"Not possible," thought Lanning before rushing over to his uncle.

"I'm fine," groaned Shafi. "Everything is as it should be for me."

"You're not fine, Uncle."

"It's not so bad. I mostly feel surprised."

"I had it handled. Why?"

"Gonzalo asked me to."

"Then you're doing a pretty shitty job, because now what will I do?"

Shafi smiled at Lanning's recognition. Felipe left the tiller unattended and reached Shafi in time to hear him answer.

"Entirely up to..."

The brothers would have to grieve their uncle later, whenever, however, and if later ever arrived.

"Get back to the wheel." Lanning stood up, kept his sword in hand and retook his post, guarding Nantucket.

"On it, but what the hell?" Felipe moved to the wheel.

Nantucket stood between worlds. He had become a figure of unexplainable sorcery. Lanning was not about to confront him with what felt like a child's toy sword.

Filippa gently let go of Shafi's head to move towards Lanning.

"Thank you," she said.

"You sure about this?" Lanning whispered.

"I hope."

"The edge of the world is an ice wall? Feels wrong. Plus, what the hell, El Afortunado?" Lorenzo had stepped closer to Lanning and Filippa. He pointed straight over the bow.

"There is no damn edge of the world," said Magellan, clearing the fog from his brain after Bellini's blow. He picked himself up off the deck.

"Explain that shit then." Lorenzo pointed ahead of the flotilla.

Magellan appeared dumbfounded.

"I cannot explain that, but that only means I do not know. Not that it is unexplainable."

"Shafi would say, sometimes things occur, and their mystery is the explanation," said Lanning.

An ice wall emerged from the dissipating fog. It rose from sea level in progressively higher, craggy, escarpments to an unfathomable height far above them. Its mass stretched from horizon to horizon. Its expanse was bordered by an infinite darkness on the edges. Its immensity further intimidated and diminished the collection of souls who now drifted below its sheer magnitude.

A deep silence overtook everyone.

Nantucket turned to face the tiny armada before lifting his gaze.

The sky radiated in fractal colors. Every hue in the rainbow appeared in brilliant strokes of sharply angled geometry, completely covering the formerly blue sky. Triangles of radiated purple pulsed next to matching angles of brilliant orange ropes weaving their way through effervescent green shards of all shades, fragments of red rippled between other blocks of pulsing yellow. The skies above them vibrated with the breath of the infinite universe, expanding and contracting in flashes of the intensifying rainbow of colors. The universe had shifted into a pulsing lava lamp of infinite complexity and multidimensional depth, trailing in all directions.

The fleet came to a gradual stop on an unseen sandbar. Lanning had long since replaced his blade in its scabbard, recognizing the magnitude of nature summoned before them. The six ships appeared to hover in infinite undulating space outside the confines of time.

Nantucket held calm and serene at the epicenter of the event.

Lanning, as did everyone assembled, held a reverent silence listening to Nantucket.

"I thank you, universe, for this most amazing day: for the leaping greenly spirits of trees and a blue true dream of sky; and for everything which is natural which is infinite which is yes.

I who have died am alive again today,

And this is the sun's birthday; this is the birth day of life and of love and wings: and of the great happening illimitably earth.

How should tasting touching hearing seeing breathing any— lifted from the no of all nothing—human merely being doubt unimaginable You?

Now the ears of my ears awake, and now the eye of my eyes are opened."

Like everyone else, Lanning wondered what would happen now. Were they doomed? Was this an end of all things? Strangely, he did not feel fear over the outcome. Neither did he feel threatened. The look on Nantucket's face somehow engendered reassurance and tranquility.

"Ask him." Filippa hunched her shoulders, as mystified by the circumstance as anyone else, yet feeling the same sentiments she witnessed on Lanning's face.

"Um, ow. You're squeezing the blood from my hand."

Working his hand loose, he gently kissed her cheek. Nantucket stepped off the bow, released from a burdensome weight he had carried over many days. He approached Lanning.

"Well, this looks like my stop," he said with a sardonic tone.

"Huh? Then, this," Lanning swept his arms across the landscape," is where we are all going?"

"No. I said it's *my* stop. This is where *I* get off, not you."

Lanning placed a finger on his chest, mouthing a silent, "me?"

Nantucket waved his arms across the fleet. "No, not you

personally. Sorry, I meant the greater you. All of you, all of them and you."

"Damn right, it's not. I told you!" said Magellan.

"But then why are *we* here?" Lanning pressed.

"I appreciate the implied romanticism about *my mystical* powers."

"You feign self-mockery. After all of this?" Lanning spanned the sight lines from sky to land with his arms.

Nantucket gave a benign smile. "Despite appearances, I am not an all-powerful being. I truly don't see this is as your stop. It's mine. Oh, and his."

Nantucket pointed directly at Bellini.

"ME?" said Bellini in shock. "Fuck that."

"*You* are with me," Nantucket replied flatly.

"YOU are Prester John?" Lorenzo asked.

A chagrined expression crossed Nantucket's face. "That is hoax born from need. It happens from time to time. More about people searching for something missing, rather than an imagined all-knowing being."

"I don't understand spiritual double-speak. Can we simply speak clearly without poetry?" Contigo expressed his frustration.

"I am, yet I am not. I can be, but you're much better off on your own."

"If this is truly the land of eternal peace and harmony, shouldn't we all be hopping off?" asked Lorenzo.

"I see the confusion. It's not my place to instruct any of you where to find that end, your end, your peace or eternal bliss or whatever. That would be egotistical and presumptuous."

Filippa looked at Lanning. She quietly whispered, "He is."

"I am not so sure."

"Well, I feel vindicated."

"I have my doubts. But...does it really matter anyway? Listen to what he's saying."

Contigo overheard Filippa's comment. "This proves only that we are in an unexplainable moment. I have had many in my life."

"As I have," agreed Destemido.

"This is an extreme example, but no less unexplainable than my daughter appearing after so many years." Contigo embraced his daughter.

"Feels bigger to me," Filippa insisted.

"Is there more?" Lanning asked.

"Oh, come on. I'm fully good. Remember, we thought El Afortunado was magic! Turns out he's a deckhand on grumpy's boat," said Lorenzo.

"But there must be more," Lanning said. "We are not without witnessing miracles. How are we still alive, given the mountain of shit we've been through?"

"For one, he's been with us the entire time!" Filippa pointed at Nantucket. "Divine intervention?"

"I helped where I could. Our paths are different," said Nantucket.

Lanning became frustrated with Nantucket's opacity. "That's a laugh. Then why are we suddenly on *your* path?"

"Easy, brother," counseled Felipe. "Don't wrestle the giant."

"Señor Elcano," Nantucket shouted up to Elcano who was hanging over the rail of the Trinidad.

"Señor Elcano, I thank you for your grace. You will be blessed in ways I cannot yet explain."

"Thanks?" answered Elcano with a weak wave.

"Then all the myths about you are false?" asked Filippa.

"That's a determination you must make. Our images of heaven, Nirvana, Shangri La, Valhalla, Spirit World, Xibalba, and Paradise are all different. Why does everyone assume all heavens are the same? None of us are the same."

"The only place everyone goes and wears the same clothing is prison and parochial school—which I guess feels like prison too."

Lorenzo had regained his irreverence. Felipe cringed.

Nantucket continued, "Our journeys may be seeking similar ends, but the routing is your own. You will find yours at some point. I'm not omnipotent. I'm a seeker like all of you."

He benignly pointed at Bellini.

"Even this scoundrel."

"You've barely spoken the entire time we've known you," Lanning said.

"Because I chose not to speak, does not mean I could not."

"I miss Uncle," said Felipe.

Lanning felt the time to yield had arrived. "If this is your 'stop,' then by all means. How do we find our way back from wherever this is?"

"The how will come. We all must learn to live with the unknowable."

"How do I know if I'm supposed to get out here too?" asked Hector.

"You want to live there? It's an ice wall Hector," said Lorenzo.

"Kid, take a good look. It's bleak," counseled Contigo.

"I guess God lives on an ice wall. It is a surprise, but if all paths lead to God and we're already here, how do I say no?"

Nantucket put his hand on Hector's shoulder and shook his head. "No one has an answer for that question."

"That's shitty," Hector fumed.

"You're right about that. The steps you take are the ones you make. Be a good brother, be a good friend. Best I can do," said Nantucket.

"What about our mother?" Felipe asked.

"Felipe, I'm not Merlin. I cannot help your mother. I do know in my heart that she will be fine."

"She's in jail!" Felipe said.

"Your mom is the baker at the palace?" asked Magellan.

"She is, "said Felipe.

"The goddess of ciabatta?"

"Yes," said Lanning.

"That stuff is heavenly. She's not in jail. I know this for certain."

"Gagnez, that bastard!" Bellini realized he had been both sacrificed and betrayed.

"I wanted to take her with us. An army travels on its stomach, you know, and your mother is perfection! The King refused. He evidently cannot live without her bread."

"You saw the King?" asked Filippa.

"Of course," Lanning said. "You are worried about *your* mother,"

"At no time. My mother knows her way around the royals. I suspected we were on a short cycle with his majesty anyway."

Filippa did not fall far from her mother's survivalist streak. Lanning did some mental gymnastics, ultimately landing on the answer. "You were never planning on going back, were you? So many clothes in that trunk."

Filippa nodded.

Magellan reiterated, "It's always about the money."

"Preaches the altruist," cracked Lorenzo.

"Money to be made is not a sin against mankind. Listen, junior, the world is not some box we're stuck inside of, never to peer over the edge. Nothing wrong with profiting from curiosity. Fear never keeps you safe; it keeps you down. Discovery sets you free!"

"We will leave you now," said Nantucket. He extended his arm while glancing back at Filippa. Doug, who had been circling the boat, gracefully floated down. "If you don't mind?"

Filippa nodded and bowed. "Take good care of him."

Nantucket bowed his head in a return gesture. "You," he said to Bellini, "are with me."

"The hell I am," he answered indignantly.

"Fine. We'll hang him right here." Felipe kneeled next to his fallen Uncle.

"You sure about that choice? It's probably a lot sunnier than it looks," Lorenzo added.

"Get me the rope." Felipe rose from the deck, walking back towards the stern.

No one moved for fear of a reprisal from Nantucket. Nantucket had moved to the starboard gunnel and swung his legs over the rail.

"I'll take that rope," he said.

Hector, holding a rope ladder, threw it over the side by Nantucket.

"Coming?" Nantucket said flatly.

"Why?" asked Lanning. "We need his confession for our mother's freedom from blackmail."

"I don't think so," Nantucket answered looking at Magellan.

"He's right. The Royals will take my word in a letter. I am happy to write it with my personal seal," said Magellan.

"What's gonna happen to him?" asked Hector.

"Don't think we get to know that," replied Lanning.

Nantucket disappeared over the side. Bellini realized his options had come to their end. Reluctant, but resigned, he climbed over the rail. He smirked at Lanning, but mostly to himself, muttering, "Don't forget the match."

Before he descended the ladder, he pulled his stiletto. Taking one last look at his constant companion, he tossed it over the rail. It made purchase in the L'Aquila's deck at the feet of Contigo.

"Souvenir for you!" shouted Bellini, dropping onto the sandbar.

Destemido surveyed the scene, shaking her head. "We all hang by a thread." She watched Bellini tag behind Nantucket.

"Which can be cut at any moment," said Contigo as he tucked the blade into his boot.

Everyone gathered at the port side gunnel to watch Nantucket and Bellini head onto the escarpment. What had been the surreal roiling sky filled with interlocking color patterns, had diffused and lifted. It returned to pale blue, dotted with remnants of the dissipated fog bank. The two lone figures faded into a distance farther than naturally expected before dissolving into a now-empty horizon line.

Felipe pointed skyward. A v-shaped chorus line of pelicans appeared overhead of the boats still lying aground. A rapidly rising tide lifted the formerly captive armada. Within seconds, they floated freely on a calm sea.

"And now?" Filippa said to Lanning.

Two more chorus lines flapped their way past the flotilla. Both brothers watched the birds and came to the same conclusion.

"Follow the birds," they said in unison.

"Hell, yes," echoed Magellan. "Elcano! Make fast your tow line to the Trinidad!"

A nod from Lanning propelled Felipe and Hector to the bow, where they secured a heavy tow line between the two boats.

"To where?" asked Lorenzo.

"I've got a feeling we're not far from somewhere," said Lanning, shielding his eyes while peering over the bow.

"See something out there?" asked Filippa.

Lanning had seen two sprays of water several hundred yards off the bow, in the same direction as the birds.

"Always," he answered.

The Trinidad hoisted its sail, as did the other four caravels in his fleet. The sound of hammering caught the attention of the crew as the Berber began work on the L'Aquila's long list of repairs.

"Redemption is at hand!" Magellan laughed at the Berber. He turned to Lanning. "Shall we not speak of this? Or does someone have a wise word to settle the matter?"

"I feel like the blind man finding an elephant. What I see may not equal what you have seen," replied Destemido.

"Yet we all saw something," added Contigo.

"That is not a log entry I can make. I will provide you with Bellini's guilt in writing, under my seal. Your mother is already free, but you must make sure the culprits of her accusations are held to account on your return to Algeciras."

Lanning heard Magellan's words, and acknowledged his generosity, while knowing accountability could be a dangerous challenge. The L'Aquila crew wrapped Shafi's body and committed it to the deep. Lanning kept his eye on the horizon, tracking the two spouts spraying in the distance.

⊷▬▬ Chapter 40 ▬▬⊶

DELAFORD

Although the pelicans had long vanished from the horizon, Lanning awoke the following morning to spy the familiar twin spouts off their port bow. He directed the fleet in the direction of his gaze. They spotted a green dot ahead of their course.

"Miracle worker!" shouted Magellan from the deck of his flagship. "How did you find such a small finger of land from the edge of the universe? We will find a suitable harbor."

Keeping an eye on the signals from his unseen guides, Lanning directed the fleet to the southwest side of the island. By late afternoon, the fleet dropped anchor in a pristine bay rimmed by verdant low hills. The Trinidad lowered its dinghy into the crystalline turquoise waters. Lanning and Felipe manned the oars. Together with Filippa and Magellan, they made their way ashore.

"Truly a bay fit for a King!" noted Magellan.

A fair-skinned, blonde woman towed a boy of about seven years old. They trailed a muscular, coffee-skinned man who led the way. They emerged from a strand of coconut palms to reach the sand a moment before the dinghy hit the beach. Lanning felt a strange sense of déjà vu seeing the woman, who appeared to be in her forties.

After taking an extended gander at Lanning, the dumbfounded woman stepped forward, extended her hand, and in a perfect English accent said, "Welcome to Delaford on the island of Tobago!"

Felipe's gaze bounced between the woman, the boy, and back to Lanning. "That kid could be you at that age. Don't you think?"

"Delaford?" repeated Lanning, "You said 'Delaford'?"

"Yes, that is my family name. We settled this place a long time ago," said the woman.

"That's my name," said Lanning.

"Is dat so?" asked the man with a strong Caribbean accent.

"Lanning? Are you Lanning Delaford?"

Lanning slowly nodded.

"But you were dead over fifteen years ago!"

The woman leaped forward to embrace Lanning.

"And yet, he is reborn!" quipped Magellan while watching the woman hug it out with the reluctant Lanning.

"You don't know? I am your Aunt Claire! This is your nephew, also Lanning! We are your family!"

"How can this possibly be true?"

"You and your father, my older brother, were on your way here so many years ago. We only knew that you did not arrive."

"We sank. There was an explosion." He stammered, "I am Andalusian, I mean, my family is in Andalusia. Sorry, this is my brother Felipe, Filippa, and Admiral Magellan, by whose grace we are here."

Lanning bent down and extended his hand to the boy. "Pleasure to meet you, namesake!"

"I am Noel, Claire's husband. Welcome home, sir!" The man gripped Lanning's hand. "But you had no idea, did you? I can see that on your face. You did not expect to find us."

Lanning stood emotionally flooded and speechless.

"Nevertheless, our home is yours as well," the man added.

"Food, supplies, repairs, shelter—these are the things we need to continue onward," said Magellan, stepping up to shake hands with Noel.

All boats anchored in the cove. Each unloaded their crewmen in the picturesque King's Bay. Repairs on all boats, especially the L'Aquila, ensued. Noel helped to guide the replenishment of the expedition's stores. Wild Boar was plentiful, and fresh fruit seemingly hung from nearly every tree on the island. Magellan's men set about the task of refilling their fleets holds.

The repairs to the L'Aquila, directed by the Berber, took over a month to complete to Felipe's satisfaction.

"We are ready to leave. Are you?" Felipe asked Lanning after a month on Tobago.

Lanning begged off, promising Felipe an answer in a couple of days. He had spent most of the time getting to know his aunt and nephew. He learned about his own history and family while sharing meals with them. They were from Bristol, a coastal town on the south-west coast of England. His father had followed in the family tradition of merchant adventurers. He traveled between England, Antwerp, and Calais, buying and selling various goods. They had made a fine living until the plague hit Bristol. The family made plans to leave England for the Caribbean. Claire had no clue what had happened to her brother's wife, but assumed the plague took her like so many others.

On horseback with Filippa the next day, they stopped by Argyle Falls, a beautiful, wooded area nearby the Delaford settlement.

"I see the pull." Filippa noted the faraway look in Lanning's eye.

"They are my family," he said.

"And yet?" Filippa grabbed his hand.

"Molly. I think about her every day. When the L'Aquila is repaired, I'm going back. What about you? You're not at all worried about your mother?"

Filippa laughed at the thought. "In a word, no. If we're all our own savior, it's my time to intervene in my own future, instead of tagging along on someone else's."

"I have to go back."

"But do you?"

"Unfinished business. So yes."

"I don't want to pin you, but when your business is finished?"

He kissed her tenderly, but offered no response.

"Understood," she said.

For Lanning, the journey ahead of him, coupled with the task of rooting out the path of treachery that had triggered their cycle of chaos, felt all-consuming. The possibility of returning to Tobago, to family, to Filippa, seemed too far off to contemplate.

Two days hence Lanning, along with his minimal crew, save Filippa, bid their farewells to the island and to Magellan. Gifted navigation tools from Magellan, the L'Aquila set course for Algeciras.

Filippa stood alone on the beach watching, as the caravel receded against the horizon.

Chapter 41

CLEVER GAL

Four short weeks, thanks to fair weather, favorable winds, and two spouts marking their way, the L'Aquila tied off on the Algeciras quay.

"Never again!" Hector embraced Lanning as he climbed over the port gunnel for the last time. "You're always welcome on my block, tiny man!"

Lorenzo offered to run interference with his father while Lanning and Felipe, clutching Magellan's sealed letter, raced up to the palace.

"Leila," Contigo using Destemido's given name, "I'm pretty sure dressing as a brigand will be frowned upon by the locals."

"I'm sure there's something decent left from Filippa's chest," suggested Lorenzo.

"Strange clothing after so many years for me," she answered.

"Maybe overdue?" gently replied Contigo.

"I look fine," she said firmly.

Destemido and Contigo headed up to the Squirrel & Mutton for anything approximating decent food and drink.

The two brothers hitched a ride on a wagon heading up the long stretch of road to the palace. Hopping off by the kitchen, they burst in the door, not knowing what they'd encounter. Apron on and fully dusted with a coat of flour, Molly looked up from her rolling pin to find her two boys.

"I was so sad," she wept.

"So sorry, Molly." Lanning smiled at her before continuing, "Felipe, I told you to tell mom we'd be caught in an ungodly storm, lost at sea, captured by brigands, fight an epic battle, be found at sea, lost yet again, and most likely be a couple weeks late getting home!

You suck."

"My bad, mom."

The three of them embraced. Lanning withdrew the letter from Magellan recounting the events and confession from Bellini.

"Do NOT take that to Goodman," counseled Molly.

"I'm going directly to the Prince," answered Lanning.

"But I'm fine. No harm done. Plus, Bellini is gone. I think I have a better idea."

Molly spoke in low tones so no one could overhear their conversation.

"That's genius!" said Felipe floored by his mother's idea.

"Where did you find such larceny in your soul?"

"I'll wait here," said Felipe, hugging his mother.

Lanning made his way to the upstairs area past the high ceilings of the main level, down the long hallway towards the side of the palace facing the grapevines. Molly had told him which of the large wooden doors to open without knocking, which he did without hesitation.

"What the devil are you doing here?" asked Gagnez.

"Yep, not dead. I believe that explains your surprise, Señor Viceroy."

"You will wait here while I call the guards."

"Whatever have I done to so displease you, sir?" Lanning was enjoying himself drawing out Gagnez' anger.

"Too numerous to mention. Stay put." He rose from the desk intending to call for the palace guards.

"Excellent sir. Perhaps we should include the King and the Prince as well. Would you perhaps have an extra pair of spectacles? Sometimes my reading requires magnification."

Lanning plopped the letter displaying the prominent seal of Magellan on Gagnez desk.

"And what do you expect me to make of that?"

Gagnez reached to grab the letter, but Lanning snatched it away. Rising while drawing his sword, he began a slow walk towards Gagnez who stood behind his desk. Gagnez began to back up towards the very window Bellini had roped his way up, over two months ago.

Lanning waved the sealed envelope at Gagnez. "It seems that my good friend Magellan bumped into your *friend* Marco Bellini while we were all, coincidently, at sea. Truly, sir, a wild tale has been put to pen and paper. It includes all the elements of a great yarn – betrayal, blackmail, murder, royalty. I promise it to be a true epic, worthy of Geoffrey Chaucer."

"You know nothing, you have nothing. You threaten me with your blade as well."

"Oh, this? Apologies." He bowed facetiously as he returned the blade to its scabbard. "Please Viceroy, I will stay put while you fetch the guards. If you prefer, I can go and get the prince as well. He may be quite entertained. I know you two are close."

Gagnez remained skeptical of the letter's true content, but also recognized the vise grip he was trapped in.

"Take it to Señor Goodman, why don't you?"

"Of course, another excellent suggestion. By all means, let's invite him to the party."

Lanning did not wish to overplay his hand, yet quite enjoyed the walls closing in on the little fat man. He decided to throw him a small lifeline.

"Señor, we are mostly victims to circumstance transpiring at elevated levels to our simple playing field. I do not begrudge your predicament, nor mine. But I do take my mother's well-being deadly serious. There are options."

"And now we come to your terms, I presume?" Resigned, Gagnez plopped down behind his desk to absorb his consequences.

Chapter 42

WHALE OF A DAY

By the time Lanning left thirty minutes later, Gagnez was a crushed and broken husk. There would be no possibility of reneging on the agreement they had struck. To safeguard against anything shifting over time, Molly would maintain possession of Magellan's letter.

Lanning returned to the palace kitchen in time to help Molly pull ten loaves of ciabatta from the woodfired oven. Snatching one for the road, Molly, Felipe, and Lanning left the palace to meet up with Contigo and Destemido at the Squirrel & Mutton.

A health hazardous pub meal out of the question, they reconvened at Molly's home for a dinner of actual mutton and ciabatta. Lorenzo appeared in time for the cheese course at the end of the meal.

"Incredible news, my friends!" said Lorenzo.

"How so?" asked Felipe.

"My father leaves tomorrow for his beloved Basque country. He will buy his castle in Azpeitia!"

"A miracle, or he simply has enough in the castle fund? Does he still wait for my payment?" asked Lanning as a Cheshire cat smile spread across his face.

"A bounty was dropped on him from a palace guard. He asked no questions, only telling me the boats now belonged to me."

"After all the schooling, you'd give up your dream?" asked Felipe.

"I'd strongly advise that, since I have not witnessed anything truly amusing about you!" quipped Destemido.

"Why thank you, PIRATE!" Lorenzo smiled. "Although I'm certain, had I graduated, my future would have been bright."

"Or brief!" said Lanning.

Lorenzo grimaced, "Proximity to power of late had dimmed my appetite for the burden of truth-telling."

"Wise choice, my friend! Is that it then?" asked Lanning.

"One last detail: Don Espinosa's son would like to make a gift to the sons of Gonzalo and Victoria Cortez!"

"A gift? This is unexpected," said Molly.

"The L'Aquila is yours to do with as you see fit. All debts are hereby forgiven."

They all raised a glass to their mutual good fortune. As they drank, there arrived another knock on the door. Lanning rose to answer.

"Good evening, Señor Delaford. Nice to see you again."

A familiar soldier stood a tenuous three feet back from the front door. In lieu of a halberd spear, the soldier needed both arms to hold the two sacks of coins he handed over to Lanning.

"Why, I'm overwhelmed, sir! Would you enjoy a glass of wine for your troubles?"

Recalling his last experience, the man cautiously checked both left and right, as well as behind him.

"I'm content to leave your door fully conscious."

With that salutation, he quickly left.

Lanning took the bags and hid them in his mother's room. He returned to enjoy several more glasses of wine with the assembled. Lorenzo, newly minted rental magnate, suffused with ample quantities of wine and joy, offered hugs all around. He departed, leaving his jester hat on the dining table as a last reminder of his former career aspirations.

Lanning stood facing father and daughter and raised his glass. "My friends, Felipe and I would like to make a gift of the L'Aquila to you both. We hope and trust you will find your way back to the home you knew together, and begin your lives anew."

Destemido and Contigo embraced the brothers, Molly, and each other.

"I have but one favor to ask," he continued.

One month later, Lanning embraced his mother and brother at the quay in front of the newly outfitted L'Aquila.

"She does look amazing! Believe me, I am tempted," said Felipe, "but Lorenzo knows shit all about boats. As his new partner, I have duties to perform! Take good care, brother."

Felipe hugged Lanning and made way for Molly.

"Your life begins again, son."

"I can never tell you how much I love and treasure you."

"Sure you can! Love and love well."

Lanning swept Molly up in a deep embrace. Kissing her on the cheek, he said, "I love you, mother."

Lanning backed away, and hopped over the rail of the L'Aquila.

"¡Suelten las líneas!" Contigo, by no means a convincing waterman, managed to give the cast-off command in Spanish. His daughter had instructed him on the few commands he'd need until they reached open waters. The crew were all former Portuguese living silently in Algeciras. Destemido determined it best to remain innocuous until they reached the open sea.

As the caravel passed the seawall exiting the Algeciras harbor Lanning, poised on the bow, spotted two telltale spouts off in the distance pointing the way forward.

ACKNOWLEDGEMENTS

324. My mother passed away during the writing of this book. Sadly, she did not get a chance to read it. She made a habit of checking in with me for the all-important, I guess, page count. I wanted to get that handled first. Thanks mom. Well north of a humble thank you, my wife and best friend, Nancy Grinstein offered total support, truthful feedback, and always, an ample supply of jet fuel to get the job done. Tess, Dia, and Nicolas are my other three lifelines. I treasure and appreciate all of them for more reasons than a simple novel. Thank you to my editor, Leslie Wells, for using her secret decoder ring to decipher my intent, and help me to achieve it with pace, clarity, and enough commas in all the right places. Huge love to Molly Green for vanquishing all my mistakes, malaprops, and assortment of addled errors.

I carved the setting for this novel out of a bevy of mostly true, historical facts. There was a 16th century, a Magellan, a Loyola, and a Spain. To ensure some semblance of believable reality, wedging a fictional tale within the confines of actual history requires a variable speed blender as opposed to a Cuisinart. I relied on lots of assistance from many sources. A few years ago, I asked, Jonathan Snyder, professor of Spanish literary and cultural history based in Madrid, a series of mundane questions about life in 16th century Spain—specifically the Andalucian region. His generous insights and recommendations proved invaluable in constructing a colorful and illuminating pallet for Flat's creation.

Appropriated Historical Figures: Renounced Portuguese explorer, Ferdinand Magellan, began his historic, Spanish funded, voyage to find a shorter route to the spice islands on September 20, 1519. Juan

Sebastian Elcano sailed with Magellan, and ended up finishing the voyage in command of the remaining fleet after Magellan met his historic end in the Philippines. Charles I was only 16 when he ascended to the Spanish throne in 1516. By 1519, as a result of a complicated weave of birthright, he was redubbed Charles V, ruler of the Holy Roman Empire. After his abdication, the throne passed to his little brother Ferdinand in 1556. In 1519, future Saint, Ignatius Loyola, was a well-established officer and courtier in the Spanish army. It would not be until 1521, when his fateful injury during the battle of Pamplona, triggered his dramatically altered path through life. Sinan Reis aka Sinan the Jew, was a Barbary corsair sailing under the Ottoman flag in the early to mid 1500s. King Manuel I was King of Portugal from 1495 – 1521.

I have used an excerpt from the E.E. Cummings poem "thank you god for this most amazing day," which my gifted friend, Tracey Rich, shared with me. I have also used a quote from J. Krishnamurti, which I found in my pal and guru, Ganga White's, memoir. Shafi thanks the poet, Rainer Rilke, for the line borrowed from his poem The Seer on page 56.

While the debate around the shape of the earth continued for many millennia, Eratosthenes, the former head librarian at Alexander's swanky papyrus bank, had it all sorted out in 241 BCE. True!

Research List: Imperial Spain—JH Elliott; Hidden Music – Rumi; Over the Edge of the World: Magellan's Terrifying Circumnavigation of the Globe - Laurence Bergreen

If this book was entertaining, please consider reading: **23 Degrees South** – *A Tropical Tale of Changing Whether*...a modern retell of Herman Hesse's *Siddhartha*.

REVIEW

"Consistently entertaining courtesy of Rabin's humor-laced prose...a witty, boisterous ride!"   —Kirkus Reviews

"Enjoy with your favorite cocktail!...23 Degrees South will capture all readers with its story of two young friends on different paths who intersect within an action packed story...An exemplary and highly entertaining read for today's hectic pace of living. Highly recommended."   —Chanticleer Reviews, 5/5 Stars

23 DEGREES SOUTH CHAPTERS 1 & 2

Chapter 1
A SIMPLE BREEZE

Feeling rather full of himself, Hart, the newly minted Senior Manager for the Maytag Corporation in Sao Paulo, Brazil sat comfortably ensconced within the safe confines of his palatial new office. He rocked back and forth, slowly checking out the deep lean of his stylish, graphite black, Aeron chair. On his faux oak desk lay an old guidebook covering all things Sao Paulo. Not even on the job one week, he still puzzled over the uncomfortable fit of his title. "How the hell can I be a senior man.ager at twenty-two?" He felt very much the impostor. "How did I rate an assistant too?" Carmen dos Reis sat at her desk a few steps down the hall. Slight, curvaceously built, dark skinned, with stunning blue eyes, and dark lustrous hair. She gave a lilting, intoxicating Brazilian rhythm to everything she did. Hart spoke three languages and none of them adequately described Carmen's beauty.

He'd been thumbing his way through the dog-eared guidebook, study.ing up on his new city. São Paulo was founded by the well meaning, goal oriented Jesuits way back in 1554. It sits on a plateau precisely 2,493 feet above sea level, forty-five miles from the Atlantic coast. For Hart, who grew up only a few miles from the ocean, he may as well have been in Iowa. He felt sure at some point he would grow to enjoy his new surround.ings, but still had nagging doubts. Putting down the book for a moment, he swallowed hard against the depression he had battled from an early age. "It's called a Dukkha, and you're lucky to have it," that was the unsolicited advice from his Buddhist Studies professor at UCLA. Depression sucked. It wasn't a gift from the gods; it was a scourge that arrived at all the wrong times. He hoped his luck would hold since he hadn't suffered a bout in quite a long time. Learning about his new surroundings helped keep things on an even keel. He never enjoyed surprises; they forced him off-balance.

Once again he paged into his new distraction. Back in the early days the Jesuits ruled all things. Jesuits were famously regarded as the Pope's Paratroopers, his First Responders, the Vatican Seal Team whose mission profile directed them to splash down amongst the unsuspecting in all corners of the world and show them the one true way of all things. These stout.hearted foot soldiers of Saint Ignatius Loyola were nicknamed Jesuits by the folks on the other side of the door. If your Renaissance doorbell rang, and the guy on the stoop wore all black, you could trust that he was not there to sell you the latest Michelangelo print. Jesuits wanted to talk about Jesus. Jesuits translates as "one who uses the name of Jesus with relentless frequency." Let us say "Jesus" at breakfast, lunch, dinner, tea time, on the way to the mall, waterfall, or nightclub. Jesuits prefer Jesus over tiramisu, mud pie, filet mignon, and any fresh fish including rare, seared Ahi. The infamous acronym— WWJD—What Would Jesus Do—originated with the Jesuits back in the darkening days of the late Renaissance.

These road warriors conceived Sao Paulo as the mission center for their frequent traveler club members: participating nationally affiliated early settlers and, reluctantly, the local heathens. If you were not a Jesuit, or well-connected royalty, then you were lumped into the category of godless nuisance native or heathen. As far as Team Jesuit was concerned, heathens served no productive purpose unless they could be converted to the right side of the holy ledger. Those that would not buy in for whatever reasons were simply designated as road kill.

They squatted in the middle of the progressive highway, disrupting the missionary victory drive towards the Holy Trinity: civilization, salvation, and incorporation. The Jesuit advance guard brought the Holy Spirit, but they also traveled with their calculators. New World Wealth Management, or the upside of global colonization, occupied a large chunk of the Jesuit mindset whether they landed in Borneo, Boston, or Brazil.

Looking out his window at the street below, Hart considered this history. He hadn't seen many black robed Jesuits cruising about the tragi.cally hip streets of modern Sao Paulo. Perhaps they were horrified by how far modern Brazil had strayed from the marquee they hung up way back when. Perhaps they considered the country a job well done and had simply moved on. A quote at the top of the next page in his guidebook stopped him cold:

"That which you are seeking is always seeking you."

Hart uttered the phrase aloud to no one in particular. He unconsciously retooled the adage into a personal question of reflection. How in the holy landslide of Roman-numeral-numbered Popes, he wondered, would a 17th century, twenty something Jesuit priest on an obligatory recruiting pilgrim.age know anything about his circumstances? Logically, of course he wouldn't, but the saying still applied to his personal life. For some time Hart had realized how much of his time had been devoted to passively hanging a line over the side of his metaphorical rowboat and waiting for a strike. His paralytic life strategy had centered on aggressive anti-seeking, at least until he fell into Brazil. Now he was simply afraid that he might have let the big one get away. He pushed those thoughts deep down into a cavern of his brain marking them for later exploration. Internally, he labeled the quote enigmatic and mysterious, but mostly too damn irritating to dwell on for longer than the two seconds he had given it. He thumbed to the next page.

It was at this precise moment of uneasy reflection that Hart's best friend Simon burst into his office, knocked over the luscious Carmen, and to the best of his recollection, shot him point-blank in the neck.

Chapter 2
FUCK IF I KNOW

A phone came to life amidst the sound of spinning blenders at the Janiero juice bar in the tony suburb of Vila Olimpia.

Carlos dos Reis had a mantra that served him. "Fuck the fuckers that fuck you before they fuck you again." Had Carlos realized what chaos had begun bearing down on him at that moment, his life might have volun.tarily veered in another direction. According to Einstein's theory, Star Trek, and all that worm hole science stuff, Carlos might have had time to execute a pre-emptive strategy, and make his way to the nearest exit before the doors were cross checked and sealed. As far back as he could remember, life had backhanded Carlos, not once but many times. Most of those knuckle slaps he created himself. Those first few rips surprised and hurt him, after that it became a matter of expectation and pain management. Like the phenomenal athlete we all knew in grade school who somehow stepped on a waist-high landmine at exactly the wrong time, Carlos fulfilled the wrong destiny. He had two choices and consistently, even redundantly, selected the worst of all possible worlds. Dark skinned, with high cheekbones and thick dark hair like his mother, Carlos also possessed a genetically chiseled body inherited from his maternal grand.father, the legendary Capoeira master known only as Mestre Bimbo. He was small, about five feet six. His height only exacerbated his anger.

The Favela jungle line had reached out a tentacle for Carlos. The line incorporated a variety of sophisticated modes. Simply put, it was a phone call from the neighborhood house of horror, Carandiru, Sao Paulo's largest prison. A call was placed to a rotating collection of telephones ranging from private homes, to decrepit, pond scum phone booths, to police headquarters, to lunch counters. Someone answered, took a message, and then set about the task of fulfilling the designated request. Beginning at the juice bar, the vine caught up with Carlos through the hands of a random eleven-year-old boy on the streets of Heliopolis. Heliopolis—one of the grand slums that dot all Brazilian cities. Chewing on a Ghirardelli bittersweet chocolate bar with hazelnuts, Carlos recognized the kid approaching him from the city's soccer pitch. The boy handed him a piece of scrunched up paper. Carlos flipped the kid a Real coin and opened the balled mass.

The only words written on the paper: "Get stupid."

He tossed the two words around in his brain. For a moment he tried to pretend that he tossed them out the virtual window of the nearest fifty-story building. Whoosh, they sailed out, smacked into gravity then headed straight down and crashed onto the pavement disintegrating into a zillion unrecoverable pieces. "Damn!" He said it aloud, then in his head, then out loud again. Not now, he whined to himself.

The last two years had been the most productive of Carlos' chosen career. His most recent accomplishments included boosting a wide assort.ment of luxury cars parked at various branches of the Brazilian Savings & Loan Bank, exploding multiple hand-crafted bombs placed near various telephone switching stations, plus his most recent escapade—a late night clean out of the recently opened Sega Super Store. Carlos had been build.ing a reputation. Welcomed back to the favela from a stint in prison by a cadre of PCC (local crime mob) members, they celebrated their mutual disdain for the present government and its growing list of inequities, alongside their love for their still-imprisoned fearless leader—the Shadow.

Carlos' shoulders drooped as the reality of the message sank in. Parolees walked a tightrope with their freedom. Carlos knew what needed to be done. It wouldn't take much. He paid his rent for the next six months, strolled down to the nearest bar, drank half a bottle of Calypso Dark Rum, marshaled his nerve and walked out of the favela.

Recently crowned junior detective Jorge Rosado had just unbuttoned the collar on his thick rayon blend uniform. He hated being hot. Sao Paulo police uniforms sadistically captured, retained, then perversely amplified the tropical heat. He also hated walking a beat. He figured that life was left in his rear view mirror until his replacement patrol officer, Paolo Girardo, called in sick with a rapidly moving case of tainted street food. Rosado had filled in one last time. His feet walked the beat while his mind wandered off to organize his new metal detective's desk and its three slightly off-track drawers. Contemplating where to put his pens, stapler, and scotch tape dispenser he entirely missed Carlos dos Reis Machado making a beeline towards his exact position. Carlos promptly smash-mouthed the unsuspecting Rosado with a roundhouse left to the jaw. Surprisingly Rosado maintained his balance, but lost his cool and came rushing back at Carlos while reaching for his gun. Carlos crouched low, like an attacking tiger, then placed his left arm down on the ground as a pivot point and windmilled his legs. The motion upended Rosado at his knees sending him crashing to the ground in a moaning heap and a permanently aching tailbone. By this time two other policemen, guns drawn, flew across the street tossing their half-drunk passion fruit smooth.ies into the fast lane of oncoming traffic. The first smoothie hit the wind.shield of a Kwik Copy delivery van, entirely blotting out the driver's vision. The driver slammed on his brakes. The van fishtailed over the median line into the opposing traffic, where it came to a stop. The driver let out a long sigh of temporary relief. Temporary, that is, until Mrs. Jaio Gilberto placed her 1984 Toyota Camry solidly into the van's midsection. The precise and potent hit launched the van and its contents skipping back onto the highway median. The gentle Sao Paulo breeze lifted and stirred the day's paper output into a Mardi Gras frenzy of ticker tape, giving the whole intersection an oblique feeling of seasonal celebration. The streets were littered with an eight-by-ten inch flyer trumpeting a speaking engagement by a Jesuit priest by the name of Lazarus. Lazarus Knows appeared in bold print across the top of the flyer. "Come Sunday morning you will too" read the rest of the now well-disbursed ad.

No real injuries, plenty of insurance claims, definitely no Mardi Gras party, and six months inside for Carlos dos Reis. But then he knew that sitting at the barstool. Once returned to the fold and re-inserted back in the starting lineup of the prison futbol squad, Carlos made the customary rounds of re-acquaintance. The Shadow, aka Julian Coelho, waited patiently.

Coelho, your standard hard case criminal boss, controlled his empire from inside the walls of Carandiru Prison. His cell came equipped with a phone line from which he maintained constant contact with the outside universe. When necessary, any direct order from the Shadow moved from thought to implementation in a matter of hours.

Carlos found Julian watching the soccer team practice game from his usual perch high in the yard. He walked up the bleacher stairs to sit down next to him. Julian sat alone. No cadre, no other inmates within twenty yards of him. He looked weathered and older. It had been two years, but seeing Julian's condition, it felt more like ten.

"Greetings Ram Dass," Carlos said.

Julian laughed. The new Che Guevara tattoo on his neck crinkled its eyes and appeared to be laughing along with its host body, "See, you have skills after all."

"I'm here for six suffocating months. What's so urgent?" Carlos made his annoyance clear.

"I'm going to get the shiv in here before too long. Sadly, the PCC is no longer the organization I'd like it to be. Too concerned with economics over cause. There is a selfish, vile, greed obsessed element that has emerged to try and dominate the old guard. There's resistance, but not enough."

"What resistance?"

"Just me, I guess."

Carlos took a deep inhale.

"I heard this priest last year." Julian smiled, sensing Carlos' surprise.

"You listened to a priest?" an incredulous Carlos asked his mentor.

"I didn't say I heard the angels singing the holy word of God and took a knee! He came in here to talk to us about the world; a guy about your age. He made sense. You should have a listen, make something more out of your own life before you end up like me."

"What's his name?"

"Father something. Just give him a listen and you'll figure it out."

"I'm confused with all this. You spent years teaching me to be like you. Now you're having second thoughts. What the hell Julian?"

"Life is unpredictable. Be aware."

"I'm doing six for that pearl of wisdom?"

"It's not all about the money. I want you to carry on the fight when I'm done, but not the same fight." Julian communicated the news with little emotion.

"That will never work. I don't want to be the heir apparent. All the fuckers that want your ass will be after mine too."

"What have I taught you?" Coelho rallied a smile.

Carlos recited the lesson by rote: "Fuck the fuckers that fuck you before they fuck you again."

Julian gave a surprise chuckle, "Not exactly how I put it, but I like your spin."

"Why don't YOU follow your own damn advice?"

"I've run out my string. There's no respect for age anymore. It's a real tragedy. See if you can do something about that sometime." Julian smiled, then got up to leave. He left a Lindt bittersweet 73% lying on the ground.

Carlos scooped it up and put it in his pocket as he walked back to the pitch, sad, irritated, and as always, angry.

ABOUT THE AUTHOR

After graduating from UCLA, Neal Rabin worked for Club Med as a tennis and surf instructor on Reunion Island, off the coast of Madagascar. He stocked refrigerators, Xeroxed scripts, and served as a 'fetch' for Time Life Films. Neal co-founded and spent fifteen years as CEO of the Santa Barbara based global software company, Miramar Systems. He continues to live in Santa Barbara with his wife, two daughters, two dogs, multiple guitars, his piano, and a flock of chickens. Neal is an instrument pilot and has an active lifestyle that includes surfing, volleyball, yoga, and tennis.

www.nealrabin.com

Printed in the USA
CPSIA information can be obtained
at www.ICGtesting.com
CBHW021530310524
9377CB00003B/43

9 780997 04682